'Your money means nothing to me, Sander, nothing at all,' she told him truthfully, adding for good measure, 'And neither do you. For me, the fact that you choose to think in terms of money simply underlines all the reasons why I am not prepared to allow my sons anywhere near you unless I am there.'

'That is how *you* feel, but what about how they might feel?' Sander pressed her. 'A good mother would never behave so selfishly. She would put her children's interests first.'

How speedily Sander had turned the tables on her, Ruby recognised. What had begun at least on her part as a challenge to him, which she had been confident would make him back down, had turned into a double-edged sword which right now he was wielding very skilfully against her, cutting what she had thought was secure ground away from under her feet.

'I am...they need their moth—' she started.

'They are my sons,' Sander interrupted her angrily. 'And I mean to have them. If I have to marry you to facilitate that, then so be it. But make no mistake, Ruby. I intend to have my sons.'

Best-selling Modern™ Romance author
Penny Jordan brings you an exciting new trilogy...

## NEEDED: THE WORLD'S MOST ELIGIBLE BILLIONAIRES

*Three penniless sisters, pure and proud...
but about to be purchased!*

With bills that need to be paid,
a house about to be repossessed and little twin boys
to feed, sisters Lizzie, Charley and Ruby refuse to drown
in their debts. They will hold their heads up high
and fight to feed their family!

But three of the richest, most ruthless men in the world
are about to enter their lives...

Pure, proud, but penniless,
how far will the sisters go to save the ones they love?

Lizzie's story—
### THE WEALTHY GREEK'S CONTRACT WIFE
*Ilios Manos is Greek and ruthless.
A dangerous combination! Lizzie owes him thousands,
but he'll take her as his wife in payment.*

Charley's story—
### THE ITALIAN DUKE'S VIRGIN MISTRESS
*When project manager Charley is hired by demanding
Raphael Della Striozzi, he's adamant she must have a
makeover! Now the dowdy frump has been transformed,
she's sexy enough for another role: his mistress!*

Ruby's story—
### MARRIAGE: TO CLAIM HIS TWINS
*Out of the blue, Alexander Konstantinakos has turned
up at Ruby's house to take his twin sons back to Greece!
Ruby will do anything to keep her boys by her side—
even marry Sander!*

# MARRIAGE: TO CLAIM HIS TWINS

BY
PENNY JORDAN

First published in Great Britain 2010
Harlequin Mills & Boon Limited,
Eton House, 18-24 Paradise Road, Richmond, Surrey TW9 1SR

© Penny Jordan 2010

ISBN: 978 0 263 21353 9

Harlequin Mills & Boon policy is to use papers that are natural, renewable and recyclable products and made from wood grown in sustainable forests. The logging and manufacturing process conform to the legal environmental regulations of the country of origin.

Printed and bound in Great Britain
by CPI Antony Rowe, Chippenham, Wiltshire

# MARRIAGE: TO CLAIM HIS TWINS

# PROLOGUE

ALEXANDER KONSTANTINAKOS, powerful, formidable, billionaire head of an internationally renowned container shipping line originally founded by his late grandfather, stood in the middle of the elegantly luxurious drawing room of his home on the Greek Ionian island of Theopolis, his gaze riveted on the faces of the twin boys in the photograph he was holding.

Two black-haired, olive-skinned and dark-eyed identical faces looked back at him, their mother kneeling down beside them. The three of them were shabbily dressed in cheap-looking clothes.

Tall, dark-haired, with the features of two thousand years of alpha-male warriors and victors sculpted into the bones of his handsome face the same way that their determination was sculpted into his psyche, he stood in the now silent room, the accusation his sister had just made was still echoing through his head.

'They have to be your sons,' she had accused Nikos, their younger brother. 'They have our family features stamped on them, and you were at university in Manchester.'

Alexander—Sander to his family—didn't need to keep gazing at the photograph Elena had taken with her mobile phone on her way through Manchester Airport after visiting her husband's family to confirm her statement, or to memorise the boys' faces. They were already carved into his memory for all time.

'I don't know anything about them,' his younger brother Nikos denied, breaking the silence. 'They aren't mine, Sander, I promise you. Please believe me.'

'Of course they're yours,' Elena corrected their younger brother. 'Just look at those faces. Nikos is lying, Sander. Those children are of our blood.'

Sander looked at his younger sister and brother, on the verge of quarrelling just as they had always done as children. There were only two years between them, but he had been born five years before Elena and seven before Nikos, and after their grandfather's death as the only adult family member left in their lives he had naturally taken on the responsibility of acting as a father figure to them. That had often meant arbitrating between them when they argued.

This time, though, it wasn't arbitration that was called for.

Sander looked at the photograph again and then announced curtly, 'Of our blood, but not of Nikos's making. Nikos is speaking the truth. The children are not his.'

Elena stared at him.

'How can you know that?'

Sander turned towards the windows and looked beyond them to where the horizon met the deep blue of the Aegean Sea. Outwardly he might appear calm, but inside his chest his heart was thudding with fury. Inside his head images were forming, memories he had thought well buried surfacing.

'I know it because they are mine,' he answered his sister, watching as her eyes widened with the shock of his disclosure.

She wasn't the only one who was shocked, Sander acknowledged. He had been shocked himself when he had looked at her phone and immediately recognised the young woman kneeling beside the two young boys who so undeniably bore the stamp of their fathering—*his* fathering. Oddly, she looked if anything younger now than she had the night he had met her in a Manchester club favoured by young footballers, and thus the haunt of the girls who chased after them. He had been taken there by a business acquaintance, who had left him to his own devices having picked up a girl himself, urging Sander to do the same.

Sander's mouth hardened. He had buried the memory of that night as deeply as he could. A one-night stand with an alcohol-fuelled girl dressed in overly tight and incredibly revealing clothes, wearing too much make-up, who had made such a deliberate play for him. At one point she had actually caught hold of his hand, as though about to drag him to bed with her. It wasn't something any real man with any pride or self-respect could ever be proud of—not even when there were the kind of extenuating circumstances there had been that night. She had been one of a clutch of such girls, openly seeking the favours of the well-paid young footballers who favoured the place. Greedy, amoral young women, whose one desire was to find themselves a rich lover or better still a rich husband. The club, he had been told, was well known for attracting such young women.

He had had sex with her out of anger and resentment—against her for pushing him, and against his grandfather for trying to control his life. He'd been refusing to allow him a greater say in the running of the business which, in his stubborn determination not to move with the times, he had been slowly destroying. And against his parents—his father for dying, even though that had been over a decade ago, leaving him without his support, and his mother, who had married his father out of duty whilst continuing to love another man. All those things, all that anger had welled up inside him, and the result was now here in front of him.

His sons.

*His.*

A feeling like nothing he had ever experienced before seized hold of him. A feeling that, until it had struck him, he would have flatly denied he would ever experience. He was a modern man—a man of logic, not emotion, and certainly not the kind of emotion he was feeling right now. Gut wrenching, instinctive, tearing at him—an emotion born of a cultural inheritance that said that a man's children, especially his sons, belonged under his roof.

Those boys were his. Their place was here with him, not in England. Here they could learn what it meant to be his sons, a Konstantinakos of Theopolis, could grow into their heritage. He could father them and guide them as his sense of responsibility demanded that he should. How much damage had they already suffered through the woman who had borne them?

He had given them life without knowing it, but now that he did know he would stop at nothing to bring them home to Theopolis, where they belonged.

# CHAPTER ONE

CURSING as she heard the doorbell ring, Ruby remained where she was, on her hands and knees, hoping that whoever it was would give up and go away, leaving her in peace to get on with her cleaning. However, the bell rang again, this time almost imperiously. Someone was pressing hard on the bell.

Cursing again under her breath, Ruby backed out of the downstairs cloakroom, feeling hot and sticky, and not in any mood to have her busy blitz on cleaning whilst her twin sons were at school interrupted. She got to her feet, pushing her soft blonde curls off her face as she did so, before marching towards the front door of the house she shared with two older sisters and her own twin sons. She yanked it open.

'Look, I'm—' Her sentence went unfinished, her voice suspended by shock as she stared at the man standing on the doorstep.

Shock, disbelief, fear, anger, panic, and a sharp spear of something else that she didn't recognise exploded inside her like a fireball, with such powerful intensity that her body was drained of so much energy that she was left feeling shaky and weak, trembling inwardly beneath the onslaught of emotions.

Of course he *would* be dressed immaculately, in a dark business suit worn over a crisp blue shirt, whilst she was wearing her old jeans and a baggy tee shirt. Not that it really mattered how she looked. After all, she had no reason to want to impress him—had she? And she certainly had no reason to want him to think of her as a desirable woman, groomed and dressed for his approval. She had to clench her stomach muscles against the shudder of revulsion that threatened to betray her. The face that had haunted her dreams and then her nightmares hadn't changed—or aged. If anything he looked even more devastatingly handsome and virile than she had remembered, the dark gold gaze that had mesmerised her so effectively every bit as compelling now as it had been then. Or was it because she was a woman now and not the girl she had been that she was so immediately and shockingly aware of what a very sexual man he was? Ruby didn't know, and she didn't *want* to know.

The disbelief that had frozen her into silence had turned like snow in the sun to a dangerous slush of fear and horror inside her head—and her heart? *No!* Whatever effect he had once had on her heart, Sander Konstantinakos had no power to touch it now.

But still the small betraying word, 'You,' slid from the fullness of the naturally warm-coloured lips that had caused her parents to name her Ruby, causing a look of mixed contempt and arrogance to flash from the intense gold of Sander's eyes. Eyes the colour of the king of the jungle—as befitted a man who was in effect the ruler of the Mediterranean island that was his home.

Instinctively Ruby started to close the door on him, wanting to shut out not just Sander himself but everything he represented, but he was too quick for her, taking hold of the door and forcing it open so that he could step into the hall—and then close the door behind him, enclosing them both in the small domestic space, with its smell of cleaning fluid. Strong as it was, it still wasn't strong enough to protect her from the scent of *him*. A rash of prickly sensation raised the hairs at the back of her neck and then ran down her spine. This was ridiculous. Sander meant nothing to her now, just as she had meant nothing to him that night... But she mustn't think about that. She must concentrate instead on what she was now, not what she had been then, and she must remember the promise she had made to the twins when they had been born—she would put the past behind her.

What she had never expected was that that past would seek her out, and now it had...

'What are you doing here?' she demanded, determined to wrest control of the situation from Sander. 'What do you want?'

His mouth might be aesthetically perfect, with that well-cut top lip balancing the promise of sensuality with his fuller bottom lip, but there was nothing sensual about the tight-lipped look he was giving her, and his words were as sharply cold as the air outside the Manchester hotel in which he had abandoned her that winter morning.

'I think you know the answer to that,' he said, his English as fluent and as accentless as she remembered. 'What I want, what I have come for and what I mean to have, are my sons.'

'*Your* sons?' Fiercely proud of her twin sons, and equally fiercely maternally protective of them, there was nothing he could have said which would have been more guaranteed to arouse Ruby's anger than his verbal claim on them. Angry colour burned in the smooth perfection of Ruby's normally calm face, and her blue-green eyes were fiery with the fierce passion of her emotions.

It was over six years since this man had taken her, used her and then abandoned her as casually as though she was a…a nothing. A cheap, impulsively bought garment which in the light of day he had discarded for its cheapness. Oh, yes, she knew that she had only herself to blame for what had happened to her that fatal night. *She* had been the one to flirt with him, even if that flirtation had been alcohol-induced, and no matter how she tried to excuse her behaviour it still shamed her. But not its result—not her beautiful, adorable, much loved sons. They could never shame her, and from the moment they had been born she had been determined to be a mother of whom they could be proud—a mother with whom they could feel secure, and a mother who, no matter how much she regretted the manner in which they had been conceived, would not for one minute even want to go back in time and avoid their conception. Her sons were her life. *Her* sons.

'My sons—' she began, only to be interrupted.

'*My* sons, you mean—since in my country it is the father who has the right to claim his children, not the mother.'

'My sons were not fathered by you,' Ruby continued firmly and of course untruthfully.

'Liar,' Sander countered, reaching inside his jacket to produce a photograph which he held up in front of her.

The blood left Ruby's face. The photograph had been taken at Manchester Airport, when they had all gone to see her middle sister off on her recent flight to Italy, and the resemblance of the twins to the man who had fathered them was cruelly and undeniably revealed. The two boys were cast perfectly in their father's image, right down to the unintentionally arrogant masculine air they could adopt at times, as though deep down somewhere in their genes there was an awareness of the man who had fathered them.

Watching the colour come and go in Ruby's face, Sander allowed himself to give her a triumphant look. Of *course* the boys were his. He had known it the first second he had looked at the image on his sister's mobile phone. Their mirror image resemblance to him had sent a jolt of emotion through him unlike anything he had previously experienced.

It hadn't taken the private agency he had contacted very long to trace Ruby—although Sander had frowned over comments in the report he had received from them that implied that Ruby was a devoted mother who dedicated herself to raising her sons and was unlikely to give them up willingly. But Sander had decided that Ruby's very devotion to his sons might be the best tool he could use to ensure that she gave them up to him.

'My sons' place is with me, on the island that is their home and which ultimately will be their inheritance. Under our laws they belong to me.'

'Belong? They are children, not possessions, and no court in this country would let you take them from me.'

She was beginning to panic, but she was determined not to let him see it.

'You think not? You are living in a house that belongs to your sister, on which she has a mortgage she can no longer afford to repay, you have no money of your own, no job. No training—nothing! I, on the other hand, can provide my sons with everything that you cannot—a home, a good education, a future.'

Although she was shaken by the knowledge of how thoroughly he had done his homework, had had her investigated, Ruby was still determined to hold her ground and not allow him to overwhelm her.

'Maybe so. But can you provide them with love and the knowledge that they are truly loved and wanted? Of course you can't—because you don't love them. How can you? You don't know them.'

There—let him answer *that*! But even as she made her defiant stand Ruby's heart was warning her that Sander had raised an issue that she could not ignore and would ultimately have to face. Honesty compelled her to admit it.

'I do know that one day they will want to know who fathered them and what their family history is,' she said.

It was hard for her to make that admission—just as it had been hard for her to answer the questions the boys had already asked, saying that they did have a daddy but he lived in a different country. Those words had reminded her of what she was denying her sons because of the circumstances in which she had conceived them. One day, though, their questions would be those of teenagers, not little boys, and far more searching, far more knowing.

Ruby looked away from Sander, instinctively wanting to hide her inner fears from him. The problem of telling the boys how she had come to have them lay across her heart and her conscience in an ever present heavy weight. At the moment they simply accepted that, like many of the other children they were at school with, they did not have a daddy living with them. But one day they would start to ask more questions, and she had hoped desperately that she would not have to tell them the truth until they were old enough to accept it without judging her. Now Sander had stirred up all the anxieties she had tried to put to one side. More than anything else she wanted to be a good mother, to give her boys the gift of a secure childhood filled with love; she wanted them to grow up knowing they were loved, confident and happy, without the burden of having to worry about adult relationships. For that reason she was determined never, ever to begin a relationship with anyone. A changing parade of 'uncles' and 'stepfathers' wasn't what she wanted for her boys.

But now Sander, with his demands and his questions, was forcing her to think about the future and her sons' reactions to the reality of their conception. The fact that they did not have a father who loved them.

Anger and panic swirled through her.

'Why are you doing this?' she demanded. 'The boys mean nothing to you. They are five years old, and you didn't even know that they existed until now.'

'That is true. But as for them meaning nothing to me—you are wrong. They are of my blood, and that alone means that I have a responsibility to ensure that they are brought up within their family.'

He wasn't going to tell her about that atavistic surge of emotion and connection he had felt the minute he had seen the twins' photograph. Sander still didn't really understand it himself. He only knew that it had brought him here, and that it would keep him here until she handed over to him his sons.

'It can't have been easy for you financially, bringing them up.'

Sander was offering her sympathy? Ruby was immediately suspicious. She longed to tell him that what *hadn't* been easy for her was discovering at seventeen that she was pregnant by a man who had slept with her and then left her, but somehow she managed to resist doing so.

Sander gestured round the hall.

'Even if your sister is able to keep up the mortgage payments on this house, have you thought about what would happen if either of your sisters wanted to marry and move out? At the moment you are financially dependent on their goodwill. As a caring mother, naturally you will want your sons to have the best possible education and a comfortable life. I can provide them with both, and provide you with the money to live your own life. It can't be much fun for you, tied to two small children all the time.'

She had been right to be suspicious, Ruby recognised, as the full meaning of Sander's offer hit her. Did he really expect her to *sell* her sons to him? Didn't he realise how obscene his offer was? Or did he simply not care?

His determination made her cautious in her response, her instincts warning her to be careful about any innocent admission she might make as to the financial hardship they were all currently going through, in case Sander tried to use that information against her at a later date. So, instead of reacting with the anger she felt, she said instead, 'The twins are only five. Now that they're at school I'm planning to continue my education. As for me having fun—the boys provide me with all the fun I want or need.'

'You'll forgive me if I say that I find that hard to believe, given the circumstances under which we met,' was Sander's smooth and cruel response.

'That was six years ago, and in circumstances that—' Ruby broke off. Why should she explain herself to him? The people closest to her—her sisters—knew and understood what had driven her to the reckless behaviour that had resulted in the twins' conception, and their love and support for her had never wavered. She owed Sander nothing after all—much less the revelation of her teenage vulnerabilities. 'That was then,' she corrected herself, adding firmly, 'This is now.'

The knowing look Sander was giving her made Ruby want to protest—*You're wrong. I'm not what you think. That wasn't the real me that night.* But common sense and pride made her hold back the words.

'I'm prepared to be very generous to you financially in return for you handing the twins over to me,' Sander continued. 'Very generous indeed. You're still young.'

In fact he had been surprised to discover that the night they had met she had been only seventeen. Dressed and made-up as she had been, he had assumed that she was much older. Sander frowned. He hadn't enjoyed the sharp spike of distaste he had experienced against himself at knowing he had taken such a young girl to bed. Had he known her age he would have… What? Given her a stern talking to and sent her home in a cab? Had he been in control of himself that night he would not have gone to bed with her at all, no matter what her age, but the unpalatable truth was that he had *not* been in control of himself. He had been in the grip of anger and a sense of frustration he had never experienced either before or since that night—a firestorm of savage, bitter emotion that had driven him into behaviour that, if he was honest, still irked his pride and sense of self. Other men might exhibit such behaviour, but he had always thought of himself as above that kind of thing. He had been wrong, and now the evidence of that behaviour was confronting him in the shape of the sons he had fathered. Sander believed he had a duty to ensure that they did not suffer because of that behaviour. That was what had brought him here.

And there was no way he was going to leave until he had got what he had come for.

And just that?

Ruby shook her head.

'Buy my children, you mean?'

Sander could hear the hostility in Ruby's voice as well as see it in her eyes.

'Because that *is* what you're talking about,' Ruby accused him, adding fiercely, 'And if I'd had any thought of allowing you into their lives, what you've just said would make me change my mind. There's nothing you could offer me that would make me want to risk my sons' emotional future by allowing *you* to have any kind of contact with them.'

Her words were having more of an effect on him than Sander liked to admit. A man of pride and power, used to commanding not just the obedience but also the respect and the admiration of others, he was stung by Ruby's criticism of him. He wasn't used to being refused anything by anyone—much less by a woman he remembered as an over-made-up and under-dressed little tart who had come on to him openly and obviously. Not that there was anything of that girl about her now, dressed in faded jeans and a loose top, her face free of make-up and her hair left to curl naturally of its own accord. The girl he remembered had smelled of cheap scent; the woman in front of him smelled of cleaning product. He would have to change his approach if he was to overcome her objections, Sander recognised.

Quickly changing tack, he challenged her. 'Nothing

I could offer *you*, maybe, but what about what I can offer my sons? You speak of their emotions. Have you thought, I wonder, how they are going to feel when they grow up to realise what you have denied them in refusing to let them know their father?'

'That's not fair,' Ruby objected angrily, knowing that Sander had found her most vulnerable spot where the twins were concerned.

'What is not fair, surely, is you denying my sons the opportunity to know their father and the culture that is their birthright?'

'As your bastards?' The horrible word tasted bitter, but it had to be said. 'Forced to stand in second place to your legitimate children, and no doubt be resented by your wife?'

'I have no other children, nor any wife.'

Why was her heart hammering so heavily, thudding into her chest wall? It didn't matter to her whether or not Sander was married, did it?

'I warn you now, Ruby, that I intend to have my sons with me. Whatever it takes to achieve that and by whatever means.'

Ruby's mouth went dry. Stories she had read about children being kidnapped by a parent and stolen away out of the country flooded into her mind. Sander was a very rich and a very powerful man. She had discovered that in the early days after she had met him, when she had stupidly imagined that he would come back to her and had avidly read everything she could about him, wanting to learn everything she could—until the reality of the situation had forced her to accept that the fantasy she had created of Sander marrying her and looking after her was just that: a fantasy created by her need to find someone to replace the parents she had lost and keep her safe.

It was true that Sander could give the boys far more than she could materially, and the unwelcome thought slid into her mind that there could come a day when, as Sander had cruelly predicted, the twins might actually resent her and blame her for preventing them from benefitting from their father's wealth and, more importantly, from knowing him. Boys needed a strong male figure in their lives they could relate to. Everyone knew that. Secretly she had been worrying about the lack of any male influence in their lives. But if at times she had been tempted to pray for a solution to that problem she had certainly not envisaged that solution coming in the form of the boys' natural father. A kindly, grandfather-type figure for them was as much as she had hoped for, because after their birth she had decided that she would never take the risk of getting involved with a man who might turn out to be only a temporary presence in her sons' lives. She would rather remain celibate than risk that.

The truth, in her opinion, was that children thrived best with two parents in a stable relationship—a mother and a father, both committed to their wellbeing.

A mother and a father. More than most, she knew the damage that could be done when that stability wasn't there.

A sense of standing on the edge of a precipice filled

her—an awareness that the decision she made now would affect her sons for the rest of their lives. Shakily she admitted to herself that she wished her sisters were there to help her, but they weren't. They had their own lives, and ultimately the boys were *her* responsibility, their happiness resting in *her* hands. Sander was determined to have them. He had said so. He was a wealthy, powerful and charismatic man who would have no difficulty whatsoever in persuading others that the boys should be with him. But she was their mother. She couldn't let him take them from her—for their sakes even more than her own. Sander didn't love them; he merely wanted them. She doubted he was capable of understanding what love was. Yes, he would provide well for them materially, but children needed far more than that, and her sons needed *her*. She had raised them from birth; they needed her even more than she needed them.

If she couldn't stop Sander from claiming his sons, then she owed it to them to make sure that she remained with them. Sander wouldn't want that, of course. He despised and disliked her.

Her heart started to thud uncomfortably heavily and far too fast as it fought against the solution proposed by her brain, but now that the thought was there it couldn't be ignored. Sander had said there was nothing he would not do to have his sons living with him. Well, maybe she should put his claim to the test, because she knew that there was no sacrifice she herself would not make for their sakes—no sacrifice at all. The challenge she intended to put to him was a huge risk for her to take, but for the boys' sake she was prepared to take it. It was, after all, a challenge she was bound to win—because Sander would never accept the terms with which she was about to confront him. She was sure of that. She let out her pent up breath.

'You say the boys' place is with you?'

'It is.'

'They are five years old and I am their mother.' Ruby took a deep breath, hoping that her voice wouldn't shake with the nervousness she was fighting to suppress and thus betray her. 'If you really care about their wellbeing as much as you claim then you must know that they are too young to be separated from me.'

She had a point, Sander was forced to admit, even though he didn't like doing so.

'You need to be very sure about why you want the twins, Sander.' Ruby pressed home her point. 'And that your desire to have them isn't merely a rich man's whim. Because the only way I will allow them to be with you is if I am there with them—as their mother and your wife.'

# CHAPTER TWO

THERE—she had said it. Thrown down the gauntlet, so to speak, and given him her challenge.

In the silence that followed Ruby could literally hear her own heart beating as she held her breath, waiting for Sander to refuse her demand—because she knew that he *would* refuse it, and having refused it he must surely be forced to step back and accept that the boys' place was with her.

Trying not to give in to the shakiness invading her body, Ruby could hardly believe that she had actually had the courage to say what she had. She could tell from Sander's expression that her demand had shocked him, although he was quick to mask his reaction.

*Marriage*, Sander thought quickly, mentally assessing his options. He wanted his sons. There was no doubt in his mind about that, nor any doubt that they were his. Marriage to their mother would give him certain rights over them, but it would also give Ruby certain rights over his wealth. That, of course, was exactly what she wanted. Marriage to him followed by an equally speedy divorce and a very generous financial divorce settlement. He could read her mind so easily. Even so, she had caught him off-guard—although he told himself cynically that he should perhaps have been prepared for her demand. He was, after all, a very wealthy man.

'I applaud your sharp-witted business acumen,' he told Ruby drily, in a neutral voice that gave away nothing of the fury he was really feeling. 'You rejected my initial offer of a generous payment under the guise of being a devoted mother, when in reality you were already planning to play for higher stakes.'

'That's not true,' Ruby denied hotly, astonished by his interpretation of her demand. 'Your money means nothing to me, Sander—nothing at all,' she told him truthfully, adding for good measure, 'And neither do you. For me, the fact that you choose to think of my offer in terms of money simply underlines all the reasons why I am not prepared to allow my sons anywhere near you unless I am there.'

'That is how *you* feel, but what about how *they* might feel?' Sander pressed her. 'A good mother would never behave so selfishly. She would put her children's interests first.'

How speedily Sander had turned the tables on her, Ruby recognised. What had begun as a challenge to him she had been confident would make him back down had now turned into a double-edged sword which right now he was wielding very skilfully against her, cutting what she had thought was secure ground away from under her feet.

'They need their mother—' she started.

'They are *my* sons,' Sander interrupted her angrily. 'And I mean to have them. If I have to marry you to facilitate that, then so be it. But make no mistake, Ruby. I intend to have my sons.'

His response stunned her. She had been expecting him to refuse, to back down, to go away and leave them alone—anything rather than marry her. Sander had called her bluff and left her defenceless.

Now Ruby could see a reality she hadn't seen before. Sander really did want the boys and he meant to have them. He was rich and powerful, well able to provide materially for his sons. What chance would she have of keeping them if he pursued her through the courts? At best all she could hope for was shared custody, with the boys passed to and fro between them, torn between two homes, and that was the last thing she wanted for them. *Why* had Sander had to discover that he had fathered them? Hadn't life been cruel enough to her as it was?

Marriage to him, which she had not in any kind of way wanted, had now devastatingly turned into the protection she was forced to recognise she might need if she was to continue to have the permanent place in her sons' lives that she had previously taken for granted.

Marriage to Sander wouldn't just provide her sons with a father, she recognised now through growing panic, it would also protect her rights as a mother. As long as they were married the twins would have both parents there for them.

Both parents. Ruby swallowed painfully. Wasn't it

true that she had spent many sleepless nights worrying about the future and the effect not having a father figure might have on her sons?

A father figure, but not their real father. She had *never* imagined them having Sander in their lives—not after those first agonising weeks of being forced to accept that she meant nothing to him.

She wasn't going to give up, though. She would fight with every bit of her strength for her sons.

Holding her head up she told him fiercely, 'Very well, then. The choice is yours, Sander. If you genuinely want the boys because they are your sons, and because you want to get to know them and be part of their lives, then you will accept that separating them from me will inflict huge emotional damage on them. You will understand, as I do, no matter how much that understanding galls you, that children need the security of having two parents they know are there for them—will always be there for them. You will be prepared to make the same sacrifice that I am prepared to make to provide them with the security that comes from having two parents committed to them and to each other through marriage.'

'Sacrifice?' Sander demanded. 'I am a billionaire. I don't think there are many women who would consider marriage to me a *sacrifice*.'

Did he really believe that? If so, it just showed how right she was to want to ensure that her sons grew up knowing there were far more important things in life than money.

'You are very cynical,' she told him. 'There are any

number of women who would be appalled by what you have just said—women who put love before money, women like me who put their children first, women who would run from a man like you. I don't want your money, and I am quite willing to sign a document saying so.'

'Oh, you will be doing that. Make no mistake about it,' Sander assured her ruthlessly. Did she really expect him to fall for her lies and her faked lack of interest in his money? 'There is no way I will abandon my sons to the care of a mother who could very soon be without a roof over her head—a mother who would have to rely on charity in order to feed and clothe them—a mother who dressed like a tart and offered herself to a man she didn't know.'

Ruby flinched as though he had physically hit her, but she still managed to ask quickly, 'Were *you* any better? Or does the fact that you are a man and I'm a woman somehow mean that my behaviour was worse than yours? I was a seventeen-year-old-girl; you were an adult male.'

A seventeen-year-old girl. Angered by the reminder, Sander reacted against it. 'You certainly weren't dressed like a schoolgirl—or an innocent. And you were the one who propositioned me, not the other way round.'

And now he was going to be forced to marry her. Sander didn't want to marry anyone—much less a woman like her.

What he had seen in his parents' marriage, the bitterness and resentment between them, had made him vow never to marry himself. That vow had been the cause of acrimony and dissent between him and his grandfather, a despot who believed he had the right to barter his own flesh and blood in marriage as though they were just another part of his fleet of tankers.

Refusing Ruby's proposal would give her an advantage. She could and would undoubtedly attempt to use his refusal against him were there to be a court case between them over the twins. But her obstinacy and her attempt to get the better of him had hardened Sander's determination to claim his sons—even if it now meant using underhand methods to do so. Once they were on his island, its laws would ensure that he, as their father, had the right to keep them.

The familiar sound of a car drawing up outside and doors opening had Ruby ignoring Sander to hurry to the door. She suddenly realised what time it was, and that the twins were being dropped off by the neighbour with whom she shared school run duties. Opening the door, she hurried down the drive to thank her neighbour and help the twins out of the car, gathering up school bags and lunchboxes as she did, clucking over the fact that neither boy had fastened his coat despite the fact that it was still only March and cold.

Identical in every way, except for the tiny mole behind Freddie's right ear, the boys stood and stared at the expensive car parked on the drive, and then looked at Ruby.

'Whose car is that?' Freddie asked, round-eyed.

Ruby couldn't answer him. Why hadn't she realised the time and got rid of Sander before the twins came home from school? Now they were bound to ask questions—questions she wasn't going to be able to answer honestly—and she hated the thought of lying to them.

Freddie was still waiting for her to answer. Forcing a reassuring smile, she told him, 'It's just...someone's. Come on, let's get inside before the two of you catch cold with your coats unfastened like that.'

'I'm hungry. Can we have toast with peanut butter?' Harry asked her hopefully.

Peanut butter was his current favourite.

'We'll see,' was Ruby's answer as she pushed then gently into the hall in front of her. 'Upstairs now, boys,' she told them both, trying to remain as calm as she could even as they stood and stared in silence at Sander, who now seemed to be taking up a good deal of space in the hallway.

He was tall, well over six foot, and in other circumstances it would have made her smile to see the way Harry tipped his head right back to look up at him. Freddie, though, suddenly very much the man of the family as the elder of the two. He moved closer to her, as if instinctively seeking to protect her, and some silent communication between the two of them caused his twin to fall back to her other side to do the same.

Unwanted emotional tears stung Ruby's eyes. Her darling boys. They didn't deserve any of this, and it was *her* fault that things were as they were. Before she could stop herself she dropped down on one knee, putting an arm around each twin, holding them to her. Freddie was the more sensitive of the two, although he tried to conceal it, and he turned into her immediately, burying his face in her neck and holding her tightly, whilst Harry looked briefly towards Sander—wanting to go to him? Ruby wondered wretchedly—before copying his brother.

Sander couldn't move. The second he had seen the two boys he had known that there was nothing he would not do for them—including tearing out his own heart and offering it to them on a plate. The sheer force of his love for them was like a tidal wave, a tsunami that swept everything else aside. They were his—of his family, of his blood, of his body. They were his. And yet, watching them, he recognised immediately how they felt about their mother. He had seen the protective stance they had taken up and his heart filled with pride to see that instinctive maleness in them.

An old memory stirred within him: strong sunlight striking down on his bare head, the raised angry voices of his parents above him. He too had turned to his mother, as his sons had turned to theirs, but there had been no loving maternal arms to hold him. Instead his mother had spun round, heading for her car, slamming the door after she'd climbed into it, leaving him behind, tyres spinning on the gravel, sending up a shower of small stones. He had turned then to his father, but he too had turned away from him and walked back to the house. His parents had been too caught up in their own lives and their resentment of one another to have time for him.

Sander looked down at his sons—and at their mother. They were all their sons had. He thought again of his own parents, and realised on another surge of emotion that there was nothing he would not do to give his sons what he had never had.

'Marriage it is, then. But I warn you now it will be a marriage that will last for life. That is the measure of my commitment to them,' he told her, looking at the boys.

If she hadn't been holding the twins Ruby thought she might well have fallen down in shock—shock and dismay. She searched Sander's face for some sign that he didn't really mean what he was saying, but all she could see was a quiet, implacable determination.

The twins were turning in her arms to look at Sander again. Any moment now they would start asking questions.

'Upstairs, you two,' she repeated, taking off their navy duffel coats. 'Change out of your uniforms and then wash your hands.'

They made a dash past Sander, deliberately ignoring him, before climbing the stairs together—a pair of sturdy, healthy male children, with lean little-boy bodies and their father's features beneath identical mops of dark curls.

'There will be two conditions,' Sander continued coldly. 'The first is that you will sign a prenuptial agreement. Our marriage will be for the benefit of our sons, not the benefit of your bank account.'

Appalled and hurt by this fresh evidence of how little he thought of her, Ruby swallowed her pride—she was doing this for her boys, after all—and demanded through gritted teeth, 'And the second condition?'

'Your confirmation and proof that you are taking the birth control pill. I've seen the evidence of how little care you have for such matters. I have no wish for another child to be conceived as carelessly as the twins were.'

Now Ruby was too outraged to conceal her feelings.

'There is no question of that happening. The last thing I want is to have to share your bed again.'

She dared to claim *that*, after the way she had already behaved?

Her outburst lashed Sander's pride into a savage need to punish her.

'But you *will* share it, and you will beg me to satisfy that hunger in you I have already witnessed. Your desire for sexual satisfaction has been honed in the arms of far too many men for you to be able to control it now.'

'No! That's not true.'

Ruby could feel her face burning. She didn't need reminding about the wanton way in which she had not only given herself to him but actively encouraged him to take her. Her memories of that night were burned into her conscience for ever. Not one of her senses would ever forget the role they had played in her self-humiliation— the way her voice had sobbed and risen on an increasing note of aching longing that had resulted in a cry of abandoned pleasure that still echoed in her ears, the greedy need of her hands to touch and know his body, the hunger of her lips to caress his flesh and taste his kisses, the increased arousal the scent of his skin had brought her. Each and all of them had added to a wild torrent of sexual longing that had taken her to the edge of her universe and then beyond it, to a place of such spectacular loss of self that she never wanted to go there again.

Shaking herself free of the memories threatening to deluge her, Ruby returned staunchly, 'That was different...a mistake.' Her hands curled into her palms in bitter self-defence as she saw the cynical look he was giving her. 'And it's one that I never want to repeat. There's no way I'd ever want to share your bed again.'

Her denial unleashed Sander's anger. She was lying, he was sure of it, and he would prove it to her. He wasn't a vain man, but he knew that women found him attractive, and Ruby had certainly done everything she could that night to make it plain to him that she wanted him. Normally he would never have even considered bedding her—he liked to do his own hunting—but her persistence had been like a piece of grit in his shoe, wearing down his resistance and helping to fuel the anger already burning inside him. *That* was why he had lost control. Because of his grandfather. Not because of Ruby herself, or because the aroused little cries she had made against his skin had proved so irresistible that he had lost sight of everything but his need to possess her. He could still remember the way she had cried out when he had finally thrust into her, as though what she was experiencing was completely new to her. She had clung to him, sobbing her pleasure into his skin as she trembled and shuddered against him.

Why was he thinking of that now?

The savagery of his fury, inflamed by both her demand for marriage and her denial of his accusation, deafened him to the note of raw pain in her voice. Before he could stop himself he had taken hold of her and was possessing her mouth in a kiss of scorching, pride-fuelled fury.

Too shocked to struggle against his possession, by the time she realised what was happening it was too late. Ruby's own anger surged in defiance, passionate enough to overwhelm her self-control and battle with the full heat of Sander's desire to punish her. Desire for him was the last thing she had expected to feel, but, shockingly, the hard possession of Sander's mouth on her own turned a key in a lock she had thought so damaged by what he had already made her endure that it could never be turned again. Turned it with frightening ease.

This shouldn't be happening. It could not be happening. But, shamefully, it was.

Her panic fought with the desire that burned through her and lost, overcome as swiftly as though molten lava was pouring through her, obliterating everything that stood in its path. Her lips parted beneath the driving pressure of Sander's probing tongue, an agonised whimper of longing drawn from her throat. She could feel the passion in Sander's kiss, and the hard arousal of his body, but instead of acting as a warning that knowledge only served to further enflame her own desire, quickening the pulse already beating within her own sex.

Somewhere within the torrent of anger motivating him Sander could hear an inner voice warning him that this was how it had been before—this same furious, aching, agonised need and arousal that was possessing him now. It should have been impossible for him to want her. It should always have been impossible. And yet, like some mythical, dark malformed creature, supposedly entombed and shut away for ever, his desire had found the superhuman strength to break the bonds imprisoning it. His tongue possessed the eager willingness of the softness of her mouth and his body was already hard, anticipating the corresponding willingness of the most intimate part of her if he didn't stop soon...

Ruby shuddered with mindless sensual delight as Sander's tongue began to thrust potently and rhythmically against her own. Beneath her clothes her nipples swelled and hardened, their ache spreading swiftly through her. Sander's hand cupped her breast, causing her to moan deep in her throat.

She was all female sensual heat, all eager willingness, her very responsiveness designed to trap, Sander recognised. If he didn't stop now he wouldn't be able to stop himself from taking her where they stood, from dragging the clothes from her body in his need to feel her bare skin against his touch, from sinking himself deep within her and feeling her body close round him, possessing him as he possessed her, both of them driven by the mindless, incessant ache that he was surely cursed to feel for her every time he touched her.

He found the buttons on her shirt, swiftly unfastening them. The feel of his hands on her body drew Ruby back into the past. Then he had undressed her expertly and swiftly, in between sensually erotic kisses that had melted away her ability to think or reason, leaving her aching for more, just as he was doing now. His left hand lifted her hair so that he could taste the warm sweetness of that place just where her neck joined her shoulder.

Ruby felt the warmth of his breath against her bare skin. Flames were erupting inside her—the eager flames of denied longing leaping upwards, consuming her resistance. Mindless shudders of hot pleasure rippled through her. Her shirt was open, her breasts exposed to Sander's gaze.

He shouldn't be doing this, Sander warned himself. He shouldn't be giving in to the demands of his pride. But that was *all* he was doing. The heat running through his veins was only caused by angry pride, nothing else.

Her breasts were as perfect as he remembered, the dark rose nipples flaring into deep aureoles that contrasted with the paleness of her skin. He watched as they lifted and fell with the increased speed of her breathing, lifting his hand to cup one, knowing already that it would fit his hand as perfectly as though it was made to be held by him. Beneath the stroke of his thumb-pad her nipple hardened. Sander closed his eyes, remembering how in that long-ago hotel bedroom it had seemed as though her nipple was pushing itself against his touch, demanding the caress of first his thumb and forefinger, then his lips and tongue. Her response had been wild and immediate, swelling and hardening his own body.

He didn't want her, not really, but his pride was now demanding her punishment, the destruction of her claim that she didn't want him.

Ruby could feel herself being dragged back to the past. A small cry of protest gave away her torment.

Abruptly Sander thrust her away from him, brought back to reality by the sound.

They stood watching one another, fighting to control the urgency of their breathing, the urgency of their need. Exposed, raw, and in Ruby's eyes ugly, it was almost a tangible force between them.

They both felt the strength of it and its danger. Ruby could see that knowledge in Sander's eyes, just as she knew he must see it reflected in her own.

The weight of her shame ached through her.

Ruby's face was drained of colour, her eyes huge with shock in her small face.

Sander was just as shocked by the intensity of the desire that had come out of nowhere to threaten his self-control—but he was better at hiding it than Ruby, and he was in no mood to find any pity for her. He was still battling with the unwanted knowledge of just how much he had wanted her.

'You will take the contraceptive pill,' he told her coldly. His heart started to pound heavily in recognition of what his words meant and invited, and the ache in his body surged against his self-control, but somehow he forced himself to ignore the demands of his own desire, to continue. 'I will not accept any consequences of you not doing so.'

Never had she felt so weak, Ruby thought shakily— and not just physically weak, but emotionally and mentally weak as well. In the space of a few short minutes the protective cover she had woven around herself had been ripped from her, exposing her to the full horror of a weakness she had thought controlled and contained. It should be impossible for her to want Sander, to be aroused by him. Should be.

Reaction to what had happened was setting in. She felt physically sick, dazed, unable to function properly, torn apart by the conflicting nature of her physical desire and her burning sense of shame and disbelief that she should feel that desire... Wild thoughts jostled through her head. Perhaps she should not merely ask her doctor for a prescription for the birth control pill but for an anti-Sander pill as well—something that would destroy her desire for him? She needed a pill for that? Surely the way he had spoken to her, the way he had treated her, should be enough to ensure that she loathed the thought of him touching her? Surely her pride and the humiliation he had heaped on her should be strong enough to protect her?

She couldn't marry him. Not now. Panic filled her.

'I've changed my mind,' she told him quickly. 'About...about us getting married.'

Sander frowned. His immediate response to her statement was a fierce surge of determination to prevent her from changing her mind. For the sake of his sons. Nothing else. And certainly not because of the ache that was still pounding through him.

'So the future of our sons is not as important to you as you claimed after all?' he challenged her.

She was trapped, Ruby acknowledged, trapped in a prison of her own making. All she could do was cling to the fragile hope that somehow she would find the strength to deny the desire he could arouse in her so easily.

'Of course it is,' she protested.

'Then we shall be married, and you will accept my terms and conditions.'

'And if I refuse?'

'Then I will move heaven and earth and the stars between them to take my sons from you.'

He meant what he was saying, Ruby could tell. She had no choice other than to bow her head in acceptance of his demands.

He had defeated her, Sander knew, but the taste of his triumph did not have the sweetness he had expected.

'The demands placed on me by my business mean that the sooner the arrangements are completed the better. I shall arrange for the necessary paperwork to be carried out with regard to the prenuptial agreement I shall require you to sign and for our marriage. You must—'

A sudden bang from upstairs, followed by a sharp cry of pain, had them both turning towards the stairs.

Anxious for the safety of her sons, Ruby rushed past Sander, hurrying up the stairs to the boys' room, unaware that Sander was right behind her as she pushed open the door to find Harry on the floor sobbing whilst Freddie stood clutching one of their toy cars.

'Freddie pushed me,' Harry told her.

'No, I didn't. He was trying to take my car.'

'Let me have a look,' Ruby instructed Harry, quickly checking to make sure that no real damage had been done before sitting back on her heels and turning to look at Freddie. But instead of coming to her for comfort Freddie was standing in front of Sander, who had obviously followed her into the room, looking up at him as though seeking his support, and Sander had his hand on Freddie's arm, as though protecting him.

The raw intensity of her emotions gripped her by the throat—grief for all that the twins had missed in not having a father, guilt because she was the cause of that, pain because she loved them so much but her love alone could not give them the tools they would need to grow into well balanced men, and fear for her own self-respect.

His hand resting protectively on the shoulder of his son, Sander looked grimly at Ruby. His sons needed him in their lives, and nothing—least of all a woman like Ruby— was going to prevent him from being there for them.

Oblivious to the atmosphere between the two grown-ups Freddie repeated, 'It's *my* car.'

'No, it's not. It's mine,' Harry argued.

Their argument pulled Ruby's attention back to them. They were devoted to one another, but every now and again they would argue like this over a toy, as though each of them was trying to seek authority over the other. It was a boy thing, other mothers had assured her, but Ruby hated to see them fall out.

'I've got a suggestion to make.' Sander's voice was calm, and yet authoritative in a way that immediately had both boys looking at him. 'If you both promise not to argue over this car again then I will buy you a new toy each, so you won't have to share.'

Ruby sucked in an outraged breath, her maternal instincts overwhelming the vulnerability she felt towards Sander as a woman. What he was doing was outright bribery. Since she didn't have the money to give the boys one each of things she had impressed on them the need to share and share alike, and now, with a handful of words, Sander had appealed to their natural acquisitive instincts with his offer.

She could see from the eager look in both pairs of dark gold eyes that her rules about sharing had been forgotten even before Harry challenged Sander excitedly, 'When...when can we have them?'

Harry was on his feet now, rushing over to join his twin and lean confidently against Sander's other leg whilst he looked up excitedly at him, his words tumbling over themselves as he told Sander, 'I want a car like the one outside...'

'So do I,' Freddie agreed, determined not to be outdone and to assert his elder brother status.

'I'm taking both of you and your mother to London.'

This was news to Ruby, but she wasn't given the chance to say anything because Sander was already continuing.

'There's a big toyshop there where we can look for your cars—but only if you promise me not to quarrel over your toys in future.'

Two dark heads nodded enthusiastically in assent, and two identical watermelon grins split her sons' faces as they gazed up worshipfully at Sander.

Ruby struggled to contain her feelings. Seeing her sons with Sander, watching the way they reacted to him, had brought home to her more effectively than a thousand arguments could ever have done just what they were missing without him—not financially, but emotionally.

Was it her imagination, or was she right in thinking that already they seemed to be standing taller, speaking more confidently, even displaying a body language they had automatically copied from their father? A small pang of sadness filled her. They weren't babies any longer, *her* babies, wholly dependent on her for everything; they were growing up, and their reaction to Sander proved what she had already known—they needed a male role model in their lives. Helplessly she submitted to the power of the wave of maternal love that surged through her, but her head lifted proudly as she returned Sander's silently challenging look.

Automatically Ruby reached out to stroke the tousled dark curls exactly at the moment that Sander did the same. Their hands touched. Immediately Ruby recoiled from the contact, unable to stop the swift rush of knowledge that slid into her head. Once Sander's hands had touched her far more intimately than they were doing now, taking her and possessing her with a potent mix of knowledge and male arousal, and something else which in her ignorance and innocence she had told herself was passionate desire for her and her alone, but which of course had been nothing of the sort.

That reality had left her emotions badly bruised. His was the only sexual male touch she had ever known. Memories she had thought sealed away for ever were trying to surface. Memories aroused by that kiss Sander had forced on her earlier. Ruby shuddered in mute loathing of her own weakness, but it was too late. The mental images her memories were painting would not be denied—images of Sander's hands on her body, the sound of his breathing against her ear and then later her skin. But, no, she must not think of those things. Instead she must be strong. She must resist and deny his ability to arouse her. She was not that young girl any more, she was a woman, a mother, and her sons' needs must come before her own.

# CHAPTER THREE

RUBY'S head was pounding with a tension headache, and her stomach cramped—familiar reactions to stress, which she knew could well result in her ending up with something close to a full-scale migraine attack. But this wasn't the time for her to be ill, or indeed to show any weakness—even if she had hardly slept since and had woken this morning feeling nauseous.

The twins were dressed in the new jumpers and jeans her sisters had bought them for Christmas, and wearing the new trainers she had spent her preciously saved money on after she had seen the frowning look Sander had given their old ones when he had called to discuss everything—'everything' being all the arrangements he had made, not just for their stay in London but for their marriage as well, before the four of them would leave for the island that would be their home. They were too excited to sit down, insisting instead on standing in front of the window so that they could see Sander arrive to pick them all up for their visit to London.

Would she have made a different decision if her

sisters had been at home? Ruby didn't see how she could have done. They had been wonderful to her, insisting that they would support her financially so that she could stay at home with the boys, but Ruby had become increasingly aware not just of the financial pressure they were under, but also the fact that one day surely her sisters would fall in love. When they did she didn't want to feel she and the twins were standing in their way because they felt duty-bound to go on supporting them.

No, she had made the right decision. For the twins, who were both wildly excited about the coming trip to London and who had happily accepted her careful announcement to them that she was going to marry Sander, and for her sisters, who had given her and the twins so much love and support.

The twins had reacted to the news that she and Sander were going to be married with excitement and delight, and Freddie had informed her hopefully, 'Luke Simpson has a daddy. He takes him to watch football, and to McDonalds, and he bought him a new bicycle.'

The reality was that everything seemed to be working in Sander's favour. She couldn't even use the excuse of saying that she couldn't take the boys out of school to refuse to go to London, since they were now on holiday for Easter.

When they went back to school it would be to the small English speaking school on the island where, Sander had informed her, those islanders who wished their children to grow up speaking English could send them.

The conversation she and Sander had had about the

twins' future had been more of a question and answer
session, with her asking the questions and Sander sup-
plying the answers. All she knew about their future life
was that Sander preferred to live and work on the island
his family had ruled for several centuries, although the
container shipping business he had built up into a worldwide concern also had offices and staff at all the world's
major commercial ports, including Felixstowe in
England. Sander had also told her that his second in
command was his younger brother, who had trained in
IT and was based in Athens.

When it came to the boys' future education, Sander
had told her that he was completely against them going
to boarding school—much to her own relief. He had
said that when the time came they would spend term
time in England as a family, returning to the island when
the boys were out of school.

In addition to the younger brother, Sander had informed her, he also had a sister—the same sister Ruby
had learned had taken the photograph of the twins that
had alerted Sander to their existence. Like his brother,
she too lived in Athens with her husband.

'So it will just be the two of us and the boys, then?'
she had pressed warily.

'That is the norm, isn't it?' he had countered. 'The
nuclear family, comprising a father, a mother and
their children.'

Stupidly, perhaps, she hadn't thought as far as how they
would live, but the way her thoughts had recoiled from
the reality of their new life together had shown her how

apprehensive she was. Because she feared him, or because she feared wanting him? Her face burned even now, remembering her inability to answer that inner question.

It had been far easier to deal with the practicalities of what lay ahead rather than allow herself to be overwhelmed by the complex emotional issues it raised.

Now, waiting for Sander to collect them, with letters for her sisters explaining what she was doing and why written and waiting for them on their return to the UK—the situation wasn't something she felt she wanted to discuss with them over the phone—Ruby could feel the pain in her temple increasing, whilst her stomach churned with anxiety. Everything would have been so very different if only she hadn't give in to that shameful physical desire Sander had somehow managed to arouse in her. In her handbag were the birth control pills Sander had demanded that she take. She had been tempted to defy him, to insist that she could rely on her own will-power to ensure that there was no further sexual intimacy between them. But she was still horrified by the memory of what had happened between them in her hallway, still struggling to take in the fact that it had happened. The speed of it, the intensity of it, had been like a fire erupting out of nowhere to blaze so fiercely that it was beyond control. It had left her feeling vulnerable and unable to trust herself.

There must not be another child, Sander had told her. And wasn't the truth that she herself did not *want* to create another new life with a man who had no respect for her, no feelings of kindness towards her, and cer-

tainly no love for her? Love? Hadn't she grown out of
the dangerous self-deceit of dressing up naked lust in
the fantasy illusion of 'love'? Clothing it in the kind of
foolish dreams that belonged to naive adolescents?
Before Sander had kissed her she would have sworn and
believed that there was nothing he could do to her, no
intimacy he could enforce on her, that would arouse her
own desire. But the searing heat of the kiss he had sub-
jected her to had burned away her defences.

She hated having to admit to herself that she couldn't
rely on her own pride and self-control, but the only
thing she could cling to was the knowledge that Sander
had been as close to losing *his* control as she had been
of losing hers. Of all the cruel tricks that nature could
play on two human beings, surely that must be the
worst? To create within them a desire for one another
that could burn away every shred of protection, leaving
them exposed to a need that neither of them wanted. If
she could have ripped her own desire out of her body
she would have done. It was an alien, unwanted presence, an enemy within her that she must find a way to
destroy.

'He's here!'

Freddie's excited announcement cut through her introspection. Both boys were racing to the door and
pulling it open, jumping up and down with eager delight
when the car door opened and Sander stepped out.

He might be dressed casually, in a black polo shirt,
beige chinos and a dark tan leather jacket, but Sander
still had that unmistakable air about him that said he was

a man other men looked up to and women wanted to be close to, Ruby was forced to admit unwillingly. It wasn't just that he was good-looking—many men were that. No, Sander had something else—something that was a mixture of an aura of power blended with raw male sexuality. She had sensed it as a naive teenager and been drawn to him because of it, and even now, when she was old enough and wise enough to know better, she still felt the pull of his sexual magnetism, its threat to suck her into treacherous waters.

A shiver that was almost a mocking caress stroked over her, making her hug her arms around her body to conceal the sudden unwanted peaking of her nipples. Not because of Sander, she assured herself. No, it was the cold from the open door that was causing her body's sensitive reactions.

Sander's brooding gaze swept over Ruby and rested momentarily on her breasts. Like a leashed cougar, the desire inside him surged against its restraint, leaping and clawing against its imprisonment, the force of its power straining the muscles he had locked against it.

These last couple of weeks he had spent more hours than he wanted to count wrestling with the ache for her that burned in his groin—possessed by it, driven by it, and half maddened by it in equal parts.

No woman had ever been allowed to control him through his desire for her, and for the space of a handful of seconds he was torn—tempted to listen to the inner voice that was warning him to walk away from her, from the desire that had erupted out of nowhere when he had kissed her. A desire like that couldn't be controlled, it could only be appeased. Like some ancient mythical god it demanded sacrifice and self-immolation on its altar.

And then he saw the twins running towards him, and any thought of protecting himself vanished, overwhelmed by the surge of love that flooded him. He hunkered down and held out his arms to them.

Watching the small scene, Ruby felt her throat threaten to close up on a huge lump of emotion. A father with his sons, holding them, protecting them, loving them. There was nothing she would not risk to give her sons that, she acknowledged fiercely.

Holding his sons, Sander knew that there was nothing more important to him than they were—no matter how much he mistrusted their mother.

'Mummy says that we can call you Daddy if we want to.'

That was Freddie, Sander recognised. He had always thought of himself as someone who could control and conceal his emotions, but right now they were definitely threatening to overwhelm him.

'And do you want to?' he asked them, his hold tightening.

'Luke at school has a daddy. He bought him a new bicycle.'

He was being tested, Sander recognised, unable to stop himself from looking towards Ruby.

'Apparently Luke's father also takes him to football

matches and to McDonalds.' She managed to answer Sander's unspoken question.

Sander looked at the twins.

'The bicycles are a maybe—once we've found bikes that are the right size for you—and the football is a definite yes. As for McDonalds—well, I think we should leave it to your mother to decide about that.'

Ruby was torn between relief and resentment. Anyone would think he'd been dealing with the twins from birth. He couldn't have given them a better answer if she had scripted it herself.

'Are you ready?' Sander asked Ruby, in the cold, distant voice he always used when he spoke to her.

Ruby looked down at the jeans and loose-fitting sweater she was wearing, the jeans tucked into the boots her sister had given her for Christmas. No doubt Sander was more used to the company of stunning-looking women dressed in designer clothes and jewels—women who had probably spent hours primping and preening themselves to impress him. A small forlorn ache came from nowhere to pierce her heart. Pretty clothes, never mind designer clothes, were a luxury she simply couldn't afford, and they would have been impractical for her life even if she could.

'Yes, we're ready. Boys, go and get your duffel coats,' she instructed, turning back into the hall to get the case she had packed, and almost being knocked over by the twins as they rushed by.

It was Sander's fingers closing round her arm that saved her from stumbling, but the shock of the physical contact with him froze her into immobility, making her feel far more in danger of losing her balance than the twins' dash past her had done.

Her arm felt thin and frail, in direct contrast to the sturdiness of the twins' limbs, he thought. And her face was pinched, as though she didn't always get enough to eat. A question hovered inside his head...an awareness of deprivation that he pushed away from himself.

Although he was standing behind her she could still smell the scent of his cologne, and feel the warmth coming off his body. Inside her head an image formed of the way he had kissed her such a short time ago. Panic and fear clawed at her stomach, adding to her existing tension. She saw Sander's gaze drop to her mouth and her whole body began to tremble.

It would be so easy to give in to the desire clawing at him—so easy to take her as quickly and wantonly as the way she was offering herself to him. His body wanted that. It wanted the heat of her eager muscles wrapped greedily round it, riding his deepening thrusts. It wanted the swift, savage release her body promised.

It might, but did he really want the kind of cheap, tawdry thrill a woman like her peddled—had been peddling the night they had met?

Ruby's small anguished moan as she pulled free of him brought him back to reality.

'Is this your only case?' he demanded, looking away from her to the shabby case on the hall floor.

Ruby nodded her head, and Sander's mouth twisted with contempt. Of course she would want to underline her poverty to him. Marriage to him was her access to a brand new bank account, filled with money. No doubt she was already planning her first spending spree. He remembered how much delight his mother had always taken in spending his father's money, buying herself couture clothes and expensive jewellery. As a child he'd thought her so beautiful, too dazzled by her glamorous exterior to recognise the corruption that it concealed.

Sander was tempted to ignore the hint Ruby was plainly intending to give him and let her travel to the island with the single shabby case, but that would mean punishing his sons as well as her, he suspected—and besides, he had no wish to make his marriage the subject of speculation and gossip, which it would be if Ruby didn't have a wardrobe commensurate with his own wealth and position.

'Our marriage will take place this Friday,' he told her. 'On Saturday we fly to the island. You've done as I instructed with regard to the birth control pill, I trust?'

'Yes,' Ruby confirmed.

'Can you prove it?'

Ruby was outraged that he should doubt her, but scorched pride had her fumbling angrily with the clasp of her handbag, both her hands shaking with the force of her emotions as she delved into her bag and produced the foil-backed pack of pills, quite plainly showing the empty spaces from the pills she had already taken.

If she had hoped to shame Sander into an apology she soon recognised that one would not be forthcoming. A curt nod of his head was the only response he seemed willing to give her before he continued cynically,

'And, having fulfilled your obligation, you now expect me to fulfil what you no doubt consider to be mine, I expect? To furnish you with the wherewithal to replace your single suitcase with a full set of new ones and clothes with which to fill them.'

The open cynicism in his voice burned Ruby's already scorched pride like salt poured into an open wound. 'Your only obligation to me is to be a good father to the twins.'

'No,' he corrected her coldly, 'that is my obligation to them.' He didn't like her response. It wasn't the one he had expected. It didn't match the profile he had mentally drawn up for her. Somehow she had managed to stray from the script he had written. The one in which she revealed herself to be an unworthy mother, leaving him holding the high ground and the moral right to continue to despise her. 'There is no need to be self-sacrificing.' Her resistance to the role he had cast for her made him feel all the more determined to prove himself right. 'As my wife, naturally you must present an appropriate appearance—although I must caution you against buying clothes of the type you were wearing the night you propositioned me. It is the role of my wife you will be playing in future. Not the role of a whore.'

Ruby had no words to refute his contemptuous insult, but she wasn't going to accept his charity. 'We already have plenty of clothes. We don't need any more,' she insisted vehemently.

She was daring to try to reject what he knew to be the truth about her. She must be taught a lesson that would ensure that she did not do so again. She *would* wear clothes bought with his money, so that they would both know just what she was. He might be forced to marry her in order to be able to lay legal claim to his sons, but he wasn't going to let her forget that she belonged to that group of women all too willing to sell their bodies to any man rich enough to provide them with the lifestyle of designer clothes and easy money they craved.

'Plenty of clothes?' he taunted her. 'In one case? When there are three of you? My sons and my wife will be dressed in a manner appropriate to their station in life, and not—'

'Not what?' Ruby challenged him.

'Do you *really* need me to answer that question?' was his silkily derisory response.

The shabby case was in the boot of a very expensive and luxurious-looking car, the twins were safely strapped into their seats, her decision had already been made—and yet now that it came to it Ruby wavered on the front doorstep, looking back into the house.

'Where's your coat?'

Sander's question distracted her.

'I don't need one,' she fibbed. The truth was that she didn't have a proper winter coat, but she wasn't going to tell Sander that—not after what he'd already said. He was waiting, holding the car door open for her. Shivering in the easterly March wind, Ruby locked the front door. Her head pounding painfully, she got into the car. Its interior smelled of expensive leather, very different from the smell inside the taxi that had transported them back to Sander's hotel that fateful night...

Her mouth went dry.

The twins were both engrossed in the TVs installed in the back of the front seats. Sander was concentrating on his driving. Now wasn't the time to think about that night, she told herself. But it was too late. The memories were already storming her defences and flooding over them.

Her parents' death in an accident had been a terrible shock, followed by her sister's decision to sell their family home. Ruby hadn't realised then that their parents had died heavily in debt. Her oldest sister had tried to protect her by not telling her, and so she had assumed that her decision to sell the house was motivated by the decision to set up her own interior design business in Cheshire. Angry with her sister, she had deliberately chosen to befriend a girl new to the area, knowing that her sister disapproved of the freedom Tracy's parents allowed her, and of Tracy herself. Although she was only eighteen months older than Ruby, Tracy had been far more worldly, dressing in tight-fitting clothes in the latest and skimpiest fashions, her hair dyed blonde and her face heavily made-up.

Secretly, although she hadn't been prepared to admit it—especially not to her older sister—Ruby had been shocked by some of the disclosures Tracy had made about the things she had done. Tracy's goal in life was to get a footballer boyfriend. She had heard that young footballers in Manchester patronised a certain club in the city, and had asked Ruby to go there with her.

Alarmed by Tracy's disclosures, Ruby hadn't really wanted to go. But when she had tried to say so, telling Tracy that she doubted her sister would give her permission, Tracy had mocked her and accused her of being a baby who needed her sister's permission for everything she did. Of course Ruby had denied that she was any such thing, whereupon Tracy had challenged her to prove it by daring her to go with her.

She had been just seventeen, and a very naive seventeen at that, with her whole world turned upside down by events over which she'd had no control. But no matter how often both her sisters had reassured her since then that her rebellion had been completely natural, understandable, and that she was not to blame for what had happened, Ruby knew that deep down inside she would always feel guilty.

Before they'd left for Manchester Tracy had promised Ruby a 'makeover' and poured them both a glass of vodka and orange juice. It had gone straight to Ruby's head as she had never drunk alcohol. The drink had left her feeling so light-headed that she hadn't protested or objected when Tracy had insisted that Ruby change into one of her own short skirts and a tight-fitting top, before making up Ruby's face in a similar style to her own, with dark eyeliner, heavy thick mascara loaded on her eyelashes and lots of deep pink lipgloss.

The girl staring back at Ruby from the mirror, with her tousled hair and her pink pout had been so unrecognisable as herself that under the effect of the vodka and orange Ruby had only been able to stare at her reflection in dizzy astonishment.

She might only have been seventeen, but she had known even before she had watched Tracy sweet talking the bouncer into letting them into the club that neither her parents nor her sisters would have approved of her being there, but by then she had been too afraid of Tracy's mockery and contempt to tell her that she had changed her mind and wanted to go home.

She'd watched other girls going in—older girls than her, dressed up to the nines in tiny little tops and skirts that revealed dark sunbed tans—and she'd known instinctively and immediately that she would feel out of place.

Inside, the club had been hot and stuffy, packed with girls with the same goal in mind as Tracy.

Several young men had come up to them as they'd stood close to the bar. Tracy had refused Ruby's suggestion that they sit down at a tucked-away table with a derisory, 'Don't be daft—no one will see us if we do that.' But Tracy had shaken her head, ignoring the boys and telling Ruby, 'They're nothing. Just ordinary lads out on the pull.'

She'd bought them both drinks—cocktails which had seemed innocuous when Ruby sipped thirstily at hers, because of the heat in the club, but which had quickly made her feel even more dizzy and disorientated than the vodka and orange juice had done.

The club had been packed and noisy, and Ruby's head had begun to ache. She had felt alien and alone, with the alcohol heightening her emotions: bringing home to her the reality of her parents' death, bringing to a head all the despair and misery she had been feeling.

Tracy had started talking to a young man, deliberately excluding Ruby from their conversation and keeping her back to her.

Suddenly and achingly Ruby had longed for the security of the home life she had lost—of knowing that there was someone in her life to take care of her and protect her, someone who loved her, instead of getting cross with her like her elder sister did. And that had been when she had looked across the bar and seen Sander.

Something about him had set him apart from the other men in the bar. For a start he'd been far more smartly dressed, in a suit, with his dark hair groomed, and an air of command and power and certainty had emanated from him that Ruby's insecure senses immediately recognised and were drawn to… In her alcohol-induced state, Sander had looked like an island of security and safety in a sea of confusion and misery. She hadn't been able to take her eyes off him, and when he had looked back at her, her mouth had gone so dry with the anticipation of speaking to him that she had had to wet her lips with the tip of her tongue. The way that Sander's gaze had followed that movement, showing her that he was singling her out from all the other girls in the bar, had reinforced Ruby's cocktail-produced belief that there was a link between them—that he was drawing her to him, that they were meant to meet, and that somehow once she was close to him she would be safe, and he would save her from her own fears and protect her just as her parents had done.

She had no memory of actually going to him, only of reaching him, feeling like a swimmer who had crested turbulent waves to reach the security of a calm sea where she could float safely. When she had smiled up at Sander she had felt as though she already knew him. But of course she hadn't. She hadn't known anything, Ruby reflected bitterly now, as she dragged her thoughts away from the past and massaged her throbbing temple as Sander drove onto the motorway slip road and the car picked up speed.

# CHAPTER FOUR

SANDER had booked them into the Carlton Towers Hotel, just off Sloane Street. They had an enormous suite of three bedrooms, each with its own bathroom, and a good-sized sitting room as well.

Ruby had felt dreadfully out of place as they'd walked through the downstairs lobby, compared with the elegantly groomed women surrounded by expensive-looking shopping bags who were having afternoon tea in the lounge. But she had soon forgotten them once they had been shown into their suite and she had realised that Sander would be staying in the suite with them.

Her heart was beating far too fast, her whole body suddenly charged and sensitised, so that she was far too aware of Sander. His presence in the room, even though there were several feet between them and he was fully dressed, somehow had the same effect on her body as though he was standing close to her and touching her. The sound of his voice made her think she could almost feel the warmth of his breath on her skin. Her body was starting to react even to her thoughts, tiny darts of sensation heightening her awareness of him.

He raised his hand, gesturing towards the bedrooms as he told her, 'I've asked for one of the rooms to be made up with twin beds for the boys.'

Inside her head she could feel that hand cupping her breast. Beneath her clothes her breasts swelled and ached whilst she tried desperately to stifle her body's arousal. Why was this happening to her? She'd lived happily without sex for nearly six years. Why was her body reacting like this now?

It was just reacting to memory, that was all. Her desire for Sander, like that memory, belonged to the past and had no place in the present. Ruby tried to convince herself, but she knew that it wasn't true. The fact that he could arouse her to intense desire for him was something she didn't want to think about. Her stomach was churning, adding to the feeling of nausea already being produced by her headache. She had actually been sick when they had stopped for a break at a motorway service station, and had had to purchase a travel pack of toothbrush and toothpaste to refresh her mouth. Now all she really wanted to do was lie down in a dark room, but of course that was impossible.

'You and I will occupy the other two rooms, of course,' Sander was saying. 'I expect that you will wish to have the room closest to the boys?'

'I could have shared a room with them,' was Ruby's response. Because sharing with the boys would surely prevent any more of those unwanted memories from surfacing? 'There was no need for you to book three rooms.'

'If I had only booked two the hotel would have assumed you would be sharing my bed, not sleeping with the twins,' was Sander's response.

Immediately another image flashed through her head: two naked bodies entwined on a large bed, the man's hands holding and caressing the woman, whilst her head was thrown back in wild ecstasy. Sander's hands and her head. Heat filled her body. Her own mental images were making her panic. What she was experiencing was probably caused by the same kind of thing that caused the victims of dreadful trauma to have flashbacks they couldn't control, she told herself. They meant nothing other than that Sander's unexpected and unwanted reappearance in her life was causing her to remember the event that had had such a dramatic effect on her life.

To her relief the twins, who had been inspecting the suite, came rushing into the sitting room. Harry ran over to her to inform her, 'Guess what? There's a TV in our bedroom, and—'

'A TV which will remain switched off whilst you are in bed,' Ruby told him firmly, relieved to be able to return to the familiar role of motherhood. 'You know the rules.' She was very strict about limiting the boys' television viewing, preferring them to make their own entertainment.

Sander's comment about the rooms had penetrated her mind and was still lodged there—a small, unnerving time bomb of a comment that was having an effect on her that was out of all proportion to its reality. The sound of Sander saying 'my bed' had made her heart jerk around inside her chest as though it was on a string—and why? She had no desire to share that bed with him; he meant nothing to her now. It was merely the result of only ever having had one sexual partner and being sexually inexperienced. It had left her reacting to a man saying the words 'my bed' as though she were a teenager, blushing at every mention of anything remotely connected to sex, Ruby derided herself.

'I thought we'd use the rest of the afternoon to get the boys kitted out with the clothes they'll need for the island. We can walk to Harrods from here, or get a cab if you wish.'

The last thing Ruby felt like doing was shopping, but she was determined not to show any weakness. Sander would only accuse of being a bad mother if she did.

Hopefully she might see a chemist, where she could get something for her headache. It had been so long since she had last had one of these debilitating attacks that she didn't have anything she could take for it. Determinedly trying to ignore her continuing feeling of nausea, she nodded her head, and then winced as the pain increased.

'The boys will need summer clothes,' Sander told her. 'Even in March the temperature on the island can be as high as twenty-two degrees centigrade, and it rises to well over thirty in the summer.'

Two hours later Ruby was battling between angry frustration at the way in which Sander had overruled all her attempts to minimise the amount of money he was spending by choosing the cheapest items she could find and a mother's natural pride in her sons, who had drawn smiles of approval from the assistants with their appearance in their new clothes: smart, boyish separates from the summer ranges that had just come in, and in which Ruby had to admit they looked adorable.

As a reward for their good behaviour Sander had insisted on taking them to the toy department, where he'd bought them both complicated-looking state-of-the-art boys' toys that had them both speechless with delight.

The whole time they had been shopping with the boys Ruby had been conscious of the admiring looks Sander had attracted from other women—women who no doubt would have been only too delighted to be marrying him in two days' time, Ruby acknowledged, and her heart gave a flurry of tense beats in response to her thoughts.

'I've got some business matters to attend to this evening,' Sander told her as they made a detour on the way back to the hotel to allow the boys to walk in Hyde Park—a suggestion from Sander which Ruby had welcomed, hoping that the fresh air would ease the pounding in her head.

After acknowledging Sander's comment Ruby focused on keeping an eye on the twins, who were walking ahead of them.

Sander continued. 'But first I've arranged for a jeweller to come to the hotel with a selection of wedding and engagement rings. I've also made an appointment for you tomorrow morning at the spa and hair salon in Harvey Nichols, and then afterwards a personal shopper will help you choose your own new wardrobe. I thought I'd take the boys to the Natural History Museum whilst you're doing that, to keep them occupied.'

Ruby stopped walking and turned to look at him, her eyes blazing with temper.

'I don't need a spa appointment, or a new hairstyle, or a new wardrobe, thank you very much. And I certainly don't want an engagement ring.'

She was lying, of course. Or did she think she could get more out of him by pretending she didn't want anything?

Oblivious to Sander's thoughts, Ruby continued, 'And if my present appearance isn't good enough for you, then too bad. Because it's good enough for me.'

Quickly hurrying after the twins, Ruby tried to ignore how unwell she was feeling. Even though she couldn't see him she knew that Sander had caught up with her and was standing behind her. Her body could feel him there, but stubbornly she refused to turn round.

'You have two choices,' Sander informed her coolly. 'Either you accept the arrangements I have made for you, or you will accept the clothes I shall instruct the store to select on your behalf. There is no option for you, as my wife, to dress as you are doing now. You are so eager to display your body to male eyes that you aren't even wearing a coat—all the better for them to assess what is on offer, no doubt.'

'That's a disgusting thing to say, and totally untrue. You must *know* the reason I'm not wearing a coat is—'

Abruptly Ruby stopped speaking realising that she had allowed her anger to betray her into making an admission she had no wish to make.

'Yes?' Sander probed.

'Is that I forgot to bring one with me,' Ruby told him lamely. The truth was that she had not been able to afford to buy herself one—not with the twins constantly outgrowing their clothes. But she wasn't going to expose herself to more humiliation by admitting that to Sander.

How could he be marrying a woman like this one? Sander wondered savagely. It would have suited his purposes far more if the report he had received from the agents he had hired to find Ruby had included something to suggest that she was a neglectful mother, thus giving him real grounds for legally removing them from their mother. The report, though, had done nothing of the sort—had actually dared to claim that Ruby was a good mother, the kind of mother whose absence from their lives would damage his sons. That was a risk he was not prepared to take.

Ignoring Ruby's defiant statement, Sander went on, 'The boys are approaching an age where they will be aware of appearance and other people's opinions. They are going to have to deal with settling into a different environment, and I'm sure that the last thing you want to do is make it harder for them. I have a duty to the Konstantinakos position as the ruling and thus most important family on the island. That duty involves a certain amount of entertaining. It will be expected that as my wife you take part in that. Additionally, my sister, her friends, and the wives of those of my executives who live in Athens are very fashion-conscious. They would be quick to sense that our marriage is not all it should be were you to make a point of dressing as you do now. And that could impact on our sons.'

*Our* sons. Ruby felt as though her heart had been squeezed by a giant hand. She was very tempted to resort to the immature tactic of pointing out that since he hadn't even been aware of the twins' existence until recently he was hardly in a position to take a stance on delivering advice to her on what might or might not affect them—but what was the point? He had won—again, she was forced to acknowledge. Because now she would be very conscious of the fact that she was being judged by her appearance, and that if she was found wanting it would reflect on the twins. Acceptance by their peers was very important to children. Ruby knew that even at the boys' young age children hated being 'different' or being embarrassed. For their sake she would have to accept Sander's charity, even though her pride hated the idea.

She hated feeling so helpless and dependent on others. She loved her sisters, and was infinitely grateful to them for all that they had done for her and the boys, but it was hard sometimes always having to depend on others, never being able to claim the pride and self-respect that came from being financially self-supporting. She had hoped that once the boys were properly settled at school she might be able to earn a degree that ultimately would allow her to find work, but now she was going to be even more dependent on the financial generosity of someone else than she was already. But it wasn't her pride that was important, Ruby reminded herself. It was her sons' emotional happiness. They hadn't asked to be born. And she hadn't asked for Sander's opinion on her appearance—or his money. She was twenty-three, and it was ridiculous of her to feel so helpless and humiliated that she was close to defeated tears.

To conceal her emotions she leaned down towards the boys, to warn them not to run too far ahead of them, watching as they nodded their heads.

It was when she straightened up that it happened. Perhaps she moved too quickly. Ruby didn't know, but one minute she was straightening up and the next she felt so dizzy from the pain in her head that she lost her balance. She would have fallen if Sander hadn't reacted so quickly, reaching out to grab hold of her so that she fell against his body rather than tumbling to the ground.

Immediately she was transported back to the past. The circumstances might be very different, but then too she had stumbled, and Sander had rescued her. Then, though, the cause of her fall had been the unfamiliar height of the borrowed shoes Tracy had insisted she should wear, and the effect of too many cocktails. The result was very much the same. Now, just as then, she could feel the steady thud of Sander's heart against her body, whilst her own raced and bounced, the frantic speed of its beat making her feel breathless and far too weak to try to struggle against the arms holding her. Then too his proximity had filled her senses with the scent of his skin, the alien maleness of hard muscle beneath warm flesh, the power of that maleness, both physically and emotionally, and most of all her own need to simply be held by him. Then she had been thrilled to be in his arms, but now… Panic curled through her. That was not how she was supposed to feel, and it certainly wasn't what she wanted to feel. Sander was her enemy—an enemy she was forced to share her sons with because he was their father, an enemy who had ripped from her the protection of her naivety with his cruel contempt for her.

Determinedly Ruby started to push herself free, but instead of releasing her Sander tightened his hold of her.

He'd seen that she was slender, Sander acknowledged, but it was only now that he was holding her and could actually feel the bones beneath her flesh that he was able to recognise how thin she was. She was shivering too, despite her claim not to need a coat. Once again he was reminded of the report he had commissioned on her. Was it possible that in order to ensure that her sons ate well and were not deprived of the nourishment they needed she herself had been going without? Sander had held his sons, and he knew just how solid and strong their bodies were. The amount of energy they possessed alone was testament to their good health. And it was *their* good health that mattered to him, not that of their mother, whose presence in his life as well as theirs was something he had told himself he would have to accept for their sakes.

Even so… He looked down into Ruby's face. Her

skin was paler than he remembered, but he had put that down to the fact that when he had first met her her face had been plastered in make-up, whilst now she wore none. Her cheekbones might be more pronounced, but her lips were still full and soft—the lips of sensual siren who knew just how to use her body to her own advantage. Sander had never been under any illusions as to why Ruby had approached him. He had heard her and her friend discussing the rich footballers they intended to target. Unable to find one, Ruby had obviously decided to target him instead.

Sander frowned, unwilling to contrast the frail vulnerability of the woman he was holding with the girl he remembered, and even more unwilling to allow himself to feel concern for her. Why should he care about her? He didn't. And yet as she struggled to pull free of him, her eyes huge in her fine boned face, a sudden gleam of March sunshine pierced the heavy grey of the late afternoon sky to reveal the perfection of her skin and stroke fingers of light through her blonde curls, Sander had sudden reluctance to let her go. In rejection of it he immediately released her.

It was the unexpected swiftness of her release after Sander's grip had seemed to be tightening on her that was causing her to feel so...confused, Ruby told herself, refusing to allow herself to use the betraying word *bereft*, which had tried to slip through her defences. Why should she feel bereft? She wanted to be free. Sander's hold had no appeal for her. She certainly hadn't spent the last six years longing to be back in his arms. Why should she, when her last memory of them had been the biting pressure of his fingers in her flesh as he thrust her away from him in a gesture of angry contempt?

It had started to rain, causing Ruby to shiver and call the boys to them. It was no good her longing for the security of home, she told herself as they headed back to the hotel in the taxi Sander had flagged down, with the twins squashed in between them so that she didn't have to come into contact with him. She must focus on the future and all that it would hold for her sons. Their happiness was far more important to her than her own, and it was obvious to her how easily they were adapting to Sander's presence in their lives. An acceptance oiled by the promise of expensive toys, Ruby thought bitterly, knowing that her sons were too young for her to be able to explain to them that a parent's love wasn't always best shown though gifts and treats, and knowing too that it would be part of her future role to ensure that they were not spoiled by their father's wealth or blinded to the reality of other people's lives and struggles.

Once they were back in their suite, in the privacy of her bathroom, Ruby tried to take two of the painkiller tablets she had bought from the chemist's she had gone into on the pretext of needing some toothpaste. But her stomach heaved at the mere thought of attempting to swallow them, nausea overwhelming her.

Still feeling sick, and weakened by her pounding headache, as soon as the twins had had something to eat she bathed them and put them to bed.

They had only been asleep a few minutes when the

jeweller Sander had summoned arrived, removing a roll of cloth from his briefcase, after Sander had introduced him to Ruby and they had all sat down.

Placing the roll on the class coffee table, he unfolded it—and Ruby had to suppress a gasp of shock when she saw the glitter of the rings inside it.

They were all beautiful, but something made Ruby recoil from them. It seemed somehow shabby and wrong to think of wearing something so precious. A ring should represent love and commitment that were equally precious and enduring instead of the hollow emptiness her marriage would be.

'You choose,' she told Sander emptily, not wanting to look at them.

Her lack of interest in the priceless gems glittering in front of her made Sander frown. His mother had loved jewellery. He could see her now, seated at her dressing table, dressed to go out for the evening, admiring the antique Cartier bangles glittering on her arms.

'Your birth paid for these,' she had told him. 'Your grandfather insisted that your father should only buy me one, so I had to remind him that I had given birth to his heir. Thank goodness you weren't a girl. Your grandfather is so mean that he would have seen to it that I got nothing if you had been. Remember when you are a man, Sander, that the more expensive the piece of jewellery you give a woman, the more willing she will be, and thus the more you can demand of her.' She had laughed then, pouting her glossy red lip-sticked lips at her own reflection and adding, 'I shouldn't really give away the secrets of my sex to you, should I?'

His beautiful, shallow, greedy mother—chosen as a bride for his father by his grandfather because of her aristocratic Greek ancestry, marrying his father because she hated her own family's poverty. When he had grown old enough to recognise the way in which his gentle academic father had been humiliated and treated with contempt by the father who had forced the marriage on him, and the wife who thought of him only as an open bank account, Sander had sworn he would never follow in his father's footsteps and allow the same thing to happen to him.

What was Ruby hoping for by pretending a lack of interest? Something more expensive? Angrily Sander looked at the rings, his hand hovering over the smallest solitaire he could see. His intention was to punish her by choosing it for her—until his attention was drawn to another ring close to it, its two perfect diamonds shimmering in the light.

Feeling too ill to care what kind of engagement ring she had, Ruby exhaled in relief when she saw Sander select one of the rings. All she wanted was for the whole distasteful charade to be over.

'We'll have this one,' Sander told the jeweller abruptly, his voice harsh with the irritation he felt against himself for his own sentimentality.

It was the jeweller who handed the ring to Ruby, not Sander. She took it unwillingly, sliding the cold metal onto her finger, her eyes widening and her heart turning over inside her chest as she looked at it properly for the first time. Two perfect diamonds nestled together on a slender band, slightly offset from one another and yet touching—twin diamonds for their twin sons. Her throat closed up, her gaze seeking Sander's despite her attempt to stop it doing so, her emotions clearly on display. But there was no answering warmth in Sander's eyes, only a cold hardness that froze her out.

'An excellent choice,' the jeweller was saying. 'Each stone weighs two carets, and they are a particularly good quality. And of course ethically mined, just as you requested,' he informed Sander.

His comment took Ruby by surprise. From what she knew of Sander she wouldn't have thought it would matter to him *how* the diamonds had been mined, but obviously it did. Meaning what? That she had mis-judged him? Meaning nothing, Ruby told herself fiercely. She didn't want to revisit her opinion of Sander, never mind re-evaluate it. Why not? Because she was afraid that if she did so, if she allowed herself to see him in a different light, then she might become even more vulnerable to him than she already was? Emotionally vulnerable as well as sexually vulnerable? No, that must not happen.

Her panic increased her existing nausea, and it was a relief when the jeweller finally left. His departure was quickly followed by Sander's, to his business meeting.

Finally she could give in to her need to go and lie down—after she had checked on the twins, of course.

# CHAPTER FIVE

'YOUR hair is lovely and thick, but since it is so curly I think it would look better if we put a few different lengths into it.' Those had been the words of the salon's senior stylist when he had first come over to examine Ruby's hair. She had simply nodded her head, not really caring how he cut her hair. She was still feeling unwell, her head still aching, and she knew from experience that these headaches could last for two and even three days once they took hold, before finally lifting.

Now, though, as the stylist stepped back from the mirror and asked, 'What do you think?' Ruby was forced to admit that she was almost lost for words over the difference his skill had made to her hair, transforming it from an untidy tumble of curls into a stunningly chic style that feathered against her face and swung softly onto her shoulders—the kind of style she had seen worn by several of the women taking tea at the hotel the previous afternoon, a deceptively simple style that breathed expense and elegance.

'I...I love it,' she admitted wanly.

'It's easy to maintain and will fall back into shape after you've washed it. You're lucky to have naturally blonde hair.'

Thanking him, Ruby allowed herself to be led away. At least she had managed to eat some dry toast this morning, and keep down a couple of the painkillers which had eased her head a little, thankfully.

Her next appointment was at the beauty spa, and when she caught other women giving her a second look as she made her way there she guessed that they must be querying the elegance of her new hairstyle set against the shabbiness of her clothes and her make-up-free face.

She hated admitting it, but it *was* true that first impressions counted, and that people—especially women—judged members of their own sex by their appearance. The last thing she wanted was for the twins to be embarrassed by a mother other women looked down on. Even young children were very perceptive and quick to notice such things.

The spa and beauty salon was ahead of her. Taking a deep breath, Ruby held her head high as she walked in.

Two hours later, when she walked out again with the personal shopper who had come to collect her and help her choose a new wardrobe, Ruby couldn't help giving quick, disbelieving glances into the mirrors she passed, still unable to totally believe that the young woman looking back at her really was her. Her nails were manicured and painted a fashionable dark shade, her eyebrows were trimmed, and her make-up was applied in such a subtle and delicate way that it barely looked as though she was wearing any at all. Yet at the same time her eyes looked larger and darker, her mouth fuller and softer, and her complexion so delicately perfect that Ruby couldn't take her eyes off the glowing face looking back at her. Although she would never admit it to Sander, her makeover had been fun once she had got over her initial discomfort at being fussed over and pampered. Now she felt like a young woman rather than an anxious mother.

'I understand you want clothes suitable for living on a Greek island, rather than merely holidaying there, and that your life there will include various social and business engagements?' Without waiting for Ruby's answer the personal shopper continued. 'Fortunately we have got some of our new season stock in as well as several designers' cruise collections, so I'm sure we shall be able to find everything you need. As for your wedding dress...'

Ruby's heart leapt inside her chest. Somehow she hadn't expected Sander to specify that she needed a wedding dress.

'It's just a very quiet registry office ceremony,' she told the personal shopper.

'But her wedding day and what she wore when she married the man she loves is still something that a woman always remembers,' the other woman insisted.

The personal shopper was only thinking of the store's profit, Ruby reminded herself. There was no real reason for her to have such an emotional reaction to the words. After all, she didn't love Sander and he certainly didn't love her. What she wore was immaterial, since neither of them was likely to want to look back in future years to remember the day they married. Her thoughts had produced a hard painful lump in her throat and an unwanted ache inside her chest. Why? She was twenty-three years old and the mother of five-year-old sons. She had long ago abandoned any thoughts of romance and love and all that went with those things, dismissing them as the emotional equivalent of chocolate—sweet on the tongue for a very short time, highly addictive and dangerously habit-forming. Best avoided in favour of a sensible and sustaining emotional diet. Like the love she had for her sons and the bond she shared with her sisters. Those were emotions and commitments that would last for a lifetime, whilst from what she had seen and heard romantic love was a delusion.

The twins were fascinated by the exhibits in the Natural History Museum. They had happily held Sander's hand and pressed gratifyingly close to him for protection, calling him Daddy and showing every indication of being happy to be with him, so why did he feel so aware of Ruby's absence, somehow incomplete? It was for the boys' sake, Sander assured himself, because he was concerned that they might be missing their mother, nothing more.

Without quite knowing how it had happened, Ruby had acquired a far more extensive and expensive wardrobe than she had wanted. Every time she had protested or objected the personal shopper had overruled her—politely and pleasantly, but nonetheless determinedly—insisting that her instructions were that Ruby must have a complete wardrobe that would cover a wide variety of situations. And of course the clothes were sinfully gorgeous—beautifully cut trousers and shorts in cream linen, with a matching waistcoat lined in the same silk as the unstructured shirt that went with them, soft flowing silk dresses, silk and cotton tops, formal fitted cocktail dresses, along with more casual but still frighteningly expensive 'leisure and beach clothes', as the personal shopper had described them. There were also shoes for every occasion and each outfit, and underwear—scraps of silk and lace that Ruby had wanted to reject in favour of something far more sensible, but which somehow or other had been added to the growing rail of clothes described by the personal shopper as 'must-haves'.

Now all that was left was the wedding dress, and the personal shopper was producing with a flourish a cream dress with a matching jacket telling Ruby proudly, 'Vera Wang, from her new collection. Since the dress is short and beautifully tailored it is ideal for a registry office wedding, and of course you could wear it afterwards as a cocktail dress. It was actually ordered by another customer, but unfortunately when it came it was too small for her. I'm sure that it will fit you, and the way the fabric is pleated will suit your body shape.'

What she meant was that the waterfall of pleated

ruching that was a feature of the cream silk-satin dress would disguise how thin she was, Ruby suspected.

The dress was beautiful, elegant and feminine, and exactly the kind of dress that a woman would remember wearing on her wedding day—which was exactly why she didn't want to wear it. But the dresser was waiting expectantly.

It fitted her perfectly. Cut by a master hand, it shaped her body in a way that made her waist appear far narrower surely than it actually was, whilst somehow adding a feminine curvaceousness to her shape that made Ruby think she was looking at someone else in the mirror and not herself: the someone else she might have been if things had been different. If Sander had loved her?

Shakily Ruby shook her head and started to take the dress off, desperate to escape from the cruel reality of the image the mirror had thrown back at her. She could never be the woman she had seen in the mirror—a woman so loved by her man that she had the right to claim everything the dress offered her and promised him.

'No. I don't want it,' she told the bewildered-looking personal shopper. 'Please take it away. I'll wear something else.'

'But it was perfect on you…'

Still Ruby shook her head.

She was in the changing room getting dressed when the personal shopper reappeared, carrying a warm-looking, casually styled off-white parka.

'I nearly forgot,' she told Ruby, 'your husband-to-be said that you had left your coat at home by accident and that you needed something warm to wear whilst you are in London.'

Wordlessly Ruby took the parka from her. It was lined with soft checked wool, and well-made as well as stylish.

'It's a new designer,' the shopper told her. 'And a line that we're just trialling. She's Italian, trained by Prada.'

Ruby bent her head so that the personal shopper wouldn't see the emotion sheening her eyes. Sander might have protected her in public by pretending to believe that she had forgotten her coat, but in private he had humiliated her—because Ruby knew that he had guessed that she didn't really possess a winter coat, and that she had been shivering with cold yesterday when they had walked in the park.

Walking back to the hotel wrapped in her new parka, Ruby reflected miserably that beneath the new hairstyle and the pretty make-up she was still exactly what she had been beforehand—they couldn't change her, could not take away the burden of the guilt she still carried because of what she had once been. Expensive clothes were only a pretence—just like her marriage to Sander would be.

For her. Yes, but not for the twins. They must never know how she felt. The last thing she wanted was for them to grow up feeling that she had sacrificed herself for them. They must believe that she was happy.

She had intended to go straight to the suite, but the assessing look a woman in the lobby gave her, before smiling slightly to herself, as though she was satisfied that Ruby couldn't compete with her, stung her pride enough to have her changing her mind and heading for the lounge instead.

A well-trained waitress showed her to a small table right at the front of the lounge. Ruby would have preferred to have hidden herself away in a dark corner, her brief surge of defiance having retreated leaving her feeling self-conscious and very alone. She wasn't used to being on her own. Normally when she went out she had the twins with her, or one of her sisters.

When the waitress came to take her order Ruby asked for tea. She hadn't eaten anything all day but she wasn't hungry. She was too on edge for that.

The lounge was filling up. Several very smart-looking women were coming in, followed by a group of businessmen in suits, one of whom gave her such a deliberate look followed by a warm smile that Ruby felt her face beginning to burn.

She was just about to pour herself a cup of tea when she saw the twins hurrying towards her followed by Sander. His hair, like the twins', was damp, as though he had just stepped out of the shower. Her heart lurched into her ribs. Her hand had started to tremble so badly that she had to put down the teapot. The twins were clamouring to tell her about their day, but even though she tried desperately to focus on them her gaze remained riveted to Sander, who had now stopped walking and was looking at her.

It wasn't her changed appearance that had brought him to an abrupt halt, though.

In Sander's eyes the new hairstyle and pretty make-up were merely window-dressing that highlighted what he already knew and what had been confirmed to him when Ruby had opened the door of her home to him a few days earlier—namely that the delicacy of her features possessed a rare beauty.

No, what had caused him to stop dead almost in mid-stride was the sense of male pride the sight of the trio in front of him brought. His sons and their mother. Not just his sons, but the *three* of them. They went together, belonged together—belonged to him? Sander shook his head, trying to dispel his atavistic and unfamiliar reactions with regard to Ruby, both angered by them and wanting to reject them. They were so astonishingly the opposite of what he wanted to feel. What was happening to him?

Her transformation passed him by other than the fact that he noticed the way she was wearing her hair revealed the slender column of her throat and that her face had a bit more colour in it.

Ruby, already self-conscious about the changes to her appearance, held her breath, waiting for Sander to make some comment. After all the sight of her had brought him to a halt. But when he reached the table he simply frowned and demanded to know why she hadn't ordered something to eat.

'Because all I wanted was a cup of tea,' she answered him. Didn't he like her new haircut? Was that why he was looking so grim? Well, she certainly wasn't going to ask him if he approved of the change. She turned to the boys, asking them, 'Did you like the Natural History Museum?'

'Yes,' Harry confirmed. 'And then Daddy took us swimming.'

Swimming? Ruby directed a concerned look at Sander.

'There's a pool here in the hotel,' he explained. 'Since the boys will be living on an island, I wanted to make sure that they can swim.'

'Daddy bought us new swimming trunks,' Freddie told her.

'There should be two adults with them when they go in a pool,' Ruby couldn't stop herself from saying. 'A child can drown in seconds and—'

'There was a lifeguard on duty.' Sander stopped her. 'They're both naturals in the water, but that will be in their genes. My brother swam for Greece as a junior.'

'Mummy's hair is different,' Harry suddenly announced.

Self-consciousness crawled along her spine. Now surely Sander must say something about her transformation, give at least some hint of approval since he was the one who had orchestrated her makeover, but instead he merely stated almost indifferently, 'I hope you got everything you are going to need, as there won't be time for any more shopping. As I said, I've arranged for us to fly to the island the day after the marriage ceremony.'

Ruby nodded her head. It was silly of her to feel disappointed because Sander hadn't said anything her new look. Silly or dangerous? His approval or lack of it shouldn't mean anything to her at all.

The boys would be hungry, and she was tired. She was their mother, though, and it was far more important that she focused on her maternal responsibilities rather than worrying about Sander's approval or lack of it.

'I'll take the boys up to the suite and organise a meal for them,' she told Sander.

'Good idea. I've got some ends to tie up with the Embassy,' he said brusquely, with a brief nod of his head.

'What about dinner?' Ruby's mouth had gone dry, and the silence that greeted her question made her feel she had committed as much of a *faux pas* as if she'd asked him to go to bed with her.

Feeling hot and angry with herself for inadvertently giving Sander the impression that she wanted to have dinner with him, she swallowed against the dry feeling in her mouth.

Why had Ruby's simple question brought back that atavistic feeling he had had earlier? Sander asked himself angrily. For a moment he let himself imagine the two of them having dinner together. The two of them? Surely he meant the four of them—for it was because of the twins and only because of them that he had decided to allow her back into his life. Sander knew better than to allow himself to be tricked by female emotions, be they maternal or sexual. As he had good cause to know, those emotions could be summoned out of nowhere and disappear back there just as quickly.

'I've already arranged to have dinner with an old friend,' he lied. 'I don't know what time I'll be back.'

An old friend, Sander had said. Did that mean he was having dinner with another woman? A lover, perhaps?

Ruby wondered later, after the boys had eaten their tea and she had forced herself to eat something with them. She knew so little about Sander's life and the people in it. A feeling of panic began to grow inside her.

'Mummy, come and look at our island,' Freddie was demanding, standing in front of a laptop that he was trying to open.

'No, Freddie, you mustn't touch that,' Ruby protested,

'It's all right, Mummy,' Harry assured her adopting a heartbreakingly familiar pose of male confidence. 'Daddy said that we could look.'

Freddie had got the laptop lid up—like all children, the twins were very at home with modern technology— and before Ruby could say anything the screen was filled with the image of an almost crescent shaped island, with what looked like a range of rugged mountains running the full length of its spine.

In the early days, after she had first met him, Ruby had tried to find out as much as she could about Sander, still refusing to believe then that all she had been to him was a one-night stand.

She had learned that the island, whose closest neighbour was Cyprus, had been invaded and conquered many times, and that in Sander's veins ran the ruling blood of conquering Moors from the time of the Crusades—even though now the island population considered itself to be Greek. She had also learned that Sander's family had ruled the island for many centuries, and that his grandfather, the current patriarch, had built up a shipping business in the wake of the Second World War which had brought new wealth and employment to the island. However, once she had been forced to recognise that she meant nothing to Sander she had stopped seeking out information about him.

'Bath time,' she told her sons firmly.

Their new clothes and her own had been delivered whilst they had been downstairs, along with some very smart new cases, and once the twins were in bed she intended to spend her evening packing in readiness for their flight to the island.

Only once the boys were bathed and in bed Ruby was drawn back to the computer, with its tantalising image of the island.

Almost without realising what she was doing she clicked on the small red dot that represented its capital. Several thumbnail images immediately appeared. Ruby clicked on the first of them to enlarge it, and revealed a dazzlingly white fortress, perched high on a cliff above an impossibly blue green sea, its Moorish-looking towers reaching up into a deep blue sky. Another thumbnail enlarged to show what she assumed was the front of the same building, looking more classically Greek in design and dominating a formal square. The royal blue of the traditionally dressed guards' jackets worn over brilliantly white skirts made a striking image.

The other images revealed a hauntingly beautiful landscape of sandy bays backed by cliffs, small fishing harbours, and white-capped mountains covered in wild flowers. These were contrasted by a modern cargo dock complex, and small towns of bright white buildings and dark shadowed alleyways. It was impossible not to be captivated by the images of the island, Ruby admitted, but at the same time viewing them had brought home to her how different and even alien the island was to everything she and the twins knew. Was she doing the right thing? She knew nothing of Sander's family, or his way of life, and once on the island she would be totally at his mercy. But if she hadn't agreed to go with them he would have tried to take the twins from her, she was sure. This way at least she would be with them.

A fierce tide of maternal love surged through her. The twins meant everything to her. Their emotional security both now and in the future was what would bring her happiness, and was far more important to her than anything else—especially the unwanted and humiliating desire that Sander was somehow able to arouse in her. Her mouth had gone dry again. At seventeen she might have been able to excuse herself for being vulnerable to Sander's sexual charisma, but she was not seventeen any more. Even if her single solitary memory of sexual passion was still limited to what she had experienced with Sander. He, of course, had no doubt shared his bed with an unending parade of women since he had ejected her so cruelly from both it and his life.

She looked at the computer, suddenly unable to resist the temptation to do a web search on Sander's name. It wasn't prying, not really. She had the boys to think of after all.

She wasn't sure what she had expected to find, but

her eyes widened over the discovery that Sander was now ruler of the island—a role that carried the title of King, although, according to the website, he had decided to dispense with its usage, preferring to adopt a more democratic approach to ruling the island than that exercised by his predecessors.

Apparently his parents had died when Sander was eighteen, in a flying accident. The plane they'd been in piloted by a cousin of Sander's mother. A shock as though she had inadvertently touched a live wire shot through her. They had both been orphaned at almost the same age. Like hers, Sander's parents had been killed in an accident. If she had known that when they had first met... What difference would it have made? None.

Sander was thirty-four, to her twenty-three; a man at the height of his powers. A small shiver raked her skin, like the sensual rasp of a lover's tongue against sensitised flesh. Inside her head an image immediately formed: Sander's dark tanned hand cupping her own naked breast, his tongue curling round her swollen nipple. The small shiver became a racking shudder. Quickly Ruby tried to banish the image, closing down the computer screen. She was feeling nauseous again. Shakily, she made her way to the bathroom.

# CHAPTER SIX

'I NOW pronounce you man and wife.'

It was over, done. There was no going back. Ruby was shaking inwardly, but she refused to let Sander see how upset she was.

Upset? A small tremor made her body shudder inside the cream Vera Wang dress she had not wanted to wear but which the personal shopper had included amongst her purchases and which for some reason she had felt obliged to wear. It was, after all, her wedding day. A fresh tremor broke through her self-control. What was the matter with her? What had she expected? Hearts and flowers? A declaration of undying devotion? This was Sander she was marrying, Sander who had not looked at her once during the brief ceremony in the anonymous register office, who couldn't have made it plainer how little he wanted her as his wife. Well, no more than she wanted him as her husband.

Sander looked down at Ruby's left hand. The ring he had just slipped onto her marriage finger was slightly loose, despite the fact that it should have fitted. She was far too thin and seemed to be getting thinner. But why should her fragility concern him?

It didn't. Women were adept at creating fictional images in order to deceive others. To her sons Ruby was no doubt a much loved mother, a constant and secure presence in their lives. At their age that had been his own feeling about his mother. Bitterness curled through him, spreading its poisonous infection.

In the years since the deaths of his parents he had often wondered if his father had given in so readily to his mother's financial demands because secretly he had loved her, even though he'd known she'd only despised him, and she, knowing that, had used his love against him. It was a fate he had sworn would never be his own.

And yet here he was married, and to a woman he already knew he could not trust—a woman who had given herself to him with such sensuality and intimacy that even now after so many years he was unable to strip from his memory the images she had left upon it. He had been a fool to let her get close enough to him once to do that. He wasn't going to let it happen again.

Neither of them spoke in the taxi taking them back to the hotel. Ruby already knew Sander had some business matters to attend to, which thankfully meant that she would have some time to herself in which to come to terms with the commitment she had just made.

After Sander had escorted them to the suite and then left without a word to her, after kissing the boys, Ruby reminded herself that she had not only walked willingly into this marriage, she was the one who had first suggested it.

The boys were tired—worn out, Ruby suspected, by the excitement of being in London. A short sleep would do them all good, and might help to ease her cramped, nauseous stomach and aching head.

After removing her wedding dress and pulling on her old dressing gown, she put the twins to bed. Once she had assured herself that they were asleep she went into her own bathroom, fumbling in her handbag for some headache tablets and accidentally removing the strip of birth control pills instead. They reminded her that although Sander might have made her take them she must not let him make her want him. Her hands shook as she replaced them to remove the pack of painkillers. Just that simple action had started her head pounding again, but thankfully this time at least she wasn't sick.

She was so tired that after a bath to help her relax she could barely dry herself, never mind bother to put on a nightdress. Instead she simply crawled beneath the duvet on her bed, falling asleep almost immediately.

Ruby woke up reluctantly, dragged from her sleep by a sense of nagging urgency. It only took her a matter of seconds to realise what had caused it. The silence. She couldn't hear the twins. How long had she been asleep? Her heart jolted anxiously into her ribs when she looked at her watch and realised that it was over three hours since she had tucked the twins into their beds. Why were they so quiet?

Trembling with apprehension, she pushed back the bedclothes, grabbing the towel she had discarded earlier and wrapping it around herself as she ran barefoot from her own room to the twins'.

It was empty. Her heart lurched sickeningly, and then started to beat frantically fast with fear.

On shaking legs Ruby ran through the suite, opening doors, calling their names, even checking the security lock on the main door to the suite just in case they had somehow opened it. All the time the hideous reality of what might have happened was lying in wait for her inside her head.

In the dreadful silence of the suite—only a parent could know and understand how a silence that should have been filled with the sound of children's voices could feel—she sank down onto one of the sofas.

The reason the twins weren't here must be because Sander had taken them. There could be no other explanation. He must have come back whilst she was asleep and seized his opportunity. He hadn't wanted to marry her any more than she had wanted to marry him. What he had wanted was the twins. His sons. And now he had them.

Were they already on a plane to the island? *His* island, where he made the laws and where she would never be able to reach them. He had their passports after all. A legal necessity, he had said, and she had stupidly accepted that.

Shock, grief, fear and anger—she could feel them all, but over and above those feelings was concern for her sons and fury that Sander could have done something so potentially harmful to them.

She could hear a noise: the sound of the main door to the suite opening, followed by the excited babble of two familiar voices.

The twins!

She was on her feet, hardly daring to believe that she wasn't simply imagining hearing them out of her own need, and then they were there, in the room with her, running towards her and telling her excitedly, 'Daddy took us to a café for our tea, because you were asleep,' bringing the smell of cold air in with them.

Dropping onto her knees, Ruby hugged them to her not trusting herself to speak, holding the small wriggling bodies tightly. They were her life, her heart, her everything. She could hardly bear to let them go.

Sander was standing watching her, making her acutely conscious as she struggled to stand up that all that covered her nudity was the towel she had wrapped round her.

Going back to her bedroom, she discarded the towel and grabbed a clean pair of knickers before reaching for her old and worn velour dressing gown. She was too worked up and too anxious to get back to the twins as quickly as she could to care what she looked like or what Sander thought. The fact that he hadn't taken them as she had initially feared paled into insignificance compared with her realisation that he could have done so. Now that she had had a taste of what it felt like to think she had lost them, she knew more than ever that there was nothing she would not do or sacrifice to keep them with her.

Her hands trembled violently as she tied the belt on

her dressing gown. From the sitting room she could hear the sound of cartoon voices from the television, and when she went back in the boys were sitting together, watching a children's TV programme, whilst Sander was seated at the small desk with his laptop open in front of him.

Neither of them had spoken, but the tension and hostility crackling in the air between them spoke a language they could both hear and understand.

Her headache might have gone, but it had been replaced with an equally sickening sense of guilt, Ruby acknowledged, when she sat down an hour later to read to the boys, now bathed and in bed. She watched them as they fell asleep after their bedtime story. Today something had happened that she had never experienced before. She had slept so deeply that she had not heard anything when Sander returned and took her sons. How could that be? How could she have been so careless of their safety?

She didn't want to leave them. She wanted to stay here all night with them.

The bedroom door opened. Immediately Ruby stiffened, whispering, 'What do you want?'

'I've come to say goodnight to my sons.'

'They're asleep.' She got up and walked to the door, intending to go through it and then close it, excluding him, but Sander was holding it and she was the one forced to leave and then watch as he went to kiss their sleeping faces.

Turning on her heel, Ruby headed for her own room. But before she stepped inside it her self-control broke and she whirled round, telling Sander, 'You had no right to take the boys out without asking me first.'

'They are my sons. I have every right. And as for telling you—'

*Telling* her, not asking her. Ruby noted his correction, consumed now by the kind of anger that followed the trauma of terrible shock and fear, which was a form of relief at discovering that the unthinkable hadn't happened after all.

'You were asleep.'

'You could have woken me. You *should* have woken me. It's my right as their mother to know where they are.'

'Your *right*? What about *their* rights? What about their right to have a mother who doesn't put her own needs first? I suppose a woman who goes out at night picking up men needs to sleep during the day. And knowing you as I do, I imagine that is what *you* do.'

Sickened by what he was implying, Ruby said fiercely, '*Knowing* me? You don't know me at all. And the unpleasant little scenario you have just outlined has never and would never take place. I have never so much as gone out at night and left the twins, never mind gone out picking up men. The reason I was asleep was because I haven't been feeling well—not that I expect you to believe me. You'd much rather make up something you can insult me with than listen to the truth.'

'I've had firsthand experience of the truth of what you are.'

Ruby's face burned. 'You're basing your judgement of me on one brief meeting, when I was—'

'Too drunk to know what you were doing?'

His cynical contempt was too much for Ruby's composure. For years she had tortured and tormented herself because of what she had done. She didn't need Sander weighing in to add to that self-punishment and pain. She shook her head in angry denial.

'Foolish and naive enough to want to create a fairy story out of something and someone belonging in reality to a horror story,' she said bitterly. Too carried away by the anger bursting past her self-control, she continued, 'You need not have wasted your contempt on me, because it can't possibly match the contempt I feel for myself, for deluding myself that you were someone special.'

Ruby felt sick and dizzy. Memories of what they once shared were rushing in, roaring over her mental barriers and springing into vivid life inside her. She had been such a fool, so willing and eager to go to him, seeking in his arms the security and safety she had lost and thinking in her naivety that she would find them by binding herself to him in the most intimate way there was.

'So much drama,' Sander taunted her, 'and all of it so unnecessary, since I know it for the deceit that it is.'

'You are the one who is deceiving yourself by believing what you do,' Ruby threw at him emotionally.

'You dare to accuse *me* of self-deception?' Sander demanded, stepping towards her as he spoke, forcing her to step back into her bedroom. She backed up so quickly that she ended up standing on the trailing belt of her dressing gown. The soft, worn fabric gave way immediately, exposing the pale curve of her breast and the darker flesh of her nipple.

Sander saw what had happened before Ruby was aware of it herself, and his voice dropped to a cynical softness as he said, 'So that's what you want, is it? Same old Ruby. Well, why not? You certainly owe me something.'

Ruby's despairing, 'No!' was lost, crushed beneath the cruel strength of his mouth as it fastened on hers, and the sound of the door slamming as he pushed it closed was a death knell on her chances of escape.

Her robe quickly gave way to the swift expertise of Sander's determined hands, sliding from Ruby's body whilst he punished her with his kiss. In the mirror Sander could see the narrow curve of her naked back. Her skin, palely luminous, reminded him of the inside of the shells washed up on the beach below his home. Against his will old memories stirred, of how beneath his touch and against it she had trembled and then shuddered, calling out to him in open pleasure, so easily aroused by even the lightest caress. A wanton who had made no attempt to conceal the passion that drove her, or her own pleasure in his satisfaction of it, crying out to him to please her.

Sander drove his tongue between her lips as fiercely as he wanted to drive out her memory. The honeyed sensuality of her mouth closed round him, inviting his tongue-tip's exploration of its sweetest hidden places. The simple plain white knickers she was wearing jarred against the raw sexuality of his own arousal. He wanted her naked and eager, stripped of the lies and deceit with which she was so keen to veil her own reality. He would make her admit to what she was, show her that he knew the true naked reality of her. His hands gripped her and held her, moving down over her body to push aside her protective covering.

Her figure was as perfect as it was possible for a woman's figure to be—or it would be if she carried a few more pounds, Sander acknowledged. From her shoulders, her torso narrowed down into a handspan waist before curving out into feminine hips and the high, rounded cheeks of her bottom. Her legs were long and slender, designed to wrap erotically and greedily around the man she chose to give her the pleasure she craved. Her breasts were full and soft, and he could remember how sensitive her nipples had been, the suckle of his mouth against them making her cry out in ecstasy.

Why was he tormenting himself with mere memories when she was here and his for the taking, her body already shivering in his hold with anticipation of the pleasure to come?

She was naked and in Sander's power. She should fight him and reject him, Ruby knew. She wanted to, but her body wanted something else. Her body wanted Sander.

Like some dark power conjured up by a master sorcerer desire swept through her, overwhelming reason and pride, igniting a need so intense that she felt as though an alien force were possessing her, dictating actions and reactions it was impossible for her to control.

It was as though in Sander's arms she became a different person—a wildly passionate, elementally sensual woman of such intensity that everything she was crystallised in the act of being taken by him and taking him in turn.

It might be her wish to fight what possessed her, but it was also her destiny to submit to it as Sander's mouth moved from its fierce possession of hers to an equally erotic exploration of her throat, lingering on the pulse there that so recklessly gave away her arousal.

It was not enough to have her naked to his gaze and his touch. He needed to have the feel of her against his own skin. She was an ache, a need, a compulsion that wouldn't allow him to rest until he had conquered her and she had submitted to his mastery of her pleasure. He wanted, needed, to hear her cry out that desire to him before he could allow himself to submit to his own desire for her. He needed her to offer up her pleasure to him before he could lose himself within her and take his own.

He was caught in a trap as old as Eve herself—caught and held in the silken web of a desire only she had the power to spin. The savagery of his anger that this should be so was only matched by the savagery of his need for the explosion of fevered sensuality now possessing them both. It was a form of madness, a fever, a possession he couldn't escape.

Scooping her up in his arms, Sander carried Ruby to the bed, watching her watch him as he placed her on it and then wrenched off his own clothes, seeing the way her eyes betrayed her reaction to the sight of him, naked and ready for her.

Her eyes dark and wide with delight, Ruby reached

out to touch the formidable thickness of Sander's erection, marvelling at the texture of his flesh beneath her fingers. Engrossed and entranced, she stroked her fingertips over the length of him, easing back the hooded cover to reveal the sensitive flesh beneath it, not the woman she knew as herself any more, but instead a Ruby who was possessed by the powerful dark force of their shared desire—a Ruby whose breath quickened and whose belly tightened in pleasurable longing.

She looked up at Sander and saw in his eyes the same need she knew was in her own. She lifted her hand from his body, and as though it had been a signal to him he pushed her back on the bed, following her down, shaping and moulding her breasts with his hands, feeding her need for the erotic pleasure she knew he could give her with the heat of his lips and his tongue on her nipples, until she arched up against him, whimpering beneath the unbearable intensity of her own pleasure.

The feel of his hand cupping her sex wasn't just something she welcomed. It was something she needed.

Her body was wet and ready for him, just as it had been before. Just for a heartbeat the mistrust that was his mother's legacy to him surfaced past Sander's desire. There must not be another unwanted conception.

'The pill—' he began,

Ruby nodded her head.

A sheen of perspiration gleamed on his tanned flesh, and the scent of his arousal was heightening her own. It was frightening, this intensity of desire, this sharpening and focusing of her senses so that only Sander filled them. It had frightened her six years ago and it still frightened her now. The need he aroused within her demanded that she gave everything of herself over to him—all that she was, every last bit of her. The verbal demand he was making now was nothing compared with that.

'Yes. I'm taking it.'

'You swear?'

'I swear…'

Sander heard the unsteady note of need trembling in her voice. She was impatient for him, but no more than he was for her. He had fought to hold back the tide of longing for her from the minute he had seen her again. It had mocked his efforts to deny it, and now it was overwhelming him, the fire burning within him consuming him. Right now, in this heartbeat of time, nothing else mattered. He was in the grip of a force so powerful that he had to submit to it.

They moved together, without the need for words, movement matching movement, a duel of shared anger and longing. Her body welcomed his, holding it, sheathing it, moving with it and against it, demanding that he move faster and deeper, driving them both to that place from which they could soar to the heavens and then fall back to earth.

It was here now—that shuddering climax of sensation, gripping her, gripping Sander, causing the spurting spill of the seeds of new life within her. Only this time there would be no new life because she was on the pill.

They lay together in the darkness, their breathing unsteady and audible in the silence.

Now—now when it was over, and his flesh was washed with the cold reality of how quickly he had given in to his need for her—Sander was forced to accept the truth. He could not control the physical desire she aroused in him. It had overwhelmed him, and it would overwhelm him again. That knowledge was a bitter blow to his pride.

Without looking at her, he told her emotionlessly, 'From now on I am the only man you will have sex with. Is that understood? I will not have my wife shaming me by offering herself to other men. And to ensure that you don't I shall make it my business to see to it that your eager appetite for sexual pleasure is kept satisfied.'

Sander knew that his words were merely a mask for the reality that he could neither bear the thought of her with another man nor control his own desire for her, no matter how much he despised himself for his weakness.

Ruby could feel her face burning with humiliation. She wanted to tell him that she didn't understand what happened to her when she was in his arms. She wanted to tell him that other men did not have the same effect on her. She wanted to tell him that he was the only man she had ever had sex with. But she knew that he wouldn't listen.

Later, alone in his own room, Sander tried to explain to himself why the minute he touched Ruby he became filled with a compulsion to possess her. His desire for her was stronger than his resolve to resist it, and he couldn't. What she made him feel and want was unique to her, loath as he was to admit that.

# CHAPTER SEVEN

GIVEN Sander's wealth, Ruby had half expected that they might fly first-class to the island—but what she had not expected was that they would be travelling in the unimagined luxury of a private jet, with them the only passengers on board. But that was exactly what had happened, and now, with the boys taken by the steward to sit with the captain for a few minutes, she and Sander were alone in the cabin, with its cream leather upholstery and off-white carpets.

'The money it must cost to own and run something like this would feed hundreds of poor families,' Ruby couldn't stop herself from saying.

Her comment, and the unspoken accusation it held, made Sander frown. He had never once heard his mother express concern for 'poor families', and the fact that Ruby had done so felt like a sharp paper cut on the tender skin of his judgement of her—something small and insignificant in one sense, but in another something he could not ignore, no matter how much he might want to do so.

To his own disbelief he found himself defending his

position, telling her, 'I don't actually own it. I merely belong to a small consortium of businessmen who share and charter it when they need it. As for feeding the poor—on the island we operate a system which ensures that no one goes hungry and that every child has access to an education matched to their skills and abilities. We also have a free health service and a good pension system—the latter two schemes put in place by my father.'

Why on earth did he think he had to justify anything he did to *Ruby*?

It was dark when their flight finally put down on the island, the darkness obscuring their surroundings apart from what they could see in the blaze of the runway lights as they stepped down from the plane and into the warm velvet embrace of the Mediterranean evening. A soft breeze ruffled the boys' hair as they clung to Ruby's sides, suddenly uncertain and unsure of themselves. A golf cart type of vehicle was their transport for the short distance to the arrivals building, where Sander shook hands with the officials waiting to greet him before ushering them outside again to the limousine waiting for them. It was Sander who lifted the sleepy children into it, settling Harry on his lap and then putting his free arm around Freddie, whilst Ruby was left to sit on her own. Her arms felt empty without the twins, and she felt a maternal urge to reach for them, but she resisted it, not wanting to disturb them now that they were asleep.

The headache and subsequent nausea it had caused

her had thankfully not returned, although she still didn't feel one hundred percent.

The car moved swiftly down a straight smooth road before eventually turning off it onto a more winding road, on one side of which Ruby could see the sea glinting in the moonlight. On the other side of them was a steep wall of rock, which eventually gave way to an old fashioned fortress-like city wall, with a gateway in it through which they drove, past tall buildings and then along a narrow street which broadened out into the large formal square Ruby had seen on the internet.

'This is the main square of the city, with the Royal Palace up ahead of us,' Sander informed her.

'Is that where we'll be living?' Ruby asked apprehensively.

Sander shook his head.

'No. The palace is used only for formal occasions now, and as an administrative centre. After my grandfather died I had my own villa built just outside the city. I don't care for pomp and circumstance. My people's quality of life is what is important to me, just as it was to my father. I cannot expect to have their respect if I do not give them mine.'

Ruby looked away from him. His comments showed the kind of attitude she admired, but how could she allow herself to admire Sander? It was bad enough that he could arouse her physically without her being vulnerable to him emotionally as well.

'The city must be very old,' she said instead.

'Very,' Sander agreed.

As always when he returned to the island after an absence, he was torn in opposing directions. He loved the island and its people, but he also had the painful memories of his childhood here to contend with.

In an effort to banish them and concentrate on something else, he told Ruby, 'The Phoenicians and the Egyptians traded here, just as they did with our nearest neighbour Cyprus. Like Cyprus, we too have large deposits of copper here, and possession of the island was fought over fiercely during the Persian wars. In the end a marriage alliance between the opposing forces brought the fighting to an end. That has traditionally been the way in which territorial disputes have been settled here—' He broke off to look at her as he heard the small sound Ruby made.

Ruby shivered, unable to stop herself from saying, 'It must have been dreadful for the poor brides who were forced into marriage.'

'It is not the exclusive right of *your* sex to detest a forced marriage.'

Sander's voice was so harsh that the twins stirred against him in their sleep, focusing Ruby's attention on her sons, although she was still able to insist defensively, 'Historically a man has always had more rights within marriage than a woman.'

'The right to freedom of choice is enshrined in the human psyche of both sexes and should be respected above all other things,' Sander insisted.

Ruby looked at him in disbelief. 'How can you say that after the way you have forced me…?'

'You were the one who insisted on marriage.'

'Because I had no other choice.'

'There is always a choice.'

'Not for a mother. She will always put her children first.'

Her voice held a conviction that Sander told himself had to be false, and the cynical look he gave her said as much, causing Ruby's face to burn as she remembered how she had fallen asleep, leaving the twins unprotected.

Looking away from her, Sander thought angrily that Ruby might *think* she had deceived him by claiming her reason for insisting he married her was that she wanted to protect her sons, but he knew perfectly well that it was the fact that she believed marriage to him would give her a share in his wealth. That was what she really wanted to protect.

But she had signed a prenuptial agreement that barred her from making any claim on his money should they ever divorce, an inner voice defended her unexpectedly. She probably thought she could have the prenup set aside, Sander argued against it. Her children loved her, the inner voice pointed out. They would not exhibit the love and trust they did if she was a bad mother. He had loved *his* mother at their age, Sander pointed out. But he had hardly seen his mother or spent much time with her. She had been an exotic stranger, someone he had longed to see, and yet when he had seen her she had made him feel anxious to please her, and wary of her sudden petulant outbursts if he accidentally touched her expensive clothes. Anna, who was now in charge of the villa's household, had been more of a true mother—not just to him, but to all of them.

As Anna had been with them, Ruby was with the twins all the time. Logically he had to admit that it simply wasn't possible for anyone to carry out the pretence of being a caring parent twenty-four seven if it was just an act. A woman who loved both money and her children? Was that possible? It galled Sander that he should even be asking himself that question. What was the matter with him? He knew exactly what she was—why should he now be finding reasons to think better of her?

Sander looked away from Ruby and out into the darkness beyond the car window. The boys were soft warm weights against his body. His sons, and he loved them utterly and completely, no matter who or what their mother was. It was for their sakes that he wanted to find some good in her, for their sakes that his inner voice was trying to insist she was a good mother—for what caring father would *not* want that for his children, especially when that father knew what it was to have a mother who did not care.

Was it her imagination, or were the twins already turning more to Sander than they did to her? Miserably Ruby stared through the car window next to her. Whilst they had been talking they had left the city behind and were now travelling along another coastal road, with the sea to one side of them. But where previously there had been steep cliffs now the land rolled more gently away from the road.

It was far too late and far too selfish of her to wish that Sander had not come back into her life, Ruby admitted as the silence between them grew, filled by Sander's contempt for her and entrapping her in her own ever-present guilt. It was that guilt for having conceived the twins so carelessly and thoughtlessly that had in part brought her here, Ruby recognised. Guilt and her overwhelming desire to give her sons the same kind of happy, unshadowed, secure childhood in a family protected by two loving parents that she herself had enjoyed until her parents' death. But that security had been ripped from her. Her heart started to thud in a mixture of remembered pain and fierce hope that her sons would never experience what she had.

On his side of the luxurious leather upholstered car Sander stared out into the darkness—a darkness that for him was populated by the ghosts of his own past. In his grandfather's day the family had lived in the palace, unable to speak to either their parents or their grandfather unless those adults chose to seek them out. Yet despite maintaining his own distance from Sander and his siblings, their grandfather had somehow managed to know every detail of his grandchildren's lives, regularly sending for them so that he could list their flaws and faults and petty childhood crimes.

His sister and brother had been afraid of their grandfather, but Sander, the eldest child and ultimately the heir to his grandfather's shipping empire, had quickly learned that the best way to deal with his grandparent was to stand up to him. Sander's pride had been honed on the whetstone of his grandfather's mockery and baiting, as he'd constantly challenged Sander to prove himself to him whilst at the same time having no compunction about seeking to destroy his pride in himself to maintain his own superiority.

An English boarding school followed by university had given him a welcome respite from his grandfather's overbearing and bullying ways, but it had been after Sander had left university and started work in the family business that the real clashes between them had begun.

The continuation of the family and the business had been all that really mattered to his grandfather. His son and his grandchildren had been merely pawns to be used to further that cause. Sander had grown up hearing his grandfather discussing the various merits of young heiresses whom Sander might be wise to marry, but what he had learned from his mother, allied to his own naturally alpha personality and the time he had spent away from the island whilst he was at school and university, had made Sander determined not to allow his grandfather to bully him into marriage as he had done his father.

There had been many arguments between them on the subject, with his grandfather constantly trying to manipulate and bully Sander into meeting one or other of the young women he'd deemed suitable to be the mother of the next heir. In the end, infuriated and sickened by his grandfather's attempts at manipulation and coercion, Sander had announced to his grandfather that he was wasting his time as he never intended to marry, since he already had an heir in his brother.

His grandfather had then threatened to disinherit him, and Sander had challenged him to go ahead, telling him that he would find employment with one of their rivals. There the matter had rested for several weeks, giving Sander the impression that finally his grandfather had realised that he was not going to be controlled as his own parents had been controlled. But then, virtually on the eve of a long planned visit by Sander to the UK, to meet with some important clients in Manchester, he had discovered that his grandfather was planning to use his absence to advise the press of an impending engagement between Sander and the young widow of another ship-owner. Apart from anything else Sander knew that the young widow in question had a string of lovers and a serious drug habit, but neither of those potential draw-backs had been of any interest to his grandfather.

Of course Sander had confronted his grandfather, and both of them had been equally angry with the other. His grandfather had refused to back down, and Sander had warned him that if he went ahead with a public an-nouncement then he would refute that announcement equally publicly.

By the time he had reached Manchester Sander's anger hadn't cooled and his resolve to live his own life had actively hardened—to the extent that he had decided that on his return to Greece he was going to cut all ties with his grandfather and set up his own rival business from scratch.

And it had been in that frame of mind, filled with a dangerous mix of emotions, that he had met Ruby. He could see her now, eyeing him up from the other side of the crowded club, her blonde hair as carefully tousled as her lipglossed mouth had been deliberately pouted. The short skirt she'd worn had revealed slender legs, her tight top had been pulled in to display her tiny waist, and the soft rounded upper curves of her breasts had been openly on display. In short she had looked no different from the dozens of other eager, willing and easily available young women who came to the club specifically because it was known to be a haunt for louche young footballers and their entourages.

The only reason Sander had been in the club had been to meet a contact who knew people Sander thought might be prepared to give his proposed new venture some business. Whilst he was there Sander had received a phone call from a friend, urging him not to act against his own best interests. Immediately Sander had known that somehow his grandfather had got wind of what he was planning, and that someone had betrayed him. Fury—against his grandfather, against all those people in his life he had trusted but who had betrayed him— had overwhelmed him, exploding through his veins, pulsing against all constraints like the molten heat of a volcano building up inside him until it could not be contained any longer, the force of it erupting to spew its dangerous contents over everything in its path. And Ruby had been in the path of that fury, a readymade sacrifice to his anger, all too willing to allow him to use her for whatever purpose he chose.

All it had taken to bring her to his side had been one

cynical and deliberately lingering glance. She had leaned close to him in the crush of the club, her breath smelling of vodka and her skin of soap. He remembered how that realisation had momentarily checked him. The other girls around her had reeked of cheap scent. He had offered to buy her a drink and she had shaken her head, looking at him with such openly hungry eyes that her lack of self-respect had further inflamed his fury. He had questioned to himself why girls like her preferred to use their bodies to support themselves instead of their brains, giving themselves to men not directly for money but in the hope that they would end up as the girlfriend of a wealthy man.

Well, there had been no place in his life for a 'girlfriend', but right then there *had* been a rage, a tension inside him that he knew the use of her body in the most basic way there was would do much to alleviate. He had reached for his drink—not his first of the evening—finished it with one swallow, before turning to her and saying brusquely, 'Come on.'

A bump in the road woke the twins up, and Harry's 'Are we there yet?' dragged Sander's thoughts from the past to the present.

'Nearly,' he answered him. 'We're turning into the drive to the villa now.'

As he spoke the car swung off the road at such a sharp angle that Ruby slid along the leather seat, almost bumping her head on the side of the car. Unlike her, though, the twins were safe, protected by the arms Sander had tightened around them the minute the car had started to turn. Sander loved the twins, but he did not love her.

The pain that gripped her caught Ruby off guard. She wasn't jealous of her own sons, was she? Of course not. The last thing she wanted was Sander's arms around *her*, she told herself angrily as they drove through a pair of ornate wrought-iron gates and then down a long straight drive bordered with Cypress trees and illuminated by lights set into the ground.

At the end of the drive was a gravelled rectangle, and beyond that the villa itself, discreetly floodlit to reveal its elegant modern lines and proportions.

'Anna, who is in charge of the household, will have everything ready for you and the twins. She and Georgiou, her husband, who has driven us here, look after the villa and its gardens between them. They have their own private quarters over the garage block, which is separate from the villa itself,' Sander informed Ruby as the car crunched to a halt over the gravel.

Almost immediately the front door to the villa was opened to reveal a tall, well-built woman with dark hair streaked with grey and a serene expression.

It gave Ruby a fierce pang of emotion to see the way the twins automatically put their hands in Sander's and not her own as they walked with their father towards her. Her smile of welcome for Sander was one of love and delight, and Ruby watched in amazement as Sander returned her warm hug with obvious affection. Somehow it was not what she had expected. Anna—Ruby assumed the woman was Anna—was plainly far more to Sander than merely the person who was in charge of his household.

Now she was bending down to greet the boys, not overwhelming them by hugging them as she had Sander, Ruby noted approvingly, but instead waiting for them to go to her.

Sander gave them a little push and told them, 'This is Anna. She looked after me when I was a boy, and now she will look after you.'

Immediately Ruby's maternal hackles rose. Her sons did not need Anna or anyone else to look after them. They had her. She stepped forward herself, placing one hand on each of her son's shoulders, and then was completely disarmed when Anna smiled warmly and approvingly at her, as though welcoming what she had done rather than seeing it as either a challenge or a warning.

When Sander introduced her to Anna as his wife, it was obvious that Anna had been expecting them. What had Sander said to his family and those who knew him about the twins? How had he explained away the fact that he was suddenly producing them—and her? Ruby didn't know but she did know that Anna at least was delighted to welcome the twins as Sander's sons. It was plain she was ready to adore and spoil them, and was going to end up completely under their thumbs.

'Anna will show you round the villa and provide you and the boys with something to eat,' Sander informed Ruby.

He said something in Greek to Anna, who beamed at him and nodded her head vigorously, and then he was gone, striding across the white limestone floor of the entrance hall and disappearing through one of the dark wooden doors set into the white walls.

That feeling gripping her wasn't a sense of loss, was it? A feeling of being abandoned? A longing for Sander to return, because without him their small family was incomplete? Because without him *she* was incomplete?

As soon as the treacherous words whispered across her mind Ruby stiffened in denial of them. But they had left an echo that wasn't easily silenced, reminding her of all that she had suffered when she had first been foolish enough to think that he cared about her.

## CHAPTER EIGHT

'I'LL show you your rooms first,' Anna told Ruby, 'and then perhaps you would like a cup of tea before you see the rest of the villa?'

There was something genuinely warm and kind and, well, *motherly* about Anna that had Ruby's initial wary hostility melting away as they walked together up the marble stairs, the twins in between them.

When they reached the top and saw the long wide landing stretching out ahead of them the twins looked at Ruby hopefully.

Shaking her head, she began, 'No—no running inside—' Only to have Anna smile broadly at her.

'This is their home now, they may run if you permit it,' she told her.

'Very well,' Ruby told them, relieved by Anna's understanding of the need of two young children to let off steam, and both women watched as the boys ran down the corridor.

'Looking at them is like looking at Sander when he

was a similar age, except that—' Anna stopped, her smile fading.

'Except that what?' Ruby asked her, sensitively defensive of any possible criticism being lodged against her precious sons.

As though she had guessed what Ruby was thinking, Anna patted Ruby on the arm.

'You are a good mother—anyone can see that. Your goodness and your love for them is reflected in your sons' smiles. Sander's mother was not like that. Her children were a duty she resented, and they all, especially Sander, learned young not to turn to their mother for love and comfort.'

Anna's quiet words formed an image inside Ruby's head she didn't want to see—an image of a young and vulnerable Sander, a child with sadness in his eyes, standing alone and hurt by his mother's lack of love for him.

The boys raced back to them, putting an end to any more confidences from Anna about Sander's childhood, and Ruby's sympathy for the child that Sander had been was swiftly pushed to one side when she discovered that the two of them were going to be sharing a bedroom and a bed.

Why did she feel so unnerved and apprehensive? Ruby asked herself later, after Anna had helped her put the twins to bed and she was in the kitchen, drinking the fresh cup of tea Anna had insisted on making for her. Sander had already made it plain that she must accept that their marriage would include sexual intimacy. They both already knew that she wanted him, and she had already suffered the humiliation *that* had brought her, so what was there left for her to fear?

There was emotional vulnerability, Ruby admitted. With her sexual vulnerability to Sander there was already a danger that she could become sexually dependent on him, and that was bad enough. If she also became emotionally vulnerable to him might she not then become emotionally dependent on him? Where had that thought come from? She was a million miles from feeling anything emotional for Sander, wasn't she?

Excusing herself to Anna, Ruby explained that she wanted to go up and check the twins were still sleeping as they had left them, not wanting them to wake alone in such new surroundings.

The twins' bedroom, like the one she was to share with Sander, looked out onto a courtyard and an infinity pool with the sea beyond it. But whilst Sander's bedroom had glass doors that opened out onto the patio area that surrounded the pool, the boys' room merely had a window—a safety feature for which she was extremely grateful. Glass bedroom doors, a swimming pool, and two adventurous five-year-olds were a mix that would arouse anxiety in any protective mother.

She needn't have worried about the twins. They were both sleeping soundly, their faces turned toward one another. Love for them filled her. But as she bent towards them to kiss them it wasn't their faces she could see but that of another young child, a child whose dark eyes, so like those of her sons, were shadowed with pain and angry pride. Sander's eyes. They still held that angry pride now, as an adult, when he looked at her. And the pain? Her question furrowed Ruby's brow. Emotional pain was not something she had previously equated with Sander. But the circumstances a child experienced growing up affected it all its life. She believed that wholeheartedly. If she hadn't done so then she would not feel as strongly as she did about Sander being a part of the twins' lives. So what had happened to Sander's pain? Was it buried somewhere deep inside him? A sad, sore place that could never heal? A wound that was the cruellest wound of all to a child—the lack of its mother's love?

Confused by her own thoughts, Ruby left her sleeping sons. She was tired and ready for bed herself. Her heart started beating unsteadily. Tired and ready for bed? Ready to share Sander's bed?

The villa was beautifully decorated. The guest suite Anna had shown Ruby, and in which she would have preferred to be sleeping, was elegantly modern, the clean lines of its furniture softened by gauzy drapes, the cool white and taupe of the colour scheme broken up with touches of Mediterranean blues and greens in the artwork adorning the walls.

From the twins' room Ruby made her way to the room she was sharing with Sander—not because she wanted to look again at the large bed and let her imagination taunt her with images of what they would share there, but because she needed to unpack, Ruby told herself firmly. Only when she opened the door to the bedroom the cases that had been there before had vanished, and from the *en suite* bathroom through the open door she could smell the sharp citrus scent of male soap and hear the sound of the shower.

Had Sander had her cases removed? Had he told Anna that he didn't want to share a room with her? Relief warred with a jolt of female protectiveness of her position as his wife. She liked Anna, but she didn't want the other woman to think that Sander was rejecting her. That would be humiliating. More humiliating than being forced in the silence of the night to cry out in longing to a husband who could arouse in her a hunger she could not control?

Ruby moved restlessly from one foot to the other, and then froze as the door to the *en suite* bathroom opened fully and Sander walked into the bedroom.

He had wrapped a towel round his hips. His body was still damp from his shower, and the white towel threw into relief the powerful tanned male V shape of his torso and the breadth of his shoulders, tapering down over strong muscles to his chest, to the hard flatness of his belly. The shadowing of dark hair slicked wetly against his skin emphasised a maleness that had Ruby trapped in its sensual spell. She wanted to look away from him. She wanted not to remember, not to feel, not to be so easily and completely overwhelmed by the need that just looking at him brought back to simmering heat. But she didn't have that kind of self-control. Instead of satiating her desire for him, what they had already shared seemed only to have increased her need for him.

Her own intense sensuality bewildered her. She had

lived for six years without ever once wanting to have sex, and yet now she only had to look at Sander to be consumed by this alien desire that seemed to have taken possession of her. Possession. Just thinking the word increased the heat licking at her body, tightening the pulse flickering eagerly deep inside her.

It was Ruby's fault that he wanted her, Sander told himself. It was she, with her soft mouth and her hungry gaze, with her eagerness, who was responsible for his own inability to control the savage surging of his need to possess her. It was because of her that he felt this ache, this driven, agonising urgency that unleashed within him something he barely recognised as part of himself.

Like a wild storm, a tornado threatening to suck them both up into its perilous grasp, Ruby could feel the pressure of their combined desire. Fear filled her. She didn't want this. It shamed and weakened her. Dragging her gaze from Sander's body, she started to run towards the door in blind panic. But Sander moved faster, reaching the door before her, and the impetus of her panic slammed her into his body, the impact shocking through her.

Tears of anger—against herself, against him, and against the aching desire flooding her—filled her eyes and she curled her hands into small fists and beat them impotently against his chest. Sander seized hold of her wrists.

'I don't want to feel like this,' she cried, agonized.

'But you do. You want this, and you want me,' he told her, before he took the denial from her lips with the ruthless pressure of his own.

Just the taste of her unleashed within him a hunger he couldn't control. The softness of her lips, the sound she made when he kissed her, the way her whole body shuddered against his with longing, drove him in what felt like a form of madness, a need, to a place where nothing else existed or mattered, where bringing her desire within the control of his ability to satisfy it felt as though it was what he had been born for.

Each sound she made, each shudder of pleasure her body gave, each urgent movement against his touch that begged silently for more became a goal he had to reach—a test of his maleness he had to master, so that he would always be the only man she desired, *his* pleasuring of her the only pleasure that could satisfy her. Something about the pale silkiness of her skin as he slid her clothes from it made him want to touch it over and over again. His hands already knew the shape and texture of her breasts, but that knowing only made him want to feel their soft weight even more. His lips and tongue and teeth might have aroused the swollen darkness of her nipples to previous pleasure, but now he wanted to recreate that pleasure. He wanted to slide his hand over the flatness of her belly and feel her suck it in as she fought to deny the effect of his touch and lost that fight. He wanted to part the slender thighs and feel them quiver, hear the small moan from between her lips, watch as she tried and failed to stop her thighs from opening eagerly to allow him the intimacy of her sex. He loved the way her soft, delicately shaped outer lips, so primly folded, opened to the slow stroke of his fingers, her wetness eagerly awaiting him.

A shocked cry of protest streaked with primitive longing burst from Ruby's throat as Sander gave in to the demand of his own arousal and moved down her body, to kiss the soft flesh on the inside of her thighs and then stroke the tip of his tongue the length of the female valley his skilled fingers had laid bare to his caress.

Waves of pleasure were racing through her, dragging her back to a level of sensuality where she was as out of her depth as a fledgling swimmer swept out by the tide into deep water. Each stroke of his tongue-tip against the most sensitive part of her took her deeper, until her own pleasure was swamping her, pulling her down into its embrace, until the rhythm it imposed on her was all that she knew, her response to it dictated and controlled by the lap of Sander's tongue as finally it overwhelmed her and she was drowning in it, giving herself over completely to it.

Later, filling her with his aching flesh, feeling her desire catch fire again as her body moved with his, inciting him towards his own destruction, Sander knew with razor-sharp clarity, in the seconds before he cried out in the exultation of release, that what he was doing might be trapping her in her desire for him but it was also feeding his need for her.

# CHAPTER NINE

FROM the shade of the vine-covered pergola, Ruby watched the twins as they splashed in the swimming pool under Sander's watchful eye. It was just over six weeks now since they had arrived on the island, and the twins were loving their new life. They worshipped Sander. He was a good father, Ruby was forced to admit, giving them his time and attention, and most important of all his love. She glanced towards the house. Anna would be bringing their lunch out to them soon. A prickle of despair trickled down her spine as chilling as cold water.

This morning she was finally forcing herself to confront the possibility that she might be pregnant! The breakfasts she had been unable to eat in the morning, the tiredness that engulfed her every afternoon, the slight swelling of her breasts—all could have other explanations, but her missed period was now adding to the body of evidence.

Could she really be pregnant? Her heart jumped sickeningly inside her chest. There must be no more children, Sander had said. She must take the contraceptive pill. She had done, without missing a single one, but her symptoms were exactly the same as those she had experienced with the twins. Sander would be angry—furious, even—but what could he do? She was his wife, they were married, and she was having his child. A child she already knew he would not want.

Ruby could feel anxiety-induced nausea clogging her throat and causing perspiration to break out on her forehead. Was she right in thinking that Anna already suspected? Anna was an angel, wonderful with the children—almost a grandmother to them. After all, she had mothered Sander and his sister and brother. Somehow she seemed to know when Ruby was feeling tired and not very well, taking charge of the twins for her, giving her a kind pat when she fell back on the fiction that her lack of energy and nausea were the result of their move to a hot climate.

Sander was getting the twins out of the pool. Anna had arrived with their lunch. Determinedly, Ruby pushed her anxiety to one side.

Sander was used to working at home when he needed to, but since he had brought Ruby and his sons to the island he had discovered that he actually preferred to work at home. So that he could be with his sons, or so that he could be with Ruby? That was nonsense. A stupid question which he could not bring himself to answer.

Angrily he tried to concentrate on the screen in front of him. This afternoon he was finding it hard to concentrate on the e-mails he should be answering. Because he was thinking about Ruby? If he was then it was because of the conversation he had had with Anna earlier in the day, when she had commented on what a good mother Ruby was.

'A good mother and a good wife,' had been her exact words. 'You are a lucky man.'

Anna was a shrewd judge of character. She had never liked his mother, and she had protected them all from their grandfather's temper whenever she could. She had given him the only female love he had ever known. Homely, loyal Anna liked and approved of Ruby, a woman with more in common with his mother than she had with her.

Sander frowned. He might have seen the financially grasping side of Ruby that echoed the behaviour of his mother, but he had also seen her with the twins, and he was forced to admit that she *was* a loving and protective mother—a mother who gave her love willingly and generously to her sons…just as she gave herself willingly and generously to him…

*Now* what was he thinking? He was a fool if he started allowing himself to believe that. But did he want to believe it? No, Sander denied himself. Why should he want to believe that she gave him anything? Only a weak man or a fool allowed himself to think like that, and he was neither. But didn't the fact that he couldn't stop himself from wanting her reveal the worst kind of male weakness?

Wasn't the truth that even though he had tried to

deny it to himself he had not been able to forget her?
From that first meeting the memory of her had lain in
his mind like a thorn in his flesh, driven in too deeply
to be easily removed, the pain activated whenever an
unwary movement caused it to make its presence felt.

He had taken her and used her as a release for his
pent-up fury after his argument with his grandfather,
telling himself that his behaviour was justified because
she herself had sought him out.

Inside his head Sander could hear his grandfather's
raised voice, see the fist he had smashed down onto his
desk in his rage that Sander should defy him.

Sander moved restlessly in his computer chair. It was
too late now to regret allowing himself to recall that final
argument with his grandfather and the events that had
followed it. Far too late. Because the past was here with
him, invading his present and filling it with unwanted
memories, and he was back in that Manchester hotel
room, watching Ruby sleep curled up against him.

His mobile had started to ring in the grey light of the
dawn. She had protested in her sleep as he'd moved
away from her but she hadn't woken up.

The call had been from Anna, her anxiety and shock
reaching him across the miles as she told him that she
had found his grandfather collapsed on the floor of his
office and that he was on his way to hospital.

Sander had moved as quickly as he could, waking
Ruby and telling her brusquely that he wanted her out
of his bed, his room and the hotel, using her yet again

as a means of expelling the mingled guilt and anger the phone call had brought him.

She had looked shocked and uncomprehending, he remembered, no doubt having hoped for rather more from him than a few brief hours in bed. Then tears had welled up in her eyes and she had tried to cling to him. Irritated that she wasn't playing by the rules, he had thrust her off, reaching into his jacket pocket for his wallet and removing several crisp fifty-pound notes from it. It had increased his irritation when she had started to play the drama queen, backing off from him, shaking her head, looking at him as though he had stamped on a kitten, not offered her a very generous payment for her services.

His terse, 'Get dressed—unless you want the hotel staff to evict you as you are,' had had the desired effect. But even so he had escorted her downstairs and out to the taxi rank outside the hotel himself, putting her into a cab and then watching to make sure that she had actually left before completing his arrangements to get home.

As it turned out his grandfather had died within minutes of reaching the hospital, from a second major heart attack.

In his office Sander had found the document his grandfather had obviously been working on before he collapsed, and had seen that it was a notice to the papers stating that Sander was on the point of announcing his engagement. His guilt had evaporated. His guilt but not his anger. And yet despite everything Sander had still mourned him. Evidence of the same weakness that was undermining him now with regard to Ruby. A leopard did not change its spots just because someone was foolish enough to want it to do so.

After his grandfather's death Sandra had renewed his vow to himself to remain single.

How fate must have been laughing at him then, knowing that the seeds of his own destiny had already been sown and had taken root.

He turned back to the computer, but it was no use. Once opened, the door to his memories of that fateful night with Ruby could not be closed.

The hotel bedroom, with its dark furniture, had been shadowed and silent, the heavy drapes deadening the sound of the traffic outside and yet somehow at the same time emphasising the unsteadiness of Ruby's breathing—small, shallow breaths that had lifted her breasts against her tight, low-cut top. The light from the standard lamp—switched on when the bed had been turned down for the night—had outlined the prominence of her nipples. When she had seen him looking at them she had lifted her hands towards her breasts, as though to protect them from his gaze. He could remember how that simple action had intensified his anger at her denial of everything she was about, infuriating him in the same way that his grandfather had. The raging argument he'd had with his grandfather earlier that day had still been fresh in his mind. The two angers had met and joined together, doubling the intensity of his fury, driving him with a ferocious and overpowering need to possess her.

He had gone to her and pulled down her hands. Her body had trembled slightly in his hold. Had he hesitated then, trying to check the raging torrent within him, or did he just want to think that he had? The image he was creating of himself was that of a man out of control, unable to halt the force of his own emotions. In another man it would have filled him with distaste. But Ruby, he remembered, had stepped closer to him, not away from him, and it had been then that he had removed her top, taking with it her bra, leaving her breasts exposed. His actions had been instinctive, born of rage rather than desire, but somehow the sight of her nakedness, her breasts so perfectly shaped, had transmuted that rage into an equally intense surge of need—to touch them and caress them, to possess the flaunting sensuality of their tip tilted temptation.

They had both drawn in a breath, as though sharing the same thoughts and the same desire, and the tension of that desire had stretched their self-control until the air around them had almost thrummed with the vibration of it. Then Ruby had made a small sound in the back of her throat, and as though it had been some kind of signal to his senses his self-control had snapped. He had reached for her, no words needed as he'd kissed her, feeling her tremble in his arms as he probed the softly closed line of her lips. She had deliberately kept them closed in order to torment him. But two could play that game, and so, instead of forcing them to give way, he had tormented them into doing so, with soft, deliberately brief kisses, until Ruby had reached for the back of his neck, her fingers curling into his hair, and whimpered with protesting need against his mouth.

Sander closed his eyes and opened them again as he recalled the surge of male triumph that had seized him then and the passion it had carried with it—a feeling he had never experienced either before Ruby or after her, surely originating from his anger against his grandfather and nothing else. Certainly not from some special effect that only Ruby could have on his senses. The very thought of that was enough to have him shifting angrily in his seat. No woman would *ever* be allowed to have that kind of power over him. Because he feared what might happen to him once he allowed himself to want a woman with that kind of intensity?

Better to return to his memories than to pursue *that* train of thought, Sander decided.

As they had kissed he had been able to feel Ruby's naked breasts pressed up against him. He had slipped his hands between their bodies, forcing her slightly away from him so that he could cup the soft weight of them. Just remembering that moment now was enough to bring back an unwanted echo of the sensation of his own desire, roaring through his body as an unstoppable force. It hadn't been enough to flick his tongue-tip against each hardened nipple and feel it quivering under its soft lash. Nothing had been enough until he had drawn the swollen flesh into his mouth, enticing its increased response with the delicate grate of his teeth.

He had heard Ruby cry out and felt her shudder. His hands had been swift to dispose of her skirt so that he could slide his hands into her unexpectedly respectable plain white knickers, to hold and knead the soft flesh of her buttocks. Swollen and stiff with the ferocity of his anger-induced arousal, he had lifted her onto the bed, plundering the softness of her plum painted mouth in between removing his own clothes, driven by the heat of his frustration against his grandfather, not caring about the girl whose body was underneath him, only knowing that within it he could find release.

Ruby had wrapped her arms round him whilst he had plundered her mouth, burying her face in his shoulder once he was naked, pretending to be too shy to look at him, never mind touch him. But he hadn't been interested in playing games. To him she had simply been a means to an end. And as for her touching him… Sander tensed his muscles against his remembered awareness of exactly what her intimate touch on him would have precipitated. His body had been in no mood to wait and in no condition to need stimulus or further arousal. That alone was something he would have claimed impossible prior to that night. No other situation had ever driven him to such a peak of erotic immediacy.

No other situation or no other woman? Grimly Sander tried to block the unwanted question. His subconscious had no business raising such an unnecessary suggestion. He didn't want to probe any further into the past. But even though he pulled the laptop back towards himself and opened his e-mails, he still couldn't concentrate on them. His mind was refusing to co-operate, returning instead to its memories. Against his will more old images Ruby began to surface, refusing to be ignored. He was back in that hotel bedroom in Manchester. Sander closed his eyes and gave in.

In the dim light Ruby's body had been alabaster-pale, her skin flawless and her body delicately female. The lamplight had thrown a shadow from the soft mound of flesh covered by her knickers, which he had swiftly removed. That, he remembered, had caused him to glance up at the tangled mass of hair surrounding her face, surprised to discover that the colour of her hair was natural. Somehow the fact that she was naturally blonde didn't go with the image she had created, with her thick make-up and tight, clinging clothes.

She had met his look and then looked away, the colour coming and going in her face as her glance rested on his body and then skittered away.

If her naturally blonde hair had been at odds with his assessment of her, then her breathy voice, unsteady and on the verge of awed apprehension, had been enough to fill him with contempt.

'You look very big,' she had delivered, within a heart-beat of her glance skittering away from his erection.

Had she really thought him both foolish and vain enough to be taken in by a ploy like that? If so he had made sure that she knew that he wasn't by taunting her deliberately, parting her legs with his hand.

'But not bigger than any of the others, I'm sure.'

She had said something—a few gasped words—but he hadn't been listening by then. He had been too busy exploring the wet eagerness of her sex, stroking his fingertip its length until he reached the hard pulse of her clitoris, and by that stage she had begun to move against his touch and moan softly at the same time, in a rising crescendo of excitement.

He had told himself that her supposed arousal was almost bound to be partly faked but unexpectedly his body had responded to it as though it was real. It had increased his own urgency, so that he had replaced his fingers with the deliberate thrust of his sex. She had tensed then, looking up at him with widened dark eyes that had filled with fake tears when he had thrust properly into her, urged by the wanton tightness of her muscles as they clung to him, as though wanting to hold and possess him. Their resistance had incited him to drive deeper and deeper into her, just for the pleasure of feeling their velvet clasp. He had come quickly and hotly, his lack of control catching him off-guard, her body tightening around him as he pulsed into her.

Sander wrenched his thoughts back to the present. What had happened with Ruby was not an interlude in his life or an aspect of himself that reflected well on him, he was forced to admit. In fact part of the reason he had chosen to lock these memories away in the first place had been because of his sense of angry distaste. Like something rotten, they carried with them the mental equivalent of a bad odour that couldn't be ignored or masked. If he judged Ruby harshly for her part in their encounter, then he judged himself even more harshly— especially now that he knew the consequences of those few out of control seconds of raw male sensuality.

It was because he didn't like the fact that his sons had been conceived in such a way that he was experiencing the regrets he was having now, Sander told himself. He owed them a better beginning to their life than that.

What was it that was gnawing at him now? Regret because his sons had been conceived so carelessly, so uncaringly, and in anger? Or something more than that? Regret that he hadn't taken more time to—? To what? To get to know the mother of his sons better or to think of the consequences of his actions? Because deep down inside he felt guilty about the way he had treated Ruby? She had only been seventeen after all.

He hadn't known that then, Sander defended himself. He had assumed she was much older. And if he had known…?

Sander stood up and paced the floor of his office, stopping abruptly as he relived how, virtually as soon as he had released her, Ruby had gone to the bathroom. He had turned on his side, ignoring her absence, even then aware of how far his behaviour had fallen short of his own normal high standards. But even though he had wanted to blot out the reality of the situation, and Ruby herself, he had still somehow been unable to stop listening to the sound of the shower running and then ceasing, had been aware against his will of her return to the bed, her skin cold and slightly damp as she pressed up against his back, shivering slightly. He had had no need for intimacy with her any more. She had served her purpose, and he preferred sleeping alone. And yet for some reason, despite all of that, he had turned over and taken her in his arms, feeling her body stiffen and then relax as he held her.

She had fallen asleep with her head on his chest, murmuring in protest in her sleep every time he tried to ease away from her, so that he had spent the night with her cuddled up against him. And wasn't it true that somehow she had done something to him during those night hours? Impressed herself against his body and his senses so that once in a while over the years that had followed he would wake up from a deep sleep, expecting to find her there lying against him and feeling as though a part of him was missing because she wasn't?

How long had he fought off that admission, denying its existence, pretending to himself that since he had returned to the island this time his sleep had never once been disturbed by that aching absence? He moved impatiently towards the window, opening it to breathe in fresh air in an attempt to clear his head.

What had brought all this on? Surely not a simple comment from Anna that she considered Ruby to be a good mother. A good mother *and* a good wife, he reminded himself.

His mobile had started to ring. He reached for it, frowning when he saw his sister's name flash up on the screen.

'Sander, we've been back from America nearly a week now. When are you going to bring Ruby to Athens so that I can meet her?'

Elena liked to talk, and it was several minutes before Sander could end the call, having agreed that, since he was due to pay one of his regular visits to the Athens office anyway, he would take Ruby with him so that she and Elena could meet.

# CHAPTER TEN

SHE had better find out for sure that she was pregnant, and if so tell Sander. She couldn't put it off much longer, Ruby warned herself. She wasn't the only one to blame after all. It took two, and she *had* taken her birth control pills.

She had also been unwell, she reminded herself, and in the anxiety and despair of everything that had been happening in London she had forgotten that that could undermine the effectiveness of the pills. Surely Sander would be able to understand that? But what if he didn't? What if he accused her of deliberately flouting his wishes? But what possible reason could she logically have for doing that? He was a successful, intelligent businessman. He would be bound to recognise that there was no logical reason for her to deliberately allow herself to become pregnant. He might be a successful, intelligent businessman, but he had also been a child whose mother had betrayed him. Would *that* have any bearing on the fact that she was pregnant? On the face of it, no—but Ruby had an instinctive feeling that it might.

She would tell him tonight, Ruby promised herself, once the boys were in bed.

Her mind made up, Ruby was just starting to relax when Sander himself appeared, striding from the house onto the patio area, quite plainly in search of her. Her heart somersaulted with guilt. Had he somehow guessed? At least if he had then her pregnancy would be out in the open and they could discuss it rationally. It was only when he told her that his sister had been on the phone, and that they would be leaving for Athens in morning and staying there for the night, that Ruby realised, cravenly, that a part of her had actually hoped that he *had* guessed, and that she would be spared the responsibility of telling him that she had once again conceived.

Since he hadn't guessed, though, it was sensible, surely, to wait until they returned from Athens to tell him? That way they would have more time to discuss the issue properly. He would be angry, she knew that, but she was clinging to the knowledge that he loved the twins, and using that knowledge to reassure herself that, angry though he would no doubt be with her, he would love this new baby as well.

'I've got a small apartment in Athens that I use when I'm there on business. We'll stay there. The twins will be safe and well looked after here, with Anna.'

'Leave them behind?' Ruby checked. 'They haven't spent a single night without me since they were born.'

Her anxious declaration couldn't possibly be fake, Sander recognised. It had been too immediate and automatic for that. He tried to imagine his own mother refusing a trip to a cosmopolitan city filled with expensive designer shops to stay with her children, and acknowledged that it would never have happened. His mother had hated living on the island, had visited it as infrequently as she could, and he himself had been sent to boarding school in England as soon as he had reached his seventh birthday.

'Elena will want to spend time with you, and I have business matters to attend to. The boys will be far happier here on the island in Anna's care than they would be in a city like Athens.'

When Ruby bit her lip, her eyes still shadowed, he continued, 'I can assure you that you can trust Anna to look after them properly. If I did not believe that myself, there would be no question of us leaving them.'

Immediately Ruby's gaze cleared.

'Oh, I know I can trust your judgement when it comes to their welfare. I know how much you love them.'

Her immediate and open admission that she accepted not only his judgement for their sons but with it his right to make such a judgement was having the most extraordinary effect on him, Sander realised. Like bright sunlight piercing a hitherto dark and impenetrable black cloud. He was bemused and dazzled by the sudden surge of pleasure her words gave him—the feeling that they were united, and that she...that she *trusted* him, Sander recognised. Ruby trusted him to make the right decision for their sons. A surge of unfamiliar emotion swamped him, and he had an alien and overpowering urge to take her in his arms and hold her tight. He took a step towards her, and then stopped as his need to protect himself cut in.

Unaware of Sander's reaction to her statement, Ruby sighed. She was being silly, she knew. The twins *would* be perfectly safe with Anna. Was it really for their sakes she wanted them with her? Or was it because she felt their presence was a form of protection and was nervous at the thought of meeting Sander's sister? Had they had a normal marriage she would have been able to admit her apprehension to Sander—but then if they were in a normal marriage she would already have told him about the new baby, and that news would have been a matter of joy and happiness for both of them.

'You will like Elena—although, as I told her often when she was a little girl, she talks all the time and sometimes forgets to let others speak.' Anna shook her head as she relayed this information to Ruby. She was helping her to pack for the trip to Athens—her offer, Ruby suspected, more because she had sensed her trepidation and wanted to reassure her than because she really felt Ruby needed help.

'She is very proud of her brothers, especially Sander, and she will be glad that he has married you when she sees how much you love him.'

Ruby dropped the pair of shoes she had been holding, glad that the act of bending down to pick them up gave her an opportunity to hide her shock. How much she loved Sander? What on earth had made Anna think and say that? She didn't love him at all.

Did she?

Of course not. After all, he hadn't exactly given her any reason to love him, had he?

Since when had love needed a reason? What reason had she needed in that Manchester club, when she had looked across the bar and felt her heart leap inside her chest, as though he himself had tugged it and her towards him?

That had been the silly, naive reaction of a girl desperate to create a fairytale hero—a saviour to rescue her from her grief, Ruby told herself, beginning to panic.

Anna was mistaken. She had to be. But when she had recovered her composure enough to look at the other woman she saw from the warm compassion in her eyes that Anna herself certainly didn't think that she was wrong.

Was it possible? *Could* she have started to love Sander without realising it? Could the aching, overwhelming physical desire for him she could not subdue be caused by love and not merely physical need? He was, after all, the father of her children, and she couldn't deny that initially when she had realised that she was pregnant a part of her had believed she had conceived because of the intensity of her emotional response to him. Because she had been naive, and frightened and alone, she had wanted to believe that the twins had been created out of love.

And this new baby—didn't it too deserve to have its mother's body accept the seed that began its life with love?

'You will like Elena,' Anna repeated, 'and she will like you.'

\* \* \*

Ruby was clinging to those words several hours later, after their plane had touched down in Athens and they were in the arrivals hall, as an extremely stylish dark-haired young woman came hurrying towards them, her eyes covered by a pair of designer sunglasses.

'Sander. I thought I was going to be late. The traffic is horrendous—and the smog! No wonder all our precious ancient buildings are in so much danger. Andreas said to tell you that he is pretty sure he has secured the Taiwan contract—oh, and I want you both to come to dinner tonight. Nothing too formal...'

'Elena, you are like a runaway train. Stop and let me introduce you to Ruby.' Sander's tone was firm but wry, causing his sister to laugh and then turn to Ruby, catching her off-guard when she immediately enveloped her in a warm hug.

'Anna has told me what a fortunate man Sander is to have married you. I can't wait to meet the twins. Wasn't I clever, spotting them at Manchester Airport? But for me you and Sander might never have made up your quarrel and been reconciled.'

They were out of the airport now, and Sander was saying, 'You'd better let me drive, Elena. I have some expensive memories of what happens when you drive and talk at the same time.'

'Oh, you.' Elena mock pouted as she handed over her car keys, and then told Ruby, 'It wasn't really my fault. The other driver should never have been parked where he was in the first place.'

Anna was right—she was going to like Elena, Ruby

acknowledged as her sister-in-law kept up a stream of inconsequential chatter and banter whilst Sander drove them through the heavy Athens traffic.

Elena had obviously questioned Sander about their relationship, and from what she had said Ruby suspected that he had made it seem as though the twins had been conceived during an established relationship between them rather than a one-night stand. That had been kind of him. Kind and thoughtful. Protecting the twins and protecting her. The warm glow she could feel inside herself couldn't possibly be happiness, could it?

The Athens night was warm, the soft air stroking Ruby's skin as she and Sander walked from the taxi that had just dropped them off to the entrance to the exclusive modern building that housed Sander's Athens apartment. They had spent the evening with Elena and Andreas at their house on the outskirts of the city, and tomorrow morning they would be returning to the island. Of course she was looking forward to seeing the twins, but... Was she simply deceiving herself, because it was what she wanted, or had there really been a softening in Sander's attitude towards her today? A kindness and a warmth that had made her feel as though she was poised on the brink of something special and wonderful?

Sander looked at Ruby. She was wearing a pale peach silk dress patterned with a design of pale grey fans. It had shoestring straps, a fitted bodice and a gently shaped slim skirt. Its gentle draping hinted at the feminine shape of her figure without revealing too much of it, and the strappy bodice revealed the tan her skin had acquired in the weeks she had spent on the island. Tonight, watching her over dinner as she had talked and smiled and laughed with his sister and her husband, he had felt pride in her as his wife, as well as desire for her as a man. Something—Sander wasn't prepared to give it a name—had begun to change. Somehow *he* had begun to change. Because Ruby was a good mother? Because she had trusted him about the twins' care? Because tonight she had shown an intelligence, a gentleness and a sense of humour that—a little to his own surprise— he had recognised were uniquely hers, setting her apart from his mother and every other woman he had known?

Sander wasn't ready to answer those questions, but he was ready and eager to make love to his wife.

To make love to her *as* his wife. A simple enough statement, but for Sander it resonated with admissions that he would have derided as impossible the day he had married her.

As they entered the apartment building Sander reached for Ruby's hand. Neither of them said anything, but Ruby's heart leapt and then thudded into the side of her chest. The hope she had been trying desperately not to let go to her head was now soaring like a helium balloon.

On the way up to the apartment in the lift she pleaded mentally, 'Please let everything be all right. Please let things work out for…for *all* of us.' And by all she included the new life she was carrying as well.

She *was* going to tell Sander, but today whilst she had had the chance she had slipped into a chemist's shop and bought a pregnancy testing kit—just to be doubly sure. She would wait until they were back on the island to use it, and then she *would* tell Sander. Then, but not now. Because she wanted tonight to be very special. Tonight she wanted for herself. Tonight she wanted to make love with Sander, knowing that she loved him.

In the small sitting room of the apartment, Sander removed the jacket of his linen suit, dropping it onto one of the chairs. The small action tightened the fabric of his shirt against the muscles of his back, and Ruby's gaze absorbed their movement, the now familiar ache of longing softening her belly and then spreading swiftly through her. Her sudden need to breathe more deeply, to take in oxygen, lifted her breasts against the lining of her dress, causing her already aroused and sensitive nipples to react even more to the unintentional drag of the fabric. When Sander straightened up and turned round he could see their swollen outline pressing eagerly against the barrier of her dress. His own body reacted to their provocation immediately, confirming the need for her he had already known he felt.

She couldn't stand here like this, Ruby warned herself. If she did Sander was bound to think she was doing so because she wanted him and was all too likely to say so. She didn't want that. She didn't want to be accused of being a woman who could not live without sexual satisfaction. What she wanted was to be told that he couldn't resist her, that he adored her and loved her.

Quickly Ruby turned towards the door, not wanting

Sander to see her expression, but to her astonishment before she could reach it he said quietly, 'You looked beautiful tonight in that dress.'

Sander was telling her she looked beautiful?

Ruby couldn't move. She couldn't do anything other than stare at him, torn between longing and disbelief.

Sander was coming towards her, standing in front of her, lifting his hands to slide the straps of her dress off her shoulders as he told her softly, 'But you will look even more beautiful without it.'

The words were nothing, and yet at the same time they were everything. Ruby trembled from head to foot, hardly daring to breathe as Sander unzipped her dress so that it could fall to the floor and then cupped the side of her face and kissed her.

She was in Sander's arms, and he was kissing her, and she was kissing him back. Kissing him back, holding him, feeling all her doubts and fears slipping away from her like sand sucked away by the sea as her love for him claimed her.

The sensation of Sander's hands on her body, shaping it and caressing it, carried her on a surging tide of her own desire, like a tribute offered to an all powerful conqueror. His lightest touch made her body shudder softly in swiftly building paroxysms of pleasure. She had hungered to have him desire her like this, without the harsh bitterness of his anger. In the deepest hidden places of her heart Ruby recognised that, even if she had hidden that need from herself. She had hungered, ached, and denied that aching—yearned for him and forbidden that yearning. But now, here tonight in his arms, the lies she had told to protect herself were melting away, burned away by the heat of his hands on her body, leaping from nerve-ending to nerve-ending. Beneath Sander's mouth Ruby moaned in heightened pleasure when his thumb-pad rubbed over her nipple, hot, sweet and aching need pulsing beneath his touch. Her body was clamouring for him to free it, to lay it bare to his eyes, his hands, his mouth, so that he could plunder its desire, feed it and feast on it, until she could endure the ache of her own need no longer and she clung to him whilst he took her to the heights and the final explosion that would give him all that she was and all that she had to give, make her helpless under the power of his possession and her own need for it, for him.

This was how it had been that first night in Manchester, with her senses overwhelmed by the intensity of what she was experiencing. So much so, in fact, that she had scarcely noticed the loss of her virginity. She'd been so desperate for his possession and for the pleasure it had brought her.

She was his, and Sander allowed himself to glory in that primeval knowledge. His body was on fire for her, aching beyond bearing with his need for her, but he wanted to draw out their pleasure—to savour it and store the unique bouquet of it in his memory for ever. He bent and picked her up, carrying her through into the bedroom, their gazes meeting and locking in the sensually charged warmth of the dimly lit room.

'I've never forgotten you—do you know that? I've

never been able to get your memory out of my head. The way you trembled against me when I touched you, the scent of your skin, the quick, unsteady way you breathed when I did this.'

Ruby fought to suppress her breathing now, as Sander caressed the side of her neck and then stroked his fingertips the length of her naked spine.

'Yes, just like that.'

Helplessly Ruby whimpered against the lash of her own pleasure, protesting that Sander was tormenting her and she couldn't bear any more, but Sander ignored her, tracing a line of kisses along her shoulderblade. When he had done that the first time she had arched her back in open delight, helpless against the onslaught of her own desire. Sander lifted her arm and began kissing the inside of her wrist and then the inside of her elbow. He had never known that it was possible for him to feel like this, Sander acknowledged. The sensual sweetness of Ruby's response to him was crashing through all the defences he had raised against the way she was making him feel.

He kissed her mouth, probing its soft, welcoming warmth with his tongue, whilst Ruby trembled against him, her naked body arching up to his, the feel of her skin through his clothes a torment he could hardly bear.

Ruby was lost beneath the hot, intimate possession of Sander's kiss—a kiss that was sending fiery darts of arousal and need rushing through her body to turn the existing dull ache low down within it into an open pulsing need. Her breasts yearned for his touch, her nipples throbbing and swollen like fruit so ripe their readiness could hardly be contained within their skin. She wanted to feel his hands on her body, stroking, caressing, satisfying her growing need. Wanted his lips kissing and sucking the ache from her breasts and transforming it to the liquid heat of pleasure. But instead he was pulling away from her, lifting his body from hers, abandoning her when she needed him so desperately. Frantically Ruby shook her head, her protest an inarticulate soft moan as she sat up in the bed.

As though he knew how she felt, and what she feared, Sander reached for her hand and carried it to his own body, laying it flat against the hard swell of his flesh under the fabric of his suit trousers, his gaze never leaving her face as it registered her passion stoked delight in his erection, and its sensual underlining of his own desire for her.

Very slowly her fingertips traced the length and thickness of his flesh, everything she was feeling visible to him in the soft parting of her mouth, the brief flick of her tongue-tip against her lips and the excitement darkening her absorbed gaze.

Impatiently Sander started to unfasten his shirt. Distracted by his movements, Ruby looked up at him and then moved closer, kneeling on the bed in front of him as she took over the task from him. She leaned forward to kiss the flesh each unfastened button exposed, and then gave in to the impulse driving her to know more than the warmth of his skin against her lips, stroking her tongue-tip along his breastbone, breathing in the pheromone-laden scent of his body as it shuddered beneath her caress. His chest was hard-muscled, his nipples flat and dark. Lost in the heady pleasure of being so close to him, Ruby reached out and touched the hard flesh with her fingertip, and then on an impulse that came out of nowhere she bent her head and kissed the same spot, exploring it with the tip of her tongue.

Reaction ricocheted through Sander, engulfing and consuming him. He'd been unfastening his trousers whilst Ruby explored him, and now he wrenched off what was left of his clothes before taking Ruby in his arms to kiss her with the full force of his building need.

The sensation of Sander's body against her, with no barriers between them, swept away what were left of Ruby's inhibitions. Wrapping her arms around Sander's neck, she clung to him, returning his kiss with equal passion, sighing her approval when his hands cupped her breasts.

*This* was what his heart had been yearning for, Sander admitted. This giving and receiving, this intimacy with no barriers, this woman above all women. Ruby was everything he wanted and more, Sander acknowledged, making his own slow voyage of rediscovery over Ruby's silk-soft body.

Sander prided himself on being a skilled lover, but he had never been in this position before. He had never felt like this before. He wasn't prepared for his own reaction to the way he felt. He wasn't prepared for the way it powered his own desire to a level he had never known before, threatening his self-control, creating within him a desire to possess and pleasure every part of her, to bring her to orgasm over and over again, until he possessed her pleasure and her with it. He wanted to imprint himself on her desire so that no other man could ever unlock its sweetness. He wanted *her*, Sander acknowledged, and he fed the fast-surging appetite of his own arousal on the sound of her unsteady breathing, interspersed with sobs of pleasure, as he sucked on the hard peaks of her nipples and kneaded the soft flesh of her breasts.

Ruby arched up towards him, her hands clasped on the back of his neck to hold him against her. She had thought that Sander had already taken her to the utmost peak of sensual pleasure, but she had been wrong. Now, with the barriers between them down, she knew that what had gone before had been a mere shadow of what she was feeling now. Lightning-fast bolts of almost unbearable erotic arousal sheeted through her body with every tug of Sander's mouth on her nipples, going to ground deep inside her, feeding the hot pulse already beating there, until merely arching up against him wasn't enough to appease the savage dragging need possessing her. Instead she had to open her legs and press herself against him, her breath catching on a grateful moan of relief when Sander responded to her need with the firm pressure of his hand over her sex.

Against his hand Sander could feel the heavy pulsing beat of Ruby's need. It drove the ache within his own flesh to a maddening desire to take her quickly and hotly, making him fight for the self-control that threatened to desert him when he parted the swollen outer lips of her sex to find the wetness within them.

It was almost more than Ruby could stand to have Sander touching her so intimately, and yet at the same time nowhere nearly intimately enough. His fingertip rimmed the opening to her sex. A fresh lightning bolt shot through her. She could feel her body opening to him in eagerness and hunger, heard a sound of agonised relief bubbling in her throat when Sander slid one and then two fingers slowly inside her.

He didn't need Ruby's fingers gripping his arm or her nails digging into his flesh to tell him what she was feeling. Sander could feel her need in his own flesh and hers as the movement of her body quickened and tightened. Even before she cried out to him he was aware of her release, and the quick, fierce pleasure of her orgasm filled his own body with fierce male satisfaction, swelling his sex to a hard urgency to play its part in more of that pleasure.

But not yet—not until he was sure that he had given her all the pleasure he could.

For Ruby, the sensation of Sander's lips caressing their way down her supine body was initially one of relaxed easy sweetness—a tender caress after the white-hot heat that had gone before it. She had no intimation, no warning of the fresh urgency to come, until Sander's lips drifted across her lower belly and the ache she had thought satisfied began to pulse and swell in a new surge of need that shocked her into an attempt to deny its existence.

But Sander wouldn't let her. Her protests were ignored, and the growing pleasure of her wanton flesh was cherished with hot swirls of desire painted on her inner thighs by the stroke of his tongue—a tongue that searched out her desire even more intimately, until its movement against the hard swollen pulse of her clitoris had her abandoning her self-control once more and offering herself up to him.

This time her orgasm was short and sharp, leaving her trembling on the edge of something more. Agonised by the ache of that need, Ruby reached out to touch Sander's body, but he stopped her, shaking his head as he told her thickly, 'No. Don't. Let me do this instead.'

She could feel the glide of his body against her own, his sex hard and slick, probing the eager moistness of hers, and her muscles quickened in eager longing, matching each slow, deliberate ever deeper thrust of his body within her own.

*Aaahhh*—how she remembered the first time he had shown her this pleasure and revealed its mystery. The way it had taken her beyond that small sharp pain which had caught at her breath and held her motionless beneath his thrust for a handful of seconds before her arousal had made its own demands on her, her muscles softening to enfold him, just as they were doing now, then firming to caress him, her body driven by its need to have him ever deeper within her.

This was what her body had yearned and hungered for—this completeness and wholeness, beyond any other, as she clung to Sander, taking him fully within her and holding him there, welcoming and matching the growing speed of his rhythm.

He was lost, Sander recognised. His self-control, his inner self stripped away, taking from him his power to do anything other than submit to his own need as it rolled over him and picked him up with its unstoppable force.

He heard himself cry out, a male sound of mingled agony and triumph, as Ruby's fresh orgasm took them both over the edge, his body flooding hers with his own release.

Her body still racked by small aftershocks of the seismic pleasure that had erupted inside her, Ruby lay silently against Sander's chest, heard their racing heart-beats gradually slowing.

Tonight they had shared something special, something precious, Ruby thought, and her heart over-flowed with love.

## CHAPTER ELEVEN

THE twins' matter-of-fact response to their return to the island proved more than any amount of words how comfortable they had been in Anna's care during her absence, Ruby reflected ruefully in her bedroom, as she changed out of the clothes she had travelled home in. Sander had gone straight to his office to check his e-mails.

But getting changed wasn't all she needed to do.

Her handbag was on the bed. She opened it and removed the pregnancy testing kit she had bought in Athens. Her hands trembled slightly as she took it from its packaging, her eyes blurring with emotion as she read the instructions. Six years ago when she had done this she had been so afraid, sick with fear, dreading the result.

She was equally anxious now, but for very different reasons.

Things had changed since she had first realised that she might be pregnant again, she tried to reassure herself. When Anna had referred to her love for Sander, initially Ruby had wanted to deny it. But once that truth had been laid bare for her to see she hadn't been able to ignore it. Of *course* she loved Sander. The real shock was that she hadn't realised that for herself but had needed Anna to tell her. Now, just thinking about him filled her with aching longing and pain.

Maybe this baby would build the bridge between them, if she lowered her own pride and told him how she felt. She had begged him to give her the possession of his body—would it really be so very difficult to plead with him to accept her love? To plead with him that this child might be born into happiness and the love of both its parents? He loved the twins—surely he would love this child as well, even if he refused to accept her love for him? Telling herself that she must have faith that the love she had seen Sander give the twins would not be reserved for the twins alone, she walked towards the bathroom.

Ten minutes later Ruby was still standing in the bathroom, her gaze fixed on the telltale line. She had known, of course—impossible for her not to have done. But nothing was the same as visible confirmation. Against Sander's explicit wishes she had conceived his child. Ruby thought of the contraceptive pills she had taken so carefully and regularly every evening, in obedience to Sander's conditions for their marriage. Perhaps this baby, conceived against all the odds, was meant to be—a gift to them both that they could share together? She put her hand on her still flat body and took a deep breath. She would have to tell Sander now, and the sooner the better.

The sudden childish scream of anger she could hear from outside had her letting the test fall onto the marble surface surrounding the hand basin as she ran to the patio doors in the bedroom in automatic response to the outraged sound. Outside on the patio, as she had expected, she found the twins quarrelling over a toy. Freddie was attempting to drag it away from Harry, whilst Harry wailed in protest. Anna, alerted as Ruby had been by the noise, wasn't far behind her, and the two of them quickly defused the situation.

Once they had done so, Anna said matter-of-factly, 'You will have your hands full if it is twins again that you are carrying.'

Ruby shook her head. She wasn't really surprised that Anna had guessed. The homemade ginger biscuits that had discreetly begun to appear with her morning cup of weak tea had already hinted to her that Anna shared her own suspicions.

Sander pushed back his chair. They had only arrived at the villa an hour ago, and yet already he was conscious of an urge to seek out Ruby, and with it an awareness that he was actually missing her company—and not just in bed. Such feelings made him feel vulnerable, something that Sander instinctively resisted and resented, and yet at the same time he was opening his office door and striding down the corridor in the direction of their bedroom.

Ruby would be outside with the twins. As their father, he could legitimately get changed and go and join them. Doing so would not betray him. And if he was there as much so that he could be with Ruby as with his sons, then only he needed to know that. The conditioning of a lifetime of fearing emotional betrayal could not be overturned in the space of a few short weeks. Others close to him, like Anna and Elena, might admire Ruby and think her a good wife, but Sander told himself that he needed more proof that he could trust her.

He noted the presence of Ruby's open handbag on their bed as he made his way to the bathroom, but it was only after he had showered and changed that he noticed the discarded pregnancy test.

The first thing Ruby saw when she went back into the bedroom was Sander's suit jacket on the bed. Her heart started to hammer too heavily and far too fast, with a mixture of guilt and fear. She walked towards the bathroom, coming to an abrupt halt when she saw Sander standing beside the basin, holding the telltale test.

There was a blank look in his eyes, as though he couldn't quite believe what he was seeing. A blank look that was soon burned away by the anger she could see replacing it as he looked at her.

'You're pregnant.'

It was an accusation, not a question, and Ruby's heart sank.

'Yes,' she admitted. 'I thought I might be, but I wanted to be sure before I told you. I know what you said when we got married about me taking the pill because you didn't want another child—and I did take it,' she told him truthfully. When he didn't say anything, but simply continued to look at her she was panicked into pleading emotionally, 'Please don't look at me like that. You love the twins, and this baby, *your* baby, deserves to be loved as well.'

'*My* child? Since you have said yourself that you were on the pill, it cannot possibly be my child. We both know that. Do you really think me such a fool that I would let you pass off a brat conceived with one of the no doubt many men who happened to be enjoying your body before I found you? If so, then you are the one who is a fool. But you are not a fool, are you, Ruby? You are a venal, lying, amoral and greedy woman.'

The words exploded into the room like randomly discharged machine gun fire, meant to destroy everything it hit. Right now she might be too numb to feel anything, but Ruby knew that she had been mortally wounded.

'You obviously knew when you demanded that I marry you that you were carrying this child,' Sander accused her savagely.

He had claimed that he was not a fool, but the opposite was true. He had allowed her to tempt him out of the security of the emotional mindset he had grown up with and to believe that maybe—just maybe—he had been wrong about her. But of course he had not been. He deserved the punishment of what he was feeling now for dropping his guard, for deliberately ignoring all the safeguards he had put in place to protect himself. The bitter, angry thoughts raked Sander's pride with poison-dipped talons.

'I thought you had married me for the financial gain you believed you could get from our marriage, but I can see now that I didn't recognise the true depth of your greed and lack of morals.'

Ruby couldn't bear any more.

'I married you for the sake of our sons,' she told him fiercely. 'And this child I am carrying now is yours. Yes, I took the pill, but if you remember I wasn't well whilst we were in London. I believe that is how I came to conceive. In some circumstances a...a stomach upset and nausea can damage the pill's efficiency.'

'A very convenient excuse,' Sander sneered. 'Do you *really* expect me to believe it, knowing you as I do? You didn't marry me for the twins' sake, Ruby. You married me for my money.'

'That's not true,' Ruby denied. How could he think so badly of her? Anger joined her pain. Sander had called himself a fool, but *she* was the fool. For loving him, and for believing that she could reach out to him with that love.

'I know you,' he repeated, and hearing those words Ruby felt her self-control break.

'No, you don't know me, Sander. All you know is your own blind prejudice. When this baby is born I shall have its DNA tested, and I can promise you now that he or she will be proved to be your child and a true sibling to the twins. However, by then it will be too late for you to know it and love it as your son or daughter, Sander, because there is no way I intend to allow my children to grow up with a father who feels and speaks as you do. You love the twins, I can see that, but as they grow to be men your attitude to me, their mother, your suspicions of me, are bound to contaminate their attitude to my sex. I will *not* have my sons growing up like you—unable to recognise love, unable to value it, unable to even see it.

'Do you know what my worst sin has been? The thing I regret the most? It's loving *you*, Sander. Because in loving you, I am not being a good mother to my children. You've constantly thrown at me my behaviour the first time we met, accusing me of being some wanton who came on to you. The truth is that I was a seventeen-year-old virgin—oh, yes you may look at me like that but it's true—a naive and recklessly silly girl who, in the aftermath of losing her parents, ached so much for love to replace what she had lost that she convinced herself a man she saw across a crowded bar was her saviour, a hero, someone special who would lift her up out of the misery of her pain and loss and hold her safe in his arms. That was the true nature of my crime, Sander—idolising you and turning you into something you could never be.

'And as for all those other men you like to accuse me of being with—they never existed. Not a single one of them. Do you *really* think I would be stupid enough to trust another man after the way you treated me? Yes, I expect I deserved it for behaving so stupidly. You wanted to teach me a lesson, I expect. I'm only surprised, knowing you as I now do, that you seem unable to accept that your lesson was successful.

'There was only one reason I asked you for marriage, Sander—because I thought it would make you back off.

But then, when I realised you genuinely wanted the twins, it was as I told you at the time—because I believe very strongly that children thrive best emotionally within the security of a family unit that contains two parents who intend to stay together. I grew up in that kind of family unit, and naturally it was what I wanted for my sons.

'What you've just accused me of changes everything. I don't want you poisoning the boys' minds with your own horrible mindset. This baby *will* be their true sibling, but somehow I doubt that even DNA evidence will convince you of that. Quite simply it isn't what you want to believe. You want to believe the worst of me. Perhaps you even need to believe it. In which case I feel very sorry for you. My job as a mother is to protect all my children. The twins are two very intelligent boys. They will quickly see that you do not accept their sister or brother and they might even mimic your behaviour. I will not allow that to happen.'

Initially he had been resolutely determined to deny that there could be any truth in Ruby's angry outburst. But beneath the complex defence system his own hurt emotions had built up to protect him from the pain caused by his mother, tendrils of something 'other' had begun to unfurl. So small at first that he thought he could brush them away. But when he tried Sander discovered that they were rooted in a bedrock of inner need it stunned him to discover. When had this yearning to throw off the defensive chains that imprisoned him taken root? How could this part of him actually be willing to take Ruby's side against himself? Struggling against the opposing forces within himself, Sander fought desperately for a way forward.

This was so much worse than anything she had imagined might happen, Ruby acknowledged. She had feared that Sander would be angry, but it had never occurred to her that he would refuse to accept that the child she had conceived was his. She should hate him for that. She wished that she could. Hatred would be cleansing and almost satisfying.

She would have to leave the island, of course. But she wasn't going anywhere without the twins. They would miss Sander dreadfully, but she couldn't risk them starting to think and feel as he did. She couldn't let his bitterness infect them.

She turned to look through the still open patio doors, her vision blurred by the tears she was determined not to let him see.

'There's no point in us continuing this discussion,' she told him. 'Since it's obvious that you prefer to think the worst of me.'

Without waiting to see if he was going to make any response Ruby headed for the patio, anxious to put as much distance between them as she could before her emotions overwhelmed her and the tears burning the backs of her eyes fell.

From the bedroom Sander watched her, his thoughts still at war with themselves. Ruby had reached the top of the flight of marble steps that led down to the lower part of the garden.

Blinking fiercely to hold back her tears, Ruby stepped forward, somehow mistiming her step, so that the heel of her shoe caught on the top step, pitching her forward.

Sander saw her stumble and then fall, tumbling down the marble steps. He raced after her, taking the steps two at a time to reach her crumpled body where it lay still at the bottom of the first flight of steps.

She was conscious—just. And her two words to him as he kneeled over her were agonized. 'My baby…'

# CHAPTER TWELVE

'SHE'S coming round now. Ruby, can you hear us?'

Her clouded vision slowly cleared and the vague outlines of white-clad figures formed into two nurses and a doctor, all three of them smiling reassuringly at her. Hospital. She was in hospital? Automatically she began to panic.

'It's all right, Ruby. You had a nasty fall, but you're all right now. We've had to keep you sedated for a few days, to give your body time to rest, and we've performed some tests, so you're bound to feel woozy and confused. Just relax.'

Relax! Ruby put her hand on top of the flat white sheet pulled tightly over her body. She was attached to some kind of drip, she realised.

'My baby?' she demanded anxiously.

The nurse closest to her looked at the doctor.

She'd lost her baby. Her fall—she remembered it now—had killed her baby. The pain was all-encompassing. She had let her baby down. She hadn't protected it properly, either from her fall or from its father's rejection. She felt too numb with grief to cry.

The nurse patted her hand. The doctor smiled at her.

'Your baby is fine, Ruby.'

She looked at them both in disbelief.

'You're just telling me that, aren't you? I've lost the baby really, haven't I?'

The doctor looked back at the nurse. 'I think we should let Ruby have a look for herself.' Turning to Ruby, he told her, 'The nurse will take you for a scan, Ruby, and then you will be able to see for yourself that your baby is perfectly well. Which is more than I will be able to say for you, if you continue to upset yourself.'

An hour later Ruby was back in her hospital room, still gazing in awed delight at the image she'd been given—an image which showed quite clearly that her baby was indeed safe.

'You and your baby have both been very lucky,' the nurse told her when she came in a few minutes later to check up on her. 'You sustained a nasty head injury, and when you were taken into hospital on Theopolis they feared that a blood clot had developed. It meant they would have to terminate your pregnancy. Your husband refused to give his consent. He arranged for you to be brought here to this hospital in Athens, and for a specialist to be brought from America to treat you. Your husband said that you would never forgive him and he would never forgive himself if your pregnancy had to be terminated.'

Sander had said that? Ruby didn't know what to think.

'I dare say he will be here soon,' the nurse continued. 'Initially he insisted on staying here in the hospital with you, but Professor Smythson told him to go home and get some rest once you were in the clear.'

As though on cue the door to her room opened and Sander was standing there. Discreetly the nurse whisked herself out of the room, leaving them alone together.

'The twins…' Ruby began anxiously.

'They know that you had a fall and that you had to come to hospital to be "mended". They're missing you, of course, but Anna is doing her best to keep them occupied.'

'The nurse was just telling me that it's thanks to you I still have my baby.'

'Our baby,' Sander corrected her quietly.

Ruby didn't know what to say—or think—so her emotions did both for her. Tears slid down her face.

'Ruby, don't,' Sander begged, leaving the foot of her bed, where he had been standing, to come and take hold of her hand, now disconnected from the drip she had been on as she no longer needed it. 'When I saw you falling down those steps I knew that no matter what I'd said, or what I thought I'd believed, the truth was that I loved you. I think I knew it that last night we spent in Athens, but I told myself that letting go of my doubts about you must be a slow and measured process. It took the realisation that I might have lost you to show me the truth. I deliberately blinded myself to what was real, just as you said. I wanted and needed to believe the very worst of you, and because of that—because of my fear of loving you and my pride in that fear—you and our child almost lost your lives.'

'My fall was an accident.'

'An accident that resulted from my blind refusal to accept what you were trying to tell me. Can you forgive me?'

'I love you, Sander. You know that. What I want now is for you to forgive yourself.' Ruby looked up at him. 'And not just forgive yourself about me.' Did she dare to say what she wanted to say? If she didn't seize this opportunity to do so she would regret it, Ruby warned herself, for Sander's sake more than for her own.

'I know your mother hurt you, Sander.'

'My mother never loved any of us. We were a duty she had to bear—literally as well as figuratively. My brother and sister and myself were the price she paid for my father's wealth, and for living the life she really wanted—a life of shallow, gaudy excess, lived in luxury at someone else's expense. The only time we saw her was when she wanted my father to give her more money. There was no room in her heart for us, no desire to make room there for us.'

Ruby's heart ached with compassion for him.

'It wasn't your fault that she rejected you, Sander. The flaw was within her, not you.'

His grip on her hand tightened convulsively.

'I guess I've always been distrustful of women— probably as a result of my relationship with my mother. When I saw you in that club I saw you in my mother's image. I didn't want to look beneath the surface. I believe now that a part of me did recognise how innocent and vulnerable you really were, but I was determined to reject it. I used you as a means of expressing my anger against my grandfather. My behaviour was unforgivable.'

'No.' Ruby shook her head. 'Under the circumstances it was predictable. Had I been the experienced party girl you thought, I suspect I would have known that something more than desire was driving you. We both made mistakes, Sander, but that doesn't mean we can't forgive ourselves and put them behind us. We were both defensive when we got married. You because of your mother, and me because I was ashamed of the way I'd behaved with you—giving away my virginity to a man who couldn't wait to throw me out of his bed and his life once he had had what he wanted.'

'Don't…' Sander groaned remorsefully. 'I'm sorry I said what I did about this new baby, Ruby. When you fell just before you lost consciousness you whispered to me—"my baby"—and I knew then that no matter what I had said, or thought I believed, the child inside you was mine, that it was impossible for it to have been fathered by anyone else. Can we start again? Can you still love me after the way I've behaved?'

In answer to his question Ruby lifted herself up off her pillows and kissed him gently, before telling him, 'It would be impossible for me not to love you, Sander.'

It was just over a month since Ruby, fully recovered from her fall, had returned to the island, and each day her happiness grew. Or so it seemed to her. Sander had already proved to her that he was a loving father to the twins, and now, in addition to proving to her that he intended to be an equally good father to the child she was carrying, he had also dedicated himself to proving to her that he was a wonderfully loving husband.

Lying next to him in their bed, Ruby felt her heart swell with joy and love. Smiling in the darkness, she turned toward Sander, pressing a loving kiss against his chin.

'You know what will happen if you keep on doing that,' he warned her mock-seriously.

Ruby laughed. 'I thought I was the one who was unable to resist you, not the other way round,' she teased as she nestled closer to him, the soft curves of her naked body a sweet, warm temptation against his own.

'Does it feel like I'm able to resist you?' Sander asked her.

His hands were already stroking her skin; his breath was warm against her lips. Eagerly Ruby moved closer to him. It was still the same—that heart-stopping feeling of anticipation and longing that filled her when she knew he was going to kiss her.

'I love you…'

The words were breathed against her ear and then repeated against her lips, before Sander finally slowly stroked his tongue-tip against them deliberately, until Ruby couldn't wait any longer and placed her hands either side of his head. Her lips parted, a little shudder of longing rippling through her.

The sound of the accelerated speed of their breathing mingled with the movement of flesh against fabric, soft whispering sounds of sensuality and expectant desire.

As always, the sweetness of Ruby's arousal increased Sander's own desire. She showed her love for him so naturally and openly, with her desire whispered in soft words of love and longing, and encouragement and promises filling the air, breathed against his skin in an erotic litany of emotion. He could now admit that part of him had responded to that in her from the very start, and had in turn loved her for it, even if he had barricaded that knowledge away from himself.

The shape of her body was changing now, and her pregnancy was a gentle swell that he caressed gently before he kissed her growing bump.

Looking down at his dark head, Ruby stroked the smooth flesh at the nape of his neck. She knew now how much both she and this new baby meant to him.

Lying down beside her, Sander cupped her breast, allowing his lips to tease her nipple provocatively, his fingertips drifting tormentingly across her lower belly in a caress he knew she loved. Ruby closed her eyes and clung to him, riding the wave of her own desire as it swelled and pulsed inside her, smiling at the now familiar torment of building pleasure, of raw, sensual need that Sander knew exactly how to stretch out until it became almost unbearable.

Sander knew that if he placed his hand over her mound now he would be able to feel the insistent pulse it covered—just as he knew that the unsteady increase in her breathing meant that the stroke of his fingers within her would bring her almost immediately to orgasm, and that after that orgasm he would re-ignite her desire so that he could satisfy them both with the thrust of his body within hers. He could feel his self-control starting to give way.

His hand moved further down her body. The soft, scented wetness of her sex and the way she offered it to him with such sensual generosity turned his heart over inside his chest. He looked up at her as he parted the folded outer lips. A shudder ripped through her eyes, dark and wild with need. His fingertips stroked slowly through her wetness and then back again, to rub against the source of her desire, hard and swollen beneath his touch, making his own body throb in increasingly insistent demand. His lips caressed her nipple more urgently, his gaze registering the flush staining her skin and the growing intensity of the small shudders gripping her body.

'San—der…'

It was the way she said his name that did it—a soft plea of longing plaited with a tormenting thread of enticement that smashed through what was left of his self-control.

Ruby shuddered wildly beneath the sensation of Sander's mouth on her skin—her breasts, her belly, her thighs, and then finally her sex, where his tongue-tip stroked and probed and possessed until the pleasure made her gasp and then cry out.

Sander couldn't wait any longer. As it was he had to fight against himself to draw out their shared pleasure instead of giving in to the demand of his own flesh and its need to lose itself within her, holding them both on the rack of their shared longing before finally thrusting slowly into her, letting the responsive muscles of her body take him and possess him until they were riding the pleasure together to the ecstasy of shared love and release.

'I love you.'

'I love you.'

'You are my life, my world, light in my darkness, my Ruby beyond price.'

Held safe in Sander's arms, Ruby closed her eyes, knowing that when she woke in the morning and for every morning, of their lives together, she would wake up held safe and loved.

# EPILOGUE

'OH, RUBY, she's beautiful.'

Smiling proudly, Ruby looked on as her sisters admired their new niece, who was now just over one month old.

It had been a wonderful surprise when Sander had told her that he had arranged for her sisters and their husbands to visit the island, and Ruby thought it the best present he could have given her—barring, of course, his love and their new daughter.

'She's the image of Sander,' Lizzie announced, with an eldest sister authority that Ruby had no desire to refute.

After all, it was true that Hebe was the image of her father and her twin brothers, and, whilst Sander had said prior to her birth that if they had a girl he would like her to look like her mother, Ruby rather thought that he didn't mind one little bit that she was a dark-haired, dark-eyed daddy's girl.

'It looks as though she can wind Sander and the boys round her little finger already.' Charlotte joined the conversation, adding ruefully, 'I'm itching to cuddle her properly, but this one—' she patted the bulge of her seven-month pregnancy ruefully '—obviously doesn't want me to. He kicked so hard when I tried.'

'Ah, so it *is* a boy, then.'

Ruby and Lizzie pounced in unison, laughing when their middle sister tried to protest and then glanced toward her husband, Raphael. He was standing with Sander, and Lizzie's husband Ilios, who was holding their two-month-old son Perry with the deftness of experienced fatherhood. The three men laughed and talked together.

'Well, yes, I think so from what I saw at the last scan!' she admitted ruefully. 'Of course I could be wrong, and the truth is that Raphael doesn't mind whether we have a boy or a girl, although personally...' She gave a small sigh and then said softly, 'I know it's silly, but I can't stop myself from imagining a little boy with Raphael's features.'

'It isn't silly at all,' Ruby immediately defended her. 'It's only natural. I love the fact that the twins and Hebe look like Sander.'

'I feel the same way about Perry,' Lizzie agreed, adding, 'That's what love does for you.'

Automatically they all turned to watch their husbands. 'It's lovely that our three babies will be so close in age—especially as the twins have one another,' Ruby added.

'Sander is so proud of the boys, Ruby. And proud of you, for the way you brought them up alone.'

'I wasn't alone,' Ruby objected, pointing out emotionally, 'They and I had both of you to support us and love us. I could never have managed without you.'

'And we would never have wanted you to—would we, Charlotte?' Lizzie told her.

'Never,' Charlotte agreed, squeezing Ruby's hand.

For a moment it was just the three of them again, sisters bonded together by the tragedy they had shared, and by their love and loyalty for one another, but then Charlotte broke the silence, enclosing them all to say softly, 'I think we must have some very special guardian angels watching over us.'

Once again they looked toward their husbands, before turning back to one another.

'We've certainly been lucky to meet and fall in love with such very special men,' Ruby said.

'And all the more special because they think *they* are the lucky ones in having met us.' Lizzie shook her head and then said ruefully, 'None of us could have imagined how things were going to turn out when I was worrying so much about having to go out to Thessalonica.'

The look she gave Ilios as she spoke said very clearly to her sisters how much she loved her husband, causing both of them to turn and look at their own husbands with similar emotion.

'There is something other than how happy we are now that we do need to discuss,' she continued, explaining when Charlotte and Ruby looked at her, 'The house. Ilios insisted on clearing the mortgage for me, because at that stage I still thought that you would both need it, and I transferred it into your joint names. Since none of us need it now, what I'd like to suggest is that we donate it to charity. I've been making a few enquiries, and there is a Cheshire-based charity that provides help for single mothers. If we deed the house to the charity then they can either use it to provide accommodation or sell it and use the money in other ways. What do you think?'

'I think it's an excellent idea.'

'I agree.'

'So that's decided, then.'

'There might be one small problem,' Ruby warned. 'Since Ilios cleared the mortgage, I rather suspect that Sander and Raphael will want to match his donation.'

Once again all three of them looked towards their husbands, exchanging smiles when the men looked back.

Three such male and strong men—strong enough to admit that they had been conquered by love and to show openly just how much that love meant to them.

'We are so very lucky,' Ruby announced, knowing that she was speaking for her sisters as well as for herself.

Sander, who had detached himself from Ilios and Raphael and was on his way towards them, overheard her, and stopped to tell her firmly, 'No, it is we who are the lucky ones. Lucky and blessed by the gods and by fate to have won the love of three such true Graces.'

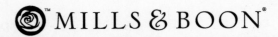

# JUNE 2010 HARDBACK TITLES

## ROMANCE

| | |
|---|---|
| Marriage: To Claim His Twins | Penny Jordan |
| The Royal Baby Revelation | Sharon Kendrick |
| Under the Spaniard's Lock and Key | Kim Lawrence |
| Sweet Surrender with the Millionaire | Helen Brooks |
| The Virgin's Proposition | Anne McAllister |
| Scandal: His Majesty's Love-Child | Annie West |
| Bride in a Gilded Cage | Abby Green |
| Innocent in the Italian's Possession | Janette Kenny |
| The Master of Highbridge Manor | Susanne James |
| The Power of the Legendary Greek | Catherine George |
| Miracle for the Girl Next Door | Rebecca Winters |
| Mother of the Bride | Caroline Anderson |
| What's A Housekeeper To Do? | Jennie Adams |
| Tipping the Waitress with Diamonds | Nina Harrington |
| Saving Cinderella! | Myrna Mackenzie |
| Their Newborn Gift | Nikki Logan |
| The Midwife and the Millionaire | Fiona McArthur |
| Knight on the Children's Ward | Carol Marinelli |

## HISTORICAL

| | |
|---|---|
| Rake Beyond Redemption | Anne O'Brien |
| A Thoroughly Compromised Lady | Bronwyn Scott |
| In the Master's Bed | Blythe Gifford |

## MEDICAL™

| | |
|---|---|
| From Single Mum to Lady | Judy Campbell |
| Children's Doctor, Shy Nurse | Molly Evans |
| Hawaiian Sunset, Dream Proposal | Joanna Neil |
| Rescued: Mother and Baby | Anne Fraser |

0510 Gen Std LP

# MILLS & BOON®

## JUNE 2010 LARGE PRINT TITLES

## ROMANCE

| | |
|---|---|
| The Wealthy Greek's Contract Wife | Penny Jordan |
| The Innocent's Surrender | Sara Craven |
| Castellano's Mistress of Revenge | Melanie Milburne |
| The Italian's One-Night Love-Child | Cathy Williams |
| Cinderella on His Doorstep | Rebecca Winters |
| Accidentally Expecting! | Lucy Gordon |
| Lights, Camera…Kiss the Boss | Nikki Logan |
| Australian Boss: Diamond Ring | Jennie Adams |

## HISTORICAL

| | |
|---|---|
| The Rogue's Disgraced Lady | Carole Mortimer |
| A Marriageable Miss | Dorothy Elbury |
| Wicked Rake, Defiant Mistress | Ann Lethbridge |

## MEDICAL™

| | |
|---|---|
| Snowbound: Miracle Marriage | Sarah Morgan |
| Christmas Eve: Doorstep Delivery | Sarah Morgan |
| Hot-Shot Doc, Christmas Bride | Joanna Neil |
| Christmas at Rivercut Manor | Gill Sanderson |
| Falling for the Playboy Millionaire | Kate Hardy |
| The Surgeon's New-Year Wedding Wish | Laura Iding |

0610 Gen Std HB

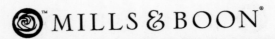

# MILLS & BOON

## JULY 2010 HARDBACK TITLES

## ROMANCE

| | |
|---|---|
| A Night, A Secret...A Child | Miranda Lee |
| His Untamed Innocent | Sara Craven |
| The Greek's Pregnant Lover | Lucy Monroe |
| The Mélendez Forgotten Marriage | Melanie Milburne |
| Sensible Housekeeper, Scandalously Pregnant | Jennie Lucas |
| The Bride's Awakening | Kate Hewitt |
| The Devil's Heart | Lynn Raye Harris |
| The Good Greek Wife? | Kate Walker |
| Propositioned by the Billionaire | Lucy King |
| Unbuttoned by Her Maverick Boss | Natalie Anderson |
| Australia's Most Eligible Bachelor | Margaret Way |
| The Bridesmaid's Secret | Fiona Harper |
| Cinderella: Hired by the Prince | Marion Lennox |
| The Sheikh's Destiny | Melissa James |
| Vegas Pregnancy Surprise | Shirley Jump |
| The Lionhearted Cowboy Returns | Patricia Thayer |
| Dare She Date the Dreamy Doc? | Sarah Morgan |
| Neurosurgeon . . . and Mum! | Kate Hardy |

## HISTORICAL

| | |
|---|---|
| Vicar's Daughter to Viscount's Lady | Louise Allen |
| Chivalrous Rake, Scandalous Lady | Mary Brendan |
| The Lord's Forced Bride | Anne Herries |

## MEDICAL™

| | |
|---|---|
| Dr Drop-Dead Gorgeous | Emily Forbes |
| Her Brooding Italian Surgeon | Fiona Lowe |
| A Father for Baby Rose | Margaret Barker |
| Wedding in Darling Downs | Leah Martyn |

0610 Gen Std LP

# MILLS & BOON

## JULY 2010 LARGE PRINT TITLES

## ROMANCE

| | |
|---|---|
| Greek Tycoon, Inexperienced Mistress | Lynne Graham |
| The Master's Mistress | Carole Mortimer |
| The Andreou Marriage Arrangement | Helen Bianchin |
| Untamed Italian, Blackmailed Innocent | Jacqueline Baird |
| Outback Bachelor | Margaret Way |
| The Cattleman's Adopted Family | Barbara Hannay |
| Oh-So-Sensible Secretary | Jessica Hart |
| Housekeeper's Happy-Ever-After | Fiona Harper |

## HISTORICAL

| | |
|---|---|
| One Unashamed Night | Sophia James |
| The Captain's Mysterious Lady | Mary Nichols |
| The Major and the Pickpocket | Lucy Ashford |

## MEDICAL™

| | |
|---|---|
| Posh Doc, Society Wedding | Joanna Neil |
| The Doctor's Rebel Knight | Melanie Milburne |
| A Mother for the Italian's Twins | Margaret McDonagh |
| Their Baby Surprise | Jennifer Taylor |
| New Boss, New-Year Bride | Lucy Clark |
| Greek Doctor Claims His Bride | Margaret Barker |

# I Am Sustainability: How the Human Body Can Save the Planet

## E.J. Wensing

Dear Mark.

Hope you enjoy
this book!

Enrico

Sept 2008

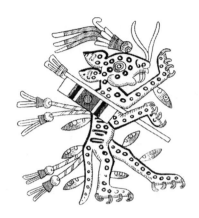

**Bäuu Press**
**PO Box 4445**
**Boulder, CO 80306**
**info@bauuinstitute.com**

1. Sustainability. 2. Psychology. 3. Personal transformation.

I Am Sustainability: How the Human Body Can Save the Planet
        / by      Enrico J. Wensing
                    p. cm.

        ISBN 10: 0-9721349-8-0
        ISBN 13: 978-0-9721349-8-9

    Printed in the United States

10 9 8 7 6 5 4 3 2 1

# I Am Sustainability: How the Human Body Can Save the Planet

E.J. Wensing

# Contents

Enrico J. Wensing

# Preface

My purpose in writing this book is to present a new approach to saving the planet. I see a wide variety of diverse yet related ideas swirling about in the literature relevant to this task. I have organized them, added some of my own insights and put them together in a scientifically and intuitively logical way that will have a very significant positive impact on global sustainability.

I think it's perhaps a foregone conclusion for many that global environmental conditions are getting worse. Also worsening are conditions for, and between, human beings. What may be a new idea to some is that if we want to save the global environment we may actually *first* need to improve conditions for, and between, each other. For instance, the UN's Millennium Project includes both environmental and human improvement goals on the same project list (Sachs and McArthur, 2005). What I describe in this book is that the best way to get conditions better for, and between, each other is to first improve conditions within ourselves. This book is about why that is necessary and how we can do it using a new approach called *"I Am Sustainability"*. This is a sustainability program that I am co-developing through a global network company called Ecosphere Net (www.ecosphere.net).

This is the first edition of this book. This book is the first of two core books. The upcoming companion book is called *We Are Sustainability*. It extends the ideas described in this book into workable programs for small groups, communities, societies and all the people of the world. Its focus is about healthy integration of the *I Am Sustainability* individual into society and how we can co-create societies and a sustainable planet. It is the goal of the Ecosphere Net project to create a global network of Sustainability Education Centers for the development and implementation of the *I Am* and *We Are Sustainability* programs.

This book is not the scholarly treatise of the subject matter one might find, say, in a doctoral dissertation. Some of the ideas in this book are my own, obtained through my own insight, subjective experience and/or speculation. Some proposals are a synthesis of things that I have learned and experienced in my own life, others are from the scientific literature, and yet others are from popular or folk literature, i.e., fiction. Folk psychology describes concepts in psychology that are often, but not always, from popular culture that have yet to be scientifically proven. Some believe that science, however, cannot prove or understand everything. Especially when it comes to what it is to be human.

Many different concepts are introduced because this book represents the interfacing of ideas from a very wide variety of sources. I have tried to reference as many as possible so that the interested can pursue them further. I have tried to minimize the introduction of terminology and obscure language and the jargon common to the disciplines from which I've derived insight for some of the concepts described in this book. Yet, at the same time, to explain my points I have to illustrate how disparate disciplines, largely isolated from each other, have been talking about the same thing. In other words there appears to be a convergence of small ideas into the "ah ha!" of a major collective insight. This book is my take on what that "ah ha!" might be and how it can serve us all.

This is a twelve-day book. This book was initially written over an eight-day period in late August 2007 at the University of the Virgin Islands. It was then edited and revised over a four-day period. I am deeply grateful to Carolyn Jones, MD for her editing and proof reading as well as her critiques and suggestions regarding the text over those four last days before it went to Peter N. Jones, PhD, the publisher at the Bäuu Press in Boulder, Colorado.

Saving the planet obviously has to be a group effort, the bigger the group the better. Luckily there is the critical mass/tipping point phenomenon. Reaching that critical point, however, begins with each one of us. More accurately stated, as described in this book, *within* each one of us. We have to develop and implement sustainable living programs cross-culturally because this planet is everyone's home and there are quite a number of us here. We all have a vested interest in its sustainability. I have begun to do this through this book and our efforts at Ecosphere Net (www.ecosphere.net).

Enrico Jacques Wensing
US Virgin Islands
August 2007

# About the Author

E nrico Wensing was born in a hospital that is now a bridal salon (at last check) in a small town just outside of Amsterdam. He has lived most of his life in Canada, spent some time in New Mexico, and now makes his home in the beautiful US Virgin Islands. Dr. Wensing holds a Master of Science degree in molecular genetics and Doctor of Dental Surgery from the University of Toronto. He is currently well underway (really... 4 years in!) completing a doctoral program in psychology at Saybrook Graduate School, California.

In 2006 he founded Ecosphere Net (www.ecosphere.net) which is a growing group of academics, teachers, and scholars developing a cross-cultural curriculum for global sustainability and creating a global network of sustainability education centers for its development and implementation. Ecosphere Net provides seminars and participatory educational sustainability programs.

Dr. Wensing is currently a member of the American Psychological Association and the Association for the Advancement of Philosophy and Psychiatry.

Enrico J. Wensing

# Dedication

To everyone, everywhere.

*"We can't solve problems by using the same kind of think-ing we used when we created them"* — Albert Einstein

# Introduction

This book is about how the human body can save the planet. In fact, it's the only way we'll be able to do it.

"Hey, that's a pretty bold statement. The body?"

It depends of course, I suppose, on what your "saved planet" and my "saved planet" look like. Maybe they're the same, maybe not. If yours includes a luxury SUV and mine a bicycle as a mode of transportation then we obviously have two different visions. This book is about how to get our visions closer to each other, maybe even similar enough to save the planet. This book is about how the human body can do that.

"Oh, there he goes with that body thing again! I don't have time for the gym!"

Nobody has time for the gym. We're too busy working. We're too busy working to make the money to buy that SUV. Why do we buy that SUV? Why do we buy anything? If you look at it—what we buy—could probably be split into two groups. Things we need and things we want. In many cases the needs and wants feel the same. Of course you want your needs.

"You gotta eat."

But, maybe surprisingly, you also need your wants.

"So I get to keep my SUV on the saved planet?"

Only if you want to. But you won't want to.

"Ya, well, who's gonna make me?! Oh, never mind, I know… MY BODY!"

Science (not a four letter word) is showing us that human wants have had survival value forever. As long as there have been humans on this planet our wants have kept us alive as a species.

"Wow. That's a long time and a lot of wanting."

So much so, in fact, that our wants are built into our DNA and they're also built into how we develop as kids. DNA is of course the blue-print that helps build our….

"SUV?"

13

Yes, no, our body. How we develop as kids is based on that DNA too, but also based on our interaction with our parents and family, our friends and the world around us. That last part is called social development.

The processes of body (biological) and social development have been going on together for so long that its impossible to really tell them apart. Maybe its even wrong to try to do that in some cases.

"What?"

For instance, how we develop our language you would think is because of our social development. Learned from the people we talk to as we're growing-up. But the basic structure for language, and how its connected to our emotions, the basic rules for that are already in our DNA blueprint! Steven Pinker at Harvard has a book out called *The Stuff of Thought: Language as a Window Into Human Nature* about this.

You might already know this, but spoken language hasn't been around all that long. We were giving each other the finger long before we were saying F#** O*&!... oh, sorry. Ok. You get it.

"Ya!"

We have used symbols to get our wants and needs fulfilled long before we could speak the language to get them. So, our wants and needs must surely be encoded somehow in our DNA.

"Ya think?"

I do. For most of us fortunate sons and daughters it turns out that we become pretty confident as kids that our first needs—the basic ones—of food, shelter and safety will be met. The main point in this book is that, individually and collectively, we are stuck in the next basic need. In fact, as I'll get into, the line between the individual and the collective is becoming increasingly blurred.

"Like how I have my cell phone with me and on all the time?"

Exactly. Yet the need to find/be "self" always remains.

"Is that a digression? Am I a digression?"

Yes.

After the basic food/shelter/safety needs, next on the ladder of priorities is our need to belong. This includes our social groups of community, friends, family and intimate partner. We all need to belong. Some people call belonging a want, but it's a need. And we are stuck there. Individually and collectively, we are stuck at the need to belong level as our guiding force behind the search for the other higher levels. Banging our behavioral heads repeatedly against that wall.

14

"Hey, that's a metaphor, I like those".

Ok, more metaphors soon. Here's the problem.

"There's a problem?"

Ya, we need to save the planet.

"Which one?"

The one somewhere in the middle that let's us still be human while also still being part of nature. Turn off your SUV engine and focus.

The problem, as I'll describe in this book, is that we look to fulfill our need for belonging in the outside, social world. Like the food/shelter/safety thing, this starts when we're developing as children.

"Hey, but we were just kids, what do you expect?"

True.

As kids we look for our belonging in, and from, the outside world. Socially. Externally. Its written in our DNA script.

"I thought it was a blueprint?"

And its how we all develop. As adults we continue to look for the fulfillment of our belonging needs through the outside. Socially. Externally. This is what is not saving the planet. Our relentless habit of seeking external fulfillment of our need to belong—and its associated fear—as I describe in this book, is what will lead this planet to its human destruction.

"Sounds serious... sorry. Focusing."

So we have to change our social development, and with time, who knows, we might even reverse our DNA.

"Don't hold your breath!"

But we'll have to save the planet long-term, make it sustainable, to see if that works.

"A true social experiment!"

In the meantime, lets' work on the social.

"But what about the body thing?!"

This book is about how the best way to change the social is through,

"let me... the body!"

The human life span has been studied by many people. Some have separated it into stages. The psychologists Erik Eriksson and Jean Piaget for example. Abraham Maslow saw life in terms of the human potential for psychological development and maturation along a hierarchy of basic human needs. The Maslow stages have been drawn as a triangle with the stages of basic human needs described along it. This is actually the stage description I was referring to previously. At the base of the Maslow Hierarchy Triangle, the biggest part, our basic needs (shelter/food/safety), next level "belonging" and so on until the top, Level 5, at the apex, where you achieve psychological health in your life and in your identity, which he called "self-actualization". This means to make/find your healthy "true-self" who you are so that you can powerfully say "My name is........and I am..........". Self-actualization is the "I am" part.

"Who you know yourself to be as a person and all the rights and privileges you see attached thereto."

Exactly.

This book is about how we have to teach everyone to flip their Maslow triangle on its top. To make self-actualization our biggest need in our way of life.

"And we're gonna do this using the body right?"

Yup, Bingo!

"See, I knew I had to go to the gym!"

No, just get involved with the *I Am Sustainability* program.

"Do I get to eat what I want?"

Sure, but what you want will likely shift dramatically. Flipping the Maslow triangle on its top means that we will make it our first priority to self-actualize and get all our other needs through that self-actualizing person.

"Ya, but your asking the kids to do it! They don't know any better, like you said its in their DNA!"

But the parents and teachers do. The late Stanford philosopher Richard Rorty wrote about this socialization and human individualization, the same in many respects as the self-actualization idea, in teaching our children.

"Does it involve Plato and Socrates?"

Yes it does, wow, impressive.

"(blush)"

But basically, lets just keep it to how Rorty described that education is stuck in a political framework, where the political right, the group that educates/civilizes the young gets access to our children first. Some call it indoctrination others socialization. This group claims: "Teach children the social truths and personal truth will come later". You get freedom later in life. While those on the opposite pole, championed by the philosophers like Plato, Nietzsche and Rousseau argue that if you take care of freedom, truth will take care of itself. Rorty, following the footsteps of another philosopher, John Dewey, suggests that a "true self" may not emerge once the societal "box" is removed because there is no "essential true self" nor "essential alienation from society". There is, according to Rorty (1998, p. 117), "only the shaping of an animal into a human being by a process of socialization, followed (with luck) by the self-individualization and self-creation of that human being through his or her own later revolt against that very process."

"Does that mean we should wait till they're 18 to teach them how to flip their triangle?"

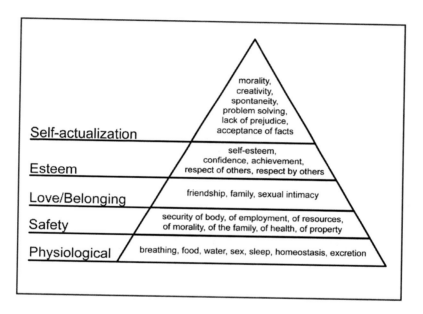

No, we should still teach the young to engage life with their triangle flipped over as much as possible so that the "revolt" that Rorty writes about isn't too difficult a process for the young as they enter adulthood. It'll be easier to wake-up to and engage the need for self-actualization and it'll be easier to counteract the society against which they have to do it. Especially if, as I describe in this book, we've helped them to develop the ability to balance their need to find belonging externally and internally.

"This is done through their body, right?"

You're good.

If we can get everyone to flip their triangle using their body we can save the planet.

"And, don't forget, our saved planets will look very similar, right?"

Yes. As I'll explain in this book it's the best way to make that happen. I'm worried that if we keep going the way we are here as humans our planet will end up looking like something else we've agreed on.

"But we can't live on that one!"

# Human Self-actualization, Sustainability and the Body

The goal of the *I Am Sustainability* program is for a person to attain sustainability as their self-actualized identity. The way I believe this can be best done is through the body. I want to explain briefly what I mean by that here, and then get into more detail in the rest of the book.

First the "self-actualized identity" part.

Abraham Maslow described that each one of us has a basic human need and motivational drive to achieve self-actualization, to achieve psychological health in our lives. When Maslow did his research he was very counter-culture because unlike all the other psychologists at the time who were studying people who had psychological dysfunction he studied highly successful individuals who were psychologically healthy. They had reached their full human potential. They were not all out saving the world, but they all were very successful personally and vocationally. He saw that self-actualization in these people manifests in identity as the final stage of a series of needs along a hierarchy as I've already described. Progression through the hierarchy is an ongoing process, with most people, according to Maslow never reaching self-actualization. Most people get stuck developmentally regardless of age in the lower levels for their entire lives. Occasionally, some people may have brief episodes of self-actualization experiences, but few reach the state and stay there in a stable psychological maturation to health, life self-fulfillment and happiness.

Self-actualization is characterized by: 1) the experience of self-lessness in life, without interference from self-consciousness or self-awareness; 2) the avoidance of fear choices, to make all life choices based toward healthy psychological and psychospiritual growth; 3) to reach and know the true voice of your authentic inner self; 4) choices made are in honesty in expression of and responsibility to that inner self; 5) to have courage in authentic self-expression; 6) to become through effort first-rate in whatever one does as a life vocation; 7) the potentiation for recog-

19

nition and incidence of peak (joy) experiences; and 8) opening yourself up to your self, knowing your self, including identifying defenses and finding the courage to give them up, "if the psychoanalytic literature has taught us nothing else, it has taught us that repression is not a good way of solving problems" (Maslow, 1968; List adapted from Maslow, 1971, p. 45). Self-actualized individuals are doers. They have a total commitment to hard work. "Working well at something they consider important" (Maslow, 1965, p.6).

## Characterization of Self-actualization

1. The experience of self-lessness in life.

2. The avoidance of fear choices, to make all life choices based toward healthy psychological and psychospiritual growth.

3. To reach and know the true voice of your authentic inner self.

4. Choices made are in honesty in expression of, and responsibility, to that inner self.

5. To have courage in authentic self-expression.

6. To become through effort first-rate in whatever one does as a life vocation.

7. The potentiation for recognition and incidence of peak (joy) experiences.

8. Opening yourself up to your self, knowing your self, including identifying defenses and finding the courage to give them up.

The concept of human individuation was introduced and extensively described by Swiss psychologist and physician Carl Jung. It is the process by which, during adulthood a person becomes a psychological integral and indivisible unity or "whole" or "whole and complete". Jung's historically earlier concept of the process of individuation parrallels that of Maslow's theoretical conceptualization of self-actualization. There are of course some important differences. For instance, while Jung described a balancing of what he saw as the masculine and feminine aspects of every individual as part of the journey to psychological health (for an excellent treatise on Carl Jung and his work see Shamdasani, 2003), Maslow's proposals made no such reference and may, it could be argued, in fact have been partially influenced by the strong patriarchal and anthropocentric social sentiment of the era in which he lived (Cullen & Gotell, 2002). Maslow's proposals, including the hierarchy of needs, are based on both empirical research and his personal hypotheses.

The realization of an autonomy of the self as distinct from society as created by the individual is what Rorty (1999) is referring to in his term individualization. While this aspect of a process toward autonomy from society is shared by Maslow and Jung's descriptions, it is *not* equivalent in that in Rorty's sense psychological maturation to health, self-fulfillment and happiness are *not* implied.

Secondly, the "sustainability as their self-actualized identity" part.

Its very important to mention here, and as I'll describe further, that the term "self-actualization" on its own means something different than the process and progress through the hierarchy of needs Maslow described (or as Jung described for the progress and process to individuation). Self-actualization in sustainability through the *I Am Sustainability* program means getting to the point of where your identity is first and foremost healthy sustainability. This identity becomes the crucible for the general and complete self-actualization Maslow described. It is the crucible in the sense that the *I Am Sustainability* becomes the health identity, the context, through which previously unhealthy behaviors are actively transformed into healthy behaviors as part of the process and progress toward complete self-actualization. Achieving an identity in sustainability through self-actualization first will make the Maslow type of self-actualization a much easier task. In fact, that is the exact premise of the *I Am Sustainability* program. The first step necessary toward a "whole person" self-actualization as Maslow described, is to become self-actualized in sustainability! It provides the foundation. As described in this book, there is a way to do that for adults and a way to do that for young people. In both cases there is a healthy guided management of the process and progress through the hierarchy of needs Maslow described. The person self-actualized in sustainability will have everything in place that Maslow described, *and more!* The only thing that will be lacking will be the identity that Maslow felt could come through what a person chose as a vocation. Their job. Maslow felt self-actualization of the whole person required commitment to a specific career. *I Am Sustainability* and its companion *We Are Sustainability* help get you ready to do that. More than that though, as I detail further, *I Am Sustainability* and its companion *We Are Sustainability* get you on your way to help save the planet in a very powerful and significant way by creating an equivalence between how you treat your self, other people and the world around you.

Lastly, some more to what I mean by "the way I believe this can best be done through the body" part.

Creating an identity in sustainability through a self-actualization process in and through the body is unique to this book and to the *I Am Sustainability* program. Allow me to use a metaphor. Everyone needs a home. Our home forms a safe haven. It provides a grounding point, a point of reference and context. The "home" for the self, its belonging, as I'll describe in this book, is for most people currently defined on the outside in our social groups. Not so for a person self-actualized in sustainability. Their self is inside. Not just inside their mind, or inside their body. It *is* the entire body. Yet, as I will detail further, the sustainability identity extends far beyond their skin into the world. A key element to saving the planet is to get individuals to ground their sustainability in their body first. The body becomes the belonging reference point, not the social groups.

There's more though. Think about it. If a person is self-actualized or self-actualizing that person will not only have/seek psychological health, but also physical health. In "physical health" I'm only referring to general personal fitness and physically healthy living, not extreme body-building. A person self-actualized in sustainability would not hurt their body. In fact a self-actualized or self-actualizing person would "ground" their self-actualized self in their body because its part of that healthy self. Now, some may suggest that you can achieve psychological health, the self-actualization that Maslow described, in an unhealthy body. Of course that is true if your physical ill health is beyond your control. But, noting the example of Marathon of Hope runner Canadian Terry Fox, you can do a lot with an unhealthy body. He ran a marathon every day, on a prosthetic leg lost to cancer, for how many days before succumbing to cancer again?

Self-actualization, either as per Maslow in general or in sustainability, inherently involves, and the process of, keeping/making the body healthy. This is a proposal, however, that Maslow did not write about and perhaps would not agree with. But there is no denying that physical fitness and mental fitness are complimentary and synergistic with regard to the achievement Maslow described for self-actualized individuals. In the case of sustainability, as I'll describe, through the *I Am Sustainability* program its about much more than just body health. Its about using the body to save the planet.

The human body has historically been a focal point for social change. Skin color, gender, sexuality, physical disability, and general body health have each provided the impetus for social change on a large scale. As I'll describe further, the body has extensive social significance. Social psychologists say that we in fact find our identity in our body, and we express our identity through our body. If we are going to begin the shift toward "being sustainability" then what better place to reference that from than from our bodies? However, environmental psychologists say that we find our identities in our environments and express our identity through our environments. Which is it then, our bodies or our environments for a home for our identity in sustainability? The answer, as I'll detail, is that at first in the *I Am Sustainability Program* it is the body, but as you self-actualize through the program in sustainability it ends-up being *both*. They are complimentary.

Personally though, as a pragmatist, I need more. I need more than a socially constructed metaphor and campfire song of, "A home for sustainability in my body and in my environment". I suppose because so many of my early life experiences were so "unreal" in a negative sense, I have always found some comfort in the predictable and reproducible reality of the physical sciences. Perhaps emotional trauma for me inspired a shift toward logical positivism. I used to think that only the sciences could ultimately describe truth. All through university I loved the life sciences, molecular genetics, especially. Still do. I like evidence based medicine too. If we're talking about me, my health, my life, I like the proof of reproducible, factual, quantitative data. So when I first discovered that we made meaning of our body and of our environments so that our identities were to some degree connected to both of them I thought, ok interesting, but that's social stuff. True, from the social sciences, but those I have until only recently considered inherently more subjective than the physical sciences. I still said internally, "Give me the biology!" I want the proof of that connection between body and environment. The science. The evidence. Well, the proof has arrived and more arrives all the time. From many diverse sources too: physics, biology, artificial systems and robotics and complex systems sciences to name a few.

Two main areas with regard to the connection of our body and our environment are very interesting and, for me, contain the proof I'm looking for. First, emerging connectionist models in dynamical systems theory described by complexity science is demonstrating the profoundly intimate connection our body systems have with environmental systems. Secondly, the emerging tenets of embodied cognition from the cognitive sciences indicate (not just "suggest") that our bodies are the central processor of everything we do, everything we are, and everything we can be in our human potential. Together, these two areas indicate that the mind, as I'll describe further, is secondary to the body in the processing of human experience department. Its true. Its science. Its through the body we learn. Its through the body we remember. Its through the body we will save the planet. Not just because of our social connection, but also because, as I'll explain, we will be acting on the physical reality of our connection.

The current environmental programs continue to have a marginal impact on the welfare of the global environment and the prospect of achieving global sustainability. Plus there are still proportionately very few people self-actualizing as Maslow described back in the 1960s. These two are connected. If we want sustainability, our environmental education has to help people self-actualize in sustainability. As I describe in this book, when a person self-actualizes in sustainability with their body as their grounding and reference point they will, as a consequence, also become more environmentally connected and more environmentally responsible than ever before.

# An Important Metaphor

Wikipedia describes the meaning of the word metaphor as: "A direct comparison between two or more seemingly unrelated subjects. A metaphor describes a first subject as *being* or *equal to* a second subject in some way. Thus, the first subject can be economically described because implicit and explicit attributes from the second subject are used to enhance the description of the first."

To begin this book I'd like to introduce a recurrent metaphor that forms a main theme in this book. It describes how one thing can be made up of two things at once, but that often, we can only see one thing at a time. Depending on how you look at it. Focus on the one; you'll lose sight of the other. The metaphor comes from the property of light.

Light, as anyone who has taken introductory physics knows has both wave and particle properties. The particle is a photon and while it is part of the energy of light it is its movement as a wave that is necessary to make light. Albert Einstein and others have called this the "wave-particle duality of light". Science has taken light apart to see its pieces, yet its pieces, by themselves, don't make light. Light is the experience of those pieces together.

This phenomenon can be used to understand how we think and how humans behave. Human thinking, it is thought, is made up of a combination of computer-like computation (particles) and what are called dynamical system processes (waves). Together they create what we experience as our thinking (light). For instance, Melanie Mitchell (1998) at the Santa Fe Institute has described how the mechanism of our thinking is best described by a computer mechanism model employing connectionism in parallel-distributed neural networks while our ability to change our minds, to adapt to new environmental information in real time can best be described by dynamical systems properties such as self-organization and chaotic attractors.

The point here is that, as described by the light metaphor, one thing can be comprised of two different things at the same time. As simple as that may sound, this is an important concept, which has a wide variety of applications, some of which will be described in this book. In other words, this concept (there are others as well of course) from physics may be actually better referred to as a general principle of nature because it shows-up, as I'll describe more in this book, in so many ways in so many different disciplines.

For instance, one way of describing human behavior can come from using the light metaphor as well. Our behavior is made up of momentary reactions (particles) and of gradually emerging systems of action (waves). Something in our environment symbolizes something, there is a coupling in which the environment represents something, and a reaction ensues. In this sense, the old "stimulus-response" lives. (Did I hear someone say, "Let the behaviorists back in the room"?). Our behavior is also made up of connected actions, systems of behaviors, such as when we are doing something like getting ready to go to work in the morning. The external environmental representation and the internal systems integrate to perpetuate human behavior (light). I use the word "perpetuate" here and not "generate" because behavior flows as a system and appears to be perpetual if you look at it from the big picture, and it appears to be generated if you are looking at the closer, smaller picture. Perpetuated implies no cause, while generated implies cause, the difference between the two is a matter of perception based on the way its described, or, as I'll discuss later, the modes of description used. Of course philosophers continue to wrangle with the question of "first cause", that is, what caused the bigger picture systems to begin in the first place?

You could say that this last example is made up of premeditated behaviors while the first example is just one of a spontaneous reaction. Turns out both originate as subconscious thoughts though. We premeditate our premeditation's subconsciously. In fact, even when we think, we are only really thinking about something that has already been thought of subconsciously. Similarly, the spontaneous reactions are not so spontaneous. They are grounded in learned behavior. A context of something previously learned from which we react. This is a good thing because otherwise there would be way too much for us to think about. We do have some conscious control of subconscious originated thoughts and behaviors. This allows us to strategize our behaviors and thinking, but only to a limited degree.

Learning too can be compared to the light metaphor. In a mechanistic sense, it involves both computational and dynamical processes (I'll explain the concept of dynamical systems more later). Variation in either particle (computational analog symbol processing following syntactical and semantic rules) and/or wave (the facility to change our thinking over time, learn from our mistakes and accommodate/assimilate new knowledge as performed by dynamical system processes) can change the properties of light (our knowledge and its related behavior).

Where does the computation and dynamical system thinking take place? If you said "In the human brain" or "In the human mind" you'd be only partially correct. If you said "In the Braind" you'd be right on target!

In their quest to find the mind within the brain scientists have dissected and stimulated a lot of brains. So far, no luck. No defined modules. No defined mind centers. No seat of the soul.

The question is, "Is the brain/mind the top organ? Is the mind all in our head?" It turns-out too that while we like to think we use our heads (well…most of us [brain/mind]) to make decisions our brain/mind (braind?) actually works *largely* from information it receives from the body. Perhaps even entirely, if you include information it has stored in it, which it learned initially through body experiences. Not only does the body's sensory experience go to the brain such as taste and smell (everybody knows those), but also the body's memory and the body's movement, and there through, are you ready for this one, its "knowing" (that's very new) act as input to the brain. In truth the body "knows" *before* the mind/brain does. Body perception precedes mental perception and mental representation.

In fact, as we develop as kids, our bodies teach our brain to create our mind. Then everything we do is just a repeat of that except that its just a lot faster. The body sets-up the context and boom, the mind/brain gets it, usually without our awareness or even our conscious involvement. So Body-brain-mind are one. Braind it is!

The braind, as I'll describe further, actually extends beyond our bodies. Beyond our skin, well into the environment.

So next time you forget something like your cell phone or car keys at home, say, "I don't know where I've left my Braind today!". You probably put them in a place that is out of the ordinary. To remember, you have to remember what? Your actions, where you have been, retrace your steps, and remember where your body was. You probably forgot them in the first place because your mind is used to another morning body routine.

By the way, just kidding about using the term "Braind". I only made that up to get the point across of how the body, mind and brain work together. In fact, if we are going to make someone the leader we'd have to give that title to the body and not the mind or brain. As I hope to convince you in this book, the body is also the leader that can give us global sustainability.

# In Case you Missed the Preface

I n case you missed the preface, here was the best part:

> I think it's perhaps a foregone conclusion for many that
> global environmental conditions are getting worse. Also
> worsening are conditions for and between human beings.
> What may be a new idea to some is that if we want to save
> the global environment we may actually *first* need to im-
> prove conditions for, and between, each other. For in-
> stance, the UN's Millennium Project includes both
> environmental and human improvement goals on the same
> project list (Sachs and McArthur, 2005). What I describe
> in this book is that the best way to get conditions better
> for, and between, each other is to first improve conditions
> within ourselves. This book is about why that is necessary
> and how we can do it using a very exciting new approach
> I call "*I Am Sustainability*".

I want to bring this back now because I think it should also be part of the
introduction. The premise of this book is that the best way to achieve
global sustainability is to first achieve identity in sustainability individually, and the best way to do that is through education programs that make
the body the central focus.

If you have an identity in sustainability you reduce your fear-based
behaviors. I believe fear is the fundamental motivator behind everything
that threatens the environment and other humans globally.

Why is the body the central focus? Its that way already anyway.
Socio-culturally the body is very important. Its central. Its all about looking good. Keeping up appearances. Not only how the physical body looks,
but how the physical body moves. As I'll describe, the body is a place not
only *with* which we identify but also a place *in* which we make our iden-

tity. Both on the surface and on the inside. It's *the* central processor of who we are and what we do (see "Braind" above). So for the *I Am Sustainability* program its not like we are going to be putting our faith in something we've made-up as humans. If we ground our new identity in sustainability in our bodies, we are doing something that is very natural.

I just snuck-in the words "new identity in sustainability". Did you catch that? I used the words "new identity" because, as I'll describe further, I believe that each one of us, by the time we reach adulthood already has an identity in sustainability. Its just that for most people currently its mostly fear-based. Its about understanding how to make it less fear-based. Self-actualization in sustainability is that "how" and the I Am Sustainability program provides the "how to". Although the "I Am Sustainability" program does incorporate some self-esteem work, like the excellent work of Nathaniel Branden, self-esteem is just part of the program.

So, "*I Am Sustainability*" refers to someone, you and I both hopefully, not only identifying with sustainability as a lot of people have started to do ("going green", recycling, etc.), but actually being sustainability. Not being "sustainable", no, I mean being "sustainability". Finding, getting, and maintaining "being sustainability". Your own personal sustainability. Whatever that looks like. Whatever that looks like? Sure, because its not about creating who you are that the *I Am Sustainability* program teaches, its about helping you make the basis of the rest of you, your foundation and your crucible sustainability.

Whatever your sustainability identity looks like, the foundation of you, I think will be similar in many respects to other peoples' "being sustainability" because, as I'll describe further, when you *are* sustainability you have reduced your fear-based behaviors, many of which we all have in common. This enables you to work better with other people and better with the environment. Yet you retain your individuality. That falls in line, by the way, with the general consensus that maintaining biodiversity is a natural process of ecosystems and is good for sustainability. Again, by retaining our individuality, our biodiversity, we will be doing something natural. We can still be "one" as a planet of people, as I'll discuss in this book, but its important to be our self. I call this collective individualism. Ok, I'll file that term with "braind".

By the way, the term "sustainability" itself, as I'll describe has various meanings. One of the more commonly understood ones has been stated by Marc Pilisuk and Linda Reibel of Saybrook Graduate School in California as, "Sustainability is defined as living in such a way that the capacity of future generations to meet their own needs is preserved." In this book I describe how each of us "being sustainability" first can get us to global sustainability.

"Being sustainability", in this book means not only doing things like recycling, building a sustainable house and so on. "Being sustainability" means going into who you are, figuring out what worries you and trying to quench the anxiety around those worries and thereby changing your behavior. That behavior will be friendlier and more authentic to self, others and the environment. With enough practice you will say "*I Am Sustainability*"! As mentioned, this is more than building your self-esteem. Its knowing who you are, what motivates you and seeing your life in a whole new way. Its not too touchy feely, and its for a good cause. You!

Enrico J. Wensing

# Life As a House: What Life is All About

Life is all about defining yourself as an individual. Each day we define ourselves, over and over and over, our inner voice (narrative) says: "I am this, but not that". Most of us define ourselves by the groups we belong to. "I am a golfer, it's cool to be a golfer" or "I am a good looking guy, I belong to the beautiful people". We also define ourselves by what we are not, "I am not greedy, I don't belong to the greedy people group", "I am not a golfer, golfers are boring, I'm not boring". We do this all the time every day. Watch yourself and you'll see that I'm right. It's the "I'm this and not that" narrative you "hear" inside your head. We are incessant judgment machines.

Who we are, who we define ourselves as, is based on external factors. As we go through our day we keep comparing our experiences with the external environment to who we think we are. Constantly judging our environment. Then comparing it to what we already know. We let someone in front of us we say, "I'm a responsible person". We call our mom, "I'm a good son".

Of course we sometimes have to redefine ourselves. We get a new job, a promotion. We lose a partner. As per the Swiss psychologist Jean Piaget we have to initially accommodate (to make room) and eventually assimilate (integrate) that new experience into that person we think of as our "self". So who we are, who we see ourselves to be, changes with our life, gradually along the course of our life cycle and sometimes rapidly following certain life events. As I'll describe later, changes in the person we think we are, are usually experienced passively. That is, they happen to us rather than us working with them to maximize the learning opportunity. Consequently, change often occurs and is engaged more along the surface of experience rather than at the level of actively engaged life experiences, which can provide deep attitudinal and behavioral change.

Strangely, some of us define ourselves in our oppression. "I am from the hard side of town, so I am going to be hard, I have to look hard." Often times, in terms of the oppression, this actually reinforces the oppressive forces. Why? Because both the oppressor and oppressed are going external, outward, *away from* their individual self to get the definition of their self based on their interaction with the other. Its like the two social groups, the oppressed and the oppressor, have this automatic, unwritten agreement. The oppressed and oppressor sometimes define themselves in the experience of being oppressed/oppressing. Conflicts can create a cause, a life's purpose for both.

For instance, environmental problems and conflicts for some environmental activists is the vehicle in which and the stage upon which they seek self-definition. They ride their self-actualization process on the back of the environmental issues. They seek meaning and purpose to their lives. Nothing wrong with that, we all do. The problem, as I'll describe further, is in the extremism. The linear right and wrong, the "us vs. them," which forms the basis to the polarized cult mentality. Again, the oppressed are defined by their oppression. As with the light metaphor, there are in many cases two things going on at once. In the extreme environmental activism I've encountered, there is often genuine true healthy motivation towards helping, but concomitantly interwoven with that there is their psychological process. The cause, whether its the environment or human rights, symbolizes something for the individual on a personal level and it is that symbolism that has activated their process. ("Process" here refers to the automatic psychological developmental path that defines each of our lives; more on that soon). The tip-off is the exaggerated emotional side to it, the romantic lamentations, the extreme behavior that is expressed in one form or another (e.g., martyrdom)…etc. This is opposed to healthy personal power, determination and engagement. I'll describe how you can understand and determine the difference by studying your narratives and knowing your schemata/stories, your "self" basically, a little later.

At their foundation though, these behaviors are actually learned coping skills on the part of both the oppressor and the oppressed. In a real way both sides get stuck in the suffering. Coping is another term used for surviving. These are socially learned survival skills. The mutual coping is like a social dance, in a real sense a social game we play. Learned? When? Since before you were born. So its more accurate to say they are inherited rather than learned.

"Wait", you think, "I define me! Sure, maybe as a kid I didn't, but now as an adult I make my own choices about who I am and what I do"! Do you?

The truth is you don't. Society defines who you are mostly. The truth is, you also shouldn't try to completely get away from that. You'll always need to belong. Its always going to be important to have times in your life when you belong to a group, belong to another, and belong to the "you" you think is your you. The trick, and the secret—the secret trick— is to become aware of *how and why* you are using these belonging relationships to explore who you are. You're doing it anyway, just wake-up. Wake-up to how you are using relationships to define yourself and how you are using them to get to know yourself. Then you can at least be a co-pilot instead of a passenger in your life. That's for young adults and on-ward.

For children (age 8 and younger), teachers (school teachers, parents etc.) can teach children to be their own best friend and to live healthy lives. I'll describe this in a lot more detail. Basically though, in teaching: no guilt, no shame, and no shock. Just balance. Don't try to create their lives to eliminate their fears, just try to find healthy developmentally appropriate balances in attitude and behavior. More on this later.

This book is about how fear is our primary individual motivator. Its helped us survive so far, it will continue to help us survive in the future. We need fear for sustainability. But it's a different approach to, and relationship with, fear that is essential to sustainability. Its about understanding it and not letting it control us. This healthier dynamic will help save the planet. This book is about how we can do that. Once we get how we can understand and work with our fears we can start to build our identity in sustainability.

Consider the metaphor of our self as a house, one we can actively build in our lives. Then I would suggest that our self needs a new home. More than ever, as more and more people populate this planet, it needs a structure it feels safe in. One it feels defined in. We will still need the external to help us build some of the walls, to define some of the structure; that will always be there. The new home, however, will be built primarily internally. This is the premise of the *I Am Sustainability* program described in this book. Using a healthy blueprint, and sometimes through trial and error, we'll be able to judge what can come from external and what can come from internal as we re-build and/or renovate who we are into "I Am Sustainability". The foundation of the new home for your new self is your body. Your self will be grounded, anchored, in your body. This is what we are trying to do anyway. That is, in part, the automatic drive toward self-actualization Malsow was talking about. Doing it with our eyes wide open we'll probably build a better home on a better piece of solid ground. Our self needs a new home. More than ever, as more and more people populate this planet, it needs a structure it feels safe in. We will still need the external to help us build some of the walls, to define some of the structure; that will always be there. The new home, however, will be built primarily internally. Using a healthy blueprint, and sometimes through trial and error, we'll be able to judge what can come from external and what can come from internal. This is what we are trying to do anyway. Doing it with our eyes open we'll probably build a better home on a better piece of solid ground.

The other night I was at dinner with my friend Jared. He was talking about a new relationship. This new relationship would require him to take-on a new lifestyle, one that he felt would, by definition reduce his mobility. He has loved being mobile. He talked about the compromises you have to make in relationships in order to have relationships. I agreed, but his "in order to" set off an alarm in me so I asked, "How do you know when your compromises aren't really sacrifices?" My idea being that in compromise you are not just trying to accommodate change but are also able to assimilate a change situation into your identity and into your life without any recurrently intrusive internal experience of loss or regret. You can truthfully say to yourself, "I am no longer a mobile person" because it is who you have really become. Sacrifice means that you only get as far as accommodating but cannot assimilate the new situation into your identity of "self" (your *I Am...*). That only works for so long. His answer went something like, "because it's a balance sheet, when you realize your life is so much more than you could ever have by being alone, then you go for it, there are no sacrifices". I thought this answer was brilliant because it falls directly into line with one of the main tenets of this book. The balance sheet compliments the house metaphor I just used. The *I Am Sustainability* program is about learning how you only assimilate the healthy things you are asked to accommodate and discard the rest. The choice is yours.

*You* build your house using healthy materials and contractors *you* choose. Healthy each step of the way, when you build your house, is when you truly experience compromise and not sacrifice each step of the way. When what the external can provide, i.e., the materials and the contractors, is something that *you* realize that you truly cannot yet give your self, but is truly something you would if you could. The *I Am Sustainability* program helps you understand yourself to the point that you see that what you currently need is reflected back to you, like a mirror, in your relationship experiences and life choices. The journey is about figuring-out how to get everything you need in your self. To become an autonomous individual that is psychologically whole and complete. A house built to completion. At the end of the journey, when the house is done (is it ever done?) in your life, when you are able to give yourself everything, when you have completed yourself, when you complete your self in your everyday then, perhaps ironically, you'll want more than ever to be with one that has built their house to the point of completion too. For a truly healthy relationship, for intimacy and for help in identifying possible minor repairs and renovations, and perhaps, together, to be guides for others who are still building their houses.

Enrico J. Wensing

# Our World, Our Values, Our Fears

Y ou have to admit, we humans are a strange bunch. We have so much intelligence and power yet we continue to struggle with a wide range of environmental problems such as global warming, pollution, and extinction (our own and other species). Are we on self-destruct, bent on suicide? Are petroleum companies and other large corporations more powerful than governments? Has real political democracy died? Is the media these days the true voice of the people? Is the free press really free?

There are so many things happening all at once nowadays its difficult, and probably incorrect to try to reduce, prioritize, single-out and categorize the problems. Yet, its something we have to do. We have to come up with solutions. Is there one fundamental problem that gives rise to the array of confusing environmental threats?

With a burgeoning global population that will, within most of our lifetimes reach 9 billion in number it would not seem too outrageous to suggest that we likely need to do better to support such growth with regard to the global environment. Do better with what though? Live in a way that is not only more environmentally friendly, but also more friendly for each other. The environment not only includes the trees and lakes and oceans of course, but also each other.

On the balance, science suggests that there are currently too many of us abusing the environment, directly or indirectly, and too many of us not doing anything to change our daily behavior to even help-out. Why is there general abuse of the environment compounded with general neglect of the environment?

The answer lies in our human values. Looking around it appears that everyone is "doing their own thing" or "living their own lives". It looks like each person has her or his own values in their own lives. Many values, like freedom and justice, are shared in civil societies. But what about our values regarding the environment, why are they so difficult to inspire? Why are some people oblivious to the needs of the environment while others become extreme activists about it?

This is because at a deeper level, as humans, we are dealing with, and have been dealing with for millions of years our basic need to survive. Our core human value is survival. All our other values stem from our need to survive. The main emotion of course behind our survival-based values is fear. Everything we do and everything we are is based on our nature and nurture of fear. Fear is the spark and the fuel of all our behavior. I'm not saying there is no such thing as courage. There is obviously. But we have to develop courage to overcome our fear. Fear is always first.

What about those that argue that there is evidence that humans by nature are good? For instance, we do not learn altruism, its merely reinforced, or not, through learning and socialization, its actually innate to our species (Warneken & Tomasello, 2006). Ok, so I have to take back the statement that "Fear is the spark and the fuel of all our behavior". We do have a built-in foundation to balance our fear. Being good has had survival value. It doesn't take long to discover, however, that there is very little balancing going on between altruism and fear. We live in a culture of fear. In fact, it appears that fear rules us. Just look around at the popular culture media for example.

In psychology Abraham Maslow (1968, 1970, 1971) wrote some time ago about our basic human hierarchy of needs and motivation while Roy Baumeister (Baumeister & Leary, 1995) has further described our need to belong. The hierarchy goes step-wise along physiological needs, safety needs, belonging needs, esteem needs, to self-actualization needs. These are *all* fear-based needs. Over the many millennia of human evolution fear has kept us alive. It has made sure, and still makes sure to this day, that our needs are met.

So what's the problem with fear? It is ruling us. Our societies. For instance, my interpretation of Jared Diamond's 2005 book *Collapse: How Societies Choose to Succeed or Fail* is that its actually a treatise of how fear has been the ultimate culprit behind the failure and collapse of every society humans have ever formed. We cannot and, perhaps surprisingly, should not even try to get rid of our basic fear drive. We just have to learn that it is out of balance and begin to understand its power and work with it in a healthier manner. Right now it rules us. Perhaps more than ever. Haven't the colors yellow, orange and red taken on a whole new meaning recently for millions of us? Orange used to be my favorite color as a kid. My kids have learned orange is a serious threat and safety concern.

On the Maslow triangle, after physical survival, belonging/fear of abandonment are our next dominant level of survival needs. While we do move up the hierarchy of needs as we mature psychologically in our lives, on average we don't move up very far. That is, while we can experience the higher levels and manifest them in who we are occasionally, on average, our behavior reflects the lower "belonging needs" level for most of our lives. Very few of us move up and stay up beyond self-esteem to full self-actualization. Therefore, while we do continue to develop during our lives, our psychological development is actually so minor that we never lose touch with the lower levels of the needs hierarchy and their supporting cast of fears. As I'll describe further, the lower needs and the fear based behaviors that attempt to satisfy them become so ingrained that the behaviors become normal, we lose sight of the underlying fears and the way we are becomes who we are. The meaning of the initial fear stimulus you made when you were young may be gone but the patterns of behavior they forged live on, day after day. The fear based drive to survive occurs at the level of the individuals and, as will be described further in the next book *We Are Sustainability*, also at the level of societies and cultures. In fact, as I'll describe further in this book, this speaks to the concept of scalar levels of identities, from a personal set of internal identities as reflected in what is sometimes called "multiplex" or the multiplicity of self to our societies which have the same identities or "characters". This is actually a good thing because, for instance, it can be used to foster empathy and compassion.

As you now know the process of psychological maturation of the self has been termed self-actualization and individuation. These are different than the individualization Richard Rorty wrote about. As we grow-up each one of us, to some extent, becomes more and more independent, more of an individual. That really is the development of the experience of an autonomous self described by Rorty. As I have mentioned too, that self is not all that autonomous. It is largely socially constructed. The premise of this book is that it doesn't have to be.

In this book I use the term "self" to mean your identity, everything you know yourself to be, and that part of yourself you don't know yet; that part that remains undiscovered. If fear is the basis of most/all of our behaviors then, as I'll describe further, beyond those fears is where there is that undiscovered part of who you are.

As I've also mentioned, at the individual level everything we do is based on a core need to survive. This is not only physical survival, but also social survival. Thus, all human behavior is at least in part and often mostly, fear-based. How we experience and deal with our needs, even

41

though there may be a hierarchy, is largely equivalent because they are all part of our repertoire of survival needs.

Their basis in survival makes our hierarchy of human needs "eternal" in the sense that they'll always be present, in our behavior and in our motivation, to some degree. Though their intensity and influence on our behavior can be shifted, if we intend on continuing our self-actualization they will always be something we have to contend with. Fear in and of itself is not a bad thing. It has survival value. Its how we act on it, how we choose to engage it behaviorally that is either healthy or unhealthy. Our choice is the element we can control. Our survival behaviors/motivations are also "internal" in the sense that our drives' emanate from our subconscious. They are so engrained in who we are and what we do, we don't even think about them most of the time. This makes them sometimes difficult to predict and often requiring the insight of hindsight.

Our fear-based behaviors that attempt to fulfill our needs develop while we are kids and quickly become our "normal" and our "tolerable" ways of being. They become aspects of our personality. Normal and healthy if the behavior fits (assimilates) well into society and satisfies our needs. Tolerable if its unhealthy/abnormal behavior with regard to the rest of our society, against the societal "gold standard", but also tolerable in the sense that if we can rationalize and/or get a way with it in such a way that it can be accommodated into our lives. In other words we survive, and thereby form our personality by being both normal and abnormal. Normal gives us belonging to society while abnormal gives us perceived independence from it. We have individualized. This curious need for polarity is common to all humans. We conform to society to satisfy our lower belonging needs, we reject society through non-conformity in an unconscious attempt at self-actualization. This is more an attempt at autonomy than self-actualization, as I'll describe further, and often manifests as reactionary unhealthy overconsumption in one form or another.

We inherit and learn our survival needs, as per the hierarchy, from both our nature and nurture. Nature is what we are biologically endowed with, our genetic blueprint. Nurture is what we learn from our parents, our peers, our schools and our society (...TV and the Internet for the most part, alas so few book readers). The process of learning is a social one and has been called socialization or, perhaps more cynically, inculturation. Nature and nurture interact as we develop throughout our lives. Although they are very interwoven, it is possible to distinguish their effect on each other. For instance, nurture can alter nature. In other words, teaching changes biology, not only developmentally, while we are teaching our children, but also in adults. For instance, psychotherapeutic teaching of adults can change an individual's neurophysiology (Thase, 2001).

As will be described in detail, the idea behind the *I Am Sustainability* curriculum is not to try to stop these natural fear-based survival drives directly. The idea is to understand them as they manifest in our lives, modify them and channel them in healthy ways whenever possible. To not resist or repress them, but rather to consciously redirect them, let them flow-out and thereby dissipate their intention, energy, and their cause. Some will be easy, some difficult and some will never go away. Through the *I Am Sustainability* programs, however, you will learn how to understand and thereby control the many drives and their associated behaviors you have adopted to survive in your life. This will help make your life a whole new powerful experience, where the power is yours, and its expressed through your choice of healthy behaviors.

This book is about shifting personal values through becoming less fearful about survival. This book, and the *I Am Sustainability* program is not about puritanical living. Importantly too, the path to sustainable living cannot become an autocratic dogma. There must be room within which to maneuver, for a person to find his or her own way. Change cannot happen by force. Environmental laws have tried to do that. Its worked in some cases and backfired in others. To be most effective change must be authentic. Genuine and self-motivated. A way of life. An authentic way of being. Thus, change must also occur from inside, and not only from outside a person. You get the various possible "how to" ways from the outside, the actual shift, however, must come from within. Through your choice.

So too, this book and the *I Am Sustainability* program is not about perfection. We will never be perfect. Nor should we try to seek it. Our best goal is health, both individually and collectively. Similarly, this book is also not about reaching some spiritually perfect paradise during life. Its not about reaching your own personal Nirvana; your very own place of freedom from karmic suffering. While attaining enlightenment in the sense of increased insight through spiritual practice in religion or otherwise can be fulfilling and healthy endeavors, the notion and proposed methods of attaining spiritual enlightenment sometimes questionable. For instance, how do I know your enlightenment is not you accidentally/purposefully faking it, you experiencing some "biopsychosociogenic" phenomenon you consider real? Is seeking to attain a state of nirvana or enlightened state of consciousness actually an attempt at generating a dissociative experience? Do I want to dissociate from human experience? No. Perhaps I am too much of a pragmatist. Who the heck do I think I am to think that I should try to dissociate from the human experience, like some spiritualists attempt to do, when it appears that I was born into that? What if my spiritual paradise is different than yours? What if I think a spiritual paradise is something we all, each one of us have inside of us already anyway. No dissociation required. In fact, I suspect its a balanced dissociation/association through conscious life engagement that is healthiest: a balance between the physical and metaphysical experiences of life. What if I can and do experience it right there, Nirvana, in front of me, in the experience of my humanity and my connection to our collective humanity (association) as well as in those spiritual moments that Hay and Nye (1998) talked about for kids and in the peak experiences (dissociation) Maslow talked about that occur in all our lives, regardless of age or psychological maturity?

This book and the *I Am Sustainability* program is about more of us living our individual lives better, to discover the individual benefits of being sustainability and thereby making sustainability a bigger possibility for all of us. That begins with us understanding where our values come from. Once we get that we can begin to make positive lasting changes to our behavior in our own lives, which, as a side-effect even right from the start will begin to improve the sustainability of the planet.

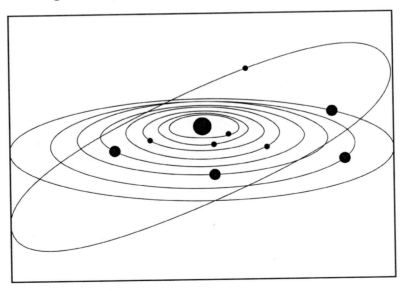

# Our Pattern of Fear: How it All Begins

Your identity is formed by systems. Who you are and who others know you to be is socially constructed by social systems interwoven with biological systems such as the genetic program in your DNA. Systems of nature and systems of nurture co-create who you are. As I've mentioned, the two are so interwoven as to be inseparable really. This is especially the case during human development. A primary social system that creates who you become as you grow-up is of course your experience of the interactions with the people that you meet in your life and the significance you ascribe to them for your survival. Your parents, your family, your friends, your communities, your world all help make up who you become as a child and who you become as an adult.

When does that begin? Well, as I've already mentioned it doesn't really begin. It just flows through from one generation to the next. Like an interwoven social/biological stream that flows through time and space. In a single lifetime the most powerful force is survival. In this mode of description this creates a purpose, a telos, for that life, one for survival through adaptation and evolution. Since the primary source of our motivation is the genetically programmed fear for survival, the first one being physical survival, it begins when we are very young. The rudimentary features of being social (socialization), like those of language, are likely genetically programmed. These rudimentary features emerge and are quickly added to by social behaviors we learn. All with the purpose very early on that we can minimize our fears by fulfilling our needs. Then we survive. Initially this is simply physical survival. The feeling of fear-based needs and the behavior strategies aimed to fulfill them continue to develop and are at their greatest intensity during our growing years. As we become adults the survival fears appear to subside from consciousness, but by that time the repetitive cycles of behavior, the strategies that fear helped create are well set-in place and on their way perpetuating themselves largely in the absence of the original survival fear stimulus. The cycles have taken-on a life of their own within the short span of our young adult life.

After food, shelter and safety, as per Maslow's Hierarchy, survival requires belonging. The opposite side of the same coin is our fear of abandonment. Our need to belong is based in and synonymous with our fear of abandonment.

Maslow wrote about belonging needs as one single level together on the hierarchy triangle. I think its more detailed than that. The three social groups we need to belong to as Maslow described (family, our friends and the world) are important at different times in our development. They are each perceived to be relevant to the fulfillment of our belonging needs at distinct times during our development. At about age 8 the importance of our parents peaks, at about age 14 our peers, and about age 21 our communities/world. These are what I call "peak points" of need. Age 8, 14 and 21 approximately is when each distinct type of need to belong is at its crest in terms of intensity/importance and the accompanying chosen (based on biological and societal factors) behavior system at its most mature and sophisticated expression. As described later, these peak points become the choice points later in life Maslow referred to. He did not propose though, like I do that choice points are actually based on childhood need to belong; behavior choices that cycle back later in life.

Obviously the pattern of behaviors that fulfill our need to belong to our parents won't be the same as those for our peers. Then the pattern of behaviors that help us belong to our peers doesn't work to fulfill our community or world belonging need. We develop three separate patterns of belonging behavior. What happens to these patterns? Does one add to the other? Do the earlier ones disappear as they're replaced by older behavior as we get older?

No. Each behavior pattern stays with us. In fact, they cycle throughout our lives. They start and then act as a cyclic system as they move forward with us. They are self-organizing and reiterative/repetitive. We are stuck with them (their experience) and for many of us, stuck in them (in our identity), as I'll explain later. They cycle with different patterns and periodicity, but remain connected, to each other and to the other needs on the triangle. Like the rotation of the planets in our solar system they each have an independent periodicity but remain codependent on the place and periodicity of the other. Just like the codependent gravitational effects between the planets in our solar system. The behavior systems of belonging cycle back and each reach peak points throughout our lives that is dependent on the place of the other. The experience of the peak points are like the light metaphor. They can come at us gradually like a wave, as part of a life cycle, or suddenly, as a particle, with a spontaneous presentation. A pattern can unfold toward a peak point, or something can suddenly symbolize our peak point without an apparent connection to a wave. More on this later.

We learn our first understanding of belonging from our parents. We learn what fulfills our need for belonging and other needs by experimenting with a variety of behaviors, although some no doubt are preordained for acceptance in the biological-social connectedness between child and parent. Whereas it was historically described as a cycle of positive reinforcement between child and parent, as I'll explain further, it has more recently been described as a self-organizing dynamical system. Both are correct.

A variety of behaviors are necessary here because, even though belonging is need number one, we still have a variety of needs as per Maslow's Hierarchy. For instance, even at a very young age we, in fact, have spiritual needs and spiritual expression. Our spirituality it appears is innate (Hay & Nye,1998). We quickly learn that some behaviors work better than others. In our trial and error development we learn through reward, punishment, and cognition (thinking/reasoning/mental processing), to develop a spectrum of behaviors that work to satisfy our needs, the primary one at age 8 being our need to belong to our parents.

As I mentioned earlier in the book, humans are a very symbolic species. We used symbols well before we used language for communication during our evolution. We remain a very symbolic species today. As with our inability to control our development as kids, we also are unable to control and readily understand what things symbolize as kids. Again, symbols are genetically and socially co-constructed without our ability to choose consciously. So our interpretation of symbols is largely preordained, yet we still have to learn to understand them and how to use them. We try to make meaning of things, to understand them, because to understand is to be less fearful (conquer mentally through dissection and/or construction of meaning). We put symbols together as stories throughout our lives, often not being totally aware of it even as adults. The fairy tales and fantasy of the child becomes the creative imagination and the "jump to conclusion" of the adult. Many of the stories have recurrent themes. In fact, as I'll mention later, there are only so many themes. West Side Story and Hamlet is an obvious example.

Carl Jung suggested that the first understanding of belonging, the one associated with our parents, is the one that creates our symbol and story of the male-female relation dynamic. Its symbolic meaning, set-up when we are 8 years old, generates how we behave in our intimate relationships throughout our lives. Not surprisingly then the expression, "Many men marry their mothers". For an interesting read on this see John A. Sanford's *The Invisible Partners*.

Of course nobody has figured out yet how to always belong all of the time. So we are constantly unfulfilled. That can create other effects such as feelings of inadequacy and self-esteem issues. However, most of us find our 60% composite average of behaviors that keep us belonging most of the time. Yet, its only 60%. Not 100%. (I say 60 here but I'm sure it varies, the point is its not 100% and its likely an average bell curve type scenario). So this creates a tension as a kid and it goes on as a tension through our adulthood.

How much tension? A lot. First, from the reality of only a 60% fulfillment of the single belonging need. Then tension from the mere fact of having to juggle all the required needs at 60%, even though belonging to mom and dad is the big one. Then tension from the constant re-shuffling required to manage the priority of needs within certain contexts to get the maximum fulfillment in the various scenarios. And you're only 8!

This tension moves on with us into adulthood. It could be given the name of suffering. We experience suffering when we cannot find completion, the complete fulfillment of our needs externally. Maybe we can for a while, some are lucky enough for a long while, but invariably, the fun is over, the thrill is gone and we're back to suffering. Why does this happen? First, because we have moved-on, grown-up a bit, and psychologically developed enough to not need the thrill anymore. Secondly, we still have all our other needs, they were always there but the thrill thing was a diversion, a distraction away from them. Now "they're back". They were never gone. Each step of psychological maturation, each step toward self-actualization, reduces our human suffering. That is why you can call the process to self-actualization an empowering one.

So, by the time we are 8 years old we have developed a repetitive survival system based in our fear of abandonment/need to belong around our parents. In this sense these systems are learned/innate games of manipulation we play to survive. They are the basis of the games most of us play for the rest of our lives. The system for belonging we arrive at by age 8 will soon be added to by two more main systems of belonging, that at age 14 and that at age 21. These three systems become the system of systems that primarily, at its most fundamental level, form the "I" of our identity. We find, form and maintain our identity in our belonging systems. They are each concerned with a different aspect of social belonging. Luckily, they retain their individuality somewhat and therefore are usually susceptible to delineation upon behavioral and psychological inspection, introspection and analysis.

The age 8 system appeases our need to belong to parents/family but, as I've mentioned, it also sets up the way we see our belonging in the partner/lover relationship dynamic. We choose our belonging to the masculine and feminine and that dynamic is based on how it is symbolized and enacted by our parents. Then we take that choice and the script connected to that choice into our intimate relationship dynamics later in life. A strict 8-year cycle, having an 8-year periodicity would imply that we would be confronted with the need to belong to a partner peak approximately every 8 years. If it were truly a cyclic process in isolation you would likely have the peak comeback at age 16, 24, 32, 40 and so on. These would be the ages you would be confronted with the same peak point (maximum point of need to belong to parents/intimate partner and maximum maturation of behavior system to get it fulfilled).

But of course its not that simple. Its not as predictable as the planets in our solar system. For one, as I've introduced and will describe further, the cycles organize with the properties of non-linear dynamical systems. Secondly, as I'll describe later, how you handle the peak point can change during life. The feature that remains consistent, however, is their recurrent nature. The systems cycle repeatedly throughout our lives making up the patterns in our lives.

In most cases the "belonging systems" are normal. Normal as defined by society, which in turn has been defined by human evolution: biological and social. In some cases though if the belonging need occurs within a dysfunctional environment, an asocial belonging system is set-up. For instance, if a child fears that her/his inadequacies will result in abandonment by parents (falls way below that theoretical 60%), for example based on repeated unsuccessful attempts to satisfy unrealistic or pathological demands, the failure can become internalized and become a life pattern (Kahn, 1989). The person grows-up and makes failure a habit. Failure is internalized in their identity. My point here is that we all internalize a habit, a pattern, a system around our belonging needs while we are growing-up that we consider to be part of our identity. We let these basic patterns, one main one that happened when we were only 8 years old, form who we are for the rest of our lives.

At the same time as we are learning what works and what doesn't with mom and dad we are developing our ego and expanding our consciousness. As our ego and consciousness expand during development we begin to see beyond our parents to the tribe. Our peers. This second peak for system formation is at about 14 years of age. By that time most of us in our socially sanctioned healthy development have set into place our self-organizing recursive survival systems with regard to our peers. In one way or another we have come to belong, to take our place within our peer group.

By the time our brains and bodies stop physically developing by age 21 we have acquired our third main pattern for belonging, that of our relation to our world. By 21 we have developed a recurrent self-organizing pattern with regard to our place in the world. Our identity, the self we "know" ourselves to be is the composite of our systems of belonging. With the ones peaking at 8, 14, and 20 being three of the main ones.

However, because we are too unaware of it and too unskilled through lack of early teaching, we can never truly get beyond our social belonging needs to that psychologically healthy experience of belonging to "self" that Maslow called self-actualization. That top goal of the pyramid that humans innately strive for but many never reach. By the time we are 21 we are so indoctrinated into the external/outside social systems that they form who we think we are. Consequently, many of us live on in tension, seemingly endlessly challenged by our repertoire of unfulfilled needs of belonging, but only knowing to look for their fulfillment externally. We go externally because for most of us that's all we know. The external has always defined us (although we may refuse to admit it), and it has always been the source for the fulfillment of our needs. for as long as we can remember. The need to self-actualize remains and also resurfaces. Some get so used to being what society prescribes that the person they think they are "told" to be becomes all they know.

Luckily (tongue in cheek), too, we have other people with their systems interacting with our systems creating what we call our societies. Some might believe that we choose our systems. I don't think so. Nature and nurture are based on subconscious self-organizing repetitive systems and these systems are everywhere. They are already in place before we are born. We choose neither our nature nor our nurture. We only want to survive. That is also not a choice. That drive forces us to step into the template set-out by our particular nature and nurture long before we are born.

At this point some of you who are still reading this book might be saying, "Wait a minute! I'm free to be who I want to be! I can chose who I want to be anytime!" The extent of your freedom is very limited in a few regards because in the end, you still want to survive. In fact, most of us want to do more than survive. We want to flourish; we need some help from the rest of society to do that. The moment we do, we fall into pre-set patterns of behavior. But are they predestined? Sure they are. They are systems that have been cycling through human societies since the very beginning.

What about small choices? Individual ones? You can choose to pick up a pencil, you can chose to put down this book (or throw it away). Small steps. Add a bunch of free choices together and you have random free will and a free life, right? Wrong. Map those "free" and "random" choices on a graph: you get the butterfly (One of the repeat graph patterns seen in self-organizing complex systems). More than that though, you are making choices based on your culture and society (nurture) and biology (nature). So even your choices in the moment are preordained and not truly free will in that sense.

Ok, so you get the free pencil move and book toss in the moment (maybe...although) but not how you move or toss them (that's cultural and biological) and not your life (that's a recurrent set of interwoven biological and social systems). Your life is a butterfly. Small linear moves of cause and effect are the fodder of great philosophical debate and rumination (also a recurrent system) about what's called free will, volition, intentionality and determinism. Go look that up. In the meantime let's assume that your actions—all of them—are based on systems that are connected to other systems that individually and collectively repeat, repeat, and repeat.

Based on our first 21 years of life we pretty much have, with some exceptions of course, the behavior system template set-up for the rest of our lives. Then all we do is repeat, repeat, repeat. Did I mention they're repetitive? All together, in society as one big connected network.

What is all this systems stuff? All human behavior and the way we develop them as kids have recently been shown to be based in a highly recurrent set of systems, which contain patterns that are the same (self-similar) that repeat over and over again. All of these systems of behavior are self-organizing, repetitive and most often occur completely automatic/subconscious (see for example Lewis, 2000; Lewis & Granic, 2000 for emotional development in childhood). That systems are self-organizing is a good thing, we don't want to have to try to keep track of everything going on.

Up until recently most scientists have been studying direct cause and effect relationships. A causes B, B can then react with C to cause D and so on. These are called linear systems. In many cases linear systems can be taken apart to examine the components and see how they work together. Lately, as I'll describe further, an increasing awareness has emerged that recognizes that many things, well, actually almost everything, organizes and behaves together in a non-linear fashion. While the A, B, and C's of linear systems are called the multiple variables in the system, the term "complex system" is used for non-linear systems with multiple variables. The majority of non-linear complex systems in nature, including everything human, are "dynamical systems". They are comprised of multiple interacting variables that together act in a non-linear fashion. Non-linear dynamical systems while they appear to be changing (and they change a lot) completely at random (no obvious "cause and effect" relationships like in linear systems) they are, in fact, highly organized and repetitive, and self-similar in how they repeat when you look at them from a new mathematical perspective. Like the "white noise" or "snow" on your T.V. that appears random and meaningless, when you take certain types of mathematical "filters" to the noise the self-similar pattern begins to emerge. (I secretly suspect that this was Carl Sagan's metaphor he used in his book *Contact*) Another example, as described by Carl Anderson at Harvard Medical School, is the "noise" of electrical impulses moving up the spinal cord during development, which were for a long time considered to be random events are actually highly ordered self-similar impulse patterns and may actually contain specific patterns that act as self-organizing developmental signals. That is a very new and very exciting proposal. Self-similar repetitive patterns have been found in an extremely wide variety of behaviors that were previously considered disordered and random: from our daily use of the Internet, our heart rhythms, our development, our rush-hour traffic and our language. Its like we've found an entire undiscovered reality to what it is to be human.

In my usage, something that affects something else creates a system. Systems describe movement and change. There are different ways to look at systems and different ways to describe them. Historically, in the pursuit of truth one mode of description has often competed against another in the sciences even though in many cases they were independently correct (For a discussion on this phenomenon see University of Amsterdam's Bram Bakker's excellent essay on the effect of the perspective of different modes and levels on the scientific explanation (Bakker & den

Dulk, 1999). This has forged different groups in science and society, especially with regard to the philosophy of what is "right and wrong" or the "best way" to look at something. No fault completely on the part of the scientists, its been difficult sometimes historically to maintain scientific rigor and accuracy, avoid conceptual confusion, conflation and homogenization, while at the same time allowing for the emergence and introduction of perhaps radical proposals, as well as novel speculation and ideas often from the periphery.

The current frontier of how systems that are multivariable (i.e. dynamical) and multidimensional (signals of space/time), that is, complex systems are connected and interact in "real life/time" is for me a very exciting one. Luckily, non-linear systems scientists from a necessary wide variety of disciplines are beginning to give us the big picture of how everything interacts, how things come about on a large scale: the scale of human biology, the scale of society, the scale of life and of living systems here on Earth all together. For instance, two current mechanisms of interactions are scaffolding of dynamical systems (from learning and language sciences) and system connectionism (from the neural sciences).

The exploration and study of the interaction between systems is a tricky business though. We are so trained in our social/biological thinking to think in terms of how things cause each other, especially when we start looking at how things interact on different levels. However, as Bram Bakker (Bakker & den Dulk, 1999) so cogently reminds us, interactions are just interactions, and that while the interaction of A and B may cause C in the mode of component observation, the linear system which contains A and B, but also C and D cannot be said to be caused by A causing B when in the mode of system observation and description. For instance, as Bram argues, while systems of atoms are obviously essential to life, life cannot be described in terms of atomic causality. Both modes are correct, atomic and life, they both describe a component of one reality, but neither one can be used to describe how it causes the other.

Similarly, in the mode of description of interactions of non-linear dynamical systems their interactions, say one level to the next, while they can be mapped cannot be used to describe causality of the system. In other words, while we can draw a map of a various interactions of dynamical systems on different scales it is incorrect to infer causality between the levels or from the environment between the different modes of description.

Interactions are systems. Systems are interactions. Sometimes those interactions are seen to "cause" something directly in the moment, sometimes something "emerges" spontaneously along the way unpredictably, sometimes something causes something further down to emerge and sometimes something further down causes something earlier on to emerge. (To mention just a few scenarios) "But then" you might ask, "doesn't everything effect and interact with everything else, ultimately?" Exactly. Everything is part of one system. That's difficult to conceptualize for some. For instance, some suggest that the human body can be seen as an autonomous self-organizing system, one that is self-contained, self-constrained, and perhaps most importantly, self-regenerated. The scientific term that has been used for this is that the human body is an autopoietic system. "Autopoiesis" is a term that was first used to describe the concept for biological self-organizing systems as a means to organism survival by the Chilean scientists the late Francisco Varela and his graduate student at the time Humberto Maturna (Maturna & Varela, 1980). The equivalent self-organizing, self-generating autopoietic systems view for social systems was first described by the late German sociologist Niklas Luhmann (see Herting & Stein, 2007). These two views consider biological organisms and societies as closed systems.

In a more expanded view, my co-member at Ecosphere Net (www.ecosphere.net) Beth Dempster (2000, 2002, 2004) has coined the term sympoietic to describe the interaction of biological systems with environmental systems, one which is actually quite co-dependent, interactive and occurs through open boundaries. This is an open system perspective. Which view is right? Autopoeitic or sympoietic? Both views are correct. They are just different views of the same system. However, as I'll describe further, to get the big picture of what is happening I generally apply the sympoietic view when considering human growth in relations to our interaction with the environment. Some choose to draw the boundary at the skin while others, myself included, choose to see that there is a boundary but that its very porous. Not that we humans are leaky; we are just influenced by and interacting with more than what's contained within our skin. My open system view of the human body and of human being includes the proposal that human psychological maturation (self-actualization, individuation) involves the interaction of self-organizing biological systems in the body and in the environment interwoven with self-organizing social systems that reside in both the constantly developing individual human psyche and the social systems of the external environment. The "oil" for this system of systems, in this mechanistic view, is the influence of language and linguistics. More on this later.

# Life Systems and the Stories We Make of Them

Back, for a moment, to the earlier discussion of symbolism and meaning making. One of the things I find really interesting is the relationship between systems and the stories we make of them. Systems are just systems. But throughout our history cultures have attached meaning to them. Joseph Campbell called this cultural mythology. Even individually we attach meaning to systems, or just take-on the meaning culturally prescribed. Often we accept the societal script attached to the system even without being aware (conscious) of it. For instance, our culture has identified six characters and their associated mythology: the orphan, the wanderer, the warrior, the altruist, the innocent, and the magician that we take on during the journey—the "hero's journey"—of our lives (Pearson, 1998). Thus, our characters in the play of our lives, on the stage of our lives, compliment each other. For instance, the hero and the villain story is replayed over and over again in our codependent relationships and, as I'll explain further, within the composite of narratives that make-up the individual self. I'm reminded of William Shakespeare's quote, "All the world's a stage and all the men and women merely players..." (From *As You Like It*).

Systems have no meaning. We make meaning of them. We make music and movies about the meaning. We make drama from them. Science tries to reveal them, for what they truly are. But we are of course much more than our inflammatory response or our DNA synthesis pathway. Maslow's description of self-actualization is one meaning to what happens in our life cycle. As is Jung's individuation and Rorty's individualization. The brilliant Joseph Campbell saw the system of life as a Hero's Journey. He characterized it with 10 stages that self-organize and cycle over and over again in our lives.

These are: 1. Separation (from the known); 2. The Call; 3. The Threshold (with guardians, helpers, and mentors); 4. Initiation and Transformation; 5. The Challenges; 6. The Abyss; 7. The Transformation; 8. The Revelation; 9. The Atonement; and 10. The Return (to the known world +/- a gift for the unknowing (adapted from J. Campbell, *The Hero's Journey*).

---

### Ten Stages of the Hero's Journey

1. Separation (from the known).

2. The Call.

3. The Threshold (with guardians, helpers, etc.).

4. Initiation and Transformation.

5. The Challenges.

6. The Abyss.

7. The Transformation.

8. The Revelation.

9. The Atonement.

10. The Return (to the known world +/- a gift).

---

Knowing these stages and understanding them creates a powerful opportunity to engage life in a healthier manner.

Whether you call it self-actualization or the hero's journey it contains a series of cyclic processes. Each cycle, as I have described, brings around peak points for "processing". Again, a system is just a system, it doesn't care if you process and its purpose is not for you to do that. If you choose to not process at the peak points (we all do invariably to some degree) it will cycle back eventually and show-up again. Repeat, repeat, repeat. Within a lifespan you may go on many hero journeys or just one.

Maslow's self-actualization process, however, is more linear, with a self-actualized person being the end point for self-actualization but certainly not the end-point for personal development. So, once again, you have systems within systems, connectionism between different levels of personal growth. There can be major cycles and minor cycles.

What does any of this have to do with sustainability? Lots. For one, we have to begin to realize most of us are living our lives based in behavior patterns/cycles without being aware of them. Secondly, these cycles are based in fear-based patterns that do not help create a sustainable world. Ironically though, we hold on tight to our systems of behavior even though many of us recognize that there are better ways of being. Better ways to keep our "self" sustainable. Perhaps its easier to be with the devil we know and than the devil we don't know.

I have just described how three major patterns, systems, of behavior develop during our first 21 years. This is a common template, but certainly not the only one. While its three peak forms are very resilient, how its forged by the time we are 21 is malleable to some degree. Nevertheless, there are only so many patterns that will work to find the social belonging we so desperately need for our very survival, as far as we're concerned, during our development. This scenario can, however, be modified to a large degree by trauma, as in the unexpected loss of a parent during childhood, for example. The three main life cycles remain intact, they are just modified by the experience of trauma. For instance, in my case, I lost my mother to suicide when I was eleven and my father who, in shock, walked-out on my sister and I on the same day. One result of this was, because it happened between the two peaks of 8 and 14, my sense of belonging to the intimate partner relationship dynamic was affected, as was the relationship dynamic to my peer group. Some might even say that this book is evidence that the belonging system that peaks further away as a 21 year-old, my relationship to the world was also affected. This is true perhaps. I have certainly had to be sustainability. Prior to the work I have done on myself to recognize, correct and shift the patterns to healthy self-actualization over the last 10 years, I originally took-on what may be called unhealthy patterns of the "*I Am Sustainability*" identity system.

The need to belong behavior cycles can be identified by their narratives. One way to look at how narratives play their roll in your life is to consider how it would sound if you were to describe it as a story giving each person in the relationship dynamic a different role. Each one of the cycles has a main narrative, a voice, a main character, and a general schema. As I've mentioned, if we portray each cycle as a story we could ascribe a title to your roll in it like "The Hero's Journey as a Sage" or "The Grand Wizard in the Hero's Journey", and so on as originally described by Joseph Campbell, Carl Jung, James Hillman and Anthony Stevens. As will be described in the *I Am Sustainability* program getting to know your narratives and their characters is an important step in understanding yourself.

Alan Combs (2006) has recently revitalized the term "heterarchy", to review human value and motivational systems from a self-organizing dynamical system/complexity science perspective. He argues, and I agree, that human behavior is difficult, if not impossible to completely predict from a linear hierarchy such as Maslow's Hierarchy of Needs. He asserts that if we view value based behavior as a complex system its more of a heterarchy, and any hope of predictability ought to be patterned as a nonlinear complex system as opposed to a direct, linear hierarchy. It remains, nonetheless, a pattern that is repetitive and self-organizing. A chaotic pattern, to be sure, but nevertheless, one that repeats in a self-similar fashion. As I assert, recognizing and understanding them is the first step to changing them in the moment. We may not be able to predict them easily, as Comb's suggests, but by knowing our self, our patterns etc., we may be able to see them coming and shift them to act on them differently. More importantly, we can learn our patterns, become pattern recognizers of our lives and through that understanding not react to them, but act on them differently in the moment. With practice we'll get to know our patterns; through knowing our "self's" we can become pattern recognizers. We don't necessarily have to be pattern predictors to be successful in shifting our behavior.

The notion of a heterarchy also speaks to my assertion that each level of the hierarchy of needs described by Maslow occurs concurrently. Thus, as will be discussed below, we may partially fulfill different needs at the same time, utilizing the same action.

As mentioned, the notion of self-organizing systems in human behavior is not a new one. Its based, in part, on the work currently being done in a discipline called complexity science. What is important here is that complexity science indicates that our patterns of behavior are deeply rooted in systems that are subconscious, both biological and social, and initially forged as our identity when we are young and then reiterated through life. There is a profound interaction between our thinking and emotions that occurs below the radar (our awareness) automatically all the time throughout our lives. This, in my view, lends credence and support to the practice of depth psychology as a means of understanding and transforming human behavior and attitudes.

Psychotherapy called cognitive behavior therapy (CBT) coupled with an analytical component has become popular most recently. This type of psychotherapeutic behavior modification stresses our ability to mentally get over our unhealthy patterns and implement healthy new ones through learning and practice. Depth psychology does that as well, but it adds the exploration and analysis of what is called a dynamic subconscious to the learning process. Science indicates that our emotions and thinking are largely bound together. For instance, we think thoughts and they give us feelings, or we have feelings and they have thoughts attached to them. So its not simply a matter of changing our thinking that will change our behavior, although that can work, and does work in some cases, but invariably in some form or another the emotions connected to that thought system need to be processed with the thoughts.

Similarly, how much can science really discover and describe about what it is to be human? We cannot talk always about what it is to be human based on a biomedical model that works largely or on an evidence basis. We will never scientifically know everything about how humans work biologically, socially, psychologically and spiritually or how theses factors interact to create what it is to be human. Therefore, understanding human behavior remains, in part, maybe a large part, an ephemeral qualitative description as related to us by the personalities in the social sciences, humanities and arts and the cultural bias' inherent to them.

With regard to the need to belong it is the qualitative aspect of social events, the individual emotional quality of experience, that are primarily contributory to the system of behavior developed during our development. It is the *feeling* of the experience of belonging that fulfills, not the quantity. Satiation cannot be truly measured; although some are trying, quality of life cannot truly only be measured quantitatively.

Imagine, "That meal was an 8 out of 10 and my quality of life today is at 9.5!" "Wow, mine too, but wait, how do you define your satiation and quality of life??" Meanwhile at the folk psychologists doorway, "I really had a great time with you today; great food, great company" "Ya, me too, want to come up for a glass of wine?" Hey, who's having more fun? Most importantly, who is closer to human reality?

The scientific research in clinical psychology in collaboration with medical research may be able to identify factors and co-factors in human behavior, but it will never get to the whole picture. Thus, some behavior modification will have to come through a social, subjective, unscientific, folk-psychological pathway. While its true, this lends the way to charlatans and therapists in denial, some of which I have met, but it is likely the best we will ever be able to achieve. So let's work with it constructively. This book is about that.

# Life Systems for Self-actualization

So far I have discussed how systems of behavior develop when we are biologically and socially developing as children and young adults. These systems are self-organizing with their biological and societal factors well in place before we are born. I have mentioned three common cycles that can be identified with regard to fear and abandonment. The experience of the need to belong to external social groups peaks at about age 8, 14 and 21 as does the maturity of the behavior systems used to attempt too fulfill them. These ages of course represent child, adolescent and adult. These social belonging needs, their associated fears and their fear-based behaviors are highly reinforced socially, more so than other fear-based needs, such as spiritual needs. We still have the spiritual needs, such as the need for ritual, but they too are often connected to and overshadowed by our need to belong to groups externally.

The particle and wave metaphor can be used to describe the human behavior systems generated by our need to belong. The event(s) that originally generated our behavior (at the peak point) can be seen as the particle while the wave represents the course (space/time) that it takes to return back repeatedly into our lives. With regard to the particle, something in our adult lives can trigger, through its symbolism, the experience of conflict with regard to our belonging need once again, one that mirrors the belonging conflicts at age 8, 14 and 21. Like a post traumatic stress episode, wham, its in our face again. The particle/peak point is usually a stressful event with a high emotional and cognitive salience, therefore the comparison to posttraumatic stress. The wave description implies the temporal nature of the systems. The wave is a different mode of metaphoric description than that of the particle. It describes how the conflict episodes (particle) from each stage of childhood development, while part of the bigger cycles of our lives, can be re-experienced as a distinct event against the others as it cycles back into our lives. The wave continues on and on as a cycle generating the repeat experience of the peak point (the particle in this metaphor). Understanding the details of the wave and the particle aspects of behavior on an individual and personal basis provides the opportunity for psychological completion and closure.

Each repeat of the cycle as we get older is actually an opportunity to deal with what set-up the cycle in the first place. "Deal with" means understanding it as a pattern, knowing how it evokes certain behaviors in us, the emotions and thoughts, and trying to consciously behave in a healthier manner. Not to resist the emotion behind the behavior, in fact its important to engage it, but to play it out on your life's stage in a healthier manner.

All cycles have a movement to them, a journey, as the cycle returns with the peak point, this in psychological terms can put you into some level of crisis and process. The crisis is the same you had as a kid and the process you undergo to handle it as an adult is your opportunity to grow-up out of that experience. In general life terms, just as you attached the meaning to the systems as a child, adolescent and young adult and they in that act became laden with emotion, you have continuously been in the process, after age 21, of dealing with the balancing of these emotions. "The process" refers to the action of understanding and extinguishing the emotionally laden meaning of each of the cycles as they come around back into your life. It's a process going on for the most part without your awareness. The systems started when you were a kid without your awareness and they continue, for the most part, in your adulthood without your awareness. That's why so few people actually evolve out of them. They are always in "recycle" because we learn so little, if anything, each time around.

Each of the smaller cycles as they provide peak points within our life actually provide an opportunity to get back and internalize an aspect of our "self". This is done by reconciling with our fears around the original need to belong reified during childhood. The cycling gives us the chance for self-reunification, a chance to move psychologically toward self-actualization and individuation. What I am saying here is that just as the abandonment fears/need to belong systems are set-up in the DNA we are going to inherit from our parents and our society/culture before we are born, so too is the process of self-actualization. But, unlike the belonging systems which are set-up for us when we are developing as kids without our input, we very much have the ability to have input, to become involved with our cycles the second, third, forth time they come around later in our lives. This is being involved, engaged in your process of self-actualization. The problem is that by the time we are adults we think our behavior is our identity. Yet it was set-up based in fear and need to belong when we were kids.

Self-actualization tries to happen as part of the blueprint of life. Most of us just don't engage it. But if it is happening anyway, why not just do it as consciously as possible? Rather than just being a passenger on the emotional roller-coaster experiences of our processes. If we can become actively, consciously, involved we can make a huge positive difference; for ourselves, those we love, and the world around us.

These are the "choice points" I believe Maslow wrote about over 35 years ago in his description of the process of self-actualization (Maslow, 1971, p.45). As the systems, with their peak points, cycle back into our life they provide challenges—opportunities really—for us to extend ourselves beyond the current way we are (which is the way we decided to be as kids), the way we see ourselves and reach out to our full human potential. We can do this by making healthy choices. The *I Am Sustainability* program shows you how.

Cycles occur during relationships, between and within the two people in the relationship. Any number of cycles/processes may be activated by the relationship partner, but its usually focused on the dynamic you experienced around your parents and the place you chose within it. In fact, you chose that partner in the first place because of their symbolism, not just because they look good in a pair of jeans. They evoke the emotional "peak point" through their symbolism. We have to choose how to react to that peak. The choice-point. We have a chance to move toward completion. Each relationship we participate in has the potential to give us back a part of our self. To give us an aspect of our "self" that was covered over by the overwhelming need to belong as a kid. That is why, especially in the case of intimate relationships, we often cannot, even if we want to, go back to an old relationship because once we have gained as much of our "self" back as a relationship has to offer, we have grown and in many cases out-grown the need for relationship. Often partners move along toward self-actualization at different speeds within the relationship. You may not be dependent on them for growth but they still maybe on you for theirs. This difference can be difficult to deal with for both.

This is also why the end of a relationship can be very quick sometimes; precipitous in its ending. The lesson is learned, the "lost" aspect (system) of self retrieved, the need for the relationship gone. The drive behind the need for relationships is, in part, the subconscious need for self-actualization. The drive behind the need for a relationship is often because of the symbolism of a person or of a relationship, not that person or relationship *per se*. The true origin of these drives, because of their subconscious location, is often initially confused with love. Big red flag signals for a "wait a minute!" is when your view of another person enters emotional extremism. You view your partner as, "the best ever" and the "only one", +/- who has ever truly understood/loved/seen into me, and who I will have to be with forever/marry now/be careful not to lose.

That may sound cold or cruel, but that is in essence what is happening in our relationships. We have made our behavior systems co-dependent because we only had the ability early on as kids to fulfill our belonging externally. So we depend on external players to collaborate with us. These systems cycle, as they do the need returns, and off we go looking externally to fulfill it. Somebody else, also going external, has the same need in the opposite complimentary sense. Throw in some tight jeans, and whamo, you've found the one!

We move that balance internally, every time we grow through our relationships. In "the end" your partner no longer needs to complete you, you complete your self. Now you can have relationships, characterized by healthy dynamics. The same dynamics you have in your self. You can only give what you have. This will not appeal to everyone because many people are stuck in co-dependencies. All fear-based. For global sustainability, however, we need to shift that to healthy non-fear-based.

Please also note that this does not mean that you do not love a person in these co-dependent relationships. There is love, both sides. Just like the light metaphor at the beginning of this book there can be two things, particle and wave, in something that looks like light. In fact, without each of the two, you can't have light. Similarly, there is both love and cycle/process in co-dependent relationships.

Interwoven social systems in our relationships are common to every person on the planet. It's the way its been going on for millions of years. We each play a part. The costumes may have changed, the scripts and language altered, and the cultural meaning varied. The systems and the meaning we make of them have, however, to a large degree remained the same. So to change, we all have to play a part as well. We will still have societies in which each person plays a part, there will still be functional economic and intellectual co-dependencies, for example, but the psychological co-dependencies will be greatly reduced.

Some people might worry that so much focus on the self may be narcissistic. It is possible to be self-oriented and self-directed without being narcissistic. Its possible to love oneself deeply, while, if one so decides, at the same time to still authentically love and believe in a God. Whether you believe your soul is from God or the transcendent aspect of your being that is up to you. Its not what you or I believe that is important, its what you do and I do with those beliefs, how we engage them into behavior that is important.

That word narcissism is Greek and means "self-love". It doesn't mean "self-love only". Who put the "only" connotation there? I've always believed that I have to truly love my self before I can truly love another. Otherwise I love the other for what I am missing in the love for my self. Said differently, I can only give another what I have myself first. I can only give what I have. Maslow and many others have agreed with this notion. Maslow, and the humanistic movement of which he was a part, has been criticized for having the focus too much on the human condition. But it is the human condition that is destroying the environment. We have to get our own internal environment healthy before we can get the external environment healthy. We can only give what we have.

For instance, why are some environmental activists so militant, so angry? They are angry because they are not yet truly engaged consciously in their process of self-actualization. That is, they are in their process and without being aware of it and responsible they are letting it control their behavior. Only they see their behavior as being passionate to a cause. But their action is really a reaction to what the situation means to them as a symbol. They are self-actualizing but they are unaware of the process, and are using the environmental crises as a vehicle to connect with their emotionally laden peak points. They are reacting to the environmental crisis as they were to the abandonment crisis they experienced as children. That, too, is a large part of what forms the basis of any extremism, whether that is suicide in a cult or suicide for a religious cause its all fear of abandonment from the group or fear of some other attachment loss. These are all merely meaning making events of systems. Systems do not inherently have meaning.

By the way, do not confuse meaning with outcome or consequences. Systems do have outcome. They move (flow) toward some point and in so doing there are outcomes. For instance, weather systems meet and create rain. However, the goat that was sacrificed to bring the rain is a meaning and consequence we attached to it. So too, as I'll describe further, a person self-actualizing in sustainability through the *I Am Sustainability* program becomes a system pattern recognizer and they retain and expand their ability to understand meanings made of systems, but they no longer attach meaning to them nor are they controlled behaviorally by that meaning.

The meaning we attach to systems begins so early, so surreptitiously when we are young and is so successfully supported by our external social environment, the one we seek belonging/identity in as kids that after a while the behavior and emotionally laden meaning belief system is just on auto-pilot.

While Malsow (1971) argued that the self-actualized person is a person who is self-determined, self-organized (he did not mean in the dynamical complex system sense), and self-directed he also considered them to be a more transpersonal individual, a person whose identity extends beyond their self, and is invariably committed to some cause external to their self. There is a concurrent self and selflessness. For instance, with regard to the humanistic psychological tradition (of which he was a leader) and psychological maturation, he wrote, "I consider Humanistic, the Third Force Psychology to be a transitional, a preparation for a still "higher" Fourth Psychology, transpersonal, transhuman, centered in the cosmos [the universe] rather than in human needs and interest, going beyond humanness, identity, self-actualization and the like." (Maslow, 1968, p iii-iv) In fact Maslow (1971) distinguished between self-actualized transcenders and non-transcenders, with the transcenders being more spiritual and self-transcendent. Consequently, Maslow speculated that because of their relatively expanded vision and insight the transcenders would be less happy in life. I suspect that in this sense he was mistaken. Being unhappy is not per se a bad thing. However, being unhappy to the extent where that unhappiness prevails in your daily life would suggest to me that the person had not reached full psychological health. It suggests personal stories of drama, victimhood, and suffering. If internal belonging needs/behaviors are in balance with external belonging needs/behaviors, if the 50/50 balance has been achieved through self-actualization and the associated psychological health attained there through, then, happiness would not be contingent on a non-variance between an individual's insight and vision (internal) and the external reality she/he perceived. Indeed, any emotionally laden story of what "should be" versus what is would indicate a story and an attachment to a cultural and/or personal mythology. In the 50/50 balance stories occur, are understood but are not reacted to. Quality of life while still of course contingent on external factors can, in the "normal" course of life be re-generated in the moment in the form of possibilities.

Unhappiness is experienced but not entirely life controlling. More on this later.

The point here, though, is that you get through to selflessness by going through a reification process of the self first. You get the "I" before the "We". You go through the "I" to get to the "We". Importantly, "reification" is more than an affirmation, its creating an autonomous self that is clearly self-defined and sustainable. You have self-actualized your ability to survive, your sustainability. It has to be a sure thing, a true self, a "this is me, and I belong here first and always" because only then can we have the courage to go forward as a healthy person, in a society and world that is currently not all that healthy. This is not a narcissistic precursor, or prerequisite "selfish" phase, in fact quiet the contrary. As described in the I Am Sustainability program it only involves shifting the fulfillment of belonging needs from the external to the internal. Not completely, just into balance, where what comes in and how needs are fulfilled is judged by the need to belong to self and to the group. In so doing the self is reified and empowered. Its through the empowerment that the self will extend beyond itself again, but this time with courage like never before and do so selflessly from a healthy ego stance as opposed to from one of sacrifice, martyrdom, suffering or unhealthy ego.

The balanced self-actualized person engages life from the place of a healthy ego, enacting what I term their "authentic self". (Although there is the word "act" in enacting, it's the least acting you have ever done.) "Balanced" here refers to the reality that we are always going to have part of our belonging needs fulfilled from external sources, even as self-actualized in sustainability. Those sources will shift, however, from fear-based dramatic co-dependencies of manipulation, entanglement, and enmeshment to healthy interactions and relationships.

As I've also mentioned, life is comprised of unstoppable systems. We can learn much from them, but we can never leave them. The best thing we can hope to do is to switch from one to another. I have also mentioned that the periodicity of systems, as they cycle, enacts what can be seen as a psycho-spiritual maturation process. "Process" here is another system. It refers to a "working through", mentally and emotionally of something that comes-up in a relationship that bugs you. (I focus on the negative processes here, but there are also ones we make to mean "positive" or "good" or "right".) It keys off something that you've felt or thought of or experienced before. This process has an automatic, self-organizing, recursive mechanism. It goes on and repeats without your awareness. That's why sometime you get the "ah ha! Not this again!" The recursiveness is just a feature of systems. It has no inherent meaning or intentionality. Its just a system. We make meaning of systems and in so doing attach our emotions. As the cycles cycle, the attached meanings and their emotions show-up again and again. Each time they do we can reconcile the meaning(s) we made which were based in fear. They come around and we can have a look at them, try to figure out what the story is, or we can just go back to the bar and have another martini. But they'll be back. In getting them we do not become fearless, we only gain more understanding. But in that understanding we gain power over our lives and ourselves. We stop being a total passenger.

I've mentioned the term "narratives" a few times in this chapter and previously. I just want to further explain what that means in itself and in relation to sustainability. Each one of us has a voice we hear inside our selves. They are of course our thoughts. For instance, "I better pick-up some milk on the way home". When you consider them together, however, our inner thoughts can also be discovered to narrate the various stories we have about people and things. Such as, "I wish I was able to go on vacation more like Bob does, when you're a manager you get all the breaks". These various narratives and the stories they support can be seen/heard/experienced independently. Sometimes you hear other types of opinion-like narratives and, if you check-in even further, you'll get that they say things about your feelings toward relationships, like "I hate it when my wife leaves the car without gas every time she uses it, she is always so absent-minded, without me things would be so disorganized" This is of course a lot different than the mental reminder about getting milk on the way home. The key distinction is the judgment(s) of other people and events in the car/gas narrative as compared to the functional nature of the milk narrative. It's the judgment narrative and its attached emotions that contain the clue to a personal story around belonging that started when you were a kid. As I'll describe, it is our stories from childhood, as manifest in our over-consumption that are in conflict with global sustainability.

The judgment narratives are like the wave in the light metaphor in that they move in and out, like waves in our lives and manifest in our attitudes, our moods and our behaviors. They are the drama story, the story of suffering, the story of the hero, etc. Our narratives manifest in behaviors such as in our competitiveness, manipulation, rivalry, our lies, our greed, our rituals, etc. Not all of them are "bad" per se. For instance, healthy competition can be psychologically healthy. The experience of rivalry can be a vehicle toward psychological health. In general terms though we are not aware of our stories, so that while they may, even with our passive passenger-like non-attendance to them, gradually help us arrive at a place of psychologically healthy self-actualization, most often they simply frame a life span with a set of belonging behavior systems inherited during childhood and young adulthood. As my adolescent daughter might say, "Dad, everyone is so retro".

It might appear that a common narrative that emerges in adulthood is an increased question about existence. The narrative becomes, "what is the meaning of my life and life in general? What is it all about? Where do I belong in the grand scheme of things". The individual ego once again, as in childhood is seeking belonging and, as before, will do so in external objects or experiences. Ultimately, therefore, a need to belong while perhaps in a somewhat revised narrative emerges, one from an adult perspective, it is really a childhood question from childhood. It's a question of survival again.

We can use our narratives to understand our personal life stories. Our stories are based on judgment because we have created them to survive. We develop the lifelong basis for our stories as kids in our need to belong. They describe our personal schemes, or schemata, that constitute our survival strategies, which, in turn forge our belief systems. However, our belief systems are actually based in our personal and cultural mythologies. Through the last 200,000 years of human history some stories have served us better than others to help us survive. We have shared our stories to create communities and societies. These stories and their narratives, as I've mentioned, are really just meaning made of systems.

One of the reasons we are often unhappy is because our stories (based in our need to belong), as I've mentioned previously often remain unfulfilled. We are disappointed when the story doesn't or hasn't played-out the way we need. In other words we have emotional attachments to specific outcomes. Disappointment comes when you live in expectations built-into your story as narrated by personal narratives. While we all get disappointed once in a while, there appears to be a pandemic of unhappiness. We all want/need more belonging. One solution, as described in the *I Am Sustainability* program, is to learn to live in a place of possibility. The way to do that is to understand and process your stories. That may sound psychotherapeutic, and it is, but many believe, myself included, in a psychotherapeutic stance in education. If you look at it, education is psychotherapeutic to a large degree anyway. Education like psychotherapy teaches us about something or other about ourselves and helps change our behavior and attitudes. In fact, I could argue that everything we learn in life in way or another, like psychotherapy, has the potential and often does so inadvertently to teach us something about our selves (our "selfs" really). Why not engage it then to maximize its potential?

Of course, too, no one person can play the part, or be the part of every character of a story at one time. Plus, as I've also mentioned, we discover very early on which characters work and which don't, that is, what we are biologically and socially most adept at to achieve that ephemeral experience of belonging. Yet, all those other possibilities exist. All those other characters. They are out there, flagrantly and subtly, as friends and associates, on T.V. As I mentioned previously, we are never fully fulfilled in our need to belong and in our hierarchy of needs, which we seek to fulfill in the external world. That continues on into adulthood and through life. We are constantly searching for something. But what? Are we searching for the meaning of life? Yes, but deeper than that, we are searching for our belonging to the grand scheme (story) of all things. Our place in the universe and its story; whatever that might be. That too, by the way, is the basis of our need for spirituality. It addresses the "whatever that might be" question of what the story of the universe is and what our place in it is. Once again, if we are able to find a universe story, say in a particular form of spirituality for instance, a mythology, we choose it because we find belonging in it. The Austrian psychiatrist and founder of existential analysis Viktor Frankl thought human life contained an inherent inner search for meaning. While I agree with this, I think that the search for meaning is at its foundation really a search for belonging. We try to find meaning so that we can judge it to find out if we can or do belong. Whatever the story we make the system mean, whatever we make of the grand scheme of things, our story of the universe, we need to belong. Our need to belong is supreme because it is what has helped us survive through the millennia as humans and in our individual lives as well.

As kids we sought belonging for our physical and social survival, gaining it in the external social world. For self-preservation, we sought belonging amongst our various relationships within our communities, thereby creating our identity based in our co-perceived place in those communities. Self-preservation led to self/identity-formation. However, and very importantly, for the rest of our lives we are in a battle to defend that identity because we believe it to be the person we actually are. We are "stuck" there, "fixed" in that system, although it is entirely formed from fear-based belonging needs and often includes unhealthy behaviors like overconsumption. Once our identity is formed, we spend the rest of our lives defending our self against the very societies and cultures that helped create them. A psychological tension between individualism (self) and collectivism (other) gradually emerges in us at each stage of identity formation. While we go external for the fulfillment for our need to belong, once its formed, the systems of our belonging need based identity; we spend a most of our life's time defending our choices, even though that occurred when we were too young to know we were making those choices. Even when we later perceive our original choices to be wrong, they are easier, in many cases to stay with (or so we perceive) than the accommodation of other new belonging behavior scenarios. Psychology has shown people like to stick with their original choices even when they know that they were wrong ones.

Now, our individuality is largely socially constructed, so its not like you have an authentic individuality in terms of individuation. Its more like the individualization, the battle for autonomy that Richard Rorty wrote about. But what are we really up to? What are we really trying to do in our Rorty individualization? What is our struggle for autonomy really about? What is the basis for our rage against the machine? That rebellion of self vs. society? We are looking to become whole and complete, to belong to and with all characters of all the stories, to belong in the universe, to not be afraid and, at the same time to be able to be recognized as an independent significant person, a unique and relevant individual self. At the risk of sounding flaky, we want to be a recognizable star amongst all the stars. We need to be a star and we want others to be stars too: so that we can fully belong. Thus, its not only about our innate altruism why we are kind. Altruism has survival value. We need to belong to a perceived equivalent "I" and a "We" concurrently. Thus, at our core, we actually all want things to workout for everyone, with no one left behind so that we can... you guessed it, belong.

Rorty's individualization is the process of "going external" for that, while Jung's individuation and Maslow's self-actualization is the "going internal" for that belonging. The first, which is the system we adopted in childhood leads to an individual unfilled feeling of despair and anger (that rage against the machine) as well as, in very real terms, our collective unsustainability. The second, while certainly not an easy system, has the best chance (yes, there's scientific proof) of developing a psychologically healthy individual balanced between belonging to self and belonging to society. When considering the first, the nonfulfillment of going external, I'm reminded of the quote by Henry David Thoreau, "Most men [and women] lead lives of quiet desperation and go to the grave with the song still in them". Its is the second going internal route, is the basis of the *I Am Sustainability* program of this book and that being developed through Ecosphere Net.

The phenomenon of multiple selves has been described, for example, by Martha Stout (2002) and Valerie Gray-Hardcastle (1999). The concept of narratives has a long history but has been extensively described by Hubert Hermans recently (for example see Hermans 2002, 2004; Salgado & Hermans, 2005) as the dialogical self.

# The Multiplicity of Self

Looking around we can see that fear is a business. Some might say its good for business. To shift to a more sustainable planet we'll have to shift our business practices. Consumers will still need to consume, but what and how they do will shift. It appears that many corporations fear that shift. For instance, in a recent *Newsweek Magazine* article Sharon Begley (2007) reported that petroleum giant Exxon is paying scientists $10,000 to write articles that question the threat of global warming.

Fear in business—as in our societies—still prevails, perhaps more than ever and very surreptitiously much of the time. Leaders have learned to lead by it and followers have learned to follow by it. Our social, cultural and educational institutions all support our fear systems.

Fear is out of balance. It is our greatest threat to global sustainability. Its time to change that. This begins with a deeper understanding of what we are all so afraid of. Yes, its fear for survival, but survival of what?

It is, at its root, survival of the self. Self-preservation. There are plenty of books and literature out there that will tell you that there is no such thing as "the self" or "a self". I'm about to tell you that there is a bunch of them and they're all inside of you.

In this book the term "self" represents the self in all its dimensions. Physical, social, mental, and spiritual. Some argue that the self is entirely socially constructed (Gergen, 1992). This group, called social constructionists, negate the first person self and suggest that, "all knowledge-claims concerning the subjects expression of the 'meaning' of self must be grounded in the institutional or social contexts of discursive negotiations" (Gergen, 1992, p. 22). However, others argue that the first-person private self is not *entirely* a social construction (Wong, 1999; Martin, 2005) and that indeed, society itself has historically recognized such autonomy based on the "separateness and inviolability" of the human body (Hunt, 2004). In his argument Wong (1999) points to the phenomenon of psychological transformation with regard to first person meaning change as an example of a private self experience and process that is independent of social performances, presentation and criteria. Wong (1999, p. 74) argues that "social constructionism lacks a convincing model to account for how a *conceptually different* psychological individual can be produced from a group of homogenous social actors."

For those interested in going deeper with this, also relevant here is the book by Steven Pinker *The Blank Slate: The Modern Denial of Human Nature*. As I've mentioned in this book dividing the self, or humans into nature and nurture, biology and psychology, is really a false dichotomy. A false separation.

Your identity, the person you are all together, your "self" is actually a composite. Your personality, which is your behaviors and attitudes, is synonymous to the word identity here. All humans have multiple dimensions, facets, or aspects to their identity. Multiple "selfs" make up your identity. Each self has a narrative that has needs and wants. It has its own identity. Although these multiple selfs result in multiple narratives, through a process called "narrative coherence", the multiplicity seems like one self, and thereby most people manage the multiplicity quiet well.

The 60% point we are as I'll describe later is not who we really are. Not that we're faking it. The 60% seems like its who we really are. It fits so tight that its like our skin and therefore who we are, but its not. It's the fear-based externally driven need to belong identity. "Authentic" only in the sense of who we are being in the here and now. Functional. Helps us to survive by fulfilling our needs. But many of us, if you look around, are not happy. Why not? I try to explain "why not" in the rest of this book.

If you like puzzles or mystery novel "who dunnits" you can begin to understand yourself better by listening to the various voices and assigning names or characters to them. They have wants and needs, and they have a characteristic age. Yes, age. In the sense they are either the 8, 14 or 21 year old. They may not be exactly those ages, but it'll be close. If like me, you have had trauma as a kid, their voice will be the loudest because it was, and remains, the most fearful. When you listen to all of them its like listening to a radio with only talk shows on the different stations. This is, in part, because each distinct self is "created" at different times during your development and is its own system doing its own thing in a sense. Pursuing its own agenda, looking for completion within the overall behavior system that "frames" your life. Completion, as I've mentioned, refers to the reconciliation available through the recurrent cycling of the various age related fear-based need to belong behavioral systems throughout the life span. In other words, multiple completion attempts by the multiple "selfs" are a feature of every life. As each self attempts to complete it revisits the emotional points you have made meaning of, the peak points like the 8, 14 and 21. Based on the fact that we are stuck at the need to belong to social groups level, the cycles from 8, 14 and 21 with their learned behaviors predominate in the overall behavior of our lives.

As I've mentioned, each time their peak meaning returns you have the opportunity to move along, to some degree, in your psycho-spiritual maturation toward a healthier more integrated composite, whole and complete self-actualization. Some peak points are easier to go through and complete than others. Some people go through their cycles quickly, some slower. The speed with which a person proceeds depends on many factors, but as you can guess, they are interwoven biological and social factors. One way to speed up the process is to actively engage the narratives of the "selfs" as much as possible. Of course many people do not live life like that. They look and live forward too far, letting their history dictate their future. So, for the most part in most of our lives, the "selfs" form that homogenous person with its seemingly coherent narrative you see in the mirror, the person you know as your "self". The processes of completion during the life span is not identified because we do not fully know or understand our "self's". The *I Am Sustainability* program is about creating an identity in sustainability. To do that you learn how the need to belong narratives influence your life. Mastering these narratives is a big step toward whole and complete self-actualization.

Let's include Freud's concept of ego here. Somewhere along the line of our evolution as a species pride and prejudice reared its ugly head. Not ugly really, but generally negative and unhealthy. So, maybe ugly. The ego became narcissistic. Survival meant more. Needs became wants. This too, in the early stages, likely had survival value. What about now, with 6 billion people? Things have to change. Don't they? They are changing even if we don't like it. We can't all get what we want, so there is increasing competition. Some people call this competition evolution. Some might even think this is good for the species. Survival of the fittest. That it's a dog eat dog world. That works until the Earth becomes an island. Guess what? The Earth is becoming an island. We are affecting each others' health and welfare more than ever by what we do. No one is immune. Now I'm dabbling in fear. Maybe not though. Maybe reality is becoming more fearful. 6 billion and counting here, with limited and depleting natural resources.

Back to the ego. This book and the *I Am Sustainability* program it describes is about getting to understand the various aspects of your self. Its about developing as healthy an ego as possible. The ego, by the way, is not a bad thing, although in many cases it can be and is. Its received a bad wrap, perhaps justifiably. You can never get rid of your ego. Even anonymous philanthropy makes you feel good. Ego. Feeling good is not a bad thing. The ego is often equated with narcissism. It doesn't have to be. It can be the seat of your authentic personal power. The healthy ego is the crucible that changes unhealthy behaviors into healthy ones in your effort to become your authentic self. Its your healthy self-esteem. The *I Am Sustainability* program explains how that is possible. A healthy ego intact and manifesting to serve and protect the authentic self is a good thing. More on this in the next chapter.

We are multiplicities. Just like Maslow's motivational needs and drives are fluid and appear to form a homogenous core, so too are and do our identities. Our identities are based on fluid/permeable borders between the various "selfs" that make-up our composite identity. It's a distribution over a range. In most cases it's a bell curve with a 60% average that dominates our way of being. Meaning that who we are is generally an average of the components. This is the "I" most of us take ourselves to be. But the average can shift, flow within certain degrees of perceived social/environmental freedom. It is a healthy ego that makes the most socially correct decision, that sets the constraints on the degrees of freedom, and that enacts the behavior. Sticking with Freudian concepts the healthy ego is somewhere in the center between the primal Id and attempting-to-be moralistically pure superego. By the way, an actual ego, superego and so on may not even exist. They have been called psychic structures. They appear to be common to all, or most, humans making them worthy metaphors for discussion even though they may be considered the topic of folk psychology.

# The Authentic Self

You might say that, strictly speaking, when a person perceives their multiplicity of self as a homogeneously constructed whole self, as many people do, that perceived self is their authentic self. They are not being deceptive when they are being who they are in their behaviors and attitudes. They are being honest and authentic as they see themselves to be in their identity. If this is the case, however, then the foundation of their authentic self is built in fear-based need to belong to external social group behaviors. A common characteristic of an identity based in fear, as I mentioned previously, is that there is a constant need for a person to define who they are and who they are not. Its like they can't believe and accept they are actually here on the planet and if they are, its as if they feel that it must be on shaky grounds somehow and therefore grounds they have to constantly defend. They need to affirm their place in the world all the time, their belonging, even if that has to occur through behaviors that are unhealthy. It's a system that repeats over and over. To make ourselves more comfortable, our "self" more secure, the psychological tension created by our fears and insecurities is often vented through expression in very stealthy self-promoting behaviors and quiet self-righteous attitudes. This is more obvious in the behavior of some people than others. Its not a bad thing per se, most (all?) of us to it to some degree. I guess you could say its an unspoken social agreement. Its just out of balance because the fear that generates it is out of balance.

Should we call it your soul? We need a focal point for discussion and a goal to achieve through our learning. Would a pure soul act responsibly here on Earth? How about your transcendent self? The one that can rise above all those seemingly spurious unhealthy survival-drives. Does the name of the healthy core really matter?

In the *I Am Sustainability* program, the "healthy core" shows-up along the journey to finding your own healthy personal balance of mind (thinking), body, spirituality (soul), and consciousness. This occurs in the evolving conversation with your self. Let's call that self, that healthy core, your authentic self. Not that you are inauthentic now, you're not. The authentic self is the person who you are right now with all your fears in balance so that your behaviors and attitudes are healthy. The healthy authentic self has a healthy ego that, as I mentioned, acts as a crucible within which behaviors and attitudes can be transformed. The healthy authentic self is attained with the help of the healthy ego and is found in the balance of the body, mind, spirit and consciousness.

In the adult *I Am Sustainability* program each person is taught how a continuous conscious (with intentionality/engagement) connection with their body, their thinking (mind), and their spirituality (spirit) can be used to create a balance that is their healthy authentic self. The healthy authentic self is the overall self that is balancing the fears that come up as they come up in a healthy manner through life. The healthy authentic self is not about eliminating all fear; it is about balancing fears as they arise. This means that as the fear based behaviors (which have already been identified) are sparked into action by the symbols that provoke them, the fear is engaged and enacted in a more responsible and healthier manner. Basically, you are trying to actively grow yourself up.

In 2000 I spoke at the University of Toronto about the authentic self and how it is found within the balance created by an ongoing internal "conversation" of mind, body, spirit and consciousness. Four points, a tetrahedron, that when in balance would generate the healthy authentic self at its core. Out of balance, say too much focus on body or mind, you would lose your authentic self and tip the balance back to be guided once again more by external factors.

The process toward a healthy authentic self identity is the process that balances the belonging needs of the self to the self (internal belonging needs of self-actualization) with the belonging needs of the self to social groups (external needs). It is the identity established in this healthy balance that generates the healthy authentic self. The identity created in maintaining that healthy balance intact is the being sustainability taught in the adult *I Am Sustainability* program.

If having an ongoing awareness of the conversation between your mind and body seems too hippy or new age-like for your palate, get in line behind me. I have to admit I thought the notion was highly suspect at first as well. That is, until I started reading about human behavior systems, the meaning we attach to them and the tenets of complexity science and embodied cognition, as I'll describe later. Your body, spirit and mind are talking anyway, might as well be aware of the conversation they're having.

At this time its also very important to know that "listening to the conversation/narratives" or "balancing toward your healthy authentic self" does not mean wallowing in these experiences. There are very practical benefits to knowing yourself and becoming authentic, as I describe throughout this book. Self-indulgent rumination is not what I'm talking about. If you do that, you are not self-actualizing, you are stuck in some coping mechanism. The only purpose of the *I Am Sustainability* program is to provide you with the tools so you can move beyond your self as you are now and do so quickly. I'll explain more about that later as well.

While Maslow wrote about a the human potential to psychologically mature through a hierarchy of human needs and motivation, other scholars have more recently debated about how and whether human consciousness is, within the general population evolving beyond our fear-based self preservation needs and if it is, how that looks. (For example Wade, 1996; Washburn, 1995, 2003; Wilber, 2001). Their overall idea is that as consciousness expands (i.e., evolves), the less fearful we become, which in turn allows us to become a self-transcendent being. In other words, we are able to move our attention to self, the personal, to the attention beyond ourselves, the transpersonal. How that occurs is the subject of their fascinating books.

So, there is relapse and "mistakes" as an adult attempts to self-actualize. Old fear-based patterns are difficult to shift and often get expressed through other substitution fear-based behaviors. The more you know your self though, the better you'll be able to avoid relapse, substitution and "mistakes". The difficulty is likely, in part, because the borders between the hierarchy of human needs is not all that solid, and in fact is often blurred. Under certain real/perceived conditions (physical and/or mental) behavior can quickly return to previous patterns for survival. That is, perceived needs flow back and forth along a perceived personal hierarchy, and often are experienced concurrently as to make them multi-dimensional. What that means is that a person's motivations are complex, often stemming from so many sources at the same time as to make them individually imperceptible. They appear as a homogenous unity. There common feature being that they are fear-based.

In the introduction I wrote about how going external to find your self, to self-actualize, is the key behavior the *I Am Sustainability* program seeks to reverse. If we can get you to go in when you self-actualize, to find the fulfillment of the need for belonging to self more rewarding, make your internal belonging more important than external belonging, then the need for external symbols such as class/group symbols (e.g., SUVs) will subside. Remember, its not about elimination, its about balancing. Right now we are externalizing so much our societies are characterized by over-consumption of our natural resources (many of which are not renewable) and exploitation of the environment and each other. The exploitation of each other actually cycles back and harms the environment even more.

As mentioned, the general process advocated by the *I Am Sustainability* program is one in which you go inside, internal, to self-actualize and in so doing, ultimately through the experiences that provides, you will go be able to go more effectively external. In a balanced healthy authentic self, one of sustainability, you will go into society and into the world with the need to make a positive difference without the need to mark your territories of belonging and not belonging. You will know who you are and as things show-up in your life you'll be able to deal with them in a healthier manner because they won't hold the same fear-based belonging value symbol they did before. Your belonging will come from within. You'll still identify with things in the external world, but you won't let them identify you. Unless, of course, you decide to. You will have the power of choice based on who you know your self to be as defined by who you know your healthy sustainable/authentic self to be.

Gradually, too, you will lose all the external stimuli, "the buttons" that set-off your emotional and behavioral reaction. It will only provoke your conscious action and healthy emotion. The external, to a large degree, will cease to rule you. Your life will be yours more than ever before. In the moments of life, be they momentary or extended, you will be a healthy self-actualized person engaged in positive actions not one in servitude to fear.

You think you have power now, just wait till you see what's really inside of you; you ain't seen nothing yet. Do you feel that truth about you? I do in everyone I meet. That human potential is alive in all of us. It wants to be heard, needs to be heard and is ready for action.

# The Sustainable Self

Once our behavior cycles are in place we can substitute players in our co-dependent social system network. In fact, we often do. That's why for most of us friends come and go and moving to a new city is not such a big deal. We sustain our network, however, in one form or another, to sustain the self we think we are. We subconsciously sustain the composite of systems created to survive. Once in place it only requires maintenance. In the usual scenario our fears shift to actions for its maintenance and sustainability. Looking back further, however, maybe primal survival needs have all been about sustainability. Are survival and sustainability equivalent? I think they are.

Let's work with that. Survival means to live. To do what it takes to make it through regardless of the conditions. Sustainability has many meanings, but doesn't it really mean to keep going? To do what it takes to keep things going so that a person can keep going.

All people are looking to fulfill their survival needs starting at the physiological and safety needs as well as all the other needs up the hierarchy concurrently, each to some degree, with most of us stuck at belonging as our predominant need. The repertoire of social behavior roles (systems) we use form the identities we assume as children to achieve our survival, our individual sustainability and the sustainability of our species. What then really does sustainability mean to us? Survival. Most of us in the affluent West are stuck primarily at the need to belong to social groups. That is our survival, our sustainability. Our social belonging need dictates the majority of our behavior, our sustainability. We create a behavior configuration with others that manages that most effectively. We sustain that configuration most of our lives. We join a network of individuals who are seeking sustainability in a society that we sustain to sustain us. We play co-dependent psychosocial games: we manipulate, entangle and enmesh each other to sustain our way of being, our fear-based system of being.

If all of these systems are fear-based, why then is the fear-based data from the environmentally aware, worried and activist quarter of society, not shocking us into new behavior? Likely because the fear we perceive is not great enough in the plus minus column of our checks and balances. Fear is the most common attempted catalyst for change currently. It doesn't have to be. In fact it shouldn't be because its pretty inefficient, especially with regard to the technique of shock and shaming people into changing their environmental behaviors.

As adults we are not only stuck in belonging and going external to fulfill it, as I've described, but more specifically, as I've also mentioned previously, we are stuck in the self-other, belonging/not-belonging judgment dynamic. Once identity formation (formed by going external) is complete, even with some possible modifications in adulthood, we spend the rest of our entire lives defending it, our self, that person we think we are, by also going external. This is found, for example, in the "I belong to this, but not that" and the "I am better/not better" judgment narratives I have mentioned previously.

Thus, while most people recognize there is an "environmental crisis" or at least some sort of environmental storm brewing on the horizon, people are merely responding to it according to their fear-based response system they have always used: that of their social belonging/not belonging system. They are using their 60% average fear-based belonging behavior system, just like how they respond to fear in all facets of their lives. Yes, to some degree we have all connected with the environmental crisis, but that is primarily because it's a social movement. A Hollywood induced and supported response to global warming and the environment. Not that the environmental problems are not real; they are very real. Many of us are making some form of reaction like recycling or reusing or reducing our consumption in certain ways. However, it's a social reaction not action, a limited emotional reaction to an identification with and not an identification in a story of crisis, a reality TV show from the realm of popular culture.

In other words, we are reacting from an emotional stance, one looking for external belonging. Currently, for most of us the environmental crisis symbolizes something, it represents something to us that we identify with. It is a story with multiple characters acting multiple parts. So, like any other story we assign ourselves (our selfs) a role(s) in it as a personal narrative(s) and story(ies), a subconscious fear-based belonging belief creating system. This is done so that we identify with (find belonging) certain characters, and perhaps even one or more of the various groups along the spectrum that identify with/or not with the environmental crisis.

On one pole are the environmental activists while on the other pole are those that question and even oppose the environmental movement. Reaction promotes social fragmentation.

On the other hand, as I'll describe further, because this is what the I Am Sustainability is all about, an individual that is able to reduce their need for external belonging is less reactionary. They take action in a cause because they identify in the cause. They do not react to stories, or attempt to fulfill a part in the story to satisfy a need for external/social belonging. They are taking action for something external as they would take action for their self. They are, and here is the key difference, taking action based on their analysis of a system. In their action they are identifying in the system not with the various stories that the system could be made to mean. For instance, in the environmental crisis, they would adhere to environmentalism with all other human beings only as much as it was healthy for them, not in order to be part of a social group. Now, in the case of environmentalism action would come from a place of trying to achieve healthy balance in systems whenever possible with all other human beings and the natural world balanced with the needs for the self. As I'll describe further, this is neither a narcissistic nor emotionally detached event for the individual in action. For instance, while they identify in the system and not in the story, they do of course understand (do not lose touch with) the stories that could be assigned to the system by different people. More on this later.

Some environmentalists have suggested that the successful movement of society toward an improved environmentalism may best be achieved through the renunciation of individualism in favor of an attitude and behavior based in collectivism (Bragg, 1996; Frantz, Mayer, Norton & Rock, 2005). These authors argue that we have put away our own needs to get together for the sake of environment. That might work to some degree. That type of self-sacrifice approach works because it perpetuates the suffering that we are all embedded in. It lets us feel good, empowers us to be the hero. That only works for the unhealthy ego.

I challenge people like Frantz, Mayer, Norton and Rock (2005) who suggest that there is "no 'I' in nature" and that an "I" grounded in narcissism and exploitativeness is counter-productive with regard to the creation of a sustainable global environment. While the "narcissism and exploitativeness" part is obviously accurate their general proposal is not. They propose that an individual self-awareness is not concurrently possible with an equal awareness of others and is, therefore, a person focused on their self is incompatible with generating and feeling a connection to nature as some environmentalists contend is one of the culprits leading to environmental destruction. There are a wide variety of reasons people are connecting/disconnecting from their environments. It need not necessarily be one caused by focusing on self. I'll describe this more in an upcoming section in this book that discusses the meaning of places as described by "place theory".

I propose that it is necessary to go through the "I" (your 'self') to get to the "We" (everybody else and the environment). You have to understand and know your self, on a daily basis, so that when you go out into the world, out into the environment and human communities, what I call the "We", you will be able to do so in a healthy not primarily fear-based manner. That is what the I Am Sustainability program is all about. My discrepancy with Cindy Frantz and company is likely because we're talking about different things. Plus whereas I take a systems view of humans and nature, she and her group do not. The "I" that Frantz, Mayer, Norton and Rock (2005) are talking about is one based in what has been called Objective Self Awareness which is basically a proposed psychological concept to describe how a person can make meaning of themselves so much that they detach from their surrounding environment, including social others. This is clearly a different "I" than described in this book. In this book, extensive self-understanding of the fear-based belonging behaviors includes a necessary self-focus. This is necessary to achieve and maintain a healthy system of behaviors, environmental and otherwise. This is a balanced connection to self that includes a connection to the environment and society and not a full detachment from either of them. In fact, in the *I Am Sustainability* program it is believed that in order to have a healthy connection to self one has to have analogous healthy connections to the environment. Somewhat surprisingly, Frantz, Mayer, Norton and Rock (2005) suggest we do not have the capacity in our attention to do that. That we do not have the capacity to pay attention to too many perceptual fields at once, especially the tow of self and environment at the same time. While this may be true in terms of absolute limits, studies have shown the absolute limit of attention at any given moment is seven objects (plus or minus two – from Princeton's George Miller), the current common "I" has evolved for millennia to survive and thrive in a variety of perceptual fields and, I propose, in so doing has adopted a variety of systems of self/other and belonging/non-belonging radar-like perceptions and associated belonging behavior systems to which we have the ability to attend.

In fact there is the growing problem of alienation for American adolescents and young adults in which control is seen as being lost to the external (forces beyond my control), more and more thereby actually fostering cynicism, individualism (in the negative unhealthy ego sense), and self-serving bias. In return these are correlated with poor school achievement, decreased self-control, depression and helplessness (Twenge, Im & Zhang, 2004). As I'll describe further, grounding children in an *I Am Sustainability* identity in which who they are, *is* healthy (psychologically health is self-actualized) and stable/resilient (sustainable) re-centralizes the control in a healthy individualism.

Historically, we've been getting it backwards. We try to get the "I" by going through the "We". We spend all our lives projecting our needs onto others trying to get the "I" back. But its never been away. Its just been overwhelmed by the fear-based need to belong to social groups. To try to get our "I" we look outward to other systems, ones that we already have and have always had within us.

The first step to creating a sustainable society is finding a different sustainable self. I believe that we already all have an identity in sustainability. Its just that its currently reified primarily in fear-based behaviors that help us maintain identity and belonging in social groups. It's our sustainable self in the sense that it helps sustain us in a system that gives us our identity based in social acceptance. The first step to global sustainability is to shift, en masse, that individual sustainable self from one that is based exclusively in behaviors satisfying belonging needs in the external social world, to one that finds a balance with what satisfies our belonging needs to the internal personal world. The words, "*I Am Sustainability*", in the program refers to someone who has achieved that balance and is being sustainability. This is not just identifying *with* sustainability as a lot of people have started to do ("going green", recycling etc.), but actually identifying in sustainability, that is, being sustainability. Not being "sustainable", but rather being "sustainability". Finding, getting, and maintaining "being sustainability" as their identity, as who they are, as who they know themselves to be. This is an important distinction, as I'll describe further.

Enrico J. Wensing

# The Ecological Self: From Shallow to Deep Ecology

A self-actualized identity in sustainability as achieved through the *I Am Sustainability* (this book) and *We Are Sustainability* (next book) programs creates a platform from which a person can further self-actualize to the extent described by Abraham Maslow. He believed that complete self-actualization requires that a person's identity be comprised in part from what they do as their chosen vocation. Maslow felt that this gives a life its sense of purpose and identity through the fulfillment of that purpose.

Invariably, following *I Am Sustainability* and *We Are Sustainability* some people will go on to self-actualize further in environmentalism and deepen their connection to become part of nature as described by the ecological self identity. This is the "healthy whole person" type of self-actualization Maslow described; only one self-actualized in the ecological self as a vocation. By the way, I use the term "vocation" because it implies what Maslow meant when he described self-actualization as involving a career path. He felt that in self-actualization the chosen career would be a true "calling", involve a true "capability", and implement an honest "skill". In other words, a self-actualized person would choose a career exclusively based on psychologically healthy and appropriate choices. Maslow also felt that each of us only had a few careers that could fulfill these requirements. That each of us had a destiny toward a finite and small set of career possibilities in which we could self-actualize. Within that chosen career, be it as a bus driver, a forest ranger, or teacher we would become what might be regarded as an elite and exemplary roll model of that career. We would truly shine in every aspect related to our career choice.

While I could use any vocation to describe what self-actualization looks like, I am going to utilize the example of the ecological self. While the ecological self is not a vocation *per se*, you would likely find an ecological self in a role very intimately related to the environment, and likely one related to sustainability in some way, on a local and/or global scale.

The ecological self is a term first used by Norwegian philosopher and deep ecologist Arne Naess and describes a profoundly deep connection with nature; a psychospiritual healthy integration with all of nature. However, as with physical health all people self-actualized in sustainability also achieve psychospiritual health but will not necessarily use a profound connection to nature to maintain it like the person who self-actualizes in the ecological self does. People who have an identity self-actualized in an ecological self maintain their psychospiritual health through their connection to all of nature. Nevertheless, people who have taken their connection to nature as far as an identity in sustainability following *I Am Sustainability* and *We Are Sustainability* programs will have an integral connection with nature through their body, as I detail in this book. The idea that someone has a connection with nature through their body does not involve getting naked in a forest, tree hugging or eating excesses of granola. It simply means they will see themselves as nature, part of its natural ecosystems. They will flow with it. Not try to prevent extinction, from a romantic stance. Extinction is part of nature. Forests become deserts.

This type of integrated connection to nature of the self-actualized in sustainability and the ecological self is important because, for example, this will shift the often politically negotiated and special interest group centered settlements of environmental policies and it will reconfigure the approach to environmental pragmatism and ecopragmatism as I describe in the *We Are Sustainability* program. It will shift these negotiations away from a human centered sustainability agenda, to one more integral with an agenda for all of nature.

The ecological self is a concept historically utilized by deep ecologists. Deep ecology is a philosophy. The deep ecology philosophy espouses an environmentally sustainable, socially equitable, and spiritually rich way of life.

My friend, Australian deep ecologist Eshana Bragg describes the ecological self as an individual whom has an emotional resonance with other life forms, which includes a perception of being similar, related to, or identical with other life forms and spontaneously behaving towards the ecosphere as one would towards one's small self; with nurture and defense (Bragg, 1995). As part of her doctoral research Eshana learned that she could identify aspects and minor expression of behaviors compatible with

90

the definition of the ecological self in every member of her study group regardless of age, gender, culture and socio-economic status.

This suggests that each of us has an element within our identity that has the potential to have a more integral connection to nature. This is likely also related to the innate altruistic behavior humans have as well as our innate spirituality that has been recognized in children. It has likely survived evolution through all the millions of years because it has survival value. Perhaps more than ever, in our current state and current rate of environmental destruction we should tap into its potential. That is what the *I Am Sustainability* program does.

For instance, I believe that we can teach children to construct an identity in sustainability, in part, by tapping into their innate altruism and spirituality. With adults, however, it is necessary to work through the established fear-based behavioral cycles. We clean up the old behavior patterns while we build-up (shift to) the new ones. As I'll describe further, this can be done utilizing a variety of techniques, including cognitive-behavioral and depth psychological approaches in an adult/environmental sustainability curriculum.

Deep ecologists equate "shallow ecology" with corporate environmentalism, which currently dominates developing and developed global societies, but especially those in the West. It is characterized by continuous economic growth and environmental protection based in technology (e.g. electric cars), scientifically based resource management (e.g. genetically modified high yield crops) and minor life changes (e.g. recycling). As Naess (1995) describes it, although like the deep ecologists they fight against pollution and resource depletion, shallow ecology's central objective is the continued affluence (sustainability of their affluence) of people in the developed countries. This is sometimes called a anthro- or andropocentric perspective, where humans (anthro means "human" while andro is a prefix that means men) are the center of the perspective around and from which all else is dictated. Some deep ecologists have adopted the term "reform ecology" instead of using the word shallow given the politically incorrect innuendo of the term "shallow ecology". But I doubt and have never read, however, that it was ever intended to describe anything but a difference in the depth of connection one could have with all of nature and the different actions one took in the service to that connection. Nevertheless, it does, in my view, also speak to the notion that deep ecology and the ecological self expression require deep psychology. That is, a deep understanding of self is the preferred healthy pre-and co-requisite to the authentic adoption of a personal deep ecological philosophy.

The deep ecologists take-on what may be thought of as a more systems perspective. They see that the entire ecosphere of the Earth as the center, instead of humans. This is a big center, and not really a center, because its too big. So deep ecologists talk in terms of a "relational, total field image" and of the human role in that field.

Naess has written of a process of self-realization toward achieving an ecological self (nature as center), which, perhaps surprisingly is actually not too dissimilar from Maslow's humanistic (a human centered approach) process of self-actualization. Both cite the value of psychological maturation of humans, both recommend a psychological process to get there, and both suggest that the person has to find their own particular way to achieve it. For instance, Naess recommends a psychological rather than a moralistic approach to achieve an improved connection to the environment and a self-realization. In other words no more shock and shame tactics in child environmental education as is currently a common approach. He suggests that this can be done through developing a caring identification with forests, nature, and the Earth as a whole. Few, if any, other deep ecologists have utilized Naess' ideas to develop programs that attempt to evoke the ecological self in participants, programs that can be utilized on the necessary cross-cultural global scale.

One exception, however, might be the program outlined in *Thinking Like a Mountain: Toward a Council of All Beings* (Seeds, Macy, Fleming, & Naess, 1988). However, it appears to be filled with exercises employing magical ideation and fantasy meditations that appear to turn the program into a confusing ego ingratiating exercise, common to the romanticism prevalent, in my experience, in new age communities. For instance, it tries to set-up a relational field in which, as part of a group exercise, an emotional/spiritual connection is attempted between each participant's sorrow and the sorrow of the Earth. Following a brief meditation on that connection of sorrow each person relates to the group, and shares his or her experience of that connection as they felt it happen for them. This is done, of course in the so-called "safe space" created by the group. Groups, of course, under these types of circumstances invariably do not evoke authenticity; instead they evoke a group dynamic of social actors. Without trying to be overly cynical, usually reaching, in my experience, about a 9 out of 10 on the "crapometer scale" (+/- 0.5 b.s. units, standard deviation).

This approach is nothing more than a group feel-good, the exact a moralistic approach Naess did not intend, and one not too far away from religious ritual with all the flair justified in the name of deep ecology (the symbolic god figure), without addressing what it is to be human and how to deal effectively with being human first.

The common deep ecological mantra "May all beings flourish!" could be seen to border on romanticism, perhaps thereby attracting iridescent gleeful romantics in the wake of its call. Not that there is anything wrong, *per se*, with romanticism, iridescence, or subjectivism. It is, however, important to not allow it to dominate as much as objectivism does in the scientific quarters. This merely accentuates the already unfortunate polarities and dichotomies.

Practical approaches are necessary as well as magical ones. Practical does not mean moralistic shock and shame. It means seeing the world, and seeing the self as a continuous interaction and integration of processes, and learning how to effectively deal with our world's problems by *first* learning how to deal effectively with our own. This is done, as described by the *I Am Sustainability,* by self-actualizing utilizing the body to find and maintain an identity in sustainability.

Magical ideation is important, it enables us to understand, believe in and learn from metaphor. It allows many of us to express our emotion and spirituality related to our human experience, to dream beyond the norm, and to imagine and create beyond the dogmatic and mainstream periphery. I suspect magical ideation has been behind the creation of many scientific hypotheses. However, the mantra, "May all beings flourish!" is not in accord with nature and natural ecosystems, in which some species, as part of the flourishing of the ecosystem, die. Species, including humans, can and do become extinct. We can't all flourish! I assume that *all* deep ecologists, perhaps more than anyone else, understand that there is a natural flux, ebb and flow, to the ecosystems of nature, and its results are not always pretty. That, however, does not justify human complacency or continued environmental destruction. Maybe we can't make it so that all beings flourish, but we can, improve the chances for everyone, including all of nature. For us humans, whatever the cycle ultimately looks like for our species, we can certainly make our human ride on it last as long as possible by doing what we can during our generation for future generations. Unfortunately, or fortunately, take your pick, we'll only be able to do that if save as many other species and their natural habitat as well. That's a scientific fact, not a magical ideation. The only way to do that is by flipping that Maslow triangle, actively engaging the process of self-actualization in sustainability and using our bodies to do it. The rest, with regard to global sustainability, if you'll pardon the pun, will come naturally.

93

In my above discredit of the "magical sharefest" group experience utilized in the *Thinking Like a Mountain* approach, my comment "evoking social actors" might have made some think that, "well, aren't we *all* social actors all the time, more or less?" Yes, we are. Of course if you are self-actualized then the social acting is minimized. (For an interesting read on the concept of "accomplished social actors" in behavioral dynamical systems, see Lane, 2004)

I think its valuable at this point to consider that what happened in the new age *Thinking Like a Mountain* group often happens in all social groups. The new age group is just a strong example of it. What happens is that leaders are often not aware of their own process and they unwittingly utilize the group experience to project and transfer their own cycle/process onto the exercise and onto the group. Often the actual group scenario, not so much the exercise that they lead, will evoke their process. Then the stage is set; the social actors take their respective places and respective roles. Who will play the martyr? Who will play the warrior? This of course is not a free, honest, or democratic environment and certainly not clear leadership.

To make it more democratic and honest, it is important for group leaders and group participants to be aware of and to own and take responsibility for the projection of their process if and when it shows-up. Projection and transferring process onto something or someone means that we often let something symbolize something it actually isn't. The symbolism provokes us into emotional reaction and into a psychological process of the emotions and thoughts around that symbol. It's a very common phenomenon.

For instance, Linda Riebel wrote about this phenomenon in her description of the overconsumption that is threatening global sustainability. She sees it as being a collective eating disorder in Western society. In this description she defined the terms *static externalization*, when an individual projects his or her own structures of personality outward, and *dynamic externalization*, when the individual projects their inner needs outward. As Riebel (1982, p. 91) describes, "In the first, the theory of human nature is a self-portrait of the theorist as he or she *is*; in the second, the theory is a self-portrait emphasizing what the theorist *needs*". Personal biases, for example, are a form of projection of, and can often be used to reveal, the story and process behind them. The bias can be recognized by statements of opinion/value judgments that include the words "have to" or "should be". As I've tried to explain, nothing inherently "has to" or "should be" anything. We've made them a "should be", because we've attached meaning to them, and have thereby created their value. Our belief systems are connected to the meaning making, and while our stories may have survival value, they are in the end, only stories. This book is about becoming more than our stories, or at least changing our stories. Its about becoming our full human potential, which I believe will break us free from our attachment to stories, or at least make our stories and our attachment to them healthier. To do that, you have to know your stories.

For instance, in this book you could say that I am projecting my life's stories onto the way in which I propose we can achieve global sustainability. That is, through the process of fulfilling each humans' potential through their self-actualization. I value human potential because I have seen it lost so many times in my life that I inherently believe (my bias) that everyone *should be* self actualized, or at least engaged in the process. The process *should be* through the body, because I believe that is the way it works best, and I value things being done at their best (the potential thing again). The curriculum teaching it *should* be based in and create a democratic structure, because I value the tenets of democracy (so everyone has the potential to reach their potential). The chimpanzees just want us to get the hell out of here. They value the quiet.

Understanding my story that I am projecting comes through analysis of the narratives and behavior connected to those stories. In my case, as with everyone else's (not sure about the chimp), my stories were formed when I was young and reinforced along the way through adulthood. Understanding my stories that I am projecting and the various behaviors I employ to carry it out has enabled me to detect when those behaviors were at anytime unhealthy. There is, as I've mentioned, healthy fear and unhealthy fear, healthy ego and unhealthy ego, and a healthy authentic self. My stories are at the point, now, that they do not control me. They still influence me; perpetuate my bias toward my value of human potential. But I am aware of them, and through that awareness (consciousness) I can make sure that they no longer carry controlling emotional and cognitive attachments to "have to" achieve specific outcomes. From being "have to's" and "should be's" they have become possibilities. The possibility of human potential. I can let go. I don't *have to* do anything or *have to* be anyone and neither does anyone else. I can let go and I will go, if I detect unhealthy and it cannot be transformed to healthy. Can I take the chimp with me though?

In reality then, can and do people really change? Yes, in terms of behavior they can change. But as I described earlier, life is comprised of a series of hero journeys within an overall life hero journey. We can get stuck for a while in parts of the journey, but once we start moving the next steps fall back into order. That is all a system. Understanding the system, by understanding the story we have attached to it will empower us to shift to a new system, new behaviors in a new hero's journey. You may never be able to stop the projection of your stories completely, but with practice you will be able to stop using the subject/object of the projection as the focal point for unhealthy aspects of your thinking and emotions you need to process. Once you have attained psychological health when you are whole and complete, projections still occur, but they do not put you readily, if ever, into process. Your emotions and thoughts you experience in a situation are authentic to that situation as defined by your authentic healthy self.

The detection of unhealthy pattern recognition and the understanding of cultural and individual meaning making is taught in the *I Am Sustainability* program. You learn to sense it with your body, hear it with your mind, and feel it with your heart. Sound flaky? Its not.

Its probably a good time to describe, briefly, one of Maslow's other ideas, which he called Eupsychian (you-sike-ian) Management. He wrote about it in 1965 during a visit to a California electronics plant on a summer break in Del Mar, California (Maslow, 1965). It's a good time to introduce eupsychian management because it relates to how a group of psychologically healthy achievers ("self-actualizers") would look like, or at least the way Maslow saw what they could look like within the management structure of a small corporation.

Eupsychian management is an approach to what has been called "enlightened management and economics" in organizations in which work conditions are set based on the fulfillment of Maslow's hierarchy so that people working within the organization have their needs met and thereby the best environment to self-actualize (Payne, 2000). People within a company take responsibility for their own self-actualization with the support of managers (who are also self-actualizing) who, amongst other things, ensure that the lower needs of food/shelter/belonging/esteem are provided for. Eupsychian management also emphasizes how Maslow considered self-actualization an active process, one requiring hard and coordinated work. In that sense, in an organization, its a social process in which people support and inspire each other.

# I Am Sustainability

While Maslow's eupsychian ideas are somewhat utopian, they are also pragmatic. Eupsychian management as part of a curriculum for global sustainability is described in the upcoming companion book to this one called *We Are Sustainability.* In it I interface eupsychian management with environmental pragmatism (Light & Katz, 1996) and ecopragmatism (Farber, 1999; Mintz, 2004).

97

Enrico J. Wensing

# A New Body Psychology: The Metaphor of Body as Place

I believe that the center of everything we are and everything we do, the "everything of what it is to be human", is centered in our bodies. This centrality then makes the body the focal point of where our fears are learned and where they can also be unlearned. The body is the center of all the cognitive (thinking) and affective (emotional) cycles I have been writing about in this book. It makes sense therefore, as I'll describe further, to use the body as the central place through which we achieve sustainability.

For those who have a more detailed foundation in psychology and philosophy, I wish to clarify that my body propositions (wink, wink) are neither a proposed form of philosophical holism nor do they equate to Kurt Goldstein's organismic theory. A body-centered approach to education for sustainability, personal and global (personal before global), as the *I Am Sustainability* program utilizes, is quite simply the most powerful teaching metaphor for the incorporation of sustainability into a learner's identity and life. Part of its power is that it has, what I call, inherent integrity (built-in integrity). It is what it says it is. Its one thing to say that the body is the center, as in a metaphor, and try to make it a social truth; but the body *is* the center of being human, biologically. In the case of the body being the center of who we are, the socially constructed truth and biologically determined scientific truth agree.

A body-centered approach to education for sustainability requires some new thinking and some new terminology/language with regard to what the role of the body is in the human experience. I present this new perspective of the body's central role in being human in my description of a new psychology I call Body Psychology and in my description of what I call a Theory of Body (ToB). First the new body psychology.

Psychology can be described as an academic and applied discipline that involves the study of mental processes, human behavior, and human experience. The American Psychological Association (APA) based in Washington, D.C. currently recognizes 54 psychological divisions that include family psychology, trauma psychology, humanistic psychology, psychoanalysis, educational psychology, and developmental psychology to name a few (see www.apa.org). With all these various disciplines there is of course some overlap of the topics they study. For instance, with regard to family issues, the School Psychology division studies the topic of family issues, as does the divisions called Society for Child and Family Policy and Practice and Family Psychology. Not surprisingly then, interfacing the various sub-disciplines in the exploration of the shared topics is becoming a growing trend in psychology. For instance, I was invited to speak by Frederick Grouzet, the Head of the Environmental Psychology Division of the Canadian Psychological Association at a symposium that considered the topic of the environment within the interface of environmental and educational psychology at the association's annual meeting in 2006.

The *I Am Sustainability* program is based in a shared psychology of the body, as I'll detail further. I propose that members of the APA divisions of environmental psychology and social psychology, amongst others, interface to form a new division called body psychology. In fact, based on the description of body psychology as I'll detail further, it is a topic relevant to educational psychologists and cognitive scientists and memory theorists as well. As I'll describe further, in the cases of environmental and social psychology, the creation of a new division called body psychology is based on the shared topic of place, place theory, the human body, and human identity. Both environmental and social psychology use the term "place" in an equivalent manner to describe the creation, maintenance, transformation and experience of human identity. This provides an opportunity for these divisions, as well as the division of educational psychology, to develop a powerful sustainability curriculum based, as I'll describe more, in a metaphor I call "body as place". As I'll detail, complexity scientists, cognitive theorists and memory theorists could support the body psychology division by relating how embodied cognition and dynamical connectionist descriptions can be used to understand body-based behavior and attitudes. The *I Am Sustainability* program is the beginning of this interface. Part of the vision for the program is the development of a multi-disciplinary textbook for students called *Body Psychology*. Now the details.

Social psychologists tell us that the human body has meaning across all cultures, acting as a "place of meaning" (Pile & Nast, 1998), a repository of an individual's conceptualization of the self (where we store our "this is who I am") (Goldenberg & Shackelford, 2005), a locus of socio-cultural expression (Burkitt, 1998) and a processor of embodied attitudes, social perception and emotion (Niedenthal, Barsalou, Winkielman, Krauth-Gruber & Ric, 2005). "Processor" means that it is a place where we "work things out", our problems/issues/upsets and the emotions and thoughts behind those problems/issues/upsets.

The use in social psychology of terms "place meaning" and "repository of self" with regard to the body is very interesting because they are equivalent to the definitions being used for physical, environmental places by the environmental psychologists. For instance, physical places can have "place meaning" (Manzo, 2005), the cognitive-affective connection to place, "place attachment" (Low & Altman, 1992), and the identification in place, "place identity" (Dixon & Durrheim, 2000).

To me this suggests that, at least socially there is plenty of important overlap between how we perceive our body and how we perceive our physical environment. This overlap means that they are relatable in a teaching by metaphor sense in a body as place metaphor based curriculum.

Environmental psychologists describe the cognitive-affective significance a place has for an individual or a culture within their term of "place meaning" and, depending on its character (i.e. the intensity of "good" or "bad" meaning) suggest that it can foster a bond to a place that they term "place attachment" (Gustafson, 2001; Manzo, 2003, 2005). Attachment to place has affective, cognitive, and what are called practice components. Affective refers to emotional aspects to the place bond, cognitive are thought, belief and knowledge aspects of the attachment, and practice refers to behaviors or action that occur within the context of place (Low & Altman, 1992). Environmental psychologists propose that place attachment may also involve a social process of identification between an individual and their environment whereby the environment comprises a portion of a person's identity and conception of self (Kyle, Graefe, Manning & Bacon, 2004).

Social psychologists are saying the same thing about the human body. The human body, like the environment as place, provides a place for meaning and attachment based primarily in socio-cultural influences, human spirituality, and the human tendency of meaning making (Cacioppo, Hawkley, Rickett, & Masi, 2005).

The human body plays a significant role in the formation, development, maintenance, and transformation(s) of human identity (Budgeon, 2003; Shroff & Thompson, 2006). Humans possess an awareness of a so-called "body self" that has both cognitive and affective dimensions. These dimensions appear to regulate the extent to which—and in what character—the self of an individual integrates with the physical body. Integration of the self with the body is, in part, regulated by the level of general self-esteem, specific self-evaluations of the body and by mortality salience (I'll describe what that means in a second) (Goldenberg & Shackelford, 2005).

Similarly, the environment is a part of the human identification of the self. Humans identify *with* the environment as a place (Kyle, Graefe, Manning & Bacon, 2004), but perhaps more importantly the environment is a part of the human identification of the self (Dixon & Durrheim, 2000). Together both an identification in and an identification with place increases the consciousness and concern of environment as place (Dixon & Durrheim, 2000; Kyle, Graefe, Manning & Bacon, 2004).

With regard to spirituality and place, environmental psychologists suggest that there is a spiritual component to place attachment that has both social and personal experiential dimensions (Mazumdar & Mazumdar, 2004). Social psychologists argue that the human body has historically been a locus for individual and cultural spirituality (Kovach, 2002).

The body is also a place where humans experience what is called mortality salience, which is the existential (the meaning of existence) implications of the immanence of the body's death (Goldenberg & Shackelford, 2005). Similarly environmental places conjure-up existential "what is life all about?" questions, because degradation of environmental place can result in a deeply emotional sense of loss and grief (Rogan, O'Connor & Horowitz, 2005).

So humans find meaning, identity, spirituality and existential experience in both their physical environments and bodies that provides the "attachment" and "place meaning" both social and environmental psychologist are talking about. The external environment and the human body with regard to meaning, identity and spirituality are equivalent. This makes achieving the "I get it" in learning easier. Take care of your body as you take care of the environment, because who you are is in both. It will be easier to get kids and big people to see that the environment is an extension of their selves because it actually is.

The overlap fulfills two dimensions of the ecological self identity as described by Arne Naess, George Sessions, Bill Devall, Eshana Bragg and others: 1) the spiritual dimension, and 2) the egalitarian dimension. In the first, the ecological self is described as a highly spiritual being, and shares that spirituality with all of nature. In the second the ecological self gives equal rights to self and the natural environment. If social psychology and environmental psychology interface with a new body psychology focus and implement that interface into an environmental curriculum we are well underway to creating sustainability, not only for the environment, but also for the learners. This gets into human flourishing and positive psychology as well, so the relevance is widespread.

So far we've looked at meaning similarities between our bodies and the environment. How they are equivalent in terms of the meaning, attachment, identity, existentialism and spirituality connected to them. The overlap goes even further.

As mentioned above, the human body is a processor of embodied attitudes, social perception and emotion (Niedenthal, Barsalou, Winkielman, Krauth-Gruber, & Ric, 2005). The human body is a place of psychosocial processing at both the individual and societal level (Baghurst, Hollander, Nardella, & Haff, 2006; Lunde, Frisen, & Hwang, 2006). The use of the body as a place for psychosocial processing changes during the human life span. It is a particularly significant place during human development, especially for adolescent females (Lunde, Frisen, & Hwang, 2006; Shroff & Thompson, 2006). Two examples of psychosocial processing with the body as place are tattooing and body art (e.g., piercing) (MacCormack, 2006) and in the expression of asceticism such as intense adherence to body purification, restriction, and control (Atkinson, 2006).

Psychosocial processing with the environment as place can take on two general forms: either internalization or externalization. With internalization a place provides something for the individual, that the person "takes-in", to help with their psychosocial process. That is why many go on vacations. What a place provides, in terms of psychosocial connection changes during the human life span (Scopelliti & Giulani, 2004; Smaldone, Harris, & Sanyal, 2005). The other type of psychosocial processing by humans utilizing environment as place, that of externalization, I've mentioned before. It is where a person or society takes their process and externalizes it onto the environment (Riebel, 1982, 2000; Williams & Parkman, 2003). The process of our psychological externalization onto the environment and each other is what I believe to be our greatest threat to global sustainability. This shows-up, as I'll detail later, as overconsumption.

We are taking-out our process on the environment. Our process of needing to belong we create as kids in external groups (parents, family, friends. etc) and get stuck there for the rest of our lives. We are never fulfilled in that quest, and as I wrote previously, we are stuck thereby in the "I am this/not that" of our everyday judgments of others and situations. We are so over-worked because of it, to buy the things that give us our sense of belonging; we are just doing instead of being much of the time. This is the human process on repeat: our need to belong utilizing the external (each other, material goods, our selves), in perpetuity. Process, however, implies change, perpetuity does not. In that sense, as per Riebel (1982) it is a static externalization, where the individual projects outward his or her own structures of personality. Structures that we constructed, through the social biological interweave during childhood and young adulthood. For the adults, Maslow contended that the inner need to self-actualize (to achieve psychological health) never goes away, only other priorities, real or imagined, get (or are they put?) in the way.

I love the way Williams and Parkman (2003, p. 450) have put it,

> On the one hand, enabled by consciousness and scientific rationality, humans produce and externalize their being into the world thus creating environmental damage, yet on the other hand consciousness provides a risk of anomie [breakdown of social structure] so great that humans must internalize the social order and thereby make it taken-for-granted and a matter of common sense. Environmental destruction, then, finds its foundation in our very being.

Who's for a little bit of social structure breakdown for the environment? Ok...Who wants ice cream?

There is, as detailed above, plenty of important overlap between how we perceive our body and how we perceive our physical environment. That enables us to teach sustainability from a whole new perspective. As I've mentioned previously, sustainability at its root is about survival. Survival of the physical self first, then the self that we want to see belonging to social groups, then survival of our self through the empowerment we get from self-esteem, and then survival as a self that is self-actualized (psychologically healthy). We want to sustain ourselves no matter where on Maslow's triangle we are. Do you see where I am going? Each step on the Maslow Hierarchy of Needs has a place in the body in the form of a fear-based meaning. We can utilize the body as place metaphor within a sustainability curriculum each step along the hierarchy of needs on the way to self-actualization. This was how Maslow saw enlightened management in corporations he called Eupsychian Management. He believed that if you make sure the hierarchy of needs is addressed and fulfilled people will self-actualize. Similarly, in the *I Am Sustainability* program each level on an individual's hierarchy of needs is fulfilled from a sustainability of identity in body/environment place perspective on the way to self-actualization in sustainability.

In the above I've discussed how the body and environment as "places" both give us our "self". This is an opportunity to develop and implement a powerful teaching metaphor. One we don't have to set-up. Its already there, naturally. We can link sustainability of self and sustainability of the environment through a new body as place metaphor. We can develop that metaphor under the auspices of a new discipline called Body Psychology. This psychological sub-discipline will be quiet intellectually challenging because it will embrace what Dutch psychologist and philosopher Huib Loren DeJong (2002, p. 441) has called "explanatory pluralism" in which he proposes that "theories at different levels [scalar] of description, like psychology and neuroscience, can co-evolve and mutually influence each other, without the higher-level theory being replaced by, or reduced to, the lower level one." Body psychology will act as a cross-disciplinary interface with the objective of creating a more sustainable future for individuals, communities and the planet.

The body as place metaphor is a powerful metaphor for teaching and learning. Metaphors can be used to help us understand things such as difficult concepts. Metaphors are more then that though. They are laden with thoughts *and* emotions. 1+1=2 is not a metaphor. "Cry me a river" is. Math is not very emotional. Metaphors often are. "Two hearts that beat as one". Metaphor? No, simile. They denote similarity. Metaphors are conceptually explanatory, "I was as 'Hungry as a horse'" and have culturally specific meaning. In other words, to understand the metaphor you had to have seen a horse eat, or at least, imagine how much they eat (it's a lot). It creates a mental picture, an understanding, and often an emotional connection. Its something you can relate to, put into context with your own experience. Now, how many of us have experiences with horses and their eating? A few. How many of us have body experiences? All of us!

See, for the metaphor to work, for one, you have to get it. You had to have had the experience first before you can use it to understand something else. We've all experienced our bodies to some degree. Now, what if you increased that experience through Eastern-based physical bodywork programs in schools? You would increase body awareness further. Of course, there's gym class. But this is way bigger than that. Think bigger. Make bodywork, body awareness, body processes and the like an integral part of the normal body psychology learning in the social environment of regular school classes. Some of these topics are already part of existing school programs. It's just at the level of a whisper, a subtle innuendo, though. Let's make it a focal point and then, once we get more of our body as place experience we can start to equate it to the environment as place experience. Not just because we'll get more of a cognitive-affective link to the environment as the deep ecologists hope for—that's great—but because its actually a true equivalency both socially (see above) and biologically (see next chapter). The metaphor is true. Its more than a metaphor, it's the truth. We don't have to hide it from the kids! And because of me, when I start blabbing, and telling them, they might be angry that you did! Need help starting-up the conversation? Ok…Its going to go something like this,

> "Well…ughmmm…Billy, there's a bit more to the birds and the bees story, that well, we haven't told you, but since that "wensling" guy (they never get my name right in this daydream) put out his books and started teaching that econut (sigh…its ecosphere net) course…well…your mom and I kinda figured…well that we'd better tell ya, so you heard it from us first…you see Billy…your body is a place, a special place…"

Body as place" is the ultimate metaphor, the most powerful, in the sense that through it we can potentially accomplish so many things, from suicide prevention to saving the planet. Those two are linked, in the body as place metaphor. Yes, suicide prevention as I'll describe further in the upcoming chapter on belonging. More than that, the metaphor is the bridge between the humanistic and the transpersonal. It is a powerful tool in connecting self to self (internalizing our need to belong) and self to other (including other people and the local/global environment) in the fulfillment of our need to belong, in a healthy way.

A new body psychology forms the basis of the *I Am Sustainability* program introduced later in this book. As will be described the program is an open-ended exploratory curriculum, based in something called social constructivism. Through this curriculum we can, individually and collectively, explore the body as place metaphor within the context of body psychology. We can explore how the body as place metaphor within the context of body psychology can help fulfill our hierarchy of needs.

By fulfilling our needs in a healthy manner we are moving toward self-actualization as individuals and as a species. Since we are the most destructive species on the planet, self-actualization in sustainability through our body is how the human body can save the planet.

# A New Theory of Body (ToB): So, Who's On First, What's On Second? Exactly!

The "Who's on first, what's on second? Exactly!" in the title of this section is of course part of the hilarious skit performed too many years ago by the comedy team of Bud Abbott and Lou Castello. For me, it symbolizes the confusion currently in the literature regarding the role the brain, mind and body each play in the human experience, especially with regard to the problem of how the human brain/mind creates the experience of human consciousness. This is an area of debate, which has been characterized by many different schools of thought over many years, all of which have their particular proof for their particular "Philosophy of Mind". I am obviously not trying to solve that debate with this book. With regard to the mind/brain problem, as I addressed at the beginning of this book and as I do so here, I merely introduce my input to the debate. The debate centers on the philosophy of mind, which is an argument about the mind, our thinking, and our consciousness as they relate to the human body. For years, many have been thinking that what is doing the thinking is between the ears, not too far away from where you eat your ice cream. The brain, with its mind intact, some believe is what is doing all the thinking and all the experiencing. Every thing you are is somewhere between your ears and that ice cream. The rest is just a vehicle. Of course that vehicle has some sensitivity, some input, but ultimately it is the mind/brain that deals with that sensory input. It's the decider. Exclusively. It chooses more ice cream, they say, not your body.

In this section I'll try to prove that its really the body. Its been the body all along. Time to talk about broccoli. It'll be better for you than that ice cream.

One of the basic arguments of this book is that the biological and social basis of who we are is really inseparable. Two areas in science are currently beginning to advocate that position more and more. The first is emerging connectionist perspectives of dynamical systems in complexity science. The second are described in the concepts of embodied cognition in the cognitive sciences.

Some relevant features of concepts of dynamical systems have already been briefly introduced earlier in this book. Quite literally, everything we do, from our use of the Internet to how we drive in traffic, can be described in terms of patterns that are self-organizing and self-similar. Another term used for self-similar is "fractal". French mathematician Benoit Mandelbrot coined the term fractal in the 1980s to describe the self-similarity seen in organizing patterns throughout nature. Turns-out, we're part of that nature. Surprise!

Next time you go to the produce section of the grocery store pick-up a broccoli and say (to someone who knows you), "you'll notice how the large structure of the broccoli is the same as the florets, which is the same as the individual smaller florets inside of those...that is the fractal pattern of broccoli". Don't tell the produce manager because he'll likely up the price.

The term fractal is important because so many things, not just broccoli, follow a self-similar pattern. For instance, everything humans do. Not just a few things, everything. How boring is that?! Self-similarity of course in human systems doesn't look so repetitive usually because it happens on a large scale. On the small scale we usually experience it at it looks like random behavior. So it of course depends on how you look at behavior, but its there. In the big picture human behavior, your behavior is a self-similar self-organizing system. Everything humans do can be described by a self-organizing repeat system. The system is pretty open and wild, but it is nevertheless a constrained system, meaning that it only goes out so far in behavior before it doesn't define that system anymore. Its chaotic pattern gives it the appearance of random, but its not random. Its a fingerprint, complex, sure, but still a defined pattern. Left "alone" the parts of the system organize and their behavior repeats, repeats, repeats.

Like the broccoli, our behavior, how we interact with others is also fractal. The electro-neurophysiological impulses during fetal development: fractal. How we use the internet: fractal. The way our hearts beat: fractal. The way we breathe: fractal. As Carl Anderson at Harvard has written in one of his articles, "Only a decade ago patterns of bunching or clustering in the opening and closing events of ion channels, quantal release of neural transmitters, or spontaneous patterns of firing neurons, heart beats, and breaths in the fetus or even cars on an expressway were perceived as random and uncorrelated noise-like processes". Not anymore. That is, not until you find a different way of looking at these things. In the case of fractals it was the application of a transform—a filter—called a Haar Wavelet transform. It is like looking into the static noise of the television screen—the "snow"—and then suddenly seeing a picture. The picture is pretty exciting.

Just above I wrote, "Left 'alone' the parts of the system organize and their behavior repeats, repeats, repeats." Obviously no system operates in isolation. Every system is obviously influenced by another, yet in that interface they do not lose their definition. Like the light metaphor, they are both a particle and wave, but together form light. For instance, our emotions influence our actions, and our actions influence our emotions. The two are connected and interwoven. Yet we often look at our emotions and actions separately. But they influence each other and self-organize around each other so that they repeat around each other in a self-similar fashion.

*When does that first begin?* Well, as I've tried to point out it never really "begins". It just flows through as a passenger along the larger system of our interwoven biological and societal systems. But in terms of our experience of the connections between our actions (behavior) and our emotions, that begins when we are very young. Its hard really to know, scientifically, when we first have emotion. When we first have awareness of emotion. When we first have consciousness. Part of that is because scientists can't really agree on what the words "conscious experience" mean.

Carl Anderson amongst others has done some really interesting experiments around the fractal nature of fetal development. Marc Lewis at the University of Toronto has done some great work around the fractal nature of emotional and behavioral development of young children. Fractal events during development can be detected *in utero* while a fetus is developing. Electro-physiological impulses and fetal heartbeats to name two are events with a self-organizing fractal character. After we are born our self-organizing self-similar life continues, including a fractal pattern to our interaction (behavior pattern) with our parents. So when do the fractal patterns begin? They never really "begin" they just flow through. Just like the biology and sociology of who we are, as I just mentioned, are carried forward in our DNA and social nurture systems, so too are the fractal patterns. They're all connected. Sure, our DNA is the blueprint for your "you", but its expression, how it is used, is in a fractal self-organizing system manner. Not random, but connected and organized with other systems, even before we are born.

What is important here is that there is a flow between systems that exist right now. Its an ongoing communication in a sense. Its already in place before you were born. There is a flow of information within and between systems that has been ongoing for a very long time. They are connected systems. Which ones are important? Which one is the most important system? Which one is the weakest link? I think we're gambling when we try to answer these questions. Of course, with regard to our personal behavior systems in the moment we can chose in those "choice points" Maslow wrote about. And that, truly, as humans is all we have in terms of power. Human power is truly in the moment, in the now.

However, even with this momentary power, we immediately "fall into" a system. This is because we are, by definition, all part of a system of systems. We are not only connected to, but *are*, literally, the human embodiment of a network of self-organizing systems.

By the way, I am not the only molecular geneticist who has made this realization. For instance, Richard Strohman from the University of California at Berkeley writes,

> The search for new laws in biology is associated with the beginnings of molecular biology and with Max Delbruck who brought the idea from physics that living systems, although ultimately reducible to universal physical laws, displayed qualities not shared by nonliving matter, and might harbor new laws unique to life itself. The rich history of twentieth century molecular biology has included a failure to find such laws, and that failure is seen as the major force driving biological research to find so-called genetic laws from which would come understanding of life and of our many diseases, inherited or otherwise. And of course, this failure has prompted the question: "If not in the genome"—and organisms are clearly programmed in some sense of that word—"then where is the program and what is its nature?"... The nature of the linkage between physical laws and phenotypes of living matter has now begun to take on new dimensions, although one such key juncture has been known for some time: the laws of thermodynamics and kinetics are linked to the phenotypes of organisms through the agency of dynamical systems [the fractal self-organizing complex type]. Sadly,

this essential point has been all but ignored in the rush to find agent-based genomic-proteomic explanations. Looking back, that substitution of agents for agency must be recognized as an epistemological error of great moment. (2003, p 4)

*So who's number one: mind, brain or body?* The answer to that is in an analogy. If we can, for the moment and purpose of explanation, compare human development to the start-up and build-up of a successful of a small business.

You rent a store space to start your business. You get a few employees to help out. Business is good so you hire a few more employees. Business becomes even better, so a few more employees. Things get really busy for your business so you hire a manager to help out. Like most managers he's a bit awkward at first, making mistakes, until finally he gets it right. Even though he's a good manager, he learns most of what he knows for the business from the employees, especially the ones who have been there since the beginning. Business continues to improve and, in fact, you win a business award. This makes the manager very proud, even though it is and was your business to begin with. You still orchestrate everything, and decide to keep the proud, now loudmouth manager because, well, things are working out. There's more but I'll stop here. I can make my point. Of course in this analogy the business owner is the body and its systems. The employees are the various systems that help run the business. As I'll get to in a minute, those are pretty elaborate...they outsource a lot! The loud mouth manager, the one everyone hears is the mind. The body, brain and systems are there long before the mind, but because of his loud mouth, he likes to take all the credit. Great manager, no question, but a big mouth. It's the body though, if anybody, who is really running the show.

Melanie Mitchell of the Santa Fe Institute has written it much better. She writes,

Dynamical approaches contribute a much-needed characterization of *continual change* in cognitive systems and a much-needed framework for describing complex couplings among brain, body and environment. Computational approaches contribute notions of mechanism and equivalence classes of mechanisms that shed light on functional and adaptive behavior in complex systems. What we need is a rapprochement between computation and dynamics (between theories of structure and theories of change) that can provide both. (1998, p.5)

*Where does it all begin?* Where do you stop and draw the boundary between what we do ourselves, as humans, and what the environment does to us? Does who I am stop at my skin? Well, from the above discussion of what social psychology and environmental psychology has determined about the equivalent meaning we give to our bodies and to our environments: our identity, our emotions, our spirituality, our belonging (i.e., all of the Maslow Hierarchy) it suggests that the border between our skin and the environment is pretty open.

Complexity science descriptions of connected networks of self-organizing dynamical systems have begun to affirm the permeability of the human skin even further. Not only do we have equal meaning of body as place and environment as place, as the interfacing of social and environmental psychology shows, we also now have complexity scientists demonstrating that the external environment and the internal environment are actually more connected than we ever realized before! Of course we have all known for quiet some time that there are certain connections. The production of vitamin D3 in our skin by ultraviolet light from the sun is one well-known example. But that is just the tip of the iceberg. Connectionist research in complexity science indicates that our bodily systems, the biological systems, are more connected to the environment than we ever imagined. The environmental systems affect us and we affect the environmental systems. That environment not only includes biological systems of nature, but also the biological and social systems of other people. For instance, Marks-Tarlow (1999, p. 311) has described the human self in an open connectionist terms suggesting that, "the boundaries of the self are dynamically fluid and ever changing, mediated by complex, recursive, feedback loops existing simultaneously at physical, social, cultural, and historical levels."

So, now for my new Theory of Body (ToB): It is my proposal, my contribution to the debate in the philosophy of mind that the body teaches the mind and keeps teaching the mind throughout our life. Everything we learn and everything we remember is through the body first. Everything we remember is in context to what the body has taught us previously. The body is a like a large processing center of systems that connect external systems and internal systems relative to our skin. As I described below, who we are though, what we use for information, for feeling, our memory, truly extends beyond our skin (and we've only begun to understand the many different ways). Without that manager of course, our mind, our development could not continue to the point it does. So, really, we need our mind, but we also need to remember, who we are, even our self-awareness (reflexive consciousness) and our ability to see that somebody else also has the ability to reflect (Theory of Mind, ToM) is all processed through the body-mind-brain system of systems. My proof is in the previous description of systems and the following description of embodied cognition.

Before the brief discussion of embodied cognition, I want to reassert what this all has to do with sustainability. Based on what I've described so far I think its important to realize how connected, and thereby co-dependent we actually are on each other and with the environment. Environmental systems are part of our systems. There are no walls really, only systems flowing through everything. This infers the best usage of the term "connectionism" in my opinion. While it has its origins in the cognitive neurosciences, system connectionism in the view of this book describes the connectedness and the effect of that connectedness of all natural systems, including humans. A shift in our thinking from our superiority to the environment to one more closely aligned with the reality of connectedness, i.e. system connectionism, will shift the conquering-type behavior tendencies of people who feel and act superior to nature, to that of equality and partnership. Not because some "overly zealous granola eating tree hugger in an organically grown cotton t-shirt" might say so, but because its actually how things really are. It's the real deal on the overall nature of reality. It's the true grip on how things really work.

While the connectionist dynamical systems concepts and nascent metaphors of complexity science give us a real picture of our connectivity, i.e., the deep connectivity of each of our body's to each other (are you ok with that? No worries. We'll get into what I call collective individualism later, it'll give you back your space) and to all of nature, the concepts described by what is known as embodied cognition go even further.

The ideas that fall under the umbrella term embodied cognition ("umbrella" here means that there are various ways "embodied cognition" can be understood, each having a slightly different implication) are being researched and developed by a wide spectrum of disciplines including cognitive science, neuroscience and the social sciences. From this interfacing have come several intriguing ideas about what drives human thinking (cognition). One such idea is termed "cognitive integration" which suggests that complimentary "external [environmental] and internal [bodily] vehicles and processes [of cognition] are integrated into a whole" (Menary, 2006). A second proposal is how the self, comprised of autobiographical narratives within an individual, comes to be forged into a single unifying collective internal "voice" that is the self, through a self-scaffolding process by external and social *embodied* resources (Clark, 2006). In this case the embodied does not refer to the human body, it means external things that have taken-on social meaning, and the meaning they become is the self we become. Wait, that is what the social psychologists and environmental psychologists are saying about the environment too.

In scientific terms what is at interest here is the "agent-environment interaction". The agent here is the whole of the body, not just the mind. The body, not the mind, is the central processor of the interaction. Others have recently described the same perspective. For instance, Keijzer (2005, p. 124) writes,

> Cognitive functioning was initially conceived as a process that occurred essentially within the head, and could in principle be replicated by computer without recurrence in the body and environment. Nowadays, it is increasingly acknowledged that many cognitive processes are also dependent on external processes and the dynamical interplay between internal, cognitive processes and bodily and situational characteristics.

Similarly, Knappett (2006, p.239) in the archeological literature writes,

> An embodied mind is one that is not restricted to some inner computational core isolated from the body, yet from the body is nonetheless controlled. Mind and body are so deeply interpenetrative that one can hardly equate 'mind' with 'brain', any more than one can equate 'cognition' with 'brain'. The whole body is implicated in cognitive processes – humans think through there bodies. One might then say that in a sense the mind stretches as far as the body's surface. The idea that cognition is also situated and distributed implies that the mind [and by inference the body] seeps out into the world, becoming co-existent with that world..."

The point of all of this is to demonstrate how central your body is to whom you are and what you experience. The implication here to is that the use of the body as place metaphor in education for sustainability is grounded in truth. Another implication here is that we know very little how we can use the body in teaching, not just as a metaphor but the physical body. Research is needed in both cases. In case of the metaphor that is why a new body psychology division of psychology is needed, to research and develop the psychology of the body. With regard to the physical body it has already been established that things like meditation, martial arts, yoga, etc. can have significant positive effects on a persons health, both physical and psychological. Bodywork and bodycare can be used as a metaphor as well, sure, but maybe, too, it has yet to be discovered direct effects on learning, especially with regard to sustainability. We've only just begun to understand embodied cognition. Lots of opportunity for research here.

What it is to be human, our human experience from the "big picture" vantage point is, from a mechanistic stance, caused by the phenomena created by the interwoven systems of all of nature, of which human systems are an integral part. Remember Bram Bakker's "Mode of Description" explanation I mentioned previously? That applies here as well in this perspective (and everywhere really). So too does the proposal of Huib Loren DeJong I mentioned previously regarding explanatory pluralism.

If we are in the mode of description of systems or that of a" being human" view any separation between body, brain and mind into categories of cause and effect is really a false one. The separation between social influences and biological influences on what it is to be human is really a false one. Their influences cannot be thought of as in the sense of the summation or in the distinction of their separate influences. Trying to do so has, for instance, created confusion and error in the practice of medicine. G. Scott Waterman M.D. (2006, p.12) uses the following example regarding depression to argue this exact point,

> The statement, "some people are depressed because of abnormalities of neurotransmission in certain brain circuits, some people are depressed because of adverse events in their lives, and some people are depressed because of a combination of those factors." Yet, a sentence of identical logical structure, "some people have myocardial infarc-

tions because of insufficient oxygen supply to their hearts, some people have myocardial infarctions because of shoveling snow, and some have myocardial infarction because of a combination of those factors," is readily seen as nonsensical. The fact that myocardial infarction necessarily entails insufficient oxygen supply to the heart, and that there is a variety of routes—including increasing the oxygen requirement of the heart by shoveling snow—by which that may occur, is well known and understood.

Scott Waterman, an associate medical school dean at the University of Vermont argues that it is erroneous and misleading to attempt to divide human mental illness into separate biological, psychological and social factors. In his Holobiological Model of mental illness Waterman takes a monist view, in other words, one in which it is claimed that it is not possible to separate and make divisions, such as between brain and mind. (From a philosophical viewpoint: monism is one, dualism is two, and pluralism is many descriptions). It is possible, however, as Bram Bakker argues that more than one explanation can work for any given phenomenon as long as there is no confusion between the various modes of explanation. In Bakker's view it is the confusion of the modes of the descriptions of phenomena that causes the conflicts in explanation, not the actual descriptions themselves. The modes are just different descriptions of the same reality. As Bakker writes,

> The relationship between mind and brain is one of the classical issues of cognitive science.... Within the modes of description perspective, the crucial step is to consider talk of the mind and talk of the brain as two different modes of description.... First of all, all modes of description are 'at best fair but limited abstractions' of reality... the brain mode description talks about regions in the brain, spiking patterns in networks of neurons, and motor neurons activating muscles...the mind mode involves...concepts such as intentions, beliefs, desires, the self, and free will...A frequently encountered intuition is that the brain somehow causes the mind. The mind may then be conceived as some sort of epiphenomenon of the brain...[However] the brain and mind mode are two ways of describing one reality, so

they do not cause each other, neither one way nor two way. Neurons firing do not cause the belief, neurons firing and belief are the same thing, but described in a different mode...If the brain does not cause the mind and the mind does not cause the brain, does this mean that the mental event of believing to see a familiar face is not caused by appropriate physical stimulation of the retina?...No, it doesn't: a causal explanation may contain mode switches, as long as cause and effect do not refer to the same thing at the same time. [That is when the confusion, and an apparent conflict in description arises] In this case, description of the different events in the causal chain is best done in different modes. Stimulation in the retina is an event described in the brain mode which causes, later in time, an event described in the mind mode: believing to see a familiar face...The notion of voluntary decisions works well in the mind mode of description: people choose freely whether or not to move a limb. In the brain mode or atom mode there is no such thing as personal choice ... we do not have to find voluntary decisions somewhere in the concepts of the brain mode for us to accept voluntary decisions as good descriptions of cognitive functioning... concepts in the mind mode may correspond to collective properties and mechanisms of large group of neurons – or even whole person, if we talk about broad concepts such as the self and voluntary decisions – that are not easily described from within the brain mode. (Bakker & den Dulk, 1999, p. 45)

So, as in the previously noted argument made by Scott Waterman, this means that the human experience and expression of mental illness cannot be described, for example, in terms of biological factors that cause that experience/expression. While something's obviously do cause the experience/expression, be they biological, social etc., to try to delineate them to implicate individual causality at the level of experience/expression is incorrect. I'll get back to this in terms of systems in the upcoming chapter "This thing called belonging".

Before we leave this section I'd like to mention another example of how our connection to environmental factors, including astrophysical ones, determine who we are and what we experience. This example you may have already heard about, as the basis of so-called biological rhythms.

Biological rhythms are cycles within the human body that are set by the environmental and planetary (astronomical) cycles. They generate an endogenous daily, weekly, monthly and annual human cycle. The most common term "circadian rhythm" describes the body cycle common to mammals (that includes you and me) of approximately 24 hours in which the natural light and darkness cycles generate a broad spectrum of physiological, endocrine (hormones) and behavioral rhythms. Daily rhythms are also found in testosterone levels, spontaneous birth, strokes, and death from cardiovascular causes. Weekly (cercaseptan) rhythms are present in spontaneous births, 17-ketosteroid levels, myocardial infarctions, and strokes (Swaab, Van Someren, Zhou & Hofman, 1996). Superimposed on these daily and weekly cycles are annual (circannual) cycles, creating the so called "birth-date effects", which manifest in aspects of social adaptation and physical and mental development. In one particular study of the birthday effect it was demonstrated that the season of the year a child was born had a significant correlation to the degree of development and flourishing of those children (Kihlbom & Johansson, 2004).

I mention biological rhythms here because most people I think are familiar with them. The environment affects our body in many ways. And we affect the environment in many ways. As the impact of the biological cycles have shown us for quiet some time, there is an integral connection between the human body, human behavior, human experience and the environment. As I've discussed above, complexity science and embodied cognition studies have begun to show us that connection is more profound, and more significant than we have ever known and perhaps ever thought possible.

# West Meets East in the Body

The implementation of a body-centered sustainability curriculum into
Eastern cultures (China, Japan, Southeast Asia, etc.) will be an interesting task. This is because the concepts of body as place, embodied cognition, body-environment connectionism, and systems concepts described
in this book are already part of their way of thinking and have been the
basis of what are called Eastern wisdom traditions, as well as Eastern
medical philosophy and practice for many years.

For instance, in Eastern thought the body is already known as "the
self", with the body being capable of thinking, feeling, and experiencing
(Tung, 1994). Moreover, "the body can feel vibrations so you can understand without words… First-hand experience is explained as: 'To truly
understand you must experience with your own body'" (Tung, 1994, p.
488).

A powerful concept in this regard too is the Eastern cultures' view
of somatization. In Eastern terms somatization is revealed in the extent to
which the language and the meaning of language is grounded in various
aspects of the body. For instance, in Mandarin Chinese, they speak of how
the heart is the center of a person, who they are and what they are like. If
a person is said to have a bad heart then the entire person is bad. Similarly,
knowing a person's heart, it is believed you know the entire person. But
to know their heart you have to see what they do. A person is seen as bad
by their actions against another. Its not what's inside that counts, their
human potential, it is what they do that defines them (adapted from Tung,
1994).

A holistic body-centered approach is also taken in the Eastern
practice of medicine. For instance, as described by Chan, Ho, and Chow
(2001):

Under the division of labor of Western medicine, the medical physician treats the body of patients, the social worker
attends to their emotions and social relations, while the

pastoral counselor provides spiritual guidance. Body, mind, cognition, emotion and spirituality are seen as discrete entities. In striking contrast, Eastern philosophies of Buddhism, Taoism and traditional Chinese medicine adopt a holistic conceptualization of an individual and his or her environment. In this view, health is perceived as a harmonious equilibrium that exists between the interplay of 'yin' and 'yang': the five internal elements (metal, wood, water, fire and earth), the six environmental conditions (dry, wet, hot, cold, wind and flame), other external sources of harm (physical injury, insect bites, poison, overeat and overwork), and the seven emotions (joy, sorrow, anger, worry, panic, anxiety and fear). The authors have adopted a body-mind-spirit integrated model of intervention to promote the health of their Chinese clients. Indeed, research results on these body-mind-spirit groups for cancer patients, bereaved wives and divorced women have shown very positive intervention outcomes. There are significant improvements in their physical health, mental health, sense of control and social support. (p.261)

Eastern approaches are being implemented into some medical schools of the West such as Harvard and UCLA (Chaitow, 2004).

Eastern medical philosophy is perhaps most noted in the West for what we call their "alternative" approach to medical practice. Berman and Strauss (2004) have divided complimentary and alternative medicine (CAM) into five categories, namely "biologically based therapies, manipulative and body-based interventions, mind-body interventions, 'energy' therapies, and alternative medical systems" (p.239).

Bodywork modalities originally from India have also proven effective adjuncts to medical and psychological treatment. Studies combining yoga bodywork (Naga Venkathesah Murthy, Janakiramaiah, Gangadhar, & Subbakrishna, 1998), meditation and psychotherapy (Derezotes, 2000) indicate the significantly greater beneficial effects on affect and behavior these therapies have when they are combined. Bodywork has been demonstrated to improve the status of diabetes with tactile massage (Andersson, Wandell, & Tornkvist, 2004), immuno-competence with yoga (Kamei, Toriumi, Kimura, & Kimura, 2001), and cystic fibrosis with massage therapy (Hernandez-Reif, Field, Krasnegor, Martinez et al., 1999).

My reason for bringing-in the Eastern philosophy with regard to the body is to demonstrate the parallel between the Eastern holistic view and the body-centered approach I describe for the *I Am Sustainability* program. In teaching body as place, embodied cognition, body-environment connectionism, and systems concepts described in this book the established Eastern bodywork programs and Eastern philosophies are a part of the program.

# Human Health and the Environment: Where Do We Draw The Line?

An important point that is made throughout this book is that the human body is connected to the environment in many different ways. So many ways, in fact, that its difficult, and maybe impossible to pull them apart to see exactly how they work. There are so many systems doing their thing at the same time. That is why its useful to use whatever we can to understand them better—consider their possibilities—but being careful to never get attached to them as absolute truths because, in the final analysis they will only ever represent the meaning we have attached to them. Not that they don't mean anything, they do, but its meaning has meaning only to us. The meanings we make are wrapped-up in our hierarchy of needs, all of which are linked to our survival, our sustainability. In their pursuit we manifest our human potential, both good and bad as we judge it toward survival.

Highly interwoven psychologically and biologically connected systems flow in and out of us our entire lives. The *I Am Sustainability* program considers humans and the environment as interactive, integrated and co-dependent.

The perspective of co-dependency of human health and environmental health acts as a mandate for the International Society of Doctors for the Environment (www.isde.org) based in Switzerland, which includes Doctors for the Environment Australia (http://www.dea.org.au). In Canada a separate, but similar organization is the Canadian Association of Physicians for the Environment (http://www.cape.ca) from their website: "Today, health should be considered a state of physical, mental, social and *ecological* well-being." In the U.S. a similar group is the Physicians for Social Responsibility (www.psr.org).

While all these organizations take the environment into consideration they do so, primarily, from a "What's the human benefit perspective?" That is, they are helping the environment when and because it helps humans. While in the short term that may appear a reasonable imperative, it becomes concerning when it's the only imperative. It is after all about balance. The "if and when" human motivation/value system is the out of balance anthropocentric perspective I mentioned earlier in which humans consider themselves the central figure of nature. I suppose we are currently the central figure in the destruction of the natural environment, and we will also be the central figure in its collapse. Alternatively, we could also be the central figure in its helping create its sustainability. That, as I'll describe further, requires us to help each other sustainability at the same time. Part of the reason we need to help each other and help the natural environment on the way to helping ourselves is because we are so highly dependent on each other and the various ecosystems of the environment. We are so highly dependent on each other and the environment because of our connections.

So, in terms of saving the natural environment to keep ourselves sustainable as the medical organizations I listed above are trying to do, where do you draw the line? Well, you don't because you can't. Its impossible to save some parts with out saving it all because you cannot be sure, most of the time, (did I just write "most of the time?") which ecosystems are necessary and which ones are not in the short and long term.

One association that appears to understand this important point is the EcoHealth Journal and Association (www.ecohealth.net). From their website:

> *EcoHealth* builds on the foundation laid by the complementary journals 'Ecosystem Health' and the 'Global Change and Human Health'. By merging these two journals and linking with the Consortium for Conservation Medicine, the journal provides an authoritative forum for research and practice that integrates human, wildlife and ecosystem health. The focus on human and wildlife health reflects their centrality as criterion for humankind's search for a sustainable future....The Association's mission is to strive for sustainable health of people, wildlife and ecosystems by promoting discovery, understanding and transdisciplinarity.

Once again, this speaks to why with regard to achieving global sustainability, it is important to resolve the "I" before engaging the "We".

Creating an identity in sustainability in yourself first, establishing sustainability in *your* healthy "I" first, gets you to a place where you will be ready to be healthier with others and the environment. From there you can be healthy and co-create our collective "We Are Sustainability".

Enrico J. Wensing

# Altruism and Ecomoralism

Over a century of neuroscience and psychological research has convinced most people that "Descartes died", leaving the old mind/brain dualism behind. The reality that we don't have a mind separate from the rest of our body has been brought home in many ways... Sophisticated behavioral analyses are also being applied to the many of the most pressing societal issues of our era. Understanding terrorism is among the most timely and challenging; equally important is the mechanisms through which poverty exerts its pervasive effects and how we might mitigate or prevent them. Advances in behavioral science are also expanding the effectiveness of our strategies for promoting public health. And research on cognitive styles and other aspects of how people learn holds promise for promoting the success of educational systems throughout the world—Alan Leshner, Executive Publisher of Science, May 2007.

In this book, so far, I have introduced that I Am Sustainability is an educational curriculum that attempts to teach behavior systems of healthy belonging in which belonging needs are fulfilled by going both internal and external. This means that in those times you are compelled to pursue social belonging (external) you will always do so within the context of and with reference to maintaining a healthy authentic self (internal). You will be "I Am Sustainability". Most importantly, it is the body that becomes the reference point for your self, in a healthy balance belonging with external social groups. The grounding of the self in the body is key to beginning to engage and reduce destructive human behaviors such as suicide and environmental exploitation. Moving forward in the world with a healthy sustainable self is, in part, also the subject of the next companion book to this one called *We Are Sustainability*. As described in the upcoming final chapters, *I Am Sustainability* is an open ended-exploratory type of education system that we at Ecosphere Net intend on making effective cross-culturally by taking that exploration through a global network of sustainability education centers.

We can no longer think of problems as being "over there" or even think of them as "other peoples' problems". We are all connected. Remember John Guare's play Six Degrees of Separation or the 1993 movie with Donald Sutherland and Will Smith? That's the idea. Whether you believe its six or not, the world, our world, is a network of connected systems (see for example Watts & Strogatz, 1998; Watts, 2003) and not only is there a world wide web of digital connection, our problems are connected too. They influence all our lives, all the time. In fact, not only are they connected to us, but they are also all connected to us all at once. For instance, poverty is not a simple single problem of the poor. There are many sides to poverty, with many consequences because of it, and all of them affect all of us all the time. In the above quote Alan Leshner correctly eludes to the connection of poverty to other social and political problems that affect us all. Similarly, Jeffrey Sachs and John McArthur heading-up the UN's Millennium Project write that the objective of the project is, "to address extreme poverty in its many dimensions—income poverty, hunger, disease, lack of adequate shelter, and exclusion- while promoting education, gender equality, and environmental sustainability with quantitative targets set for the year 2015" (Sachs & McArthur, 2005, p. 347). So, while the primary goal of the Millennium project is to address extreme poverty; it does so through a necessary broad spectrum of approaches, which includes the environment, education, human health and basic human rights.

---

**UN Millennium Development Goals by 2015**

1. Reduce extreme poverty and hunger by half relative to 1990.
2. Achieve universal primary education.
3. Promote gender equality and empowerment of women.
4. Reduce child mortality by two-thirds relative to 1990.
5. Improve maternal health, including reducing maternal mortality by three quarters relative to 1990.
6. Prevent the spread of HIV/AIDS, malaria and other diseases.
7. Ensure environmental sustainability.
8. Develop a global partnership for development.

Sachs & McArthur, 2005, p. 347

---

Environmentalism is therefore much more than recycling and carbon credits and it is much bigger than local environmental projects. While these are of course all important, it is obviously a bigger project that requires many people acting to connect the local and global levels. This too, as will be described in the final chapters on *I Am Sustainability*, requires a shift in the fundamental psychology (systems of mind with regard to human behavior and attitudes) of who we are and who we see ourselves to be at a basic level.

But how can you get a person to begin to think of others enough to be motivated enough to change the way they are behaving, when that other person is far away or environmental problems do not have direct obvious immediate impact on their everyday life? You have to start with the fundamentals of human motivation. What are the fundamentals of human motivation?

What is our core motivation for doing the things we do? Is there one cause? If you have a single neuron cell on a dish you can see the "single cause" that causes the neuron cell to move: an electric shock of about 15 mV. Do that to a conscious human being: nothing. What motivates humans into action? A higher voltage? Nice try. That's unethical. Besides electroshock, is there a single cause for human action? Of course Maslow proposed a hierarchy of need-fulfillment that motivates humans into action. But what is the driver behind need fulfillment? Is there a unifying theory of human motivation?

According to "Terror Management Theory" (TMT) the underlying goal of all of our motivations is self-preservation (Pyszczynski, Greenberg, & Solomon, 1997). Its all about survival. All our motivations and all our behavior, according to the TMT, is based in our fear of death. In sharp contrast, "Self-Determination Theory" (SDT), proposes that other types of human motivations exist (Deci & Ryan, 2000). It suggests that the underlying goal of some human motivation is the growth oriented needs for autonomy, competence, and relatedness. Does this sound familiar? It does to me. Autonomy and competence certainly could be thought of as being part of a growth oriented self-actualization while the term, "relatedness" in my view is really another way of saying belonging.

But doesn't personal growth, as suggested by Deci and Ryan and their SDT, have survival value in its creation of an evolutionary competitive advantage? Of course it has, but as described below, that's only a part of it. Certainly, the underlying current of self-preservation, as described by the TMT, is simply our oldest, and most innate form of motivation. Its our "default" system behind many, perhaps currently most of our motivations. It is behind the fear associated with our need to belong (belonging/relatedness has had survival value). As I've described the narratives of our fear-based belonging behavior systems begin during our childhood, adolescence and young adulthood. The initial belonging is fear-based survival as described by the TMT. But is it behind all motivation? Is it our "master motive"? No. Although most times it can be found in the mix, we do have motives unrelated to survival.

The Maslow hierarchy as illustrated earlier in this book looks the way it does and is the way it is, with its base, which covers the largest area, describing our need for basic survival as being preeminent because in nomadic hunting and gathering societies, long before our current attempts at civil societies, basic survival had been a large part, and still is, of the last approximately 200,000 human years here on the Earth. Initially and permanently engrained through human evolution, survival is likewise engrained in our individual development. Management of our fears for survival has been with us for a long time as a species and is with us during our entire individual lives.

While the TMT may more obviously help explain the darker side of human nature and behavior it may also play a part in our best behaviors. Perhaps our best behaviors, altruism, for instance, have evolved to help us mange our terror and support our survival. The true source of the motivation behind altruism has been the topic of a long-standing debate with some suggesting that there are selfish reasons, both from an evolutionary long distance perspective as well as an immediate psychological gratification perspective. Our distant evolution informs our current response patterns. They are systems that flow together, interwoven through space and time.

Let's look at a famous example of altruism, taken from one of my favorite movies Casablanca. This is the scene where Victor Laszlo and Ilsa Lund have gone to the Blue Parrot Café to speak with Signor Ferrari about buying two exit visas on the black market. They need the Visas to leave Casablanca for America. Ferrari has just informed them that he might be able to get one visa for Ilsa, but never one for someone as notorious (to the Germans) as Victor. Here's the script from the scene that follows:

Laszlo: We've decided, Signor Ferrari.
For the present we'll go on looking for two exit visas.
Thank you very much.

Ferrari: Well, good luck. But be careful.
(a flick of his eyes in the direction of the bazaar)
You know you're being shadowed?

Laszlo glances in the direction of the bazaar.

Laszlo: Of course. It becomes an instinct.

Ferrari looks shrewdly at the Ilsa

Ferrari: I observe that you in one respect are a very fortunate man, Monsieur. I am moved to make a suggestion, why, I do not know, because it cannot possibly profit me, but, have you heard about Signor Ugarte and the letters of transit?

Laszlo: Yes, something.

Ferrari: Those letters were not found on Urgate when they arrested him.

There's a moments pause as this sinks in.

Laszlo: Do you know where they are?

Ferrari: Not for sure, Monsieur, but I will venture to guess that Urgate left those letters with Monsieur Rick.

Ilsa's face darkens. Laszlo quietly observes.

Laszlo: Rick?

Ferrari: He is a difficult customer, that Rick. One never knows what he'll do or why. But its worth a chance.

Laszlo: Thank you very much. Good day.

From Casablanca, Screenplay by Julius. J. Epstein,
Philip G. Epstein, and Howard Koch,
Warner Bros., 1942

I love that movie. Of course not lost is the notion that Ilsa (played, need I say, by the beautiful Ingrid Bergman) has to face her past (her feelings for Rick) before she can go forward to freedom and prosperity to the American dream. Whispers of depth psychology? Ok. Digressing.

The point here is Ferrari's tip-off about the letters of transit. This is not the typical behavior of a businessman dealing in the black market as he has been portrayed in the movie prior to this scene. His choice to help, even though it serves him no benefit is an act of altruism. And we the movie watchers like him more because of it. But why did he do it? Was it his compassion? He describes that he " is moved" suggesting emotions, empathy. Is empathy behind altruism?

Just as with the fundamentals of language, it appears we are born with the fundamentals of altruism (action) and empathy (emotion). Acts of altruism appear and the experience and expression of empathy occurs at about the same time during infancy (Altruism: Warneken & Tomassalo, 2006; Warneken, Hare, Melis, Hanus, & Tomasello, 2007; Empathy: Johnson, 1992; Zahn-Waxler, Radke-Yarrow, Wagner, & Chapman, 1992). Their expression also coincides with the neurocognitive developmental time-line profile of self-other awareness that emerges in infancy (Reddy, 2003).

It helps you get ahead and makes you feel good to be altruistic. There are biological, social and psychological long and short-term benefits. Even if it is through an anonymous philanthropic act, you reap some benefit. For instance, because it fulfills your need to belong to your personal narrative and its associated story about who you are and your place in the world. It is part of your hero's journey. It feels good to be Robin Hood. There's nothing wrong with being philanthropic of course, or feeling good about it. The point here is that motivation is a multi-layered system. It is, to borrow a term from George Engel, a biopsychosocial phenomenon and separation of the biological, social and the psychological to determine their individual contribution to the causality of motivation, whether evolutionary (long-term) or in the moment if we decide to be or not to be motivated, will inherently lead to incorrect conclusions. So, whether or not altruism is really a selfish act, or whether there is pure "altruism" separate from empathy as in the notion of "unconditional love" is really an impossible inquiry because you will be restricted to using social judgments, not empirical, scientific evidence as provided by reproducible experiments to answer those questions. You may find the neural correlates of altruism and you might find a psychological measure, a psychometric of altruism, but you will only ever be able to describe the phenomenon of altruism from a personal, social and cultural stance. Are you ok with that? I am. They are all valid modes of description.

The current popular culture environmentalism is for the most part, as I mentioned previously, what has been called a reform ecology. It is the "going green" movement. It is characterized by recycling, carbon trading and energy conservation efforts. There's nothing wrong with that. It's a good thing. Ok, there is one problem. Maybe two. First, it is not enough. It's great, but we have to do more, and many are trying to do more as quickly as possible. Secondly, we have to actually be careful how we incite the "we have to do more". This is what the focus of this book and the upcoming *We Are Sustainability* book is about. We are currently setting-up a polarizing moralism, a collective guilt with regard to sustainability and the environment. There's nothing wrong with a little guilt (just ask some mom's, mine included).

Moralistic approaches, through guilt, through social pressure, and law enforcement only work to some degree. Too much and you lose the very thing the UN Millennium project is fighting for: human rights. As things get worse with our climate/environment we must not increase the "enviromoralistic" pressure, the "ecomoralism" to a religious fervor. Totalitarianism, Marxist or otherwise, will not work. Nor will extreme liberalism. We cannot cut-off human rights by polarizing either too far left or right in our effort to save the environment. There is a better way. There is a way to save human rights and save the environment at the same time. I Am Sustainability is all about that.

Deep ecologist Bill Devall (2001b) suggests that with regard to the environment and sustainability it boils down to two generally held incompatible viewpoints with regard to sustainability. So-called progressives believe that the environment serves humans. Although there are variations, progressives contend that nature can be remade to be more sustainable for the purpose of serving humans better. In contrast, so-called realists on the other hand, which includes many scientists, assert that nature is real and that humans live within the "rhythm of natural systems as part of the system, not masters of it". Devall (2001b) also writes,

Progressives believe that the future will be better than the past because humans invent new technology and advance human rights. For many Progressives, nature must be molded to serve human needs. Realists point to the fact that no human civilization has sustained itself for more than a few centuries. Civilizations overshoot the carrying capacity of their resource base, and due to changes in weather patterns, overcutting of forests, etc., go into decline. The use of contested meanings of sustainability among progressives shows that they have remained dangerously anthropocentric, impractical, and that they have failed to address the moral ambiguities of both technology and their own ideological agendas... In the past, during so-called dark ages of human civilizations, nature was able to renew its vitality after centuries of abuse by human civilizations. However, past civilizations were regional in location. Humans have never before experienced a globalized civilization which is causing massive human-caused extinction of other species and human-caused massive changes in global climate patterns... What can we expect in political discourse? Progressives continue to attack the Realists as they have for two hundred years. However, perhaps Progressives will give up their anthropocentric bias and their belief in human Progress and embrace a systems approach... At the very least, Progressives could stop slapping the word sustainable onto every harebrained scheme and political agenda that is currently fashionable or politically correct. Most likely Progressives will continue to assert that if the people can control corporations or control the WTO or the World Bank, then we can have "sustainable development." And they will continue to miss the whole point about the unsustainability of sustainability.

Do you see the moralism and judgment? The polarization? Instead, why not take those who are making an effort with regard to the environment (and everyone else) and take them further. Deeper. Is there something more fundamental we can consider in our lives than our impact on this planet simply in terms of local consumption, energy conservation, and carbon trading? Yes there is. Can we find a healthy balance between being part of nature and the need to fulfill our humanistic potential? Absolutely. That is what *I Am Sustainability* is about.

*I Am Sustainability* helps the individual form a new identity in sustainability. Each individual will develop her or his courage and commitment toward healthy altruism through this identity. As described in *We Are Sustainability* this will shift how a person deals with life situations and with others in problem solving.

What the above commentary by Bill Devall really describes is our human struggle to find our place in nature. If we say that we are part of nature then even our destructive impact is therefore, by definition, natural. Is the state of the environment or global warming then part of a natural process? Obviously we want to stop the destruction of the environment. But who gets to decide what is done to do that? Who gets to say what is right? Some choices are easy. For instance, reducing carbon emissions. Others are complex and highly political. We live in an era (postmodernism) where many believe truth is relative, socially constructed and that every individual has an inherent right to seek their full human potential. However, inherent individual and cultural differences can lead to big problems, especially with regard to the "truth is socially constructed and relative (relativism)" idea. On the one hand we want to allow for these differences, we want to embrace diversity, individualism and multiculturalism, while on the other we may feel the need to reduce or limit diversity if we disagree with their environmental or human rights practices or we perceive their ideologies as a threat to ours. We want people, including ourselves, to be free and live democratically, to have the freedom to seek all of our full human potential. Yet there are too many of us here now on this planet to do that without irreversibly damaging the very ground we live on, the air we breathe, the water we drink and the food we eat. Are we being forced into a corner by the limits of nature to look at the boundaries of our selves?

One last thing. Someone recently asked me, "Isn't it too late for this planet?" I don't think they liked my answer.

I responded, "Is it too late? It depends on your definition of an acceptable endpoint I suppose, which will in fact really just be a new beginning of something else. Some might suggest that it would be an act of selfish arrogance on our part to knowingly choose to not to do anything because, in our judgment, we think the end is imminent and we know what that looks like. You may have to shift your paradigm, but its never too late."

# There's Self-actualization and Then There's Self-actualization

Before we go into the *I Am Sustainability* programs at the end of this book its worth a quick look at what "self-actualization" means again.

Self-actualization can sometimes appear to be a partial process. One in which a person affirms their self in a group. Or one in which somebody actualizes something for their self, plus or minus the group. For instance, a student learning science with her or his classmates in a group exercise in which that student is empowered by the curriculum and the teacher to pursue their particular potential by creating "their own knowledge, to develop in directions unique to their needs, interests, abilities and perspectives: that is to become *self-actualized*" (Bencze, 2000, p.728). That student is self-actualized in science. This type of learning while fulfilling some of the criteria for self-actualization as described by Maslow is missing several other important elements for it to really be called self-actualization. The individual pursuit and fulfillment of "needs, interests, abilities and perspectives" is only part of the self-actualization Maslow described.

As I wrote previously, self-actualization as Maslow described also includes elements that children may find difficult to experience because they lack the physiological and psychological maturity. As I mentioned at the beginning of this book, Rorty and many others have realized that rebellion against society at various ages during young adulthood are necessary steps in the process of maturation and individualization. Self-actualization as per Maslow cannot happen until adulthood.

Even for adults self-actualization is difficult. As I'll detail, it really is the "Hero's Journey"! For instance, Maslow wrote about opening yourself up to your self, knowing your self, including identifying defenses and finding the courage to give them up.

Self-actualization as per Maslow involves becoming selfless in life by becoming in a sense "invisible". You become invisible when you

139

can no longer make and project meaning and thereby can be controlled into emotional reactions. In other words, you no longer have emotional "buttons" that people can readily push. The buttons are still there, you still feel, but you do not react, you only act.

Self-actualization as per Maslow involves making healthy choices. *All* choices are made with regard to your healthy psychological and psychospiritual growth. Fear-based choices are gone. You still can feel fear; you of course can still feel that emotion. But you do not base your actions out of those unless they coincide with your health.

Self-actualization involves knowing the voice of your authentic self. As I'll describe in more detail this involves being whole and complete rather than fragmented into the various ages to which your fear-based behaviors coincide.

The hero's journey is often a solo one. You have to go it alone, especially currently while many others are not self-actualizing. So you have to have courage in authentic self-expression.

There's a difference between the expression of authentic power and unhealthy ego. You begin to learn that during self-actualization. Your authentic power will drive you to become first-rate in whatever you do as your vocation. Becoming first-rate is made easier because of the authenticity of your power and the authenticity of your choice in vocation. You love what you do because you have made a career choice based on who you really are, not on who you thought you were in your fear-based behaviors.

The *I Am Sustainability* for children and young people, as will be described further, follows the previous Bencze (2000) description of self-actualization in science. That is, the individual pursuit and fulfillment of "needs, interests, abilities and perspectives" within the context of a body-based sustainability program. The young students become self-actualized in sustainability. They are however not self-actualized as Maslow described, nor should they be, as self-actualization requires physiological and psychological maturation. Being self-actualized in sustainability, however, they have the skills to make the transition toward self-actualization as adults a healthier and more effective process.

Maslow, on the basis of a study of persons (living and dead) selected as being self-actualizing persons on the basis of a general definition, described the self-actualizing person as follows, as compared to ordinary or average people (Maslow, 1956):

1. More efficient perception of reality and more comfortable relations with it. This characteristic includes the detection of the phoney and dishonest person and the accurate perception of what exists rather than a distortion of perception by one's needs. Self-actualizing people are more aware of their environment, both human and nonhuman. They are not afraid of the unknown and can tolerate the doubt, uncertainty, and tentativeness accompanying the perception of the new and unfamiliar. This is clearly the characteristic described by Combs and Snygg and Rogers as awareness of perceptions or openness to experience.

2. Acceptance of self, others, and nature. Self-actualizing persons are not ashamed or guilty about their human nature, with its shortcoming, imperfections, frailties, and weaknesses. Nor are they critical of these aspects of other people. They respect and esteem themselves and others. Moreover, they are honest, open, genuine, without pose or facade. They are not, however, self-satisfied but are concerned about discrepancies between what is and what might be or should be in themselves, others, and society. Again, these characteristics are those which Kelly, Rogers, and Combs and Snygg include in their descriptions.

3. Spontaneity. Self-actualizing persons are not hampered by convention, but they do not flout it. They are not conformists, but neither are they anti-conformist for the sake of being so. They are not externally motivated or even goal-directed- rather their motivation is the internal one of growth and development, the actualization of themselves and their potentialities. Rogers and Kelly both speak of growth, development and maturation, change and fluidity.

4. Problem-centering. Self-actualizing persons are not ego-centered but focus on problems outside themselves. They are mission-oriented, often on the basis of a sense of responsibility, duty, or obligation rather than personal choice. This characteristic would appear to be related to the security and lack of defensiveness leading to compassionateness emphasized by Combs and Snygg.

5. The quality of detachment; the need for privacy. The self-actualizing person enjoys solitude and privacy. It is possible for him [or her] to remain unruffled and undisturbed by what upsets others. He [or she] may even appear to be asocial. This is a characteristic that does not appear in other descriptions. It is perhaps related to a sense of security and self-sufficiency.

6. Autonomy, independence of culture and environment. Self-actualizing persons, though dependent on others for the satisfaction of the basic needs of love, safety, respect and belongingness, "are not dependent for their main satisfactions on the real world, or other people or culture or means-to-ends, or in general, on extrinsic satisfactions. Rather they are dependent for their own development and continued growth upon their own potentialities and latent resources." Combs and Snygg and Rogers include independence in their descriptions, and Rogers also speaks of an internal locus of control.

7. Continued freshness of appreciation. Self-actualizing persons repeatedly, though not continuously, experience awe, pleasure, and wonder in their everyday world.

8. The mystic experience, the oceanic feeling. In varying degrees and with varying frequencies, self-actualizing persons have experiences of ecstasy, awe, and wonder with feelings of limitless horizons opening up, followed by the conviction that the experience was important and had a carry-over into everyday life. This and the preceding characteristic appear to be related and to add something not in other descriptions, except perhaps as it may be included in the existential living of Rogers. Maslow further elaborates: "Feelings of limitless horizons opening up to the vision, the feeling of being simultaneously more powerful and also more helpless than one ever was before, the feeling of ecstasy and wonder and awe, the loss of placement in time and space with, finally, the conviction that something extremely important and valuable had happened, so that the subject was to some extent transformed and strengthened even in his daily life by such experiences."

9. Gemeinschaftsgefuhl. Self-actualizing persons have a deep feeling of empathy, sympathy, or compassion for human beings in general. This feeling is, in a sense, unconditional in that it exists along with the recognition of the existence in others of negative qualities that provoke occasional anger, impatience, and disgust. Although empathy is not specifically listed by others (Combs and Snygg include compassion), it would seem to be implicit in other descriptions including acceptance and respect.

10. Interpersonal relations. Self-actualizing people deep interpersonal relations with others. They are selective, however, and their

circle of friends may be small, usually consisting of other self-actualizing persons, but the capacity is there. They attract others to them as admirers or disciples. This characteristic, again, is at least implicit in the formulations of others.

11. The democratic character structure. The self-actualizing person does not discriminate on the basis of class, education, race, or color. He [or she] is humble in his recognition of what he knows in comparison with what could be known, and he is ready and willing to learn from anyone. He respects everyone as potential contributors to his knowledge, merely because they are human beings.

12. Means and ends. Self-actualizing persons are highly ethical. They clearly distinguish between means and ends and subordinate means to ends.

13. Philosophical, unhostile sense of humor. Although the self-actualizing persons studied by Maslow had a sense of humor, it was not of the ordinary type. Their sense of humor was the spontaneous, thoughtful type, intrinsic to the situation. Their humor did not involve hostility, superiority, or sarcasm. Many have noted that a sense of humor characterizes people who could be described as self-actualizing persons, though it is not mentioned by those cited here.

14. Creativeness. All of Maslow's subjects were judged to be creative, each in his own way. The creativity involved here is not special-talent creativeness. It is a creativeness potentially inherent in everyone but usually suffocated by acculturation. It is a fresh, naive, direct way of looking at things. Creativeness is a characteristic most would agree to as characterizing self-actualizing persons.

15. Polar opposites merge into a third, higher phenomenon as though the two have united; therefore, opposite forces are no longer felt as conflict. To the self-actualized person work becomes play and desires are in excellent accord with reason. The self-actualized person retains his childlike qualities yet is very wise.

According to Maslow, there are two processes necessary for self-actualization: self exploration and action. The deeper the self exploration, the closer one comes to self-actualization.

Later in life, realizing the episodic nature of self-realization, Maslow redefined self-actualization in terms of frequency of peak experiences.

In other words, any person in any of the peak experiences takes on temporarily many of the characteristics which I found in self-actualizing individuals. That is, for the time they become self-actualizers. We may think of it as a passing characterological change if we wish, and not just as an emotional-cognitive-expressive state. Not only are these his happiest and most thrilling moments, but they are also moments of greatest maturity, individuation, fulfilment—in a word, his healthiest moments.

This makes it possible for us to redefine self-actualization in such a way as to purge it of its static and typological shortcomings, and to make it less a kind of all-or-none pantheon into which some rare people enter at the age of 60. We may define it as an episode, or a spurt in which the powers of the person come together in a particularly efficient and intensely enjoyable way, and in which he is more integrated and less split, more open for experience, more idiosyncratic, more perfectly expressive or spontaneous, or fully functioning, more creative, more humorous, more ego-transcending, more independent of his lower needs, etc. He becomes in these episodes more truly himself, more perfectly actualizing his potentialities, closer to the core of his Being, more fully human.

Such states or episodes can, in theory, come at any time in life to any person. What seems to distinguish those individuals I have called self-actualizing people, is that in them these episodes seem to come far more frequently, and intensely and perfectly than in average people. This makes self-actualization a matter of degree and of frequency rather than an all-or-none affair, and thereby makes it more amenable to available research procedures. We need no longer be limited to searching for those rare subjects who may be said to be fulfilling themselves most of the time. In theory at least we may also search any life history for episodes of self-actualization, especially those of artists, intellectuals and other especially creative people, of profoundly religious people, and of people experiencing great insights in psychotherapy, or in other important growth experiences.

Personally, I don't regard self-actualization as the "healthiest" or "highest state", though it is a necessary "intermediate state" onto even higher states; there are states well beyond self-actualization that psychologists have neither identified, nor experienced, yet. In general, I think self-actualization is a term that's plagued with ambiguity because people understand different things by the term, partly due to the fact that one's understanding of the term is crucially dependent on one's own experiences. Do you think someone who knows nothing about the experience of self-actualization is going to understand anything by mere verbal definitions of the term? The point I'm trying to make is that a person's understanding of the term 'self-actualization' is crucially dependent on that person's own self-actualization-like experiences. If someone hasn't experienced self-actualization, that person will never understand what it's all about.

Now, let's talk about polar opposites in an individual, without resorting to dry or ambiguous statements. Consider the following polar opposites: 1) regarding everything as infinitely meaningful vs regarding everything as completely meaningless or absurd, 2) having a deadly serious temperament vs having a playful, joking temperament, 3) the experience of Being vs the experience of Nothingness or Non-Being, 4) Identifying oneself with everything vs nothing, 5) the experience of freely-willed actions vs the experience of actions beyond one's will, 6) the experience of being passionate and attached vs the experience of detachment... the list goes on, but let me stop here. The point is that the self-actualized individual will have or experience many of these polar opposites, at different times, but more importantly, simultaneously. I don't doubt that experiencing polar opposites simultaneously can be a disturbing thing for some, but the reconciliation of these opposites is one of the keys, I think, to self-actualization because it allows one to go beyond opposites and contradictions. One is no longer trapped within one or another 'perspective', but instead realizes all of them simultaneously.

(Adapted from Dr. Mikula's website www.brainmeta.com with permission)

As will be described in the upcoming *We Are Sustainability* book, beyond self-actualization Maslow, Asagoli and Frankel as well as many others have described further transpersonal growth called transcendent actualization. It basically describes a deeper state of selflessness and spiritual realization, one imbued with aestheticism and not all that dissimilar actually from that described by Arne Naess as part of the quality of the ecological self. Just as empathy is felt as a physiological response in the body, although perhaps in a different way, so too is aestheticism. Renowned personality psychologist Robert McCrae has recently confirmed the connection between transient physical and emotional responses, the so-called "aesthetic chills" some people get to the experience of beauty (music for example) and the personality dimension called "openness to experience". In American and 51 other cultures he tested worldwide the two were high predictors of each other (McCrae, 2007).

Note the many times openness is utilized in Shawn's description of self-actualization above. Although the function of the aesthetic chill may yet be unknown, for the *I Am Sustainability* program it is assumed that an emotional appreciation of beauty and openness to experiences are important gateways to full self-actualization. A deeper connection, collaboration and grounding of self to body is an important part of that. Once achieved, it becomes easier to connect and collaborate with other people and all of nature in a healthier manner.

# Gettin' it Done: From Ideation to Implementation

Two events led to the creation of this very short chapter. Well, maybe more. Whatever. The first was a book that I scanned over quickly a few days ago that is, well, just bad. The book is full of theory about human possibilities in our new millennium. Unfortunately its what I guess you could call a good example of extreme folk psychology. A book that has too much magical ideation, too much conflation of ideas and principles (both real and the magic make-believe type), little real substance and no real practical ideas that can work at the real world level. Enough said.

The second event that led to the creation of this chapter is IBM's Innovation Man. (No magical ideation there!) He is part of a series of recent local TV commercials touting implementation over ideation. The basic premise being that while its great to go around and come up with ideas and frame those ideas in words such as "innovation" and "ideation", that's really all just insubstantial techno-jargon at corporate meetings and seminars. By contrast, of course, putting ideas to work is implementation.

I would have never founded Ecosphere Net and began to co-develop its programs if for a moment I thought it was just going to be about ideation, magical or otherwise. I am a hugely practical person. Sustainability is about doing. Self-actualization is about doing the hard work on your self, many times against the current trends of society.

The next three chapters are about implementation. Part of the deal, however, with the programs—the adult and the child *I Am Sustainability* programs—is that by design they have some element of open-ended exploration. This may make it seem to have less structure and, as a consequence, give it the appearance of being a less rigorous (easier) implementation than traditional learning. As I'll describe, the *I Am Sustainability* programs are different, to be sure, but they are a powerful way to change your life for the better and help save the planet on the way.

# Adult Sustainability Education
# Body-centered Systems Psychotherapy

Experiential learning in the paradoxical postmodern moment: a period offering unparalleled opportunities for diverse groups to experiment with identities. But this in a context of frightening uncertainties and insecurities at an environmental, socioeconomic and personal level. The struggle to experiment must also be located within a powerful consumerism which can offer illusions of choice, but substitutes appearance for substance, manic materialism for purpose. Using cultural theory and psychoanalysis, I argue that experiential learning, in the postmodern moment, requires a holistic cultural psychology of human agency transcending the narrow vocationalist, short-term discourse of lifelong learning. In a culture where inherited templates have fractured, experiential learning has become a vital necessity, offering, potentially, some supportive space, emotional as well as critical literacy, for those peoples at the margins, and nearer the core, to recompose selves, stories and communities, on more of their own terms. — Linden West, University of Kent

The above quote by Linden West (1998) to a large degree describes, in both form and philosophy, the Adult version of the *I Am Sustainability* program. While its definition and origin is debated, postmodernism refers to the cultural movement and philosophy that amongst other things embraces the concepts of relativism, diversity and complexity as opposed to hierarchy and the contemporary living that prevailed in the period prior known as modernism. Experiential learning, also known as action learning, is the process of making meaning through direct experience. When it makes up a curriculum in an exploratory form it is called action research. As will be described, the exact way *I Am Sustainability* is taught is different than traditional courses. *I Am Sustainability* has various components the implementation of which depending on what the learning situation calls for. Similarly, the group at Ecosphere Net that provide the *I Am Sustainability* program have a wide variety of experience and expertise. Generally speaking though the *I Am Sustainability* program is exploratory and open-ended learning that has one-on-one mentorship and group components. As described further, its basis is a balanced non-coercive, positive, social constructivist approach.

The self-actualization Malsow wrote about and the self-actualization in sustainability as taught in the *I Am Sustainability* program have some similarities and some distinct differences. In the *I Am Sustainability* program self-actualization means that you get to actualize your self with the help of people to guide you. Maslow's self-actualization simply referred to a life process that somehow some people are able to get through while others, most others, are not. Self-actualization in sustainability through the *I Am Sustainability* program provides you with all the tools to get to your own personal sustainability; a solid and stable overall self that, like all sustainable ecosystems is highly resilient. You will be well on your way to full self-actualization as Maslow described, but unlike Maslow's description, you will be extremely aware of the process and engaged in its healthy active achievement.

Maslow never considered the role of the human body. As will be described in this and the following chapters, the *I Am Sustainability* program is all about the body. Its about creating a healthy home for yourself, your sustainability, in your body. Self-actualization in sustainability through the adult *I Am Sustainability* program is therefore much more than self-actualization as Maslow described. Perhaps most importantly, it not only creates the platform from which more people can fully self-actualize, but also creates one from which people can immediately start living healthier and happier lives because the primary blockage to that life, the fear-based need to belong to the external social group behaviors have been largely reduced in their influence. They are not totally eliminated. They are brought back into balance.

For adults the *I Am Sustainability* program utilizes a system I call *body-centered systems psychotherapy* and for children, adolescents and young adults *body-centered systems constructivism*. In the adult program *you* are retrieving and building your *I Am Sustainability*. You are going into you, and getting that lost but not forgotten part of you. You know its there. In the children, adolescent and young adult program we are helping *them* construct the groundwork for the system of *I Am Sustainability*. Of course we should not and cannot stop them or the adults from going external, to the social for the social. For both kids and adults its not about eliminating the going external, its about balancing going external with going internal for identification, and consciously engaging the conversation between the two to decide what are the healthy choices in the choice points. The remainder of this chapter concerns the adult program.

It is not an easy task to prioritize the many environmental problems. There are many big environmental problems, global warming while currently very much in the media, is only one of them. Global warming/climate change is part of a group of environmental problems like air/water pollution, depletion of renewable resources, ecosystem disruption and other exploitative behaviors against the environment. They are occurring concomitantly and are to a large degree interconnected. They are interwoven systems of destruction resulting from systems of human activity.

All are caused, to a significant degree, by excessive human consumption. One way to scientifically measure the human impact on the Earth's natural environment is by what is called the ecological footprint. It is a measure of the use by humans of the Earth's renewable natural resources (Wackernagel, Onisto, Linares, & Falfan, 1997). The ecological footprint has grown by 80 per cent between 1961 and 1999 to an estimated level 20 percent above the Earth's biological capacity (WWF, 2004). In other words, back in 1999 we were already using natural resources faster than they could be renewed. Things have not gotten any better. On its current trajectory it is estimated that by 2050 we will need two earths to sustain our footprint (WWF, 2006).

Ok, so maybe those guys down at the World Wildlife Federation (WWF) are a bunch of pessimists. There are some people out there saying "Relax, don't worry, everything is fine". (They're the ones in the plaid suit jackets). As my 11-year-old daughter would say, "Dad, that's so yesterday!" What if the thousands of people, many of whom are brilliant environmental scientists, are only partially correct? Doesn't it make sense to start doing as much as we can as soon as we can so future generations, our sons and daughters, our nieces and nephews don't have to clean up our garbage? To give them a fresh start, a clean shake? Who cares, if its 2050 or 2075? Our kids, and their kids do! And you know its coming. If from 1961, when the Beatles first broke the scene, to 1999, which was just yesterday (not "so yesterday"), we increased our global environmental impact to 80%—what do you really think is going to happen over the next 50 years if we stay on the pot?

Environmental problems are based in human overconsumption. Of course some environmental problems are also based, in part, in natural cycles. For instance, global warming is a natural cycle. The excessive global warming we've been seeing since the 1980s is not. Loss of biodiversity through extinction is a natural phenomenon. Strange lizards and freaky monkeys in tropical places die-out. Who cares, right? The rate of extinction we are seeing now is not a natural phenomenon. In fact, we humans are moving rapidly up the list to be cut from the team and cut from the scene. We have to reduce our impact. Our biggest impact is made through our pattern/system of overconsumption.

Overconsumption is not the only human behavior causing the environmental problems, there's overpopulation, but it's the big one in the developed world.

Overconsumption is our monster. Nearly half of our environmentally destructive human impact is caused by our overconsumption of fossil fuels to meet our energy needs.

Overconsumption is a big system, and big business, did I say big? *A huge system, huge business* (picture "the Donald" saying that), that is destroying our earth's ecosystems and future sustainability. But remember, systems are interwoven. If we deal with the overconsumption system the other systems will improve. A lot. Through system connections other systems, like biodiversity and global warming will be positively affected. ("That's smart economics, good ROI.") That way we, and those that inherit our real estate, can live longer here on planet earth. ("That's smart long-term economic investing!") (Was that Donald?)

Overconsumption is the individual monster too. We attempt to fulfill our fear-based belonging needs through consumption, but because these needs are never truly fulfilled, or at least not for long, it soon becomes overconsumption. We buy the bigger house, the bigger boat, the bigger car under the guise of entitlement to reward, but at its core its all about affirming your belonging to the identity you want to be or think you are as seen by your family, friends, peers, intimate partner. What good is a luxury SUV if people don't see you in it? If you belong to the soccer mom group you have a luxury minivan. Lawyer? Sports car/luxury car. We're entitled, we deserve it. Some can't keep up. They over consume into massive credit card debt. Others can keep up but they are so stressed-out they over consume alcohol or drugs. Others over consume food.

Remember back in the 1650s when it was a sign of social affluence and health to be overweight? Now we know better right? So why is obesity such a problem? Of course, yes, there is a biological basis in many cases. No debate. But in more cases its because of what's behind our general problem of overconsumption is behind our overconsumption of food. Let's consider a possible metaphor. Could it be we over consume food to build a wall around the self, that little amount of self we have left, to fortify and grow big around? For protection in a sense? Because you feel everyone wants a piece of you and/or because you can't keep up so you use it to escape that reality and/or because food is your reward/entitlement, but it only fulfills temporarily? And/or is it like some revolt of some sort against a society you can't seem to be a part of? Are we using our bodies as a last stand against the machine? Is food our last "my choice" weapon against it?

It is the same reason why there is overconsumption in general. It is because each of us is individually experiencing an identity crisis. Each of our "I"s is vanishing. That bugs some of us more than others of course. Nevertheless, it is becoming harder and harder to self-actualize because the forces of society have become so increasingly intense that its nearly impossible not to conform. Cell phones are with us and on all the time, not only because its more convenient, but because we don't want to be alone anymore. We can't be alone anymore. We can't disconnect from the Internet anymore. We can't truly unplug. We've forgotten how to be good alone. To be with your "self" because we are becoming only a social self.

Our overconsumption is directly related to our fear-based need of belonging and our system/cycle of going external to fulfill it we developed as kids. It continues as we go through our lives. We try to belong but we just can't keep up. So we disconnect by over consuming alcohol, or go for the big take through gambling, or indulge in over eating. Those who can afford to stay-up over consume in other ways. Bigger cars, bigger yachts and bigger houses. Many just concede certain losses and find their niche, a fragment, where they can stake their claim to belonging.

How do we reduce overconsumption? We have to go back to when the systems first started. What possible learning system could be effective for adults to learn about sustainability and overconsumption?

It is one in which they learn how to *become* sustainability, as in identity and personality (attitudes and behavior). As I'll describe, in becoming sustainability the problem of overconsumption is solved.

Importantly, its not just about learning what sustainability or environmentalism is, that is not working enough. Just turn on the TV, flip through those channels and chances are within the first few you'll learn about an environmental crisis of some type. What do we do? Do we turn on ESPN or get on our coat and head out the door to join the environmental movement? We don't even join the environmental movement the next day. Why are there not more people becoming heroes for the environment? Some are, but not many; and many of those are running around in circles because there are so many things to do for the few. We need something more effective. We need to go deeper.

There's a hero in each one of us. We're all on a hero's journey. Each day we all do hero behaviors to "be good" or "philanthropic". For most this confirms that we belong in society, that we are making a difference, that we are part of the solution. "And the beat goes on, bad da boom, ba dah boom". Yet we are still overconsuming and destroying. Why are these individual acts of kindness—these hero moves—not working to help the environment?

We know that each one of us daily and/or weekly and/or monthly and/or yearly and/or over even longer periods over our lifespan go on the hero's journey. The mini journeys (daily) are the cycles that help us get to the big prize of self-actualization. Within a single lifetime some hero journeys are easy and short, some are complicated and prolonged. They are the various systems cycling through your life. Some people seem to go through many hero journeys before they ultimately get it, the self-actualization, while others only go through a few. I agree with Maslow, it takes hard work anyway it comes at you. And it does "come at you". The hero's journey is a system of nature experienced by humans, not created by them (only their meaning is). Even after we're self-actualized and we have the big prize we will still experience the journey in cycles. This time, however, we'll manage it from the healthiest stance we ever have in our lives.

But what is the key? What is the key to becoming self-actualized, to making it happen as fast as possible? The "fast as possible" is important to remember because systems have their own rate of moving, their own periodicity: they are the master. But in a word, the key to becoming self-actualized as expeditiously as possible is *engagement*. There are others factors like focus, trust, commitment, courage, consciousness, and compassion but engagement is the key. If you have engagement, the rest will follow. With engagement in your journey, you will thereby experience maximum progression through the journey.

The so-called "rules of engagement", to unfortunately use a military expression, are described, in part, by eupsychian self-management. I do not want to use a military metaphor any further because we are not going in to kill aspects of ourselves or take any aspects of ourselves prisoner to instill an internal democracy within the composite that is our self. Although we sometimes have to be tough with ourselves, we will never have to kill aspects of our self. In our engagement of our self-actualization we manage aspects of ourselves just as we would manage the transformation to democracy with other people: through eupsychian management of the hero's journey.

As mentioned before the hero's journey consists of: 1) Separation (from the known); 2) The call; 3) The threshold (with guardians, helpers, and mentor); 4) Initiation and Transformation; 5) The Challenges; 6) The Abyss; 7) The Transformation; 8) The Revelation; 9) The Atonement; and 10) The Return (to the known world +/- a gift).

Eupsychian self-management within the *I Am Sustainability* program proposes that the current self is understood and managed as a composite. Each aspect of that composite is given a "voice" with which to express itself; a voice inside yourself. It may at first sound like one voice; it could sound like several. The wants and needs of each voice are discovered by writing them out like a story. Each voice is given a character; there is usually a predominant one. The wants and needs along the Maslow hierarchy are provided for each character in a healthy manner so that each character within a person can self-actualize. For guidance the path and narrative for each characters story is compared to the hero's journey. Each character of self wants to self-actualize and does so through the hero's journey. That is the shared system of systems of human psychological development. We *all* are in it. Joseph Campbell knew it as did Carl Jung, as have many others.

Just the act alone, of listening to yourself, being with yourself and honoring yourself will begin to build your sustainability. Its like meeting a long lost friend. You make sure you get their number, email address, all of it so you can stay in touch. Its kind of a weird exercise at first—"listening to yourself"—but it rings true for some reason. It works, and you find yourself wanting more.

The ultimate goal is to bring those voices and their journeys together. This is the "whole and complete" I was referring to earlier. Once whole and complete you will still be in the hero's journey that goes on and on, but you will be doing so from a healthy and powerful place you likely never thought possible. Its easier to stay healthy with a unified focus than an erratic scatter of stories.

So what do these "voices" manifest as in the normal person in Western society? (For the sake of brevity and clarity in this section I'll make it a male, a him/he, it could just as well be a her/she.) Remember, the narratives with their voices tell the stories that are made-up to make meaning around the need to belong within the different stages of development of childhood. The only thing that makes a person "normal" is that the separation between the voices in the normal adult person is not so clear. He sees them and experiences them (voices/narratives/stories) as the homogenized person he calls "self". He confuses and conflates his "inner voice" as one person. He sometimes goes out on a limb and speaks about his "bad self" at parties, but never gets that his composite is actually a serially constructed person he made-up coping with the lack of belonging he experienced while growing up. "Why can't I belong here…or there? he asked…then he made up a story and gave it meaning". Each aspect, from each age/stage during development is a survival/coping system. Each system is stuck in the repeat behavior/emotional/thought pattern he created at the time he was a kid. This pattern continues over and over again with only minor modifications to make them a bit more age appropriate as an adult. Yet the child story is never far behind. He is literally stuck in childhood. Most of the time his self-esteem can cover it up to himself, the fact that he is really a kid. For the external, to others, he's managed to find some successful behaviors, some winning ways, to cover it up. Yet, he is very much stuck in the systems and has never really grown-up. He has never left the need to belong to the external and has never moved further toward self-actualization. He walks around being ruled by fear-based child behavior and doesn't even know it. Strangely, in societies eyes', he's considered normal. Perhaps only because he is well adjusted to the way everyone, everywhere is. Childlike.

Childlike works because we are all childlike in our network of co-dependent social systems. It's the social norm. To grow-up, to really grow-up, is to detach from society as you now know it. Its the first step on the hero's journey to self-actualization. Once you do, the only new society you can go to, at first, for complete understanding and complete belonging is the society you create within yourself. You do end up coming back to society of course, but this time its in a much healthier, whole and complete format.

By saying childlike I am not saying people are bad. I am not attempting a defamation of the social character en masse. We are, however, each a composite of behavior systems developed when we were kids. We are using schoolyard tactics, maybe somewhat more sophisticated, but at their base, still childlike. To shift that at the societal level, a critical tipping point needs to be reached within a certain number of individuals, and for the sake of the global environment, it needs to be reached soon. This book is a call to that tipping point. This too, the call, hearing it, engaging it, is part of the hero's journey.

The first steps in the hero's journey are the separation from the known and the engagement of the call you hear. That call can take many forms, it can be a simple call for change you hear within yourself or it can be the welling-up of a strong call for personal transformation. That is when this book and the *I Am Sustainability* program can work for you. As per the hero's journey Joseph Campbell described, then you will cross the threshold with the assistance of mentors in the *I Am Sustainability* program. Through the program and our mentorship *you* will uncover and discover which initiations, transformations and challenges *you* have to face to process the fear-basis of the behavior systems you chose as a child. Next, in your abyss you will be alone, but not unequipped or unsupported. You will have many skills of management and support from the Ecosphere Net group. Following the revelation and the atonement, whatever that looks like for you, you will return to the known world with a self-actualized identity in sustainability and well on your way to the self-actualization Maslow described.

As with all systems there are choice points, tipping points, a "critical mass" where a shift can occur either as a gradual emergence or as a seemingly spontaneous shift. A gradual change and spontaneous change, both are possible along the hero's journey. Neither is more correct, although given our scientific environmental forecasts, we had better get on the ball quickly. That sense of urgency is part of "the call" aspect of the hero's journey.

The system of the hero's journey, the system of self-actualization and the system of the eupsychian management of that self-actualization are all part of the systems psychotherapy used in the body-centered adult *I Am Sustainability* program.

Eupsychian management of the self by a self-actualized or actualizing individual can also be called eupsychian self-management. This entails managing the various aspects of the self by fulfilling their hierarchy of needs. This is of course done in a healthy way, in a way that poses no threat or harm to self or other.

Systems psychotherapy considers, as I described in this book, the unhealthy behavior systems currently in your life. The systems that make you happy, the systems that make you sad. It also considers the system dynamics of your relationships and considers the role each person plays in the co-dependencies. This is a personal first few steps of your journey toward self-actualization in sustainability. Therefore, the *I Am Sustainability* program primarily uses one-on-one and very small group scenarios to do this. The groups are more instructional and conversational than "sharefesting". The one-on-ones are for analysis and guidance. The *We Are Sustainability* program takes place in groups primarily. Analysis and guidance in *I Am Sustainability* takes place through individuals who have already self-actualized as system analyzers and guides.

The self, as I wrote earlier, is made up of a composite of selves, each with their own wants and needs hierarchy, and their own story about what belonging means. In the *I Am Sustainability* you learn how to see their behavior systems and how to fulfill their belonging needs in alternative healthier ways than those that you have been using in your life. You do this by learning how to use your body to center your new behavior patterns in, as opposed to the externalization that you were attempting to use to fulfill your needs previously. Your body becomes the center of your sustainability, and because nobody can take that away from you, they can't take away your sustainability either. Your body becomes the center of your new healthier life systems. Your body becomes the true place—your body as place—of your identity in sustainability.

It is part of the Ecosphere Net project to create a global network of connected sustainability education centers that are accessible to everyone, everywhere regardless of geographic location or socioeconomic status. So it is our goal to ensure that you'll never be disconnected from a healthy society of self-actualizers within the Ecosphere Net global network.

Systems psychotherapy is also the interfacing of older psychoanalytical methods and newer cognitive analytical methods interfaced with the systems descriptions I have used in this book. In other words it is an interfacing of the entire psychotherapeutic lineage within a self-organizing systems perspective of human behavior and attitudes. The *We Are Sustainability* program is, in part, about teaching pluralism (the benefits of diversity) but that already begins with the *I Am Sustainability* in its use of the full spectrum of psychotherapeutic learning approaches.

Unfortunately, each successive school of the psychotherapeutic lineage has historically dismissed the previous schools. This may have been largely because psychotherapy has always been trying to affirm its place within the framework of a medical/scientific model. Did it have a problem with unhealthy self-actualization? Looks like it did, doesn't it? The way it has historically rebelled against its past to seek identity and meaning completely in the external highly valued medical model. Perhaps each successive school was not secure in its own authenticity, as indicated by its serial dismissal of previous schools.

Nevertheless, the *I Am Sustainability* program utilizes some of each of them all, and in an open-ended exploratory process. The open exploratory process is similar to the social constructivism approach utilized in the children's *I Am Sustainability* program. The only difference is that the self-actualization process and learning group for the children are classmates in school whereas for adults its working with the multiple narratives from childhood and onward that make-up the self. This is an important addition to the eupsychian self-management previously described.

Systems Psychotherapy proposes the perspective that everything we are is part of a system. Some of the characteristics of the systems metaphor in human behavior as used in the adult *I Am Sustainability* program are:

1) Everything can be described by a system or as being part of a system.

2) Humans attach meaning to systems creating ritual, mythology, narrative, stories, belief systems and schemata.

3) Human behavior systems are repetitive, habitual and in its most extensive case compulsive, obsessive and addictive.

4) Human behavior systems are to some extent "hardwired" neurophysiologically into a locus of behaviors associated within the cultural description called a personality trait to index the meaning of that locus.

5) While much of the "hardwiring" of reiterative systems of personality occurs during the first twenty years of life during brain maturation it is reversible through new "hardwiring" within the confines of neuroplasticity

6) The "hardwiring" of the behavior system used to attempt to fulfill the insatiable need to belong to external social groups occurs in stages during development setting-up at least three distinguishable behavior sys-

tems with regard to belonging.

7) Each of these systems has a narrative that is associated with the behavior system. In this sense the individual self is a self-organizing multi-agent system (mas). Currently, because of the insatiable external need to belong the overconsumptive self is predominately defined by an overconsumptive external mas. In this sense the composite mas of self is a fractal image of the composite mas of society.

8) The notion of balance as being right and imbalance as being wrong is only relative when taken in context within a cultural mythology. Systems are in constant flux and are thereby better described by the metaphor of flow, resilience (degrees of freedom), and sustainability through that resilience.

9) Psychological crisis episodes are viewed as points of chaos, maximal creativity, and are points for optimal learning. They are what Maslow describes as "choice points" and what I have called "peak points" that cycles back into life experience.

10) Human systems of experience and behavior are connected to each other and to the environment. Individual systems of behavior and experience are grounded in and flow through the body. The body is the central processor of human experience.

As with the social constructivism approach taken in the child/young adult version of the program, the objective of the systems psychotherapeutic approach for adults in the *I Am Sustainability* program is to start the hero's journey toward self-actualization ultimately and self-actualization in sustainability initially.

The word "systems" in systems psychotherapy means that we use many different systems of psychotherapy from the lineage of Western psychotherapeutic culture and Eastern philosophical, so-called wisdom cultural traditions. A truly pluralistic approach. "Systems" also means, as described in the above list, that the implications of systems metaphors are used to understand life events.

If the word "psychotherapy" in systems psychotherapy concerns you, then replace it with "education" or "learning". I have yet to read about or experience a psychotherapeutic approach in which learning was not a key component. Conversely, the transmissive teaching I received during my education was to some degree psychotherapeutic. So, psychotherapy is educational and conversely education is psychotherapeutic. The only difference of course is that in psychotherapy you learn a lot about yourself and your life. In education, especially the transmissive type, as I describe more later, you learn much less about yourself and you often learn about other people's lives.

Incidentally, we use "education" instead of "psychotherapy" at Ecosphere Net to improve consistency given that our project at Ecosphere Net is to set-up a global network of sustainability education centers (SEC's). So our *I Am Sustainability* program for adults is often called "Adult Sustainability Education – Body-centered Systems Education".

# Body-centered Child and Young Adult Sustainability Constructivism

I just read the passage below this week. Its written by a college instructor and speaks to what he sees as the mental state and mental experience of American young people today.

> "We are numbered in billions," Merton writes, (Thomas Merton, *Conjectures of a Guilty Bystander*)... "worked to the point of insensibility, dazed by information, drugged by entertainment, surfeited with everything, nauseated with the human race and with ourselves, nauseated with life".
>
> The nausea of which Merton writes is what we used to call 'despair' or 'angst,' that which experts today refer to by an array of psychiatric names: anxiety, clinical depression, bipolar disorder, post-traumatic stress disorder, and attention-deficit disorder – not to mention erectile dysfunction. You can take an assortment of pills for the nausea of modern despair: the pain of lost love, the fear of failure, the dread of poor sexual performance. Many of my students [the author is an English composition college instructor in Pennsylvania] take such medications. These pills are pushed on network television in slick, long-winded commercials interspersed with brief news segments calculated to *cause* anxiety—reports of suicide bombers, child molesters, suspected threats to national security, nascent pandemics, kidnappings, genocide. This mind numbing, socially engineered cocktail has left many young people tone-deaf to prophetic nuance. It is as if they have arrived at adulthood with their alarm systems disabled. In the classes I teach, I must take care to avoid any

negative statements that might label me as antagonistic to popular culture. Having been taught to assess attitude rather than substance, young people have developed an eagle eye for affect. For them, affect *is* substance. I get around this problem by cheerfully assigning stories about suffering and death. And I never lecture. (Smith, 2007, p.20)

We need something new. Remember the quote at the beginning of this book?

*"We can't solve problems by using the same kind of thinking we used when we created them"* — Albert Einstein

The children and young adult *I Am Sustainability* program flips Maslow's triangle on its top. On its self-actualization apex. Our current socialization in and out of schools is what is increasing our environmental impact and decreasing our chances for global sustainability. If we want things to change for the better, toward sustainability, then we have to teach our kids how to self-actualize in sustainability and that its ok to start doing so early. In the *I Am Sustainability* program we are teaching kids to self-actualize in sustainability. This will empower them to fully self-actualize as adults in a healthy and effective manner. It will also help the growing-up years become easier to manage for child and family.

Self-actualization in sustainability can be achieved through a teaching technique called social constructivism. This technique has been used successfully for years in small-scale pilot research based teaching exercises. We don't have to reinvent the wheel. J. Lawrence Bencze at the Ontario Institute for Secondary Education, University of Toronto has extensively developed the self-actualization of students using a secondary-school science curriculum based in social constructivism (see Bencze, 2000a, b, 2001, 2004; Bencze, Bowen, & Aslop, 2006; Bencze, Di Giuseppe, Hodson, Pedretti, Serebin, & Descoito, 2003).

Its time to open-up the social constructivist approach to make it available through all schools to all kids within an *I Am Sustainability* and *We Are Sustainability* based environmental curriculum. An *I Am Sustainability* and *We Are Sustainability* based environmental curriculum includes, and in fact focuses on, the environment of "self" first, utilizes a body as place metaphor, introduces systems learning, self-actualization, and personal sustainability as well as education in body psychology, body-work, and bodycare.

Most kids are taught through a transmissive-type educational program. A knowledgeable teacher speaks from a socially constructed curriculum and children take in the knowledge. There is a passive intake, a consumption and later at test time, a regurgitation of information. Transmission/receiver/rebroadcast. Social constructivist education is the merger of minimal instruction with maximal student inquiry and exploration. The experience of discovery and the self-actualization in the social constructivist approach has many more benefits than that of a transmissive approach. Transmissive approaches maintain the social status quo of the social dogma. The student plays a passive, consumptive role in the learning process.

Carefully orchestrated social constructivist learning fosters the experience of self-actualization, democracy and pluralism in students. "Carefully orchestrated" because teachers can quickly engineer away the students' freedom to construct their own knowledge and stir it back toward the social dogma imbued in their own personal biases. Bencze calls this latter subversive and coercive constructivist practices.

Social constructivism teaches students to not just consume information, but to do so with the intent to construct their own knowledge. By constructing their own knowledge they self-actualize. They develop themselves "in ways unique to their needs, interests, abilities, and perspectives" (Bencze, 2000a, p. 852). This freedom is the basis and experience of democracy. It also provides tremendous empowerment and self-esteem in the student, necessary to be a sustainable healthy self-actualized individual.

As a guideline Bencze has described a 3-step constructivist learning cycle. There is the inner conceptual domain through which a concept is cycled by the learning group and an outer procedural domain in which the methods/procedures to process the concepts are learned by the students. The inner conceptual domain is described by 3 stages.

These are: 1) Expressing current conceptions, interests, attitudes; 2) Sharing and learning new conceptions from peers and professionals (such as teacher, invited guest, etc.); and 3) Applying and testing conceptions in authentic problem solving situations for their own evaluation and possible construction of new ones based on their needs, interests, abilities and perspectives. The outer procedural domain follows the inner conceptual domain. After Step 1 the student may learn new methods to express ideas to facilitate movement to Step 2. After Step 2 the student may learn new methods to share and learn ideas to facilitate movement to Step 3. After Step 3 the student may learn new methods to apply and test their ideas (adapted from Bencze, 2000a, p. 853).

These latter three promote procedural understanding of the democratic constructivist learning process. This procedural component is key to empowering students to construct and produce their own knowledge. Bencze points out, however, that the 3-step cycle is as an outline only and that the constructivist process in learning be an "idiosyncratic, spontaneous, intuitive, counter-intuitive, random, context dependent and ideological". He goes onto describe the social constructivist learning process as open ended and exploratory emphasizing learning through creativity and problem solving.

If you just said, "Hey, that all sounds like a self-organizing system as you've described in this book!" you get a gold star in your workbook. Just like the body as place metaphor works because it is inherently in integrity with social and biological systems that exist (i.e., those of nature), so too a constructivist learning systems is a system that is inherently in integrity with how systems work in nature. Constructivism learning flows and self-organizes, like social systems, like biological systems. However, it is social learning regardless if its transmissive or social constructivism and it's a system regardless of which approach taken, that's not the point here. The point is that social constructivism is a learning system for kids that is empowering and fosters self-actualization (outside of the creativity/diplomacy skills). If we go with nature, how nature works instead of fighting it, instead of fighting "city hall" we're likely to be better off long-term as a species. When are we fighting it? Well, we never are really, in any scenario we're going with one system or another all of which are natural. The only difference is that when it comes to environmental education and education for sustainability the transmissive approach and variations thereof are not working. Scientifically proven, our current environmental education systems are not working. Why?

They are not working because we are using the same old education systems that created the environmental problems to solve them. We need to balance transmissive and social constructivism approaches. The transmissive type has historically dominated Western education. Transmissive type of education promotes a socially submissive life. Follow the group, conform to the curriculum and you'll get good grades. Or at least grades that will let you pass and stay with the group. You get the chance for authentic self-expression and authentic self-empowerment when you are fully grown. By then, however, it is too late. If you like to think you are free after school to do what you want, you are so indoctrinated in the culture that your freedom is locked into a social mindset. For many, however, life goes on too quickly and the question of autonomy and free- thinking is lost to more socially appropriate rituals such as marriage and family. There are too many lemmings. There are too many followers, too few creative thinkers and far too few self-actualizers. This is why the attack on our reason, as Al Gore recently wrote in his book by the same name, has been so successful. We are too busy trying to fulfill our need to belong in the external social world through overconsumption to ever consider we have lost our true selves and we have lost our ability to reason and think critically. If we want that back, then we need to balance transmissive type education with the social constructivism type. We need wide sweeping educational reform. Not just a symbolic gesture. In the end we get young people that are able to reason, think critically, and utilize their own skills in finding and working with information. Most importantly, if we utilize the social constructivism approach in a body-centered sustainability curriculum, we get future generations of young adults that consume less, live healthier, and embrace global sustainability and human rights from a healthier social stance than ever before. That won't be good of course for the luxury SUV companies and the oil industry and their view on what the sustainability of the global economy should look like.

We cannot solve our problems with the same systems (kind of thinking) we used to create them in the first place. We need something new. We can never get away from our interwoven social and biological systems. We can, however, teach our kids and ourselves how to better understand and manage them. That is what the *I Am* and *We Are Sustainability* programs are all about.

Whereas Lawrence Bencze's work at the University of Toronto has focused on self-actualizing within a science curriculum (which is really hard to do by the way because it goes against the "social grain" in several ways), the *I Am Sustainability* program does so within a body-centered sustainability curriculum. The definition of the term "sustainability" utilized in the curriculum takes-on all variations of meaning including: self-sustainability (including each level of Maslow's Hierarchy), other sustainability (including cross-cultural differences), and environmental sustainability. The *I Am Sustainability* program also explores five aspects of existing environmental education, but does so within a social constructivist approach to teaching and learning. These are:

1) "Nature as relation" rather than "Nature as object" awareness (Bonnett, 2002; Loughland, Reid & Petocz, 2002).

2) Ecological consciousness (Low, 2003; Uhl, 2003). Ecological literacy (Cutter-Mackenzie & Smith, 2003; Orr, 1992, 2004).

3) Ecological self as an identity (Bragg, 1995, 1996; Diehm, 2003; Devall (2001); Naess, 1988).

Nature as relation refers to the development of a different attitude towards nature, one of relatedness rather than objectifying it. Fostering a deeper connection, one that promotes an ecological self identity. Ecological consciousness of course relates to the students awareness of ecology. Ecological literacy refers to the students becoming well versed in the language of deep ecology and sustainability, both personal and global; especially with regard to overconsumption. Therefore 1 and 2 above are about an identification *with* nature. The *I Am Sustainability* program attempts to take this even further by generating an identification *in* sustainability; one that is connected and balanced in a healthy manner to self, others, and the environment and the Earth.

# The *I Am Sustainability* Program

What healthy is and what unhealthy is, is sometimes a matter of opinion. Standing in the middle of traffic on a busy street in dark clothing with no overhead lights at night is obviously an unhealthy choice. Other behaviors whether they are healthy or not is a matter of debate, a matter of personal preference. You'll soon discover if that preference ends-up being an unhealthy choice.

The *I Am Sustainability* program while helping you to understand your authentic self and understand how to achieve and maintain that authentic self, in your sustainability, does not tell you how that should specifically look like. This differs from the linear "right/wrong" judgments and occasional acrimony that is present in the various schools of psychology, such as the humanistic one Maslow co-created. Maslow's ideas are over 40 years old, and to some degree therefore represent the cultural mind-set at that time.

While Maslow's ideas are old they are not outdated or antiquated. They remain relevant and perhaps more so than ever in our unsustainable overconsumptive Western society. Maslow's work was all about human potential. That's exactly what we need to get back to before we can go forward. We have to go back to the self, what it is we are each capable of in a positive sense in terms of self-actualization, before we can go forward to a healthier "we", one that aspires to global sustainability. Since Maslow's time there have been many other truly great writers and talented thinkers about human potential. Some of this is described in what is called transpersonal psychology or existential-humanistic psychology. Its also in positive psychology, appreciative inquiry, and human flourishing. These newer approaches are all part of the *I Am Sustainability* program. They form the pluralistic basis of the program. That is why the people at Ecosphere Net who teach the *I Am Sustainability* program do so from a wide variety of perspectives and, to keep it culturally sensitive and appropriate, they do so in an open-ended collaborative and exploratory manner.

As far as self-actualization goes Abraham Maslow and I differ on one important point. His idea was that a person could and in fact *should* find and focus their identity in their work. What a person does as their vocation would be the identity centerpiece. In so doing the internal would merge with the external as the person self-actualized in their work, and thereby invariably contribute to an external cause. In this sense, for Maslow, the internal and external become one. The *I Am Sustainability* program extends those ideas and utilizes a different centerpiece. There is more room in your identity than just your work, yet, having identification in your work, is important. But unlike being a centerpiece of who you are, your vocation is an expression of who you are. You are sustainability. If you have become self-actualized in sustainability then everything else falls into place, because there is, as Maslow describes, no need for separation, for compartmentalization, because who you are is in everything you do. You identify "you" in everything you do. If you happen to be skilled as a pilot you conduct yourself to the same standard as if you were a forest ranger or an apple farmer. You live by a commitment to healthy excellence and achievement in everything you do. Body health, social health, psychological health as one. You are strong and resilient, not perfect. Nor do you seek perfection. You have healthy courage, compassion and celebration in your life. Whether an unhealthy society agrees with that to you is secondary.

I wrote earlier: "The only purpose of the *I Am Sustainability* program is to provide the tools so you can move beyond your self and do so quickly." I want to explain more clearly what I meant by that. Throughout this book I have tried to emphasize the achievement of balance. We are currently out of balance in our overconsumptive Western society. This is because we are psychologically unbalanced trying to find our meaning in life, our purpose and our belonging outside of ourselves. The *I Am Sustainability* program corrects that. It reconnects you with your authentic self, your healthy core, and sets you on your way to self-actualization in whatever you want to do. Nevertheless, regardless of what you do it will be as *your* healthy *I Am Sustainability* self so that you can maintain your new balance.

We cannot win against certain realities. We cannot overcome all our fears. In fact, some fear is healthy. We cannot overcome all of our external need to belong. We can, however, fight the tendency of our fears to overwhelm and control us. Its not about becoming a master over your own life. System flow is the master. Besides being a *total* master would be boring for you and those around you. You want some surprises and spontane-ity don't you? Likely. Its about becoming a master of your self in whatever life brings you. Yes, you can create your life to a large degree in the mo-ment of choice points, but you cannot completely predict it. So you have to be ready with your own identity in sustainability. Its about becoming a pattern recognizer of the systems that flow/cycle in your life and under-standing them so that you can exercise your authentic healthy power in the moment, at your choice points.

We all want to be hero's. Each and everyone of us is on, as Joseph Campbell has described, a hero's journey. Although he makes no mention of Campbell in his work, that is why, I suppose, Abraham Maslow put such an emphasis on achievement and goal orientation in the description of self-actualizers. Having a goal in which we identify provides that which we inherently need: the Hero's Journey. My contribution to that would be that, for personal and global sustainability, it needs to be a balanced hero, a conscious hero. One aware of him or herself. Hero's often become mar-tyrs, stuck in the suffering. Hero's often bear crosses or grind axes. These are hero's out of balance. Hero's out of balance are often elected to lead-ership spots in times of social hope and social fear. That is not working well for global sustainability. That is another reason for the emphasis in the *I Am Sustainability* program for achieving an identity in sustainability. The sustainability maintains the balance, and the balance maintains the sustainability.

Self-actualizing in sustainability through *I Am Sustainability* is about becoming a healthy hero. A powerful person, engaged in life, not held-up by your self(s), and not indulging in prolonged existential quests without practical results of some sort. Self-actualizers in sustainability are spiritual, to be sure, wherever and however they attain that spirituality is up to them. They are sensitive and magnanimous, but they also have a strong penchant for industry and pragmatism. When I wrote that *the only* "purpose of the *I Am Sustainability* program is to provide the tools to move beyond your self and do so quickly", I tried to reflect the intention and energy of the self-actualizer. As I have written, the "I" is vanishing in our current Western society, we are becoming frantic because of it, and in our attempts to appease our need for belonging we are overconsuming. To fight that system, just to achieve a new balance, takes hard work and some powerful insights, powerful goals and initial guidance. That is what *I Am Sustainability* is all about.

While the *I Am Sustainability* program has been described throughout this book, and in particular in the last two sections, the idea of it being "body-centered" needs more elaboration. I want to elaborate on how the human body can save the planet.

The term "body-centered" is common to both the adult and child/young adult *I Am Sustainability* programs. Quiet simply, if we do not center the sustainability education in the body then everything else we do, all our efforts, will not be as effective. The actualized self needs a home. The actualizing self needs a reference point. That home and that reference point is the body. We *must* (a rare use of the word "must")... we must include use of a "body as place metaphor" and we must include "hands-on"... physical bodywork and bodycare as our means of centering sustainability in the body. Both, not either. Not more of one. Both equally.

Going through the body when learning and becoming sustainability creates an essential social and biological personal reference point and context. Humans need what I call "collective individualism". We need diversity, a sense of autonomy balanced with a sense of belonging. What but the body, our body, can give us that individualism. What but our body can help us relate to the environment and too each other. Its what makes us unique and its what we all have in common.

Sustainability grounded in the body will help (all) the environment(s) more than ever before. Here "environment" means the body's environment, the community environment and the natural environment. A reduction of overconsumption and suicide. A reduction in violence towards self and others. Saving the planet. These are all achievable goals if we ground our sustainability curriculum, the one that self-actualizes an *I Am Sustainability* identity, in the body.

This is possible through the development of a new branch in psychology, a unified multi-disciplinary branch called Body Psychology, which takes the lead to develop a social constructivism curriculum for children/young adults and a systems psychotherapeutic approach for adults.

As it is being developed in the *I Am and We Are Sustainability* programs, body psychology extends well beyond mainstream science-based psychology into folk psychology and the so-called Eastern wisdom traditions. It includes Western and Eastern medical philosophy from specialized medical practitioners. Which body work practices are utilized: yoga, martial arts, and marathon running to name a few are part of the exploratory process of self-actualization in the *I Am Sustainability* program.

Lastly, some more clarification of how the *I Am Sustainability* is being developed through action research, i.e., more about the how we can bridge the idea of sustainability with the needed result of sustainability; both personal and global. This last section of this chapter attempts to answer the "how do we get there?" question some more. Short answer? We can do it by using action research.

Action research bridges the artificial dichotomy between rigorous human science research and informed and excellent professional practices such as in teaching and education. At Ecosphere Net we assume action research can, 1) provide a significant research contribution toward understanding and transforming human attitudes and behaviors with regard to their relationship with the environment and with each other, and 2) that it can provide the most efficacious methodological vehicle for the development and implementation of a valid cross-cultural curriculum for global sustainability. Quite simply, the generative and creative participatory process unique to action research is currently much needed to help save the planet. In terms of generating global sustainability it can do so more efficaciously than the currently popular transmissive approaches to the teaching and learning of environmentalism. The formation and development of an aspect of an individual's identity in sustainability we call "I Am Sustainability" through the generative process of action research will shift societies from the current inadequate behaviors and attitudes of reform ecology to those more closely aligned with the tenets of deep ecology and their description of the ecological self, thereby ultimately being key to the fulfillment of the UN Millennium Project goals. Our action research at Ecosphere Net seeks to improve the sustainability systems of human-self interaction, human-human interaction and human-environment interaction.

The intention of action research is to reach new understanding and engage in new action. While action research is an umbrella term for a variety of types of social research, one powerful format of action research is the focus group method. In general terms the purpose of the focus group is to engage participants to learn through their involvement in the consideration of and focus on a problem. It is a group conversation that attempts to solve or make a problem better while utilizing and actually embracing the inherently biased individual interpretative process.

The collaborative and generative focus group dialogical process (conversation) is initiated following a brief presentation of the primary researcher's interpretation and proposed solution to the problem. In general terms, the desired result, ultimately, is to generate a practical change that affects the lives of the participants and thereby those around them over the long term. Ideally, in the case of generating global sustainability through action research this includes an empowerment of participants to take action in their communities and for them to continue to perpetuate and expand the generative process of action research (the conversation) within themselves and within those communities. In essence thereby becoming collaboratively and creatively generative in the system of sustainable democratic civil societies.

Action research engages a multi-disciplinary and multi-cultural interface. By bringing the various opinions, belief systems, and expertise together for contribution in the conversation this type of diverse interface becomes inherently consistent and remains in integrity with what action research claims to do. That is, it employs pluralism (diversity, and equal power of diverse groups), egalitarianism (equal rights) and democracy (community/global choices are made by the people, not the elite or special interest group) in the conversation to generate a pluralistic, egalitarian and democratic construction of reality. Importantly, in the particular case of generating a curriculum that will work on a global level, multi-disciplinary and multi-cultural interfacing in action research opens the door to cross-cultural contribution to that construction. In its broad-based approach it becomes a vehicle that likely not only has general relevance but also wide and mass appeal.

This is exactly how the *I Am Sustainability* is being developed. Through an ever expanding focus group conversation, which will eventually be the focus of the majority of the group of all humans on the planet. This book is the starting reference point of that global conversation. At Ecosphere Net we assume that education and social action research can be interfaced effectively, that this interface can have a valid sociopolitical agenda and that this interface within a constructivist participatory research methodology utilizing a global network of sustainability education centers (SEC's) and a continuing pluralistic conversation is the best cross-cultural approach to shift human values and behaviors toward global sustainability.

Ecosphere Net will carry the results of each conversation forward from all the venues it participates in; involving different cultures such as young and adult learners, corporations and scientific groups. In the near future, for example, we are scheduled to be part of conversations at Wesleyan University in Connecticut and at Cambridge University, UK. We will regularly publish the outcomes from the ever-expanding *I Am Sustainability* conversations in our book entitled Ecosphere Net: Global Conversations for Global Sustainability.

Enrico J. Wensing

# Final Thoughts

As I have attempted to describe in this book, the basic assumption of the "I Am Sustainability" program is that all of the human impediments to global sustainability begin in a single human problem, that is, the psychology of the currently disproportionate human need to belong to social groups.

This assumption asserts that all humans need to have a sense of self-identity and that they gain that self-identity during their development through their perceived belonging to specific social groups. Even the well-known brief counter-culture episodes during teenage years and young adulthood represent identification with and belonging to a social group in one form of social group or another. Thereafter, the need to belong to the mainstream social groups, for the vast majority, ultimately subsumes any truly counter-cultural or authentic identity. Thus, the self is socially created.

The problem for the environment and global sustainability is that the human attempt to find belonging continues to be disproportionately sought-after and maintained in social groups even in adulthood. In affluent consumer oriented and developing societies it is occurring nearly exclusively within the realm of socially competitive groups. This results in exploitive behaviors with regard to the environment and other humans, overconsumption and the unequal distribution of wealth. In undemocratic countries autocratic governmental rule dictates social belonging. In these cases you have all the same environmentally exploitative behaviors of the affluent countries plus an over-abundance of exploitation of human rights and freedoms. In the poverty stricken societies the search for self identity is occurring in such a way that the self identity lives and gains belonging vicariously through the socially based group practice of excessive procreation, thereby resulting in overpopulation. In both cases the self is socially maintained at the expense of the environment and any hope for global sustainability.

As the environmental crisis becomes more of a social trend in the West, Western society, the often self-presumptive global leader in social propriety, is slowly changing from within and thereby creating new individuals with a more environmentally friendly identity. However, this is occurring too slowly and too infrequently. Perhaps most importantly, the level at which this is occurring is too shallow. This means that while pro-environmental talk can be found in abundance, pro-environmental lifestyle is disproportionately much lower in frequency.

Thus, although an increased awareness and knowledge of environmental problems by individuals and groups through environmental education does generate novel affirmations of reformed environmental attitudes and declarations of intentions for affirmative environmental action, these verbal claims are often inconsistent with actual nascent positive environmental behaviors, in both the short and long-term (Jurin & Fortner 2002; Kollmuss, & Agyeman, 2002). Stated more colloquially, for the most part people do not continue to walk their pro-environmental talk following environmental education.

At the individual level this could be seen as accomplished environmental social actors, or more bluntly, simple hypocrisy. At the corporate level this is termed "greenwashing", or more bluntly, corporate hypocrisy.

According to Wikipedia the term greenwashing is generally used,

> When significantly more money or time has been spent advertising being green (that is, operating with consideration for the environment) rather than spending resources on environmentally sound practices. This is often portrayed by changing the name or label of a product, to give the feeling of nature, for example putting an image of a forest on a bottle of harmful chemicals. Environmentalists often use greenwashing to describe the actions of energy companies, which are traditionally the largest polluters.

One of the main points in this book is that this talking and not walking phenomenon is due to a critical difference between "identification with" and "identification in" sustainability, with too little being currently done to promote the "identification in" aspect. These are two different gateways toward attitudes and behaviors that are consistent with global environmental sustainability. In the "identification with" gateway pro-environmental and sustainability attitudes and behaviors are generated through efforts that create an ecological consciousness (awareness) of the environment such as we see generated by the important work of Al Gore or the television station, CNN 's "Planet in Peril" program etc. "Identification with" sustainability can also be generated by efforts that create a "nature as relation", that is, relationship experience such as current environmental education efforts toward ecological literacy and environmental experiences such through ecotourism etc.

By contrast, "identification in" the environment and sustainability is about identity formation. Pro-environmental and sustainability attitudes and behaviors become part of an individual's identity. This is found in the work of Arne Naess and the deep ecology movement and their rendition of the ecological self. Similarly, it is also the objective of the *I Am Sustainability* program by Ecosphere Net as described in this book. But, as noted earlier in this book, *I Am Sustainability* is a balanced healthy body-centered identity that will by default be pro-environmental. This includes the environment of self, other and all of nature. This describes self-actualization in sustainability. By contrast, the ecological self, as described by the deep ecology movement would be a self-actualization in nature. As I mentioned previously, while everyone can form "I Am Sustainability" within their identity, only some will go on to self-actualize in nature as an ecological self.

As I've also tried to describe in this book, the action and movement of all of nature can be described in terms of non-linear self-organizing dynamical systems. Everything is part of a system, in what appears to be a highly connected system of systems. The properties of these systems, individually and collectively, are being explored by a broad spectrum of disciplines not just the complexity sciences. One fundamental property of all systems discovered so far, besides their ubiquity and connectedness, is that all systems, including the system of systems, self-organize spontaneously without a central control. Humans, too, even though we have our conscious brain, what appears to be a central controller, which, while having linear free choice in the moment, our actions are spontaneously subsumed beyond free will in the moment by subconscious self-organizing non-linear dynamical systems before and after the moment. Human systems are embedded within the systems of all of nature. If all the systems are embedded within each other and are thereby interacting, the question then becomes, what defines a system? In particular, what defines a human system? Maybe that definition and that reality is all a matter of perspective and not truth. So, sure, we can and should draw boundaries, we have to sometimes, no argument there, but maybe the best way to do that is as a group, defined by the very diversity we are trying to draw borders around.

We currently continue to move, however, both within countries and globally, toward what can be seen as deeper and continued social "us and them" distinctions, and "the have and have not" social structures, and the created and perpetuated "the enemy" consensus.

This is social polarization. While social hierarchy and diversity is a phenomenon found in nature, social polarization is not. While social hierarchy fosters mutualism (a biological term meaning that the fitness of all species benefits from the hierarchy) and synergy (combined action of diversity produces a stronger result than each can individually) social polarization does not. Polarization is a social construct we are making-up and together we keep it going. Guess what it is based-in? Fear. (I know you knew that :-) As many people have tried to explain, polarization is not a good thing. For instance, to the infrastructure, including the social, economic as well as the individual quality of life in the United States, preventing the loss of the middle class (polarization into rich and poor classes) has been a key emphasis in the political career of the democratic representative (and marathon runner) John Edwards.

Similarly, polarization is also occurring within the environmental movement toward those who are involved and doing something to those who are not because, in many cases they cannot because they have more immediate pressing priorities such as finding a job and feeding their families (that's the bottom of the Maslow hierarchy again). Yale Law graduate and social activist Van Jones calls this situation eco-apartheid (Google him...he's up to some great things!). In this scenario the 20% who are involved will not outweigh the 80% who are not (many of whom have the more immediate priorities) and thereby the efforts of the environmental movement will likely fail. How do we get more of the 80% involved? Van Jones would likely say "Two words, 'green economy'". (google that too) ("Ugh...dad, that's so like homework!") (Who said that?)

The "enemy consensus", which is a variation of the "us and them" scenario, is the idea that there is an enemy and somehow what they value is something different and wrong and may even be weird. This is what keeps cults a cohesive group; they have to keep the fear of the enemy going within the group. That tension. The idea includes the narrative, "Don't talk to them, until they somehow agree with and take-on our ideas and ideals as we see and express them." As Barack Obama has suggested, it is part of the current culture and politics of fear in the United States.

Fear and divisiveness is not the way to global sustainability.

As I finish this book I have some second thoughts. I am confronted by some of my narratives. They say, "Is it smart to put out a book written so quickly?" "Its too casual, too many topics, you'll never get an academic appointment at a university after this book!" I think of people who might say, "Who the hell do you think you are to think that you have the answer to saving the planet?" But then I hear my response to them, "Who the hell am I to think I should withhold it? Should it be based on *my* judgment that it is not our best way to sustainability? Besides, it is."

12 quick days. Done. The days, and the book. Pheuw. Written quickly, written to provide a starting point for bigger conversations. The biggest we've ever needed.

My friends and I continue this conversation and work in what we call the Ecosphere Net project. The goal of our project at Ecosphere Net is to further develop the ideas of this book, and those that are in the upcoming *We Are Sustainability* book as well as many others, interface them into a curriculum for global sustainability, and develop that curriculum through a cross-cultural network of sustainability education centers worldwide.

The closing quote below by Albert Einstein may best be read while listening to music of depth and meaning to you. Art in any form is all about what it is to be human. In music, the writer, player, and singer show us what we as humans are capable of creating together. Our human potential. There is more in music though. We all have music selections that can move us deeply. This is because we are all human. That is how music unites us. Our human potential and who we are is right there in our music. I love that.

Music like that, about the human potential and about what it is to be human, for me, comes from a wide variety of sources. I find both in the magnificent interpretation of Chopin's Piano Concerto No.1 by the young and very brilliant Yundi Li. I also find them in the powerful voice and lyrics of Bono singing to a guitar that only the Edge can play, in the song "Where the streets have no name". As the song suggests—tear down those walls that hold you inside—and feel the sunlight on your face!

*"A human being is a part of a whole, called by us 'universe', a part limited in time and space. He experiences himself, his thoughts and feelings as something separated from the rest... a kind of optical delusion of his consciousness. This delusion is a kind of prison for us, restricting us to our personal desires and to affection for a few persons nearest to us. Our task must be to free ourselves from this prison by widening our circle of compassion to embrace all living creatures and the whole of nature in its beauty."*

Albert Einstein

ejwensing@ecosphere.net


www.ecosphere.net

Enrico J. Wensing

# References

Atkinson, M. (2006) Straightedge bodies and civilizing processes. *Body & Society*, 12(1), 69-95.

Baghurst, T., Hollander, D.B., Nardella, B., & Haff, G.G. (2006). Change in sociocultural ideal male physique: An examination of past and present action figures. *Body Image*, 3, 87-91.

Bakker, B. & den Dulk, P. (1999). Casual relationships between levels: The modes of description perspective. Proceedings of the Twenty-first Annual Conference of the Cognitive Science Society. M. Hahn and S.C. Stoness (Eds.). 43-48.

Baumeister, R.F. & Leary, M.R. (1995). The need to belong: Desire for interpersonal attachments as a fundamental human motivation. *Psychological Bulletin*, 117, 497-529.

Begley, S. (2007, August 13). The Truth About Denial. *Newsweek Magazine*, 7, 21-29.

Bencze, J.L. (2000a). Democratic constructivist science education: Enabling egalitarian literacy and self-actualization. *Journal Curriculum Studies*, 32(6). 847-865.

Bencze, J.L. (2000b). Procedural apprenticeship in school science: Constructivist enabling of connoisseurship. *Science Education*, 84, 727-739.

Bencze, J.L. (2001, June 5). Perspectives & Practices Promoting a Just Science education: Facilitating Student Self-actualization. Keynote address Conference of the Science Coordinators' and Consultants' Association of Ontario, Barrie, Ontario, Canada.

Bencze, J.L., Di Giuseppe, Hodson, D., Pedretti, E. Serebin, L., & De-scoito, I. (2003). Paradigmatic road blocks in elementary school science 'reform': Reconsidering nature-of-science teaching within a rationalist milieu. *Systemic Practice and Action Research*, 16(5), 285-308.

Bencze, J.L. (2004). Science teachers as metascientists: An inductive-deductive dialectic immersion in northern alpine field ecology. *International Journal of Science Education*, 26(12), 1507-1526.

Bencze, J.L., Bowen, G.M. & Aslop, S. (2006). Teachers' tendencies to promote student-led science projects: Associations with their views about science. *Science Education*, 3, 400-419.

Bonnett, M. (2002). Education for sustainability as a frame of mind. *Environmental Education Research* 18(1), 9-20.

Bragg, E.A. (1995). Towards ecological self: individual and shared understandings of the relationship between self and the natural environment. Doctoral dissertation, James Cook University of North Queensland, Townsville, Australia.

Bragg, E.A. (1996). Towards ecological self: Deep ecology meets constructionist self-theory. *Journal of Environmental Psychology*, 16, 93-108.

Budgeon, S. (2003). Identity as an embodied event. *Body & Society*, 9(1), 35-55.

Cacioppo, Hawkley, Rickett, & Masi, (2005). Sociality, spirituality, and meaning making: Chicago health, aging, and social relations study. *Review of General Psychology*, 9, 143-155.

Chew, S. (2001). World ecological degradation: Accumulation, urbanization, and deforestation, 3000 BC - 2000 AD. Walnut Creek, CA: AltaMira Press.

Combs, A. (2006). Daddy, why are people so complex? *World Futures*, 62, 464-472.

Cullen, D. & Gotell, L. (2002). From orgasms to organizations: Maslow, women's sexuality and the gendered foundations of the needs hierarchy. *Gender, Work and Organization*, 9, 538-555.

De Jong, H.L. (2002). Levels of explanation in biological psychology. *Philosophical Psychology*, 15, 441- 462.

Deci, E.L. & Ryan, R.M. (2000). The "what" and "why" of goal pursuits: Human needs and self-determination of behavior. *Psychological Inquiry*, 11, 227-268.

Dempster, B. (2000) Sympoietic and autopoietic systems: A new distinction for self-organizing systems, in Allen JK and Wilby J (eds.). Proceedings of the World Congress of the Systems Sciences and ISSS. [Presented at the International Society for Systems Studies Annual Conference, Toronto, Canada, July 2000]

Dempster, B. (2002). Boundarylessness: introducing a systems heuristic for conceptualizing complexity. Presented at The Land Institute, Kansas. http://www.ejournal.ca/beth/ubs/boundaries2002.pdf [Accessed July 12, 2005; revised version forthcoming in Toward a Taxonomy of Boundaries, Charles Brown and Ted Toadvine, eds. New York, SUNY Press].

Dempster, B. (2004). Canadian biosphere reserves: Idealizations and realizations. *Environments*, 32, 94-99.

Devall, B. (2001). The deep, long range ecology movement 1960 – 2000 a review. *Ethics & The Environment*, 6(1), 18- 41.

Devall, B. (2001b). The unsustainability of sustainability. Issue #19. Obtained June 15, 2004 from www.culturechange.org.

Devall, B & Sessions, G. (1985). Deep ecology: Living as if nature mattered. Salt Lake City, UT: Gibbs Smith

de Waal, F. (2007). With a little help from a friend. *PloS Bio*, 5, 1406-1408.

de Waal, F. (2007b). Putting the altruism back into altruism: The evolution of empathy.

Diamond, J. (2005). Collapse: How Societies Chose to Fail or Succeed. New York: Penguin

Diehm, C. (2003). The self of stars and stone: Ecofeminism, Deep ecology, and the ecological self. *The Trumpeter*, 19(3), 31-45.

Dixon, D. & Durrheim, K. (2000). Displacing place identity: A discursive approach to locating self and other. *British Journal of Social Psychology*, 39, 27-44.

Farber, D. (1999). Eco-pragmatism: Making sensible environmental decisions in an uncertain world. Chicago: University of Chicago Press

Frantz, C., Mayer, S.F., Norton, C., Rock, M. (2005). There is no "I" in nature: The influence of self-awareness on connectedness to nature. *Journal of Environmentalism*, 25, 427-436.

Gergen, K. (1992). Social construction and moral action. In D. Robinson (Ed.), Social discourse and moral judgment, 10-27. London: Academic Press.

Goldenberg, J.L. & Shackelford, T. I. (2005). Is it me or is it mine? Body-self integration as a function of self-esteem, body-esteem, and mortality salience. *Self and Identity*, 4, 227-241.

Gray-Hardcastle, V.(1999). Multiplex vs multiplex selves. *Monist*, 82, 645-658.

Hay, D. & Nye, R. (1998).The Spirit of the Child. New York: Harper Collins.

Hermans, H.J.M. (2002). The dialogical self as a society of mind. *Theory & Psychology*, 12, 147-160.

Hermans, H.J.M. (2004). Introduction: The dialogical self in a global digital age. *Identity: An International Journal of Theory and Research*, 4, 297-320.

Hertig, S. & Stein, L. (2007). The evolution of Luhmann's systems theory with the focus on the constructivist influence. *International Journal of General Systems*, 36, 1-17.

Johnson, D.B. (1992). Altruistic behavior and the development of self in infants. *Merrill-Palmer Quarterly of Behavioral Development*, 28, 379-388.

Jurin, R.R. & Fortner, R.W. (2002). Symbolic beliefs as barriers to responsible environmental behavior. *Environmental Education Research*, 8(4), 373-394.

Knappett, C. (2006). Beyond the skin: Layering and networking in art and archeology. *Cambridge Archaeological Journal*, 16, 239-251.

Kollmuss, A. & Agyeman, J. (2002). Mind the gap: Why do people act environmentally and what are the barriers to pro-environmental behavior? *Environmental Education Research*, 8(3), 239-260.

Kovach, J. (2002). The body as the ground of religion, science and self. *Zygon*, 37, 941-961.

Kyle, G., Graefe, A., Manning, R., & Bacon, J. (2004). Effects of place attachment on users' perception of social and environmental conditions in a natural setting. *Journal of Environmental Psychology*, 24, 213-225.

Lane, D.C. (2004). Irrational agents or accomplished social actors. *Systems Research and Behavioral Science*, 21, 433-438.

Lewis, M. (2000). The promise of dynamic systems approaches for an integrated account of human development. *Child Development*, 71, 36-43.

Lewis, M.D. & Granic, I. (2000). (Eds.), Emotion, development, and self-organization: Dynamic systems approaches to emotional development.

New York: Cambridge University Press.

Light, A & Katz, E. [Eds.] (1996). Environmental Pragmatism. Routledge: New York.

Loughland, T. Reid, A. & Petocz, P. (2002). Young people's conception of environment: A phenomenographic analysis. *Environmental Education Research*, 8(2), 187-197.

Mandelbrot, B. B. (1983). The fractal geometry of nature. New York, NY: W.H. Freeman and Company.

Marks-Tarlow, T. (1999). The self as a dynamical system. *Nonlinear dynamics, Psychology and Life Sciences*, 3, 311-345.

Maslow, A.H. (1965). Eupsychian Management. Homewood, Illinois: Dorsey Press.

Maslow, A.H. (1968). Toward a psychology of being. 2nd Ed. Princeton, NJ: Van Nostrand.

Maslow, A. H. (1970). Motivation and personality. 2nd Ed. New York: Harper and Row.

Maslow, A. H. (1971). The farther reaches of human nature. New York: Viking.

Maturana, H. R., and Varela, F. J. (1980). Autopoiesis and cognition: The realization of the living. New York: Kluwer.

Mazumdar, S. & Mazumdar, S. (2004). Religion and place attachment: A study of sacred places. *Journal of Environmental Psychology*, 24, 385-397.

McCrae, R. (2007). Aesthetic chills as a universal marker of openness to experience. *Motivation and Emotion*, 31, 5-11.

Mintz, J.A. (2004). Some thoughts on the merits of pragmatism as a guide to environmental protection. *Boston College Environmental Affairs Law Review*, 31(1), 1-26.

Mitchell, M. (1998). A complex -systems perspective on the "computation vs. dynamics" debate in cognitive science. In M.A. Gernsbacher & S.J. Derry (Eds.), Proceedings of the 20th Annual Conference of the Cognitive Science Society-Cogsci98 (pp. 710-715).

Muraven, M. & Baumeister R.F. (1997). Suicide, sex, terror, paralysis, and other pitfalls of reductionisst self-preservation theory. *Psychological Inquiry*, 8, 36-40.

Naess, A. (1988). Self realization: An ecological approach to being in the world. In J. Seed, J. Macy, & A. Naess (Eds.), Thinking like a mountain: Towards a council of all beings. Philadelphia, PA: New Society Publishers.

Niedenthal, P.M., Barsalou, L.W., Winkielman, P., Krauth-Gruber, S. & Ric, F. (2005). Embodiment in attitudes, social perception, and emotion. *Personality and Social Psychology*, 9, 184-211.

Orr, D. (1992). Ecological Literacy. New York: SUNY Press.

Orr, D. (2004). Earth in mind: on education, environment, and the human prospect. 10th Ed. Washington, DC: Island Press

Payne, R.L. (2000). Eupsychian management and the new millennium. *Journal of Managerial Psychology*, 15, 219-226.

Pearson, C. (1998). The Hero Within: Six Archetypes We Live By. San Francisco: Harper

Pile, S. & Nast, H.J. (1998) (Eds.). Places through the body. New York: Routledge.

Pockett, S. (2004). Does consciousness cause behavior? *Journal of Consciousness Studies*, 11(2), 23-40.

Pyszczynski, Greenberg, & Solomon. (1997). Why do we need what we need? A terror management perspective on the roots of human social motivation. *Psychological Inquiry*, 8, 1-20.

Reddy, V. (2003). On being the object off attention: Implications for self-other consciousness. *TRENDS in Cognitive Sciences*, 7, 397-402.

Riebel, L. (1982). Humanistic psychology: How realistic? *Small Group Behavior*, 13, 349-371.

Riebel, L. (2000). Consuming the Earth: Eating disorders and ecopsychology. *Journal of Humanistic Psychology*, 41, 38-58.

Rorty, R. (1999). Philosophy and Social Hope. London: Penguin

Sachs, J.D. & McArthur, J.W. (2005). The millennium project: A plan for meeting the millennium development goals. *Lancet*, 365, 347-353.

Salgado, J. & Hermans, H.J.M. (2005). The return of subjectivity: from Multiplicity of selves to the dialogical self. *E-journal of Applied Psychology*, 1, 3-13.

Scopelliti, M. & Giulani, M.V. (2004). Choosing restorative environments across the lifespan: A matter of place experience. *Journal of Environmental Psychology*, 24, 423-437.

Shamdasani, S. (2003). Jung and the Making of Modern Psychology. Cambridege: Cambridge University Press.

Smith, D.B. (2007). Shade: A letter from Gettysburg. *The Sun*, 377, 16-23.

Stout, M. (2002). The Myth of Sanity: Divided consciousness and the Promise of Awareness. New York: Penguin

Sutton, J. (2007).Children's' dreaming and the theories of dreams. Abstract of a paper in progress. Obtained June 15, 2007 from http://www.phil.mq.edu.au/staff/jsutton/ChildrensDreams.html

Tung, P. M. (1994). Symbolic meanings of the body in Chinese culture and 'Somatization'. *Culture, Medicine, and Psychiatry*, 18, 483-492.

Wackernagel, M., Onisto, L., Linares, A.C., Falfan, I.S., Garcia, J.M., Guerrero, A.I.S. et.al., (1997). Ecological Footprints of Nations: How much nature do they use? –how much nature do they have? Retrieved September 20, 2006 http//:www.ecouncil.ac.cr/rio/focus/report/english/footprint.

Wade, J. (1996). Changes of Mind: A Holonomic Theory of the Evolution of Human Consciousness. Albany, NY: State University of New York Press.

Warneken, F. Hare, B. Melis, A. P., Hanus, D. & Tomasello, M. (2007).Spontaneous altruism by chimpanzees and young children. *PloS Bio*, 5, 1414- 1420.

Warneken, F. & Tomasello, M. (2006). Altruistic helping in human infants and young chimpanzees. *Science*, 311, 1301-1303.

Washburn, M. (1995). The Ego and the Dynamic ground: A Transpersonal Theory of Human Development. 2nd Ed. Albany, NY: State University of New York Press

Washburn, M. (2003). Embodied Spirituality in a Sacred World. Albany, NY: State University of New York Press

Waterman, G. S. (2006). Does the biopsychosocial model help or hinder our efforts to understand and teach psychiatry? *Psychiatric Times*, **Volume** 12-13.

Watts, D.J. & Strogatz, S. (1998). Collective dynamics of 'small-world' networks. Nature, *393*, 440-442.

Watts, D.J. (2003). Six degrees: The science of a connected age. NY: W.W. Norton.

West, L. (1998). The edge of a new story? On paradox, postmodernism and the cultural psychology of experiential learning. *Studies In Continuing Education*, 20, 235- 249.

Wilber, K. (2001). Eye to Eye: The Quest for the New Paradigm. 3rd Ed. Boston: Shambala.

Williams, J. & Parkman, S. (2003). On humans and environment: the role of consciousness in environmental problems. *Human Studies*, 26, 449-460.

Wong, K. N. (1999). The residual problem of the self: a re-evaluation of Vygotsky and social constructionism. *New Ideas in Psychology*, 17, 71-82.

Zahn-Waxler, C., Radke-Yarrow, M., Wagner, E., & Chapman, M. (1992). Development of concern for others. *Developmental Psychology*, 28, 126-136.

# Bauu Press Sustainability Practices

## Values

Bauu Institute and Press works with a wide variety of clients but we especially seek out businesses that are committed to values beyond profit. It's our goal to do business the way we live: by using no more than we need, respect those around us and tread lightly with a small footprint. Although this is hard to accomplish in the modern world; we believe that design, creativity and innovation can drive change, generate new ideas and leave things in a better state than the way we found them.

## Practices

Our values put into daily practice can be expressed through four areas: Energy, Health, Resources and Respect.

- *Energy*
- Purchase Energy Star® rated equipment and appliances
- Use low energy lighting (CFLs or dimmers on other lights)
- Use electric lighting only when necessary in favor of natural lighting
- Turn off all non-essential equipment when not in use
- Cut power to appliances when not in use with a power strip
- Use public transportation or walk before using a car
- Purchase carbon offset credits for car usage
- *Health*
- Use products that don't off-gas toxic chemicals into the work space
- Use cleaning products that are biodegradable and not tested on animals
- Discard toxic materials and products that contain them properly
- *Resources*
- Purchase supplies made with recycled content
- Purchase products & supplies that can be used more than once and/or recycled
- Discard only things that cannot be re-used, recycled or composted
- Use electronic or digital communications (telephone, email, instant messaging or PDFs) before using paper/print based communications like faxes or printed copies sent through the mail.
- *Respect*
- Treat our customers, employees, vendors and contractors with the dignity and respect they deserve
- Put money into Socially Responsible Investments
- Conserve energy and resources for future generations

Printed in the United States
203194BV00004B/1-114/P

Brian Sewell

# The Man Who Built the
# Best Car in
# the World

ALSO BY BRIAN SEWELL

*Naked Emperors*
*Outsider*
*Outsider II*
*Sleeping with Dogs*
*The White Umbrella*

Brian Sewell

The Man Who Built the
# Best Car in the World
# the World

Illustrated by Stefan Marjoram

**QUARTET**

First published in 2015 by Quartet Books Limited
A member of the Namara Group
27 Goodge Street, London W1T 2LD
Text © Brian Sewell 2015
Illustrations © Stefan Marjoram 2015
The right of Brian Sewell to be identified
as the author of this work has been asserted
by him in accordance with the
Copyright, Designs and Patents Act 1988
All rights reserved
No part of this book may be reproduced in
any form or by any means without prior
written permission from the publisher
A catalogue record for this book
is available from the British Library
ISBN 978 0 7043 7360 0
Typeset by Josh Bryson
Printed and bound in Great Britain by
T J International Ltd, Padstow, Cornwall

The author owes a considerable debt to both Philip Hall, Trustee and Director of the Sir Henry Royce Memorial Foundation, and to the encyclopaedic archival resources in his care, without reference to which no book on Royce or Rolls should be written, nor television account be attempted.

For the small fictions in this tale, the author is entirely responsible.

# Contents

## Appendices

It was a dark and stormy night...

# The Man Who Built the Best Car in the World

All over England on 27 March 1903, it was a dark and stormy night.

Rain was pelting down in Manchester, the city on which it falls more often than any other, and Mr Frederick Henry Royce (who hated to be called Fred) was muttering dark oaths between clenched teeth.

He was swearing because it was his fortieth birthday, and no one ever likes to be so old.

He was swearing more because he had a tummy-ache – he always had a tummy-ache and this was to last another thirty years until the day he died in 1933.

And he was swearing most because his shiny new car, a birthday present to himself, had broken down and he was very, very wet.

He was wet because most cars at the beginning of the twentieth century, though taller than Range Rovers now, had no roof, no doors, no windows and no windscreen, and looked like four-buttoned leather armchairs on a cart without a horse.

Fun when the weather was dry, this was foul when it was not – and poor Mr Royce was soaked to the skin.

Though Mr Royce was a famous engineer who knew everything about electricity and cranes and owned a factory in which he made everything to do with both, he knew nothing about cars.

He lifted the bonnet, but looking at the engine did not make it work, and with such a tummy-ache he could not even find the strength to push his new toy out of the way of the horse-drawn traffic trying to pass.

Then two boys came to his rescue – at least he thought of them as boys for he had first known them as boys, but they were now senior apprentices in his factory and had learned how to make his cranes.

They were Eric Platford and Tommy Haldenbury.

They had also learned to boil eggs and milk on the factory furnaces, for these were all that Mr Royce could eat when his tummy was really tiresome.

They had grown fond of him and called him 'Pa'.

'There's Pa,' said Eric to Tommy, seeing the glistening car across the road with Mr Royce peering at the silent engine, 'we'd better sort him out.'

And so they did.

While he steered it, they pushed the car to the side of the road, and found a horse-drawn cab to take him home.

The following morning the car was brought back to Pa's factory by a great grey drayhorse borrowed from a brewery, and the horse was very proud.

Pa – or Henry, as we might begin, respectfully to call him, for we are not yet on boiled egg terms and should not be too familiar – thought that all cars should be like his cranes – reliable.

This car was not.

It was handsome, but most of the time it would not start, and when it did, the engine over-heated and the water that should have cooled it, boiled and turned to steam.

It was expensive – it had cost enough to buy two comfortable houses in Manchester or pay the wages of Eric and Tommy for ten years.

And as it had been made in Paris – it was called a 'Decauville' – it was not easy to get sensible advice or send it back.

Instead, Henry spent weeks making a list of all his comments and complaints, and then he sent for Eric and Tommy.

How would you like to build a motor car?

I WILL GIVE YOU A WORKSHOP TO YOURSELVES...

'How would you like,' he asked, 'to build a motor car?'

They looked at him, wide-eyed, too surprised to speak.

They had spent years learning about electricity and cranes (which they did not particularly like), and now Pa was asking them to make a car.

'I will give you a workshop to yourselves,' said Henry, 'and you must take the Decauville to pieces, learning how it works, why some bits of it go up and down and others round and round, and when you've done that we shall build a better car, a car that will never break down – the best car in the world.'

And that is how the very first Royce car was made.

To look at it was very like the Decauville, but they ensured that every part of it, down to the smallest screw and bolt and nut, was of great strength and of the highest quality.

They made and re-made the engine until the fit and finish of every moving part of it was as accurate as the finest watch made by the finest watchmaker.

And instead of the clatter, rattle and occasional explosive bang of all other early cars, the Royce was whisper quiet – it made no more noise than the tick-tock of Henry's pocket watch.

Henry, Eric and Tommy made three identical cars – the first was ready for the road within a year.

On 1 April 1904, April Fool's Day (though Henry, who was superstitious and did not walk under ladders, insisted on recording it as 31 March), he drove it through the gates of his factory, and all his men stopped building cranes and rushed into the yard to see it go, making a triumphant racket by banging their spanners on the railings.

Henry kept this first car for himself and never once did it break down – indeed it was so reliable that in 1908, when young Eric decided to marry his sweetheart, Henry lent him the car so that he could have a honeymoon in style.

The second car went to Henry's friend Ernest Claremont, who had little interest in cars and preferred running Henry's factory and making cranes; he only drove his Royce when he could persuade a horse-drawn cab to follow close behind.

THE BOY WAS ONLY INTERESTED IN CARS

When rumours reached London that on the streets of Manchester there were cars that made no noise, these were heard by a young man named Charles Rolls, and it was he who claimed the third.

Charles Rolls was himself the third son of a rich Lord, Llangattock by name, who had a huge house and a huge estate in Wales, a collection of paintings and a marvellous library – but the boy was only interested in cars.

At Cambridge he studied engineering and was the very first student there to own a car, a Peugeot.

He knew about cars.

He had a workshop in his father's house, and there he took them to pieces and put them together again.

He particularly liked French cars – more cars were then made in France than anywhere else – and his first real job was selling them.

The only thing he disliked was the terrible noise that they all made, and when told of the silence of the three Royces in Manchester, he went there straight away to talk to Henry.

They met for lunch in the Grand Central Hotel.

Imagine that lunch under the great chandeliers, with deep red carpets under foot and deep red damask on the walls.

Imagine the waiters bowing and scraping.

Imagine the oysters, the roast beef, the Yorkshire pudding and the gravy.

Imagine the finest wines from Burgundy and Bordeaux.

And imagine these two engineers putting their heads together – Charles the educated aristocrat aged twenty-seven, Henry aged forty-one, the self-taught builder of cranes who had been to school for only a year as a child, had been a paperboy and a telegraph-boy, yet had risen from direst poverty to become a builder of great cranes.

They swallowed their oysters, they chewed their beef and they quaffed their claret (as wine from Bordeaux is properly called), and they talked of cars, the prize a car of supreme quality bearing both their names.

Henry was to make it and Charles to sell it.

It was to be fit for kings and emperors, despots, dictators and every kind of hospodar and potentate and, of course, for Charles's aristocratic friends.

It took a little time.

The first Rolls-Royce proved to be too small for potentates and they made only sixteen – but, and it is a very important but, it bore the outline of the classic radiator that all Rolls-Royces ever since have borne.

# Classical Architecture

Palladio

British Museum

Greek Temple

Italy 1470

U 44

This was inspired by such great buildings in London as Buckingham Palace and the British Museum, and is the first thing we see when a Rolls-Royce approaches.

Then they made the car longer, tried bigger engines and sent it rallying and racing, at which it was very good.

And then they made it longer still and gave it an engine almost four times the size of the original Royce, and when in 1907 they had made a dozen, they painted the thirteenth silver and gave it a silver radiator and silver handles to the doors, and called it the 'Silver Ghost'.

Thirteen is not always an unlucky number – this really was the Best Car in the World and for eighteen years Henry continued to make it until, in 1925, he made his second Best Car in the World.

In all this development both Eric and Tommy played their part.

Eric proved to be a brilliant driver and was responsible for many victories in racing and rallying; he eventually became Chief Tester of engines for both cars and aeroplanes.

And Tommy was so full of ideas for the future that he was one of the two men responsible for mad experiments that, if successful, might make the Silver Ghost better still – a sort of Dr Who.

In the Great War of 1914–18 the Silver Ghost served the British Army very well and was made into wonderful armoured cars.

Racing and rallying had made it a very tough car and it did not bog down in the trenches of the Western Front, nor in the deserts of Iraq and Palestine.

Kings and Emperors bought them by the dozen, and so did Indian Rajahs and Arab sheiks – even Lenin, Communist master of the Russian Revolution, had one.

With American millionaires it was so successful that Henry was persuaded to set up a factory in Massachusetts.

In those days no two Rolls-Royces looked alike because the owner could ask for, and be given, any kind of body that he wished.

Rolls-Royce sold him what was called a 'bare chassis', that is an engine, four wheels, all the important hidden parts that ordinary people never see, and a stout frame on which to hold them all together.

It had one seat, and sitting on that seat with nothing to protect him from the weather, a driver drove it from the factory to the workshop of the coachbuilder.

The coachbuilder then constructed on the frame exactly the body that the buyer wanted.

If he was an old fuddy-duddy accustomed to a horse-drawn coach of the kind in which the Queen rides to open Parliament, then the coachbuilder built a 'horseless carriage' – a carriage with an engine at the front instead of a horse.

If he was a family man he might ask for a 'Limousine', a body with four big doors, lots of windows and seats for seven passengers.

If he was young and wanted to drive very fast, he commissioned an open two-seater – and that is what Charles Rolls did, for he had taken to hot-air ballooning and needed space for the balloon, the passenger basket and all the equipment necessary to produce a vast quantity of hot air.

Alas, poor Charles…

As a boy he had a bicycle; as a student he had a car – and then more cars; and then he bought a balloon and was blown about all over the country, with a man in his Rolls-Royce chasing after him to come to the rescue when the hot air cooled.

Having taken to the skies, he lost interest in cars.

# Silver Ghost Chassis

## Double Phaeton

## Balloon Car

## Touring

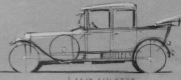

## Landaulette

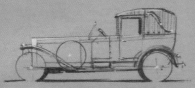

## Sedanca De Ville/Town Car

## Double Pullman

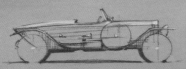

## Boat-Tailed Torpedo/Skiff

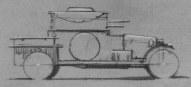

## Armoured Car

THE SILVER GHOST!

The Silver Ghost was the Best Car in the World, Henry Royce was in charge of the factory, Eric was racing and rallying, Tom was bubbling with ideas, and Charles could spend his time doing far more thrilling things than messing about with motors.

Tired of the balloon, which he could not steer, stop or make go faster than the wind, and which had occasionally tangled in a tree or dropped into a pig sty, making him feel ridiculous (for he had no sense of humour), he tasted the pleasures of the airship.

This Leviathan of the air could do everything that the balloon could not, and Charles was thrilled as never before, but not even he could afford to own one – so he bought an aeroplane, learned to fly, and immediately became so expert an airman that he could entertain the crowds who gathered at air displays.

In the first years of the twentieth century aeroplanes were tiny fragile things compared with aeroplanes now, and looked as though they were made of paper and string.

They had four wings (sometimes more), small engines, were very slow, and pilots had to be very careful not to challenge a strong or turbulent wind – but in July 1910, that is exactly what Charles did.

Here was a man who could loop-the-loop and who had, only five weeks earlier, twice crossed the English Channel (then an act of great courage), but during an air display at Bournemouth where he had to land in a white circle on the grass, a gusty wind caught his plane, broke away its tail end and sent it plummeting to the ground.

Unconscious but still breathing faintly, Charles died where he fell.

He was thirty-two and would now have been forgotten, had he not persuaded Henry Royce to build the Best Car in the World and give it both their surnames.

TIRED OF THE BALLOON, CHARLE
BOUGHT AN AEROPLANE...

We might have assumed that with the success of the Silver Ghost, Henry's tummy ceased to trouble him, but it did not.

Instead, it worsened.

Sometimes he stayed at home all day and let his factory make cars and cranes without him while he grew roses and fruit trees in his garden.

This he did very well, though these simple pleasures did not soothe his aching tummy, and with the death of Charles Rolls, which shocked and deeply saddened him, this worsened even more.

He became ill.

Friends took him to Egypt for a holiday, but looking at pyramids and camels is what is known as a distraction, not a cure for tummy upsets or any other illnesses – and in Egypt there were no interesting cars to see and the King had not yet bought a Silver Ghost.

Only when his friends took him to the South of France did Henry cease to be miserable, for there he fell in love with the blue skies, the blue sea, the warm sun and the fine French food.

Staying in a comfortable hotel in a village named Le Canadel, almost the southernmost point of the French Riviera, looking across the Mediterranean towards the island of Corsica, mountains shrugging their shoulders to the north, he said one morning – dreamily and to no one in particular while buttering his breakfast croissants – 'I would like to build a house here.'

A friend casually drained the dregs of his coffee, rose to his feet, muttered something about letters to write and disappeared.

He came back for lunch waving enormous documents in dark brown ink on sheets of parchment, and presented them to Henry – they were the title deeds to a parcel of land overlooking the sea and a permit to build whatever he wished on it.

He built a handsome villa for himself and another for the draughtsmen and engineers who so often came from the factory to consult him, and who never returned to England without sheaves of blueprints to consider (in the days before computers were invented, industrial ideas were always recorded on Full Imperial sheets of blue paper – then the largest size that could be had before metric measurements were adopted).

Friends came to stay and as some of them were artists, he learned to draw and paint the landscape from his windows; and, as in England he had grown roses and fruit trees in his garden, so he did in France, and he planted so many mimosa trees to perfume the air with their delicate yellow blossoms that he called his villa by their name – La Mimosa.

Henry was never idle.

He might prune his roses for an hour, but his brain was always working, and he often put down his secateurs and hurried down the slope to the smaller villa, there to make notes and drawings of some idea that had occurred to him for better brakes, a smoother means of changing gear, or adapting the springs for rougher French roads.

In 1904 he knew nothing about cars, yet within three years his factory was making the Best Car in the World and, until his death in April 1933, many thought him the greatest living motor engineer.

Even so, he did not quite forget the cranes that first made his fortune, and was much amused in 1931, when the American Henry Ford first made cars in England, to be told that Rolls-Royce cranes had been installed in the Ford factory in Dagenham.

Henry spent the winters in La Mimosa, returning to England for the cooler summers (in the South of France it can be as hot as Africa).

He had an old rambling house called Elmstead, which he had seen advertised in a magazine while waiting in his doctor's surgery.

HE BUILT A HANDSOME VILLA FOR HIMSELF

It was near West Wittering, in Sussex, where the sea is never blue, but the air was said by doctors to be good for anyone whose health was fragile.

And there life was much the same as in France, though not nearly so hot, and the food was English.

There were roses to prune, more pictures to paint, more engineering ideas to explore and develop, and friends from the factory far away in Derby were always driving down to discuss his thoughts and blueprints.

It was in West Wittering that he died, almost to the very end still drawing the working parts of cars on a neat little table over his tummy as he lay in bed.

The news at once reached the factory by telephone, and among the many mourners Eric Platford and Tommy Haldenbury were particularly stricken.

Thirty years earlier they had been the apprentices who warmed his milk, boiled his eggs, helped him build his very first car, and called him Pa – and he had changed their lives and made their fortunes.

They had been trained to make cranes, but instead had helped to build the Best Car in the World.

IT COULD REACH 100MPH, CROSS MOUNTAINS AND DESERTS

Eric had become Chief Tester of all Rolls-Royce motor cars and aero-engines, and Tommy was, within three years, to be appointed the great firm's General Manager.

The last Silver Ghost was made in 1925.

By then there were 6,220 of them, all made by hand.

The earliest cars were all open to the elements but within two years the coachbuilders were giving the chassis elegant saloon bodies as comfortable as little drawing-rooms, and cabriolets and laundaulettes to replace the horse-drawn carriages of kings and queens who must be seen in public; and for those who liked the idea of getting cold and wet, there were open two-seaters and what were called 'Torpedo' tourers in which four or five passengers could be thrillingly uncomfortable.

As early as 1911, when the Ghost was still young, it proved that it could reach 100 mph.

In sporting events it climbed mountains, crossed deserts and was not dismayed by ice and snow.

In 1913, when it won the Spanish Grand Prix against cars with much larger engines, Henry Royce was even a little alarmed in case the Rolls-Royce might be mistaken for a sporting car when he had always striven to give the Silver Ghost silence and serenity.

Henry and his friends constantly improved it; a little tinkering with the engine might make it quieter still, the tiniest improvement in precision might silence the transmission or make the gears easier to change, brakes could always be made more powerful and electrical equipment more reliable, a change to the springs might make the car glide even more smoothly over a humpback bridge … the tinkering never ceased.

But after eighteen years in production it was time for the Best Car in the World to give way to a successor, and Henry was the man to make it – but the Phantoms and the Wraiths, the Dawns and Clouds and Shadows, the Spurs and Spirits, are another story.

# Appendices

# A Note on
# Charles Stewart Rolls

As the Best Car in the World carries the name of Rolls before that of Royce (Royce-Rolls is not nearly so mellifluous), it may seem a trifle negligent to have said so little about Charles Stewart Rolls, who is, perhaps, a great 'What if?' of English history.

What if, at the age of twenty-seven, he had not taken the train to Manchester to meet Henry Royce? What if, two years later, he had failed to persuade Royce to build only one chassis instead of three or four, and to make that chassis the foundation of a car that was big, beautiful, silent, reliable and so expensive that only the very grand and the very rich could afford it? What if, at the age of thirty-two, and by then one of three founders of the Royal Aero Club, he had not been killed in a flying accident? What if he had lived the full biblical life span of three score years and ten, and had died in 1947?

At the time of his death, Rolls was regarded as one of England's most courageous and successful aviators, 'the stuff of which the best Englishmen are formed', yet the newspapers of the day had difficulty in assessing his achievements, seeming to suggest that, because he was an aristocrat, he must be an amateur. In the class-ridden years of the early twentieth century it was, perhaps, too soon for anyone to recognise that Rolls was a visionary, single-minded first with the possibilities of motor transport, and then transferring his concentration to the aeroplane.

He was not a man who sought acclaim through reckless derring-do; he was as capable as any driver and raced cars from Paris to Berlin, Vienna and Madrid – or would have, had they not been French and too often unreliable – but he stands apart from other competitors in that he was not merely skilled at the wheel, but had a profound understanding of engines, suspensions and all the functions of a car, and was as often up to his elbows under the bonnet as ensconced in the driving seat.

An old lady, seeing his legs projecting from under a car, mistook him for the mortal victim of an accident, and he was indeed once run over by his own car when swinging the starting-handle with a gear engaged. In his mechanical knowledge and his willingness to roll up his sleeves he was, if not crossing the boundaries of class, ignoring them.

As a boy his most passionate interest was electricity and, in rejecting the classical education offered at Eton, where he stayed for only two years and was very much a loner, showed little aptitude for Latin, mathematics, history or geography, but at fifteen had supervised the installation of electric light in The Hendre, the gloomy and disagreeable house in which the Llangattock family lived. At Cambridge (Trinity) he took a degree in Mechanics and Applied Science in 1898 and a career involved with the car became inevitable.

The rule at his level in society – nobility on his father's side reaching back to Charles I, and on his mother's to the first Plantagenets – dictated that he should be a gentleman of leisure, a soldier or a politician, but Rolls ignored it.

He was happy to sell cars to his peers, and that is what compelled him to persuade Royce to make the Best Car in the World, but he cared not at all for their society, preferring a sandwich to a formal dinner.

Rolls lived in the family's London house, South Lodge, Kensington, across the road from the Barracks in Hyde Park. His rooms were bleak and he played no intimate part in family life. Only his father's constant generosity in financing his son's sales and service company in Lillie Road, Fulham (holding the agency for Panhard and Mors), and paying for his competition cars (one Mors cost as much as £2,000 in 1902 – it had a 9236 cc engine and was a very early example of a boat-tailed racer), suggests that there must have been considerable fondness in their relationship.

Charles seems to have had few friends; perhaps there were envious enemies – his fast driving earned him the nickname 'the young Kaiser'. He had no small talk. His letters express no emotion. He did not marry, nor did his brothers, though he and John, the heir to the peerage, must have been most eligible bachelors (Henry, the middle brother, was an invalid). Of him, many conventional photographs survive in which he is at the wheel of a car or the controls of an aircraft, but in a handful the photographer has captured him in what seems a mood of introspection and reflection; these strongly suggest the visionary, the man who sees beyond the moment.

What then, if young Rolls had not travelled to Manchester to share a platter of oysters with Henry Royce? Royce, the successful manufacturer of cranes and lifting-gear, might have made no more cars, content with having made his point in the first three. There were hundreds of other hopeful engineers making cars as sidelines to bicycles and boats, and Royce did not need to join them.

What if Rolls had not persuaded Royce to build the Best Car in the World? Royce would probably have persisted in making too many different cars, appealing to a wider market, too well made, too expensive, and swiftly gone out of business, as so many early manufacturers did.

What if, at thirty-two, Rolls had not been the first British aviator to be killed? Having hob-nobbed with the Wright Brothers and Blériot, and having already flown the Channel, he would, without doubt, have flown the Atlantic, flown to Australia and flown around the world, either in competition or in the quest to improve the aeroplane.

What if he had survived until he was seventy and died in 1947? Given that as early as 1902 he had brought the car to the notice of the army and within a year the Motor Volunteer Corps had been formed, so he would have played a part in the establishment of the Royal Flying Corps (subsequently the RAF) and perhaps shortened the First World War. In the Thirties he might have argued early for re-armament, stockpiled Spitfires and Hurricanes, and shortened the Second World War, too.

Nothing of this was to be. Charles Rolls died in 1910; his father died in 1913; Henry, the second son, died shortly after; John, the eldest son, the last to bear the title Lord Llangattock, was killed in action in 1916; their sister, Eleanor, lived on until 1961.

Charles Stewart Rolls is buried in the churchyard at Llangattock, quite forgotten, but we who know the true story of the Best Car in the World must ask another question – would Henry Royce have made it without the vision of Charles Rolls?

# Coachbuilders

Of all the crafts and trades involved in constructing the first motor cars, the coachbuilder was far and away the oldest, and he lived in Hungary in a very small town called Kocs. More or less pronounced 'coach', the town gave its name to this horse-drawn vehicle not only in the English language, but in French and Spanish, German and Dutch too. It is to be found just south of the M1 motorway to Vienna, 60 kilometres in a straight line west of Budapest.

We do not know the coachbuilder's name. It is possible that he made the first coach for Matthew Corvinus, who was, perhaps, the bravest King of Hungary (1458–90), victorious in great battles against the Turks, who established a university, an observatory and one of the finest libraries the world has ever known.

Demand for coaches spread fast across Western Europe among the rich and powerful, and they were deemed a suitably extravagant gift from one monarch to another. Queen Elizabeth I commissioned one for Boris

Godunov, the Tsar of Russia, in 1603. It was a great thing of carved and gilded timber, painted with hunting scenes and battles and decorated with hangings of red velvet; in outline and proportion it has an astonishing resemblance to many early Silver Ghosts. Its constructor was possibly Walter Rippon, one of Elizabeth's favoured coachbuilders who, in 1555, had built the first ever coach in England (for the Earl of Rutland), and whose direct descendants were still constructing coachbuilt bodies for Rolls-Royce chassis as late as 1958.

One particular limousine built by Rippon in 1911 is an amusing echo of the great Moscow coach of 1603. When it came to cladding the chassis with a body, it was on the skills and traditions of the coachbuilder that Henry Royce depended. His Silver Ghost inherited from the era of the horse and the Grand Tour the aristocratic style and mode of the eighteenth-century carriage, and in their very names these capsules of plate glass, polished wood and buttoned leather recalled the past, rather than evoked the future – the phaeton, the landaulette, the sedanca and the brougham entrenching class distinctions and setting benchmarks for social aspiration.

It can, perhaps, be argued that the coachbuilder delayed the development of the car by loading it with status symbols, but once the horseless carriage period was over, he was also the artist-craftsman who could make a car, if not go faster, look as though it could. He could lower and lengthen the bonnet, fare the wings, incorporate the boot, split and rake the windscreen, dispense with runningboards, and with the deliberate use of line and balance, contrasting colours and hand-drawn coachlines, create an impression of high performance, deceptive but often very beautiful.

In the 1930s, coachbuilders brought the car into the forefront of twentieth-century design, and no computer since has ever matched their inspiration. Most English coachbuilders were based in London and the first to body a Silver Ghost chassis was Barker and Co. – indeed, as early as 1905 Charles Rolls had unwisely announced that 'all Rolls-Royces will be fitted with Barker's bodies'. This, in the event, was not true. In Manchester, where the early cars were made, the firm of Joseph Cockshoot, long known, no doubt, to Henry Royce, which had been building bodies for Renault, was given the Rolls-Royce agency for Lancashire and Cheshire, then very wealthy counties; it was Cockshoot who bodied the Pearl of the East. Across the Pennines, in Huddersfield,

Rippon Brothers bodied their first Rolls-Royce, a Type A chassis of two cylinders and 10 hp, in 1905.

Among other prominent coachbuilders of the Silver Ghost chassis were Hooper, H. J. Mulliner (who built the Silver Rogue, the special two-seater in which Rolls carried his balloon equipment), Park Ward and Windovers. In America, Brewsters bodied some very late Ghost chassis in 1925; only a handful were bodied by European coachbuilders – these were to swing into action with the Phantoms and smaller-engined chassis that succeeded the Ghost. Some remarkable and fantastic bodies were built in India by unnamed craftsmen of some genius.

All sorts of bodies, from what were in essence small drawing-rooms on wheels to the Silver Rogue, were built on the Silver Ghost chassis – but most fell into the following definitions:

**Roi des Belges**: a very early open body with low doors in which two or three rows of passengers, each rather higher towards the rear, sit on buttoned-leather seats entirely exposed to the weather and assassins. The King of Belgium was visiting his coachbuilder with his mistress and it seems that she, having re-arranged his furniture, declared, 'That's how a car should be.'

**Landaulet and Landaulette**: originally a closed horse-drawn carriage, the rear section of which was akin to a drop-head coupé that could be opened only for the benefit of rear-seat passengers.

**Limousine**: a long enclosed body carrying three rows of passengers under a fixed roof, the driver's compartment separated by a fixed division and possibly, in early examples, not enclosed under the roof.

**Cabriolet**: a four-door body that could either be as completely closed as a saloon, or as completely open as a tourer. (Sometimes confused with the all-weather body, which had removable windows rather than windows dropping into the doors.)

**Tourer**: an open body with two or four doors, for four or five passengers, with a collapsible hood and detachable lightweight side-screens instead of windows.

**Torpedo**: an early term for a four-door tourer from which the only distinctions are a straight unbroken line running from nose to tail, and a secondary scuttle (and even a second windscreen) between front and rear passengers; the tail is occasionally shaped like a boat and even made of wood.

**Phaeton**: originally a light four-wheeled carriage drawn by a pair of horses, it is a term adopted in America for tourers and torpedoes.

# Rolls-Royce:
# The Early Cars

## 1905

The Type A was exhibited at the Paris Salon (driven there from London and back without a hitch).

Based on the three prototypes constructed by Royce in 1903-04, the engine was of two cylinders and 1809 cc, later increased to 2059 cc. It was the first car to bear the classic (and classical) Rolls-Royce radiator. According to one source twenty cars were intended, but only sixteen built; according to another the figures are nineteen and seventeen. The model was withdrawn from production in 1906. Only four are believed to survive, one in the Science Museum, London, one in the Bentley Motors Heritage Collection, the others in private possession.

The prototypes of three other cars were also exhibited at this Paris Salon, all their engines based on the same cylinder dimensions as the Type A, rated at 10 hp – that is 101.6 x 137 cm, 1029.5 cc. These were the 15 hp with three cylinders, shown only as a chassis, of which only six were made and production ended in 1905, the 20 hp with four cylinders and a capacity of 4118 cc, of which forty were made, and the 30 hp of six cylinders and 6177 cc, of which thirty-seven were made.

All four were listed in the first Rolls-Royce catalogue. The 20 hp continued in production until 1908. Three additional 20 hp chassis were adapted to take V-8 engines of 3535 cc, the cylinders 82.6 – with equal bore and stroke an astonishingly modern design and the first V-8 designed from scratch – but only three were made and none survives. It was capable of only 20 mph.

## 1906

The 30 hp six-cylinder car, large, impressive, expensive and, potentially, capable of high performance, was the model that Rolls thought more suitable for his clientele.

There was serious debate among other manufacturers about the superiority of the six-cylinder engine, and at the Scottish Reliability Trials that year the so-called 'Battle of the Cylinders' took place between a 30 hp Rolls-

Royce and a four-cylinder Martini of equal capacity, a Swiss car of high quality that had won a gold medal in the British 1000-Mile Reliability Trial. Over another thousand miles, with a further 671 in the Highlands, the Rolls-Royce lost no marks and was victorious with 396 points for reliability, silence and smooth running.

In a successful attempt to break the unofficial record for the London-Monte Carlo run, Rolls and two companions drove the 771 miles from Monte Carlo to Boulogne in 28 hours, 14 minutes, including stops for refreshment, hot baths and changes of clothes, for the car was open and unprotected and they had driven through a night of drenching thunderstorms. Their average speed was 27.5 mph.

Two 20 hp cars were officially entered for the Tourist Trophy Race on the Isle of Man; one driven by Rolls was the outright winner – 208.5 miles at an average speed of 39.5 mph. Royce, meanwhile, was designing a big six-cylinder engine to replace the 30 hp in which, despite its proven reliability, he identified significant weaknesses – in crude terms it was three 10 hp engines in a row with a long crankshaft that was not robust enough. Convinced that a big six could be superior to all other engines, he designed one that, like the discarded V-8, was of equal bore and stroke, 114-114 mm, the capacity 7036 cc, developing 48 bhp. It was called the 40 hp, but when first exhibited at the Olympia Motor Show in December 1906, it had become the 40/50; later it became the Silver Ghost – though purists obstinately stick to the 40/50 designation.

# Rolls-Royce:
# The Silver Ghost

## 1904

The 40/50 engine was introduced, with a much improved chassis with a very long wheelbase of either 135.5 or 143.5 inches, and a much stronger gearbox that in top gave 48 mph at 1000 rpm.

It was not released to the public until nine months of severe road testing had proved its reliability and quality, but even before these tests began the car was advertised (*Autocar*, 30 March 1907) as: 'The most graceful, the most attractive, the most silent, the most reliable, the most flexible, the most smooth-running, in fact, the best six-cylinder car yet produced.' From this it was only a short step to being the 'Best Car in the World'.

The thirteenth chassis was completed and despatched to Barkers for the silver body that was at once dubbed the 'Silver Ghost'. Another 40/50 was entered for the RAC-monitored Scottish Reliability Trial, which involved not only

740 miles of mountain roads, but 15,000 miles of continuous driving between London and Glasgow, without mechanical servicing or over-haul of any kind – this at a time when 3,000 miles was regarded as the longest possible interval between services, and 5,000 miles was thought to be the average annual mileage.

By the time of Royce's death in 1933 this test car had been driven 350,000 miles. Rolls and Eric Platford were two of the four drivers at the wheel throughout the test – they did not drive on Sundays.

With the successful completion of this and other trials, the factory prepared to build fifty chassis for sale to the public; over the next eighteen years it was to construct 6,173 Silver Ghosts.

# 1908

Demand for the 40/50 was so great that the original Royce works in Manchester were immediately inadequate and a new factory had to be found for its manufacture; a site was selected and developed in Derby.

At the same time it was decided that the firm should concentrate its resources on only one model, aiming at perfection, the 40/50 to be constantly improved and developed, the 20 hp dropped. After the initial rush to purchase, the firm built some seven chassis a week until August 1914.

Two cars were prepared for the Scottish Reliability Trials, the engines tuned to give 70 bhp instead of 48 bhp. Only one was entered; first known as White Ghost, it was re-christened White Knave. With Eric Platford as driver it won a gold medal and was exhibited at the opening ceremony of the Derby factory in July. The second car was known as the Silver Silence, and later, after a piston seized, preventing it from competing in the Scottish Trials, as the Silver Rogue.

These names and Silver Ghost were the first of a long line of names in which silver and various spectres were prominent. For these two cars Royce lengthened the stroke of the cylinders by a small margin to improve the torque, increasing engine capacity to 7428 cc, power output to 70 bhp, and maximum speed to 70 mph. Most of these larger engines developed 60 bhp, but a handful, known as Type 70, including the car built for Rolls to carry his balloon equipment, had the more powerful version. The thirty-seventh 40/50, ordered with a limousine body from the Manchester coachbuilder Joseph Cockshoot, the property of Frank Norhury, a merchant, reached Bombay and was entered in the Bombay-Kolhapur Reliability Trial, a gruelling 620 miles of mountain climbing. It won outright, and went on to win other awards, including the Mysore Cup. It was then bought by the Maharaja of Gwalior and became known as the 'Pearl of the East' when he had it repainted with crushed pearls. It was the first of over eight hundred Rolls-Royces to be exported to India before Independence in 1947.

# 1909

This was the year of the 7428 cc engine now standard in all chassis, now with a three-speed gearbox and a lower top ratio – this in response to owners who disliked changing gear (synchromesh gears had not then been invented) and preferred to start their cars in top and stay in top, even on the steepest hills.

# 1910

Royce was gravely ill for much of the year, perhaps with bowel cancer (the nature of the illness was never revealed).

On 12 July Charles Rolls was killed in a flying accident.

No major changes were made to the 40/50.

# 1911

A Napier, the most serious rival of the Rolls-Royce, had in 1910 been driven from London to Edinburgh and back in top gear and then tested at Brooklands at a maximum speed of 76.42 mph.

A 40/50 was prepared to meet this challenge, the suspension modified, the engine given a higher compression ratio and larger carburettor, the body light, simple and without a windscreen but nevertheless a full four-seater weighing well over 2.25 tons.

On 6 September the drive to Edinburgh and back began. The RAC observers would not allow the car to exceed the then legal limit of 20 mph, and its average speed for the journey, wholly in top gear, was 19.59 mph;

but at Brooklands, after the run, it reached a maximum of 78.26 mph. For this, it was wryly nicknamed the Sluggard.

Rolls-Royce shipped eight Silver Ghosts with identical landaulette bodies to Delhi for the use of King George V while in India for the Durbar and his coronation as Emperor. Their outstanding reliability impressed and, after the United States, India became the largest market for Rolls-Royce and for coachbuilders willing to construct bodies that were often extraordinary, extravagant and exquisite.

# 1912

Demand for replicas of the Sluggard was satisfied with a short production run of the L-E or London to Edinburgh model until, in 1914, all the L-E improvements were standardised on all chassis.

The Sluggard, stripped of its touring body and fitted with a single-seater of rudimentary streamlined design and a removable cone over its upright radiator, the engine in now even more modified form, was persuaded to break the 100 mph barrier; at Brooklands it reached 101.8 mph.

# 1913

Four-speed gearboxes were again available, designed by Royce to suit the L-E engine.

Four cars were prepared for the Austrian Alpine Trials on an improved chassis designated the Continental. After winning seven awards, including the Archduke Leopold Cup, replicas of these cars were marketed and became known, unofficially, as Alpine Eagles.

Later in the year, with Don Carlos Salamanca at the wheel, an Alpine Eagle won the Spanish Grand Prix in the Guadarrama Mountains north-west of Madrid, in summer temperatures of 90 degrees and more; Eric Platford, in another Alpine Eagle, came third. Yet another Alpine Eagle broke the still unofficial record from London to Monte Carlo, cutting the time to 26 hours, 4 minutes, including the Channel crossing.

# 1914

L-E improvements were standardised. August saw the outbreak of the First World War, the Great War.

Some younger owners were drafted into the army with their cars, particularly for the

King's Messenger Service. Existing Silver Ghosts served as staff cars, but new chassis with stronger springs were equipped as supply vehicles capable of carrying 750 kilos, and as armoured cars. They campaigned in France, Egypt, Palestine, Mesopotamia, Arabia, Gallipoli and East Africa (where Tanzania was then a German colony).

The opinion of Lawrence of Arabia was that 'a Rolls-Royce in the desert is above rubies'. Support crews of skilled Rolls-Royce mechanics were recruited from the factory.

# 1918

The war was brought to an end.

# 1919

The Silver Ghost chassis was back in production, its reputation provoking great demand. To satisfy American demand, a factory in Springfield, Massachusetts, was established.

# 1921

The first Springfield Silver Ghost was made.

# 1925

Production of the Silver Ghost in Derby ceased. The total made in Manchester and Derby was 5,173.

# 1926

Production of the Silver Ghost in Springfield ceased. The number made there was 1,703.

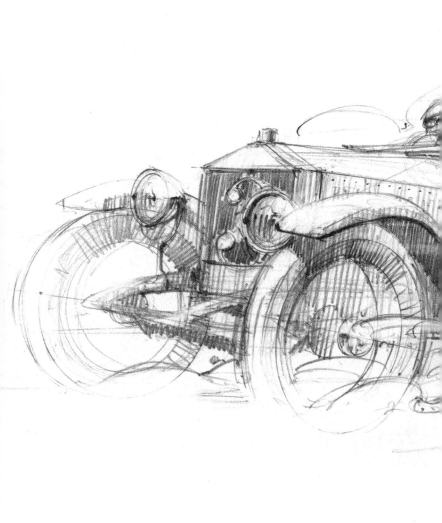